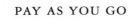

PAY AS YOU GO

McSWEENEY'S
SAN FRANCISCO

McSweeney's and colophon are registered trademarks of
McSweeney's, an independent publisher based in San Francisco.

Cover illustration by Kento Iida

ISBN: 978-1-952119-74-3

10   9   8   7   6   5   4   3   2   1

www.mcsweeneys.net

Printed in the United States.

PAY AS YOU GO

A FABLE

ESKOR DAVID JOHNSON

McSWEENEY'S
SAN FRANCISCO

For my family. My parents, Dawn and David, and my sister, Micere.
Thank you for your faith, your love, and your gift of courage.

The sun shines on me as well as on others, and I should be very happy to see the clause in Adam's will which excluded me from my share when the world was being divided.

—Francis I, king of France

The city never sleeps,
full of villains and creeps.
That's where I learned to do my hustle:
had to scuffle with freaks.

—Nas

POINT
JAMES

MIDDLETON

THE COAST

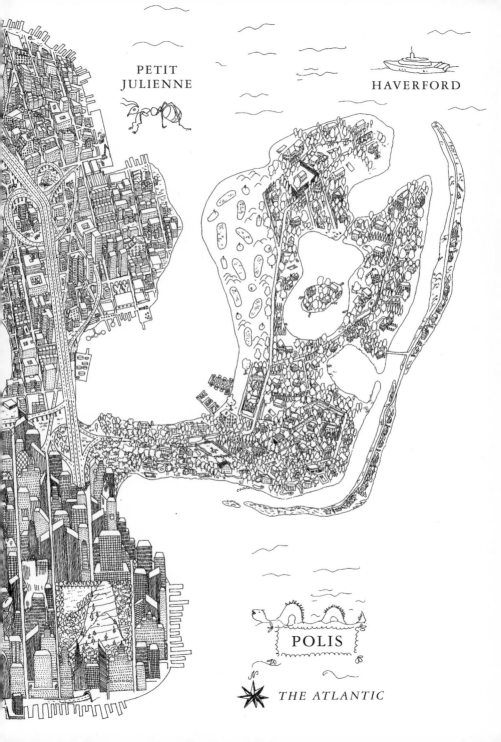

PETIT
JULIENNE

HAVERFORD

POLIS

THE ATLANTIC

MIDDLETON

(in which the Polis is first exposed as an infernal dead end
and—in a midnight tale—a prodigal daughter
returns, to the detriment of high-story hopes)

ELECTRIC DAY

My first apartment in Polis, it was shit, complete shit. I used to say to the man Calumet, Hey, Calumet, how come we're here living like shit, huh? Calumet would say, What you mean "shit"?, and I would say, I mean *shit* shit. I mean: look: the toilet isn't flushing properly, and this shitty paint job, it's peeling in all the wrong places. I swear, sometimes at night, pieces of paint are landing in my mouth and I wake up choking. There's never any juice in the fridge. And I don't like the sound of the doorbell, when the doorbell rings it makes me jump, we should get a gentler doorbell is all. The windows are dusty and they don't look out onto anything. It's like the *sky's* never blue when I look out any of these windows—they're filtering out all the hope. The one in the living room looks out onto a wall. The stairway smells. There's that woman next door who hides when you see her and I think she may be a fugitive. We only have one chair. If I'm sitting in the chair and someone else wants to sit we have to argue about it. I'd like a few plants for the countertops if that's not too much to ask, an orchid or something like that. Have you ever smelled an orchid, Calumet? And why is the TV remote always dead? I swear it was just Tuesday that I bought new batteries for the TV remote and now it's dead and I have to get up if I want to change the TV channel like I'm some kind of a savage and by the time I do that someone has taken my seat in the chair. All the mirrors lie. The floor creaks. We have carpet instead of rugs. The microwave never heats up my food. I used to think, Fine, it's not heaven or anything, but it's where the heart is. But here in this place, Calumet, it's like I can't quite hear my heart anymore. It's like my heart isn't feeling very welcome and it's getting quiet like a guest who doesn't want to bother anyone. I feel meek. What's going to happen in the winter when the frost comes for us? I don't trust the radiator. Are you ready to lose a toe? You down for that, Calumet? What kind of a life is this…? And then Calumet would say, "Ooh-wee, for fuck's sake, man, you've only been here for a week."

True, I was no expert, but it doesn't take a whole week to recognize shit. I was tired already. I didn't like that there was no elevator and we lived on the ninth floor. I didn't like that we had to wash our clothes at the laundromat where the orphans stole my socks. I didn't like that we were so far north in Middleton that the rest of Polis could forget us there, and that every dozen hours it seemed another body whose soul had abandoned it was pulled up from the piers. I was tired of the June heat that wrapped our throats like pythons. I was tired of the one thousand lamps on in the middle of the day just because Eustace had a few phobias. My *eyes* were tired.

"Seriously, Calumet, what's the big deal if we turn off just a few of these lights?" I said.

I was out in the living room suffering beneath the glare. Lamps were on in every corner, bunches of them plugged a dozen at a time into struggling surge protectors and shining on the walls such that they were extremely bright. Two small ones on the kitchenette countertop, and another on the stand next to me in case you needed some extra light for reading. There were forty-seven lamps in that apartment, I'd counted. I had to shout for Calumet to hear me because his bedroom was the last of the three, all the way down the hall.

"Don't," said Calumet. "Believe me."

"I can't just *believe* you over something like that, Calumet. This is unnatural. What about the bill?" I said.

I heard him rustling as though he was coming over. But maybe he changed his mind, for he just yelled again instead. "Eustace pays the bill," he said.

I said, "He's not even *here* right now, Calumet."

"Slide," he said. "Please, just stop bringing it up. Reread the rules already." I turned to the big poster on the wall. Okay, okay: I'll reread the rules.

RULE 1: SHOES OFF AT THE DOOR.
RULE 2: ONE FLUSH PER BATHROOM USE.
RULE 3: FAMILY DINNER ON SUNDAY EVENINGS.
RULE 4: LAMPS STAY ON.
RULE 5: NO COOKING FISH IN THE OVEN.
RULE 6: RECYCLE.

Oh Lord. That whole thing made me want to cry.

Eustace's name was the one on the lease, so Eustace got to make rules about lamps being on and to have the big bedroom at the start of the hall; mine was in the middle. He was an unlikely tyrant. Every evening he burst through the door as if escaping an ambush and headed straight to the bathroom, where he groaned in delight while showering. The trail of his multicolored uniform lay in a line—I think he worked at a toy store assembling robots. He never got fully dressed after; he'd come back out into the living room wearing a pair of white briefs and blend himself a glass of milk, raw eggs, and cinnamon, part of some liquid diet he was on. He was a fat man who had lost weight, with flaps of loose skin, transparent hair, and wet, unblinking eyes. I'd never seen anyone so pale. He seemed some kind of a deep fish from those parts of the water the sun cannot reach. After finishing his milk in the kitchenette he'd inspect all his lamps, then come stand beside the chair I was on and try the same shit (Eustace, he was always trying the same shit): he'd say, "I think there might be a game on," which was a trick to make me get up and change the channel so he could take my seat in the chair. I'd fallen for that once. He never even said what kind of a game it was. Now all I did was tell him I wasn't interested. I had to double down on whatever I was watching, even if it was shit, and he would start fidgeting in all manner of ways. He cleared his throat, he took two-steps-here two-steps-there, he went down the hall to ask Calumet if he wanted to watch the game, he swapped in a new bulb on a lamp (*that* made him hold his breath for a few seconds), his allergies kicked in and he sneezed sneezed sneezed, he donned a mask and gloves and sprayed bleach in the air, he decided right now was a good time to vacuum on the loudest setting. *Geez* already. Fine, I got up. He'd settle between the arms with a satisfied squish. Once, when he took the seat, he retrieved a pair of batteries from beneath the cushion and popped them into the remote to change the channel to what he liked, documentaries about aliens. Storming off to my room—it didn't help: I'd hate the place all the same: the green of the carpet was faded and dingy, the cheap furnishings gave the impression of termites. For all my time there I never once slept properly on that skinny bed. And every morning my door was a little bit open even though I'd closed it for sure.

"You know, Slide," Eustace said one time in that needling voice of a TV commercial, "I've been putting some thought into why you don't sleep well."

"Who says I don't sleep well?" I said. I was pouring cereal for dinner. We were quite close in the kitchenette and the lights lit up the veins in his arms.

"I see that you sleep on your back and have a hard time turning."

"You *see?*"

"Perhaps a simple remedy of spinal alignment might help. It's a problem with evolution, really, fascinating stuff. If you'd like—"

"You been opening my door at night, Eustace? You come in and breathe over me on some sick shit?"

Right away he lifted his shake to his lips and finished the rest of it in three *glug glug glug*s.

"No."

"I'm serious, Eustace," I said. "My room is my room and that's it. *Something* in here has to be sacred."

"Well, of course, Slide," he said, running water over his glass. Then added, "But it *is* very dark in there."

So that night I moved the dresser to block the door while I slept and that next week Eustace began inviting friends over from work for a tour of the apartment, stopping at my bedroom for a particularly long time to list the dimensions, as if it was up for lease. "Hey, Eustace, why're you always showing them my bedroom like it's up for lease?" I said. He laughed that off. Eustace, he was always trying to laugh things off. In his own room the door was forever open and the lights on even while he slept. His bedding was all white, a multitude of lotions arranged on the nightstand, and he had a stack of spare light bulbs in a neat pile in the corner. The whole place had a glow of unreality—just *knowing* it was so bright in there made

it hard for me to sleep. You'll have to excuse where the floorboards are a little bendy here, he'd be saying to whoever it was,
it's where I do my jumping jacks on mornings. Which was
another thing: he wouldn't shut up about all-the-weight he'd
lost. He thought he was being real slick about it, too, bringing
it up by-the-way. He'd ask, Did anyone notice the fourth-floor
stairs are a little steeper than the rest? That's why so many
people have tripped on them, oh goodness, which used to happen to him, too, before he lost all-the-weight. Or: Oh, what's
in this jar I've been shaking for the past fifteen minutes?
Funny you should ask, these are all the replacement buttons
I used to keep around for when one would pop off my shirt before I lost all-the-weight, here, you can have a few, I don't need
them anymore. Also, was anyone else thinking of running the
half-marathon in a couple months? The thought just occurred,
is all. (*That* one I would have liked to see!) I was walking by
once when I saw him tugging at the sides of his belly in the
bathroom. He twisted and twirled before the mirror, then pre-
tended he'd just seen me: "Oh my, Slide! I didn't see you. Since
you are there, help me with this one thing. People are saying
I should get a tummy tuck now that I've lost all-the-weight.
Well, I'm hardly taking them seriously. I think I'm just fine.
In any case, I'm trying to see what they mean." He reached
around to his lower back and grabbed handfuls of skin, pulling
it tight. "Here, would you mind?" he said, offering me the
folds. He was already looking in the mirror to see the results.
Me I'd just eaten. "That's quite alright, Eustace," I said. "I'm
sure you're fine as is." Our eyes met through our reflections.
He unclenched and let the skin drop. "Right, that's okay, I'm
not taking it seriously, of course," he said, and clicked on the
electric razor he used to shave. He hummed an oblivious tune

while he worked and put on a face like he hadn't a care in the entire world. But when I went to brush my teeth that night, I found all my toothpaste had been used up.

That's how he was. A vicious coward. Nipping at the edges instead of biting anything. "Hey, Calumet," I'd say, knocking on the wall between our rooms, "I'm telling you, if ever I turn up missing, Eustace is the one who did it." I heard him moving over to the thin spot we used to talk, clearing his throat before saying anything. He said, "Learn to coexist, Slide," in his sad cadence of a funeral dirge. I harrumphed onto my bed and flicked away some paint crumbs. Tired old Calumet. Easy for him to say, he was the smart one. He hardly ever left that room.

All that summer the subway up in Middleton had been under renovation and I hadn't had a chance to use it not even once. Polis had sent a horde of buses to serve as a temporary fix, but they were janky and full of problems. The one time I'd tried riding one, it was getting harder and harder to breathe until a boy toward the back began yelling, "Smoke! It's smoke! The engine's melting!," and a woman with a metal bar in her forearm used it to smash open a window. Everyone poured out, cutting themselves on glass and running to the front to curse at the driver and take pictures of her face. Well, that was frustrating. We hadn't made it more than five blocks from where I'd had to wait in line a full hour just to get on. My only other options if I wanted to go anywhere were taking a taxi, which were as rare and expensive as amber jewels, or walking south through the stretch of neighborhoods where the gangs were in the midst of a spat. All day long they flew different-colored kites depending on their street and eyed the world with suspicion. I'd ended up there without knowing anything, one Wednesday afternoon, admiring the brown-stones and looking like the perfect idiot. The houses had boarded-up windows and gardens of dried grass. A few people were out on the stoops calling to each other or playing music. At my side there appeared a black girl on a tiny bike.

"You with Ray and them?" she said, keeping pace.

I looked at her politely and said, "I don't know any Rays, so no, I'm afraid not."

She cut me off with her bike. She said, "Why you have to answer all complicated? I didn't ask for a biography. Hey, Patricio, Steve, this guy is with Ray and them."

From a few of the stoops stood up a sudden group of nine, all in orange. They called to each other in bird noises and ran down the steps. Soon I was surrounded.

"You with Ray and them?" one of them repeated. I said, "I don't know any Rays! I don't have anything to do with Ray!" Another one nodded as I spoke, convincing himself. "Yeh, yeh, that's just some shit Ray would have his people say." "Well, who you with then?" said another. "You with Z-Town? With X-Block? With the Bam Bams? With Ghost?" I said no, no, no, and no, none of those either. "You a JagHead Boy? An East Town Shade? You run with Gulag? Uncle Death? One Shot? Diablos? Why're you wearing shorts? Where's your kite? You think we won't know who you are? You down with Slice? The Pharaohs? You with Red Light? With Dwarf? You like all your toes, my dude? Which toe you don't like? You have a favorite..."

They were teens and younger, their expressions varying from the brightly eager to the hollow, as if a wind flickered the candlelight of their eyes. They had dry, cracked lips, and the meanest looking of them all was a big-shouldered rogue whose tongue was a sticky pink for being so parched. In all their hands were the thin strings leading upward to a cluster of orange kites bobbing in the air like buoys. Me I was panicking:

"You have to believe me... it's some kind of a mistake... give me a chance and I won't come back... come on, I mean, please..."

"Listen, my guy," said the girl on the bike, leaning in with a bit of pity, "you can't just be walking all around like you don't know anything. It's a *crisis* going on."

"A crisis?" I asked, stalling for time.

"That's what I said. Don't you know there's no water in the pipes? Don't you know my grandma hasn't showered? Where you from? You with H-Zone? With the Destroyers? You can't just be nobody if you're walking around here. You can't not know about the drought. It's been *months* we're talking about— what are you? The last person on earth? You up from a coma? Things is serious around here, you understand me? That hydrant by the corner is ours. We saw you walking for it. You with Bomb Teeth? You down with Sniper King? Tell them no deal. Tell them we still need the juice. Tell them End Times are moving in on the XGs and it's about to get hot. I'm being serious now, no more playing. You with Yup Yup? With Ratatat? You rep for Ozone? For Karma? Why's your face familiar? Why were your hands in your pockets? You know Plimpton? Mantis? Glass Jaw? Shortie? Du-Wop? Vault? Fifty Cal? Vamps? Phoenix? Marty? Red Bite? Rook? This ringing a bell, my guy? Gortat? Poison? Fried Blood? Mr. Midnight? Cheebo..." I must have nearly broken my neck trying to convince her, shaking my head like a maniac. Please, I was saying, I'm being serious, I was only here for a walk. She seemed to settle at last and consider me for the first time. In the sky above, sprawling toward the

horizon's every direction, a rainbow of dangling kites. "Fine,"
she said. "Then take off your shoes."

Stranded! I was stranded. Two months in and I hadn't *seen* anything. All day long traffic jams clogged the streets of Upper
Middleton and sometimes drivers fainted onto their horns just
from the waiting. The rats had left for the sewers to try cool-
ing off. Hot garbage flavored the air. Most of the buildings
in that part were the hopeless brown of government concrete,
none of the skyscrapers, none of the lights, the things you *hear
about*. Stepping out of ours and onto Aramaya Street, you were
struck at once by a brain-numbing heat that made everyone
shuffle like zombies. Indigenous boys wove through the crowd
selling spray bottles of ice water and fat people were catching
their breath on every bench in sight. The hustlers on the corners had taken to holding parasols over their heads. Everything
looked yellow. On my way back to work from lunch one day,
I was walking past the protesters in front of the subway when a
blackman on a cane stopped me. "Young blackman, you see it,
don't you? You see what's happening," he said. I didn't know
what that meant. The protesters were holding up signs like NO
SUBWAY, NO PEACE! and trying to start a chant. As the man
went on, his head doddered at an odd angle and a trickle of
spit ran along his chin. "I've tried to be reasonable but they
wouldn't listen. Wouldn't listen! Even when I laid out my concerns. Now, when you get home it's very important that you
transcribe a message. That way they'll listen. We're starting a
petition. Linda, she never used to listen. What's that? I've been
putting on my shoes for sixty-five years, same as anyone, now
let me explain..." Oh: he was just another crazy. I swear, there
was no one there who wasn't crazy. "Hey, man," I had to cut

by him and say, "I gotta be getting back to work..." *Then* at
the barbershop where I worked the two other barbers Rex and
Reginald mocked all the cuts I gave and people never wanted
to sit in my chair! It was a long, narrow space with cream walls
and pictures of great boxing matches hung up everywhere. The
ceiling had two fans, one spinning above each of their chairs,
mine was the chair without a ceiling fan. Rex and Reginald,
they were both Jamaican, always laughing. They would have
laughed on a sinking ship. Watch out! they'd tell people, New
Boy couldn't cut your head if you had five heads! *Hya hya hya.*
Watch it! New Boy needs an instruction manual! *Hya hya hya.*
He cuts hair from a stencil! *Hya hya hya.* Careful! New Boy
only knows one kind of cut! *Hya hya hya hyaa...* Now, it is true
I knew only one kind of cut, a bald fade with a line-up around
the sides, but I knew that cut very well. I could go toe-to-toe
with the best of them. Me what I liked to do was have a stack
of clean washcloths chilling in a cooler with ice that I used to
wipe everyone's neck of sweat and hang around their shoulders
before I got started. I'd gone and bought a mobile fan for my
countertop that I'd adjust to their liking or even turn it off if
that's what they wanted for whatever reason. I did my business
with a razor *plus* a comb and always made sure to say No-really-
it's-okay before accepting any tips. I looked very handsome in
my black apron, my afro patted down. Still, everyone sat in
my chair as if for electrocution. Rex and Reginald would warn
them, Easy, easy, we only hired New Boy because he begged!
We don't know his credentials! The finicky Dominicans, the
woman who came for her eyebrows, they were all nervous. One
time it got so bad that a little boy in my chair started to cry.

"You two are not helping me build a clientele!" I told Rex
and Reginald while sweeping up that afternoon.

"And you," they said, "are lucky the client can't tell what you ah do them!"

They spun in their seats, cackling, stopping only to open the little fridge in the corner, where they kept the black stouts to end their day. Rex he was very dark but had pink arms from burns; Reginald was short, with a clown's agile face, and always wore a mesh shirt through which you could see his nipples. When they laughed it was as if their whole jaws came unhinged. They'd sit, sip, and look through the glass storefront as if it were a screen. Across the street was a hospice with a fenced-in courtyard where the nurses took the old people out to sun. Come afternoon, they wheeled them out and left them in a face-to-face clump, then stood to the side talking on their phones. Those old folks would remain endlessly slouched, stagnant as reptiles, watching the world in disbelief. That made me want to cry. Who had organized all this? Where was the planning? There was no planning. It didn't matter if you went left or right: the drugstore was next to another drugstore, the United Arms High School was on the same block as a tattoo parlor, there were too many dry cleaners, every liquor shop had lines stretching outside, the gutters ran with sweat, sometimes we looked to the sky to see if any clouds were coming but they never were. No one cared anymore. No one bothered putting on their good clothes; phone-snatchers materialized from thin air; tired fights were breaking out, rabble-rousing, conspiracy theories; only one jogger remained, an erect woman who ran at night, talking to herself; and every, single, day, there was a new story on the front page of the *Looker* about some fed-up person who had gone a couple blocks north to the edge of the peninsula and dove headfirst into the rocky water below. *I know what you mean*, people would say, picking up a copy. One night an old Jew lost his mind and started throwing a barrage of china from his upper-floor window and calling to God. That one drew an audience of about forty people clapping their hands. I was next to a woman with braids who was narrating the whole thing as she recorded it on her phone. "Ooh there go another one," she'd say, and trace the arc of a saucer until it smashed to bits. On the other end of the crowd I saw Soup-Eye and his friends trying to catch teacups and bumped through the crowd quick to get to him before he saw me. I snuck up close; he hadn't seen me.

"Listen, Soup-Eye," I grabbed him and said, "I know it's one of you who's been stealing my socks from the dryers at the laundromat. There are security cameras. You should know: taking innocent people's clothes from the dryer, it's a nasty way to start your life."

"It's too hot for socks, fool," Soup-Eye said as he shrugged me off. He was big for a ten-year-old, extremely stocky. We had started off on good enough terms until I saw some of his friends wearing my favorite pair as headbands. The old Jew chanted a loud Yiddish curse and threw something else, then Soup-Eye and the other orphans ran to where it might land, only to lose their nerve at the last moment and jump aside, giggling.

I said, "Whatever, Soup-Eye. One of you is going to cut yourself. And why isn't there a curfew at that home? What if someone comes to adopt y'all in the middle of the night and you aren't there?" A teacup smashed to the ground.

"Motherfucker. No one's coming for us," said Soup-Eye, facing the sky.

*   *   *

That night I walked up and up and up, beyond the fracas and all the way to the piers where the boats came in. It smelled like dead fish, lazy gulls floated overhead. Even at that moment another ferry was coming in from across the ocean with a fresh cargo of faces. I went up on the wooden pier and watched as the ferry docked and a team of men in gray overalls tethered it with ropes. A drawbridge lowered from the back, and after a few loudspeaker commands from the captain, everyone started disembarking in single file. They were carrying bags and holding on to loved ones. Children on shoulders squealed in delight. Everyone had the dream of Polis in their eyes. Those dummies: that's how they get you. You catch a glimpse of the skyline rising from the water's horizon and you're finished. Just *looking* at that beat-up boat made me feel like I was back there again, climbing onto the deck railing with my arms wide open, as if it hadn't been three months already—a salty wind whipping my hair, a thousand and one promises titillating my soul, a mighty *woo-hoo!* escaping my chest until a crewman in a white hat had to come say I wasn't allowed up there, for liability reasons. That should've been a clue.

"Don't even bother!" I yelled to the newbies from where I was standing now. "It's a fucking conspiracy! Save your money, go somewhere else, invest in stocks or something."

But none of them were listening. I might as well have been talking to an echo. A woman in an official uniform approached me gently. "Are we feeling alright today, sir?" Geez. You seriously couldn't stand around anywhere without someone thinking you weren't okay. I felt exhausted; my throat hurt. I moved from the edge and started to walk away.

"You don't have to worry about me being one of those jumpers, ma'am," I told her as I shuffled off. "I'm not sure it's any better in the next life either."

Then all the way back: past the side streets where ancient grandfathers sat outside and smoked long pipes, past the machos arguing in nine kinds of Spanish, past the bodegas where the fruit wilted outside, along Aramaya Street, swollen with traffic, a stop in the deli for a greasy dinner sandwich, then to our building, through the lobby door, up the eight flights of smelly stairs, past the hooded woman who was always just turning the corner, and into that apartment where it was daytime even if it wasn't daytime, where there was no juice in the fridge, where every night on that slim bed my teeth fell out in my dreams.

"Hey, Calumet," I'd say.

"I know, I know," he'd say.

A Doomed Seduction

Fine, there were some good days. One time a girl in a bar said she liked my ears, Reginald had food poisoning and I got half his customers, Calumet would come out of his room and we'd get to *talk* for once. But my life was a two-mile radius shrinking every day, and I could think of nothing else to talk about. I'd hear the slow croaks of him leaving his room and scramble from my bed, where I'd been trying to touch my toes or something, poking my head out just as he locked his door with a small key. Seeing him outside, it never ceased to amaze me. Calumet was one of those loping giants the world does not make anymore. Looking into his eyes required you to tilt your head back, and even then you were met only by the morose gaze of a doe. He had a gaunt face, jowls for a neck, limp black hair. A long-gone beard had stained a shadow onto his cheeks forever. And something about the mechanics of his gait, it gave the impression of slow motion even if he had somewhere to go. On the Sunday I am talking about, he had on a set of denim overalls so loose he seemed naked, and greeted me by shyly tapping my shoulder as he headed toward the kitchenette. I followed him in quick steps, hovering about his elbows.

I said: "I don't know about you, Calumet, but me I'm heading out of this dump, I swear. I've been saving up. As soon as I get even half a wind I'm out of here, so long, sayonara, I mean." He was reaching for the good glasses so I turned on the faucet to help him rinse them. In his hands the glasses looked like toys for a tea party. "You might want to get your goodbyes in now is all I'm saying. You're going to be missing ol' Slide when it's just you and Eustace again, I'm telling you."

He said: "That's very brave."

"*Someone* here has to be. All I'm waiting for is the trains to open and that's it."

"And then what?"

"And *then* what?" I said. "You got to be kidding me, Calumet." I went on telling him that there was more than this, that life would bloom only if you watered it, that Polis was a gauntlet brimful with nectar but here where we are we're getting only the dribbles running down the side, I've been hearing things, Calumet, there are rumors of better happenings farther south, if only we could go look, but what things like this take is a Leap-of-Faith, a Seizing-of-the-Day, if you will, *chutzpah*, I mean... Yet from his great height the only thing Calumet did was shake his head. He considered me with the regret of a watchman who cannot help the strangers below. "My days for that are gone," he said.

I decided to switch the subject.

"How old *are* you, anyway, Calumet?" I said, taking a seat on the counter. He finished with the glasses and tore off some paper towels to dry them.

"I am thirty-four years old."

"What!" I said. I got off the counter. "Geez-us, man."

"Ah, so you thought I was your peer?" he said, smiling behind slabs of teeth.

"*Peer?* Man, I've been here thinking you were my uncle or something. You don't look too good for being in your thirties, Calumet. You need to get out more and that's the truth."

The glass had started to squeak, it was so dry already. I looked in a cupboard and took out four plates.

"Thir-tee-four! Damn, you really had me fooled. I really had you on some uncle shit, Calumet. What's it that's so great in your room that you don't get out more? When're you gonna let me see inside like you said?"

He readied his face for a joke. "Something in here has to be sacred," he said.

"Look, he has quips now. The eavesdropper. All this *privacy*, gosh, I could be living with spies for all I know. You have the right idea, Calumet, but I wouldn't worry if I were you, even Eustace knows better than to bother you. It wouldn't be fair."

"Fair?"

"Yeh. Me on the other hand I get all the bad stuff. Nowadays when I come home I feel like he's tried on my deodorant. Things of that nature. You have the right idea though, staying indoors. I wouldn't leave my room either if my clientele wasn't growing. I'd find something online like you."

"I see," he said.

Everything he did looked like he'd thought it over ten times. When the towel fell from his hands he gave a tiny *oh* and bent all the way down to pick it up between his thumb and forefinger. Poor Calumet. He walked through life barely touching it.

"You know, Slide," he said. "It's all out there, everything you mention. Just not in the way you mention it." And before I could ask what he meant by that Eustace exploded through the door in a series of jostling steps and ran straight for his shower while stripping bare. He groaned. That put me in a funk right away. Calumet went on, "And when are you going to tell me what was so bad before that you had to come here at all?"

"Come on, Calumet," I said as I looked for coasters. "You know that stuff is private."

"Oh, I see," he said, and continued to set up.

Sunday was family dinner, which was another name for Eustace's doomed seductions. Oh boy. He'd invite some girl from the internet over for the evening and spend the hours before making a whole production out of it. He'd order food from an Italian place, put wine to chill, play jazz on the TV, and all-of-a-sudden procure four plastic chairs and a table from his room. (The first time that happened, I looked at Calumet like *What the Fuck*.) The tablecloth was a blue-and-yellow paisley print with lace edges and the cutlery was kept in a mahogany case. There'd be a lot of fussing for us to help set things up and pick off pieces of lint. He even got a candle for the table and lit it. In all that lamplight he lit a candle. At seven the girl came, to the screech of the doorbell. Eustace, dressed in his tie and blazer, looking like a great baby, would grandly open the door, for her to step into the room and squint against the lamps. She was tall or short, black or white, sometimes shy, sometimes very shy. Invariably they were plump. They all had the stupefied air of having been invited for something else. "Oh, you're here already?" he'd say, dabbing his neck with a kerchief. "We were just hanging around." Eustace, he was always trying to hang around. He offered to take her purse only after she took off her shoes. There'd be a quick tour with a stop by my bedroom to list the dimensions as if it was up for lease, then during dinner he'd try cramming a week's worth of friendship into a scant few minutes, asking me to retell that joke about the tulips that he liked so much or nudging Calumet on the arm like that was their thing. Really we were his hostages. If ever we spoke to the girl for too long, he'd panic, cut in quickly. Anything else you need, Marie? Linneth? Polly-Ann? Gwendolyn? Some garlic bread, perhaps? A warm towel? There's sparkling water, too, there's ice... Burying her in a flurry of suggestions until she forgot us. I don't know what he was so worried about—from the time they arrived, Calumet only regarded them with a bird's indifference, and *I* was too scared of anyone nuts enough to accept an invite from Eustace. Everyone ate, minding their own business for the most part. Then it always came: Eustace's hand inched across the table toward hers finger by finger like a team of white slugs. The whole thing gave me the heebie-jeebies. I felt like we were extras in a perverse sort of play. Calumet and I finished eating quickly just to get out of there. From my room I could hear Eustace bumbling through a few more pleasantries, her hesitant laughter, the undeniable cadence of bargaining, and then the resolute steps of her departure. It was always the same. For the rest of the night he would make sporadic stops at my doorway, haranguing me with questions, finding meaning in anything. We had talked too much, we hadn't talked at all, the room was too dark, Slide, you are always chewing with your mouth open, what did I think of the linguine? She probably wasn't hungry in the first place, yes, she wasn't even hungry. He wore a lightless sadness in his eyes and would have burst at the smallest of hugs. I could have cried. It was the same, I swear, everything in that apartment was always the same. But the evening I am talking about, when Calumet and I were washing glasses in the kitchenette, was the evening that Eustace had invited Monica Iñes over, a woman who would not take off her shoes, no matter how strong the suggestion.

She was a short tea-brown girl who arrived late and offered no excuse. She had hair to her waist, a cowboy's way of entering a room, and the scandalous gaze of a tattletale. Eustace could hardly believe the buckled sandals in which she sauntered across the floor. "No, Eustace, I'd rather not," she said, cruising past him in his ascot. "I don't know what's been on this carpet." From there, he was forever two steps behind. She did her introductions herself, kept her purse close, and, when it came time to sit, replaced her plastic seat with the armchair that had been in front of the TV, dragging it. Up close, from my seat, I saw she wore a smooth mask of makeup; her face seemed shaped from a uniform layer of clay. The long forehead, her eyebrows frozen into an arch, lips painted a wet red. As if noticing, she turned to the lamp on the stand next to her and asked, "Are we under a microscope here?," then switched it off. From the kitchenette came a tiny muffled yelp. Me I was grinning a little to see all the damage so quickly done, but Calumet had already fixed her with a look of disbelief. His lips tightened and his eyes seemed to sink farther back, peering out from a faraway place. Monica Iñes, who had not noticed, surveyed the neatly arranged food. That day we had risotto primavera with crushed walnuts, linguine in seafood marinara sauce, grilled lamb chops, baby spinach salad dressed in balsamic vinaigrette, garlic rolls, apple cider, and individual slices of tiramisu waiting in the fridge. She poured a glass of cider and dipped her finger into the marinara to taste it. Her clothes were all white, her earrings in the shape of golden dice. "Pagliai's," she said, naming the restaurant. "I would've hoped they'd at least have redone their menu by now." It was a violet eve in the last days of August. Oh yes, she was putting on quite the show.

Even by the usual standards it was an off-kilter dinner. With each bite of food, her appetite for chatter seemed to increase. This began with her pointing around the table with a bread roll and asking everyone a little about themselves, offering quick appraisals. I was "not too bad-looking, even with your big ears"; Eustace was "too kind for organizing all this, too kind, really"; and of Calumet she said, "You are quite tall, I used to know someone that tall," at which he clenched his teeth and looked like he was about to say something. In truth it was an opportunity for her to get going about herself. She lived down near Hempel Square, close to the arch, and had a job in PR on the eighteenth floor of the Redson Tower. She shopped in Waterloo when she had the time but mostly preferred the smaller boutiques around Yarbots. Her life was her favorite subject; she ended sentences in useless questions. Eustace could scarcely get a word in:

Monica Iñes had a story about being mistaken for a billboard girl while strolling around Battery: "And I couldn't get them to stop following me even when I showed my ID, you know?"

Monica Iñes had a story about walking in heels all the way from Avenue II to the Phantom District: "The taxis in that part, really, they are the worst. Always on a smoke break, isn't that so?"

Monica Iñes had a twin sister who was thinking of moving apartments: "Although I keep telling her, Listen, Marissa, Haverford is not the hot market right now. What's so bad about Point James, right?"

Her sweeping gestures from within the big chair gave her the air of a monarch. She spoke of Polis with the false boredom of true love. Eustace was bloodless and sweating (he kept looking to the extinguished lamp beside her), and Calumet continued regarding her with an irregular suspicion, getting up often to use the bathroom, from which he'd return with a splashed face. Me: I was having a good time. I'd never heard of any of those places. With every next story, a new part of Polis would light up in my mind's eye, working me into a fire of imagination. She seemed a kind of merchant bringing missives from another land. Soon it was clear that Eustace was caught in a trap of his own design, for when the hour came when he should have been reaching for her hand, only Calumet had gone to his room in a huff, my plate still half-full, a third bottle of wine open and pouring…

"…and looking for gallery space around Point James is the newest nightmare, let-me-just-tell-you," Monica Iñes was saying. "Fabricio hardly wanted to cut us a deal, even after all he and Julia had been through, you know?"

"So what did she *do*?" I insisted, my chin propped in both hands. She leaned in, spoke as if scheming.

"Would you believe? I convinced her to do it outdoors in the end!"

"Did you!"

"Oh yes. I got a couple permits and we closed off that section of Dryer Road, from the rink to the gardens, you know? Right there. In front of some of those same galleries!"

"Ah! I can only imagine."

"Oh, it was the biggest outrage! No one had seen that many people in the nude around those parts for quite some time, people wrote complaints. Terrible, isn't it?" She settled back and finished another glass. "'You should get into event planning, Monica.' Daddy's words. But it can be such a hassle. You alright, Eustace?"

He looked up from the bread roll he'd been shredding into crumbs. "What? Fine! No, no, no, I'm fine, no, go on, please."

"See now that's what I mean, Monica Iñes, when I was talking about *initiative* earlier," I went on. "For example, I've been mentioning having a party, too, in this place here for quite some time, but you think anyone listens?"

"Have you?" she asked.

"I know, I know. It's a shit place. But it wouldn't be anything big, the thing I'm thinking of. It's more of a soirée, even. Conversation, music, things of that nature. Do you know how many times I've said to everyone here, How about we get a few plants? Some rhododendrons. Or African violets, even, *those* come in all kinds of colors. Are you seeing any plants here?" I pointed around. "It's like casting your prose before swine, you know? They wouldn't even know how to read it."

Eustace got up and folded Calumet's empty chair, smiling intently. "Would you like a slice of cake?" he asked.

"I'm fine, thanks," I said.

"I meant Monica," he said.

"That's okay, Eustace, I'm barely managing as is."

He went to the kitchenette and turned on the faucet.

"But perhaps I'm wasting my time, Monica Iñes. Some places are beyond hope. What are a few flowers going to change in here, huh? It takes more than that to give your life some dignity."

"Yes, I know what you mean. It really is a shame, you know? And there are such charming little spots around here, too, where you could do so much."

"Here? In Middleton? No, you have it mistaken. I've never heard of anything good here in all my time."

"Well, it's no Point James, of course, but I did attend the most delightful housewarming not even a year ago, and you'd be surprised what's on the other side of some of these walls."

"Oh?"

"Oh yes." She told me of a place. It wasn't too far from here. I saw a wooden hallway leading to a red door. The door had a brass knocker shaped like a lion's mouth. When you knocked, it knocked quietly. Inside were curved ceilings, Aztec paintings on the walls, a kitchen with an island, and super-huge windows with a view of the water. A pot of soup was waiting on the stove, made of ingredients I'd picked up at the market earlier. Latest editions of my favorite magazines were neatly arranged on a coffee table in front of the seating area, where there were leather chairs and a beanbag just for kicks. When guests came over they hung their coats in a little walk-in closet and enjoyed a seltzer with a wedge of lime. We would complain about the commute and ask about so-and-so. The toilets had heated seats. My bed adjusted for the position of my spine. I kept watches on my dresser and had presets for the shower. And in the winter there was even a fireplace I was not supposed to use, but, with the way things worked out...

"the landlord tended to turn a blind eye to all that," she finished. I looked up, blinking, still sitting at that plastic table. Someone had refilled my glass and I took a long gulp.

"That sounds nice," I said.

"Yes, Slide, it does," she said. Satisfied, she reclined and retrieved a pocket mirror from her purse to touch up the lipstick at the corners of her lips. "I don't usually make it out this far. All this heat. But at least some of it is salvageable, you know?"

The night had filled every crevice of outside. I wanted to look into her eyes, which were as bright as limpid pools. I felt drowsy.

"Monica Iñes," I said, "do you know that you are in the one good chair?"

"I know, Slide."

"Why's it so much to ask, Monica Iñes?" I said. "Why? It's not so hard. A little decency is all I'm asking for. Something to let me walk around with my back straighter, you know? I'm not done with that." Eustace had returned to take my plate but I still had a couple forkfuls of risotto left.

"It's cold," he said, and took it anyway.

"Are you seeing this?" I said. "Did you see that? Look, it's like I'm a baby."

"I saw, Slide," said Monica Iñes, the red of her lips shining.

"Not to intrude on your date or anything, Monica Iñes, but this whole place, it's too much. Look at what he just did. He's inhumane is what."

Eustace, who had stopped a few paces away, seemed to weigh many responses at once. The TV had stopped playing music some time ago.

"The food is cold, Slide. Are you going to eat cold food?"

"What if I was? Am I not allowed? Some cold food might do me good seeing how hot it is in here. As a matter of fact, give me that plate." I was getting up but Monica Iñes held my wrist.

"Sit down a little longer, dear," she said. "Tell me about the plants." She handed me my wineglass. Eustace went to the sink. I huffed, I puffed.

"I keep telling everyone, Monica Iñes," I said distractedly, "even a single plant. There are studies that show. It's good for the mood is what I mean. Why can't we be civil?"

"We have the most lovely gardens in Tipton Lane, really, you must call me sometime. They are private but a friend of mine has the key. Here, let me write you down my number, Slide."

"Yes, of course, thank you. I'll save it in my phone right now. Is that a four or a nine? You have nice handwriting, this is just the kind of handwriting I expected you to have. I have a client, Monica Iñes, he's a horticulturist, he knows I like plants. He's been telling me he can get some starters for us at a good rate. All it'll take is a stop by his showroom to—"

"He cuts hair." I turned. It was Eustace again. He held two saucers of tiramisu.

Monica Iñes said, "Eustace?" as if he had raised his hand in class.

"What he means by his 'client,'" Eustace continued, "is someone whose hair he cuts. He's a barber. That's what Slide does." His head looked like a large dollop of toothpaste squeezed from a tube. The saucers shook in his hands.

"You know what, Eustace," I said, "I'd appreciate it if you focused on drinking your milk instead."

"His milk?" Monica Iñes gleefully said.

A panic washed over his face. He looked to Monica Iñes (or maybe again to the lamp she'd turned off) and said:

"He is always complaining when all I have done is what? Given him a place to stay. Yet always he makes a fuss, even while eating my food."

"You add that to the rent!" I said. I looked to her too. "Have you ever heard of anything like this? He buys all this food and says we *have* to come eat it, and then at the end of the month," the cost of everything, he adds it to the rent. It's not even a choice, look, it's one of the rules."

My glass was full again. I got up, gulped the wine down, and walked over to the poster. I was really annoyed.

"'Rule three,'" I read. "'Family dinner on Sunday evenings.' You ever seen anything like this, Monica Iñes? And here's another one about the lamps. We're not allowed to turn off the lamps."

"Oh yes, yes, I saw that," she said.

Something was giving me a headache, probably all those lights in my face. "All these lights in my face are giving me a headache," I said, and bent down and yanked one of them from its socket. Eustace uttered a choked cry and bustled over just as I stomped to the other side of the room.

"What kind of a family would this be, anyway?" I asked.

"Don't you dare!" Eustace said. "Don't you dare!" He'd gotten only the first light plugged back in by the time I'd undone three more. Monica Iñes had her phone out and was typing something even as she looked around smiling.

"Do you know I am getting spots behind my eyes?"

Eustace's voice had reached the falsetto of a damsel. "Stop it! Cut it out or I'll, I'll... Please, sorry, no, stop. Stop it, you rat!"

I'd made it over to the bunch near the hallway. "No one needs this many lights. That's not rocket surgery." Then I reached for the socket of the surge protector where twelve lamps were plugged in at once.

"Slide! No! Stop!" It was Calumet, galloping down the hall behind an outstretched hand. But he was too late to thwart me, for I had yanked the plug from the socket, half the room had gone dim, and something was already happening to Eustace.

*   *   *

A burst of color swelled to the surface of his face, the virulent green of nausea. He became a quick blob of a man, barreling through the table and chairs until we were suddenly facing each other, and caught me with a meaty left hook to the jaw. For a second I thought the lights had turned back on. With one hand he pinned me by my throat against the wall and with the other he flailed my ribs, all the while sweating from his every pore. His eyes had the madman's look; from his open jaw there came a most frightful howl. I thought some sort of a devil was being summoned into the world through his throat. Punch after punch landed on my chest, my left cheek, that part on your sides where the ribs don't reach. It was very unfair. I kept ducking my head beneath my hands and telling him we needed to restart. I don't know how long it was, but finally Calumet plugged the lights back in and the bright daze struck Eustace silly. He tottered back and blinked without knowing anyone, like a sleepwalker just woken up, his pants smeared with tiramisu. Then he collapsed.

I realized I was a bit drunk. And when had it gotten so late? Eustace was slumped to the floor and Monica Iñes got up like it was a good time to get going. Her face was two parts excitement with a dash of fear—as far as she knew, we could *all* have been like this. "Wait!" I said. "That wasn't really a good show of my skills just now. It was an ambush." A swollen lip was fumbling some of my words. "And I'm more of a hairstylist, really, *barber* is an outdated term."

"Oh, is that so?" she said. I could tell she wasn't going to leave. Yes, she would stay. We could talk some more about other places where the rent was good and the decor in fine taste. Later that night we'd walk around in the heat and find somewhere private to hold hands. But her smile faded when Calumet spoke again.

"*You* have done this," he said. He fixed her with a fiery gaze.

"Me?" she said. He walked, trembling, through the debris until he was looming over her with his perilous height. He seemed somehow both determined and timorous, like a nervous mongoose facing its first cobra. She reached his hip.

"Yes. You are the one, Monica Iñes. And now it is best that you go."

"Well," she said, "that's just what I was doing," and with an affronted strut she cleared the distance to the front door and disappeared through it like a gust of wind. Ah, shit. How had that gone so downhill? What gives, Calumet? And, hey, as a matter of fact, why is Eustace of all people the one that's moaning?

Spiders in the Suitcase

I refused to help in any way at all, filled to the brim with too many bad passions to lift a finger. Even as Calumet swept up the broken plates and righted the table, I could only trounce in circles like a headless ox, glaring at the limp Eustace, raging up an awful calamity. So you think it's funny that I cut hair? It's an insult now when a man makes a living? I work a noble profession, I would have you know, one of the noblest! But he had faded from the world and responded to nothing. And you, I said as Calumet hoisted him up, oh yes, of course he's the one you would be helping! Our petty bully! Our round despot! Yes, it is always the fate of the oppressed to love that which oppresses them, you should know better, Calumet... Calumet, too, said nothing. Even as I exhausted myself of mean epithets, then thundered to my room to begin packing my things.

*   *   *

Nasty day! Evil place! My friends, I was a wound-up coil of venom and shed skin. No kind of lullaby would have soothed me. If I'd had a pistol, I would have used it to shoot at the moon. Oh yes: I was badder than bad. I had a leather suitcase that I pulled out from under the bed and shook free of spiders. I wasn't going to need much, only the quick essentials that would allow me to get going. In fact now would be a good time to pare down my wardrobe and leave space for nicer things in my new life. I folded in four sets of underwear from my top drawer and another five from the dirty pile in the corner. I had one other pair of jeans besides the one I was wearing, a black pair with weakened threading around the crotch. I decided to leave them. Three black T-shirts and five gray, my steel-toe boots, dress shoes, several pairs of socks, a good white button-down, khaki pants, swim trunks, a tanned leather belt and a woven blue one, my ten-pound dumbbell, a picture of someone I used to know, my towel, an unopened toiletry kit, phone charger and laptop, green mittens, a book of haircuts, and my favorite electric clippers—all those I packed. Out in Polis I would find somewhere to hold me over while I oriented myself. Maybe one of those hostels I'd heard of, a week max, just enough time to find somewhere permanent. I was sure there were some nice studios I could check out. I'd even risk roommates again, so long as I had a chance to vet everyone and ensure they weren't weirdos. We'd have to spend a night doing something regular, like bowling. Absolutely no family dinners. Anyway, I wouldn't turn my nose up at anything until I'd seen it all. A whole land of apartments! What had I even been waiting for? Dizzy on imagined futures, I paused my packing only to spit out the window. Minutes passed before I noticed my injuries—my right hand couldn't clench, it hurt to breathe, my forehead throbbed. Fucking Eustace, fat people have heavy bones. We would need a rematch. I had a nap. I woke up. The night was no closer to ending than when it began. "Alright, Calumet, this is it," I said through our spot on the wall. "It's been okay, I got to say, but I can't say any more than that. You were one of the highlights if that means anything. Me I'm do- ing what I said I would. So long, okay?" I didn't hear anything from his end. It made me worry that something was wrong. "Fine, hold your peace if that's what you want. You on Eustace's side? Well screw that too then, I don't need this." I clicked my suitcase shut. Then I heard rustling from the other side. When he spoke, his voice was deeper, he must have been cupping his hands around his mouth. "Slide, come in here," he said. I recoiled as if bitten. "Really?" I yelled. He said, "Yes. Now, please." "Now's not the best time." More silence. I hemmed, I delayed, I swallowed three waves of curiosity. But let me not lie to you and say I did not take my suitcase with me and end up before that last door along the hallway, my head still throb- bing, my pride a bit bruised, turning his knob with all the wonder of a voyager entering a hidden tomb.

It was another world. Tapestries hung on every wall and the floor was covered in rows of books, turned edge-down such that their spines faced upward. There were so many that they formed a sort of platform, and if not for the scant pathway left open, I would have had to step on them to get anywhere. The path ran straight, then split toward the desk on the right and the bed on the left—a wide, king-size mattress on a box spring alone, covered in a red duvet. Beside the bed was a small stand for medicine bottles and a miniature ship atop a plate. Calumet was at the desk, a polished antique facing the corner, sitting on a swivel chair as he picked from a bag of pistachios in his lap and added to a mound of empty shells. Beneath his eyes were pools of deep melancholy; he had the august presence of a patriarch. All the room's light came from a single warm bulb. I remained in the doorway and looked around, half-impressed, half-annoyed. "Quick, close it!" he said, and just when I was about to ask why, I caught an orange blur dashing across the books and toward my legs. A cat! I shut the door. It stopped a few paces away and regarded me with disappointment. Then it slunk to the window straight ahead, leaped onto the sill, and yawned in an arch. That was why Eustace sneezed so much. Geez, it was like everyone in that place had some sort of secret...

"I'll tell you what's *not* going to happen right now, you're not going to convince me to change my mind, let me just recommend you give *that* up right away," I said. "I've decided already: I'm leaving. I won't spend another night in this place."

"No," he said. "I wasn't going to try any of that." He cracked two pistachios and popped them into his mouth. He had one leg crossed over the other, both of them splayed out full length across the books. "What you have done tonight cannot be undone, and now you must go. One way or the other, Eustace will not have you anymore."

"What *I've* done?" I said. "Well, how's that for something. What about the part where he rocked me in the facial?"

"Slide—"

"Look: my jaw clicks. I'd sue for damages if Eustace wasn't such a sad sack already. And I have to say, Calumet, you were acting pretty strange tonight yourself. You know there are professionals the two of you can go see."

"Slide! Do not be cruel."

I crossed my arms.

Looking at some of the books by my feet, I saw they were mostly brown hardcovers, no jackets, the titles stamped in gold. I couldn't figure out any order—there was a thin one called *Us, Liberated!* right next to a thick volume titled *Modes of Birdsong IV*.

Calumet spoke: "Do you know where you will go?"

"I have a few ideas," I said.

"Have you a place to stay yet?"

"I have some *ideas*," I said. He looked me over doubtfully.

"Slide. When you go out there, it is not like you imagine. Polis is a friend to no one. It will only take what you give and spit back the bones, even your past, which it holds in reserve to taunt you."

"Yes, you've mentioned all that," I said, looking at my watch, though I had no watch.

He reclined, crossed his legs the other way. The beginnings of wrinkles tugged at the corners of his lips. "Well. You lasted longer here than the others, at least."

"That one takes me for a trip! So it's some kind of wager then? You two cast bets to see how long until Eustace assaults someone?"

"I suppose it is a bit absurd," he said, shaking his head, "though it is something. And, no, no bets were placed, beyond the private measure I kept to myself. You were past your limit weeks ago."

He cracked a pistachio. Outside, the night was at its darkest hour and every sound was of someone up to no good: the slow growl of a car turning a corner, an old voice serenading.

The cat was prowling after shadows between the furniture. Calumet shifted imperceptibly and began again.

"For some people, it is best if the world does not come to disturb us. Eustace and I can coexist, for whatever reason. Polis brought us to each other, if not as friends then at the very least as cellmates. It will have to do. Anyway, I have learned that a friend is not what you want living beneath the same roof as you." The thought caught him up for a moment. Then a wild light burst in his eyes. "Oh, why has everything I have ever touched turned to dust! Why have I never known respite! Now another one of you must pass through while I remain here, burdened? No. Come, take a seat, Slide. You asked me before why I never want to talk about my time out there. Tonight you will get your wish."

"Now?" I said, though I was already walking the path to the bed. "I'm a bit busy, Calumet."

"Yes, now. You see, some of us, we die before we die. Others are like you who can live a thousand lives without touching a grave. The price you pay is to keep our old stories with you. It is only fair."

I pouted my bottom lip as I settled on the bed. "Alright, alright, man, go ahead. Geez. What a day I'm having."

He then readied himself. His hands were dusted clean of pistachio salt and the shells swept into a wastebasket at the side of the desk. It took him two tries to clear his throat. As he began speaking, he addressed the window as much as he did me, as if all of Polis was the audience to which he gave testimony. His voice was low and rolling, rising from a great depth within his chest. Already I could see he was looking into the past.

"This, what I am talking about, was ten years ago," he began. "Okay then. Alright. Well, we were an all-purpose wait-staff in one of those old buildings in Point James..."

THE LONE BALLAD OF THE MAN CALUMET

They were an all-purpose waitstaff in one of those old buildings in Point James. The Rudolf. A tower of beige bricks high
up on Avenue XV, where the boulevards were shaded by wil-
lows and mannequins struck poses in the windows. They wore
purple pants and white shirts with silver buttons, kept their
nails trimmed, doused each other with nicknames, and learned
to smile just-so. Their shoes were expected to shine. There was
a superintendent, Madame Lupont, who organized the schedule and mothered anyone who cried. Did they cry? Sometimes:
yes. The hours were long and did not pay well. They were
the world's dregs, down to their last chances; those without
tattoos had scars. Stepping out onto the sidewalks of Point
James, as they sometimes did (only to retreat as if struck), they
were stunned by the stainless streets, the gourmet smells, the
rarefied air and the people breathing it, who seemed to shim-
mer as if varnished. None of them trusted the too-polite way
passersby asked if they needed help getting anywhere. Back
indoors, they shook their fists at the injustice. At the very
least they could save money on rent, for the second floor of the
Rudolf had been given over entirely to their quarters, so that
those with no other recourse could cry right there and never
have to worry about being late. They lived two to a room,
slept on bunk beds, and smoked indoors until the walls stank.
On one end of the floor was a single big kitchen and on the
other was a large room with showers where the water was cold
and the tiles cut their feet. A partition ran down the center
to separate the sexes. Still, there were incidents. How many
hopeless young girls fled that building with nothing but the
bruises of love and a swollen belly, Slide, I do not want to count.

Happy? Who was happy. Sad? Who had time to be sad. We never asked anything of luck because we never knew which kind would answer the call. Every night people collapsed onto those beds like felled trees in a forest where no one listened. Certainly not the residents, whose elevators had no button for the second floor. The same space down there, which held nineteen rooms, two people each, was on every other floor divided into but two apartments, a family apiece. Ah, that's some funny math, isn't it?

Fit. Madame Lupont was always talking about Fit. She did up the schedule in a ledger she kept on her person at all times, using a meticulous pencil to make changes on the fly. A tight-skinned, neckless woman with a jaw that reached past her brow, that's how she was. She kept her hair in a silver bun and something about her features seemed Eskimo. When she had to make a change, she unfolded a pair of gold-rimmed spectacles from the breast pocket of her blouse and said, *Let's see.* Always rearranging, trying new matches. Perhaps she could have this-one-here work the pool this week and that-one-there do deliveries instead. Or let's go with what's-her-name as one of the afternoon drivers and so-and-so to trim the balcony hedges. There was a staff meeting every Sunday evening in the courtyard by the pool, where everyone sat in wicker chairs while she read from motivational texts, tapping her finger on the podium for effect. "Onward!" she might say. Or "No day is wasted. The best is yet to come." What she desired most was a seamless harmony between all the building's moving parts, where every worker fit into his or her role like a cog and every solution arrived before the problem. Really, it was a fool's errand, for two things stood in her way. One: the old men on staff, who were fixed in their habits and budged for neither women nor time. If they had worked the doors twenty years ago, they would be working the doors today. Two: the young men on staff, who ended up in all manner of trouble. Every few weeks it seemed she needed another batch of them to replace the ones lost to the red lights of the Phantom District. Other buildings with smaller staffs contracted out much of their work, or let residents figure it out themselves. But the Rudolph had once been a hotel, and Madame Lupont still envisioned it as a kind of subsistent utopia, where the only thing the outside world could offer was a change of scenery. Calumet and the others, they were the drivers, porters, doormen, valets, couriers, housekeepers, movers, maids, babysitters, nannies, dog walkers, deliverymen, electricians, plumbers, emergency contacts, and everything else not yet stipulated on the day they first shook Madame Lupont's hand. They had not known it then, but they had given her the hours of their lives.

Yet, and this is important, too, she was not cruel or even cold. She simply loved the schedule. Nights would find her up late, pencil in hand, erasing and rewriting every minute of tomorrow. Some of them suspected that some awful wreck in life had thrown her heart off course, leaving her crippled, dependent on work like one of those old moguls you hear about. Though what it could be was anyone's guess: she had three bubbling grandchildren and a husband who brought her a box of éclairs every Sunday before the meeting, her mother had just turned one hundred with all the sense still in her brain, and the rumor was that when Madame Lupont left to go home, that home was on Waterman Street, where an entirely different staff opened the front door upon her arrival. She was even known to make jokes;

one time she said, "Calumet, we will have you change all the bulbs in here and get rid of our ladders. That's how you will fit!"

Such a thing was funny only in retrospect (or perhaps not at all), because if you did not fit, a pink slip saying as much would snake its way beneath your door one morning, and then you would have to go. Perhaps that was her third problem: she was forever trying to change the hand she'd been dealt. "And if you keep doing that," said Calumet's first roommate on the day he, Claudius, received his slip, "the deck is going to run out." He was a mean-faced Chinese man with a bear's physique and a silver tooth tucked far into the back of his mouth. For the weeks they shared the room, Calumet had held his breath on the bottom bunk, cringing at every groan of the frame as he waited to be splattered. Claudius secured all his plastic bags with twine and donned his cap. Staring at the ceiling, he said, "What an old cunt," then spat on the ground. That was the last time Calumet saw him. The new roommate arrived the next morning (by which time Calumet had switched to the top bunk), a pimpled blond boy who hardly disturbed the air with his tourist's smile, and whose name Calumet did not catch on his way out for the day.

That October, Calumet was being tried all over the place. Washing cars in the garage (I was so scared I'd scratch them, I hardly cleaned anything, Slide), trimming hedges in the courtyard (we always had to do some fancy shape, an R or something like that), moving a mattress up twenty flights (obscene, it wouldn't fit in the elevator, who needs all that?), and once spending an entire day dragged around by a herd of dogs whose shit they barked for him to pick up. On evenings he preferred to smoke his cigarettes with the rest of the younger staff in President's room. Everyone smoked a dark blend with vanilla flavoring and ate fried oysters and tartar sauce from the Sea King, a greasy establishment around the corner. They'd find a space on the floor or lean against the wall and eat and smoke and listen to President speak. "That's not even the half of it," President would say, patrolling the room, "my brothers and sisters, some of you don't even want to hear the other half, I can see it in your faces. You would rather turn the lights off and not have to know what your reflections tell you. That you have come to love your servitude, you have grown accustomed, the kowtow is now your natural posture, is it not? Yeeessss." He was an Asiatic blackman with many piercings and the noble repose of an ancestor. Really he should have been on a coin. Each day after work he switched from his uniform into a tight black shirt and pants, a gold ankh around his neck, and recited his dogma while touching his congregation on their shoulders, some of them spilling out into the hall just to catch his words. "Look at Sister Bones over there by the radiator, who comes to me every evening and says, 'Brother President, I think I'm ready to burn this whole place down, I am fed up! All I need is a single match!' Oh, she was quite brave. But, my brothers and sisters, I ask you, how many fires have there been over the last week? What smoke have you seen other than the one with which you poison yourselves in this very room?" and so on. The haze of their smoke gave him an aura of the clandestine, and no matter whose turn it was to be made an example of, they all responded as if handed a precious cargo, such as the girl Bones, who hung her head and muttered, "It's true, he's right." President alone took pride in the baseness of their situation, for what better position was there from which to topple a tower?

He was their bannerman for the long-promised revolution. If he'd asked for their blood they would've bitten open their veins no-problem. But when the morning came, President would report to his shift fixing leaks, just like everyone else, and in that room on evenings he, too, ate from his styrofoam box of oysters, drank from a cup of soda with the ice melting.

"President was the first of such Brothers Seven I would come to see around Polis street corners, yelling their prophecies from megaphones. I could not know it then, but I'd soon grow tired of the sight of them. Black from head to toe, saying Nubian this, World Order that. Always pointing to their foreheads. You can find them on Avenue VII holding mysterious books and arguing with financiers. Look, I may have a copy there. I used to read it and think of joining. Now I know they are an inflexible bunch, with an impenetrable rhetoric behind which they hide themselves. But ah! At the time, at the time... we didn't know any better, Slide."

Back then, Calumet was practically a spring chicken, with a beard out to here and no wrinkles at all. If he seems quiet now, it's only because he got most of his talking out of the way then. That's not to say that he was the life of the *party* or anything, but at least he knew where they were. On weekend nights a big host of them would move as a pack out toward the Phantom District. They'd cause a ruckus even on the subway and emerge into the neon lights like divers coming up for air. The leader of their procession was one called Ragabond, barely twenty, gruff like a Viking, who yelled, "Showtime, showtime, showtime!" as they paraded the alleyways. At the cafés where big-bosomed ladies sang cabaret hits, they'd buy cheap whiskey with a bucket of ice to share. In the pool halls amongst the prowling hustlers, they'd watch Piggy lose all her week's wages to a dwarf with glorious hair. They'd mingle with the sailors, the carousers, the freaks in costume, the dope boys in low cars who say they've got what-you-need. Tuxedoed dandies, arm-wrestlers playing for pennies, the goths holding snakes, the women in red windows whom John Boy couldn't resist. With them was Big Yup, whose evening always ended in a fight. Drippy-Fats exchanged nods with a crew of bikers from his previous life. Even Calumet's pimply new roommate came along, whose breathless way of speaking and delicate movements had so quickly earned him the nickname Wisp that the real name was lost forever. He was a two-drink kind of guy, after which he began declaring his love to strangers. They'd dance a rough salsa and sweat through their shirts. They'd make a shield around Fox when she had to piss in a corner. They'd stand on tabletops and laugh from their bellies. Toward the night's end, stupefied by excess, they'd find in their feet the endless stamina of zombies and use it to walk back to Point James with whoever was left. Along the way they worried about Fit. Wisp, for example, had spent the past week in the laundry room, a gray nowhere place in the basement generally accepted as a limbo between the Rudolph and dismissal. He fed a line of gleaming industrial machines with robotic servitude and scrubbed the finer things by hand until his knuckles turned red. He admitted to dreams in which his brother's arm was trapped in one of the washers but he could not get it out. If worse came to worst, he would head for Petit Julienne, from where a friend of his had once sent him a postcard. Bones shared an unlikely story of an old couple on a ferry inviting her to Singapore, should she want to go, because she reminded them of someone dead. Perhaps she would go there once her back broke from all the lifting, and start a new life as their adopted daughter. Their eyes settled on Calumet. "Legs," they said, "what about you..." "Me?" said Calumet. Well, for Calumet, if this didn't work out, the next stop would have to be one of those Downtown shelters, or, worse yet, back to that childhood home out west, where sand from the desert eroded everyone's throats, and his cousins drank themselves into demons, and his mother would be waiting with a long list of *I-told-you-so*s and cuffs to the back of his head and call him a worthless etcetera for abandoning her after all she had done, hadn't she been so good to him for so long, only to be repaid with an empty room and a typo-ridden note in the morning saying he'd gone, which, if you don't mind, Slide, and also seeing as it's not really necessary to what I'm talking about, I don't really want to get into right now.

But he must have been doing something right, for one day it was announced on the schedule that Calumet would be installing storm windows for winter. This was a big deal. Not many jobs involved entering the homes of the residents. Those that did, Madame Lupont handed out to a select few rather than risk ruination by letting every other wretch trounce upstairs with their paws of mud. That is to say, it was the sort of job usually given to the immovable old men, who did it now because they'd done it already, and whose faces the residents had grown accustomed to without realizing it. For the most part those men kept to themselves, chewing tobacco and debating cricket matches in the big kitchen. But one of them, named Mr. Terry, had recently suffered a strange two-toothed bite on the ankle and was fighting a fever for his life. His deliriums were keeping people up at night, and the joint task of installing the windows had been left for some days now to Mr. Gifford alone. Doable, yes, but Mr. Gifford was prideful, and in that obstinate way particular to Caribbean men, he let Madame Lupont know he would not be working on his own a minute longer. Either an exorcism needed to be arranged to rid Mr. Terry of the ghosts that plagued him, or someone needed to come help. Preferably one of them young fellas always staring at the stars, or talking into their phones at all hours of the day.

Their work went like this: Storm windows of various sizes were shelved in neat rows in a storage room in the basement. Some were light, most were heavy. There were cans of weather sealant to be applied with a heat gun to the window edges once they were affixed in the frame. What's more, because this was really the sort of work that should have been done from the outside of the building, using a window washer's trolley, tricky compromises had to be made. They had a box of plastic suction cups with finger loops to attach to the storm windows and hold them in place while the sealant was applied, and in some of the older apartments the entire original window itself had to be removed before anything could be done, leaving a hole in the wall through which one could easily plummet. "If you are scared of heights, now would be a good time to say," Mr. Gifford concluded his tutorial by mentioning. He had loaded Calumet with the necessary boxes while twirling a screwdriver in his hand. Calumet, tall as the day is long, couldn't afford to be scared of heights since the time he hit puberty. He said he was not. Mr. Gifford had already completed two floors on his own before presenting Madame Lupont with his ultimatum, so they started on the fifth.

*   *   *

Calumet, he lacks a certain *panache* when telling a story, I've never seen anything like it. His tone is always the same; he skips over the juicy bits in a roll of mumbles. I started asking him what it was like the first time going up into those apartments. Did he see the marble foyers? The crystal lights? Wainscoting on the lower walls? The chintz curtains? The record collections on the shelf? Any abstract sculptures, perhaps? How about one of those mudrooms where you leave your footwear before proceeding in, I've always wondered about those. What were their sofas like? Seriously, man, anything at all, do you not even care... On his desk lay a fresh mound of pistachio shells, which the cat would occasionally lick. I had my elbows on my knees, sitting on the corner of the bed closest to him. The night went on. But Calumet, all he did after all that was rub his cheek with the back of his hand and, tracing some invisible pattern on the wall with his eyes, say, "Yes. You know, it was quite nice." *Geeez-uuus, man...*

What he truly remembered was this: There was no clutter. Not only in the apartments themselves—where there were no socks on the floors, no styrofoam boxes, no pictures of saints crowding the mantelpieces, and the kitchen sinks held not a single plate—but also on the very faces of those inside, who seemed to look through the world with unclouded eyes. The first woman was a pretty brunette with a bob cut and a tiny stud in her nose. She lived alone and had decorated with wooden furniture and rustic greens, reggae music playing from hidden speakers. She asked their names and offered cucumber sandwiches while they worked. After that there was an older couple,

Mr. Greenly and Ms. Alpu, a German and a Bangladeshi, who had met by clutching each other's thighs during a turbulent flight over the Java Sea. Now she handled investments with private clients in the Financial Plaza and he composed musicals for a touring troupe, so they could not decide whether the extra room down the hall should be made into an office, a studio, or a bedroom for visiting grandchildren, information they shared freely from reclined chairs. On the seventh floor there were children. A chubby girl of ten with red hair and a bump on her forehead, and her brother of seven, whose eyes opened wide upon seeing Calumet. He ran away. He came back. He asked Calumet in a squeaky voice, "Can I climb your leg?," then did it anyway, getting as far up as the knee before sliding bottom-first back to the floor and looking up and giggling. His sister ran and scolded him in another person's voice: "Erold! No, Erold, you cannot do that." She was practicing being in charge. Their parents were away for a week and they were under the care of a frivolous auntie, a silver-haired woman who read gossip columns in her bedroom all day and whom they did not respect. "I'm sorry," the girl told Calumet, pulling Erold by the wrist. "He's not usually like this. May I offer you something to drink?" Etcetera: a neat architect with models of amusement parks that he presented to Calumet; three women in pantsuits who asked after Mr. Gifford's sister and sent their best wishes; a pair of young couples, no older than Calumet, who ate bursting prawns and exuded the sensuous air of debauchery; a curious tinkerer entertaining some friends and who wanted to try his hand at installing a storm window himself; a man from Aruba who was late for a lunch and so left while they were working and asked them to close the door after themselves; a Japanese family of five plus three yipping dogs that recognized Calumet and nibbled the hem of his pants. Nowhere at all did he experience the impenetrable wall he had expected, unless it was in the severe gaze of that gentleman on the eighteenth floor who was in the midst of scolding his typist when they entered. "Why, would, you, choose, that, of, all, the, words?" he asked the fumbling boy, rapping his fist on the desk in an incessant rhythm. He stood close to his shoulder and pointed out mistakes with the eraser end of a pencil. But even he warmed up when, in try-anything desperation, he turned to the two workmen and asked what name they would give to a green boat, were they in the position, and Calumet answered "Esmerelda" without thinking, to which the gentleman gave a pensive frown and thought it over, and then agreed, with a light like dawn spreading over his face, and then asked Calumet his name, followed by a series of slow, probing questions while they installed the windows, and then even took the liberty of measuring the length of Calumet's fingers, saying, "These are good…"

They all moved with the surety that nothing could happen to them. Not a single one of their doors were locked; they said "Come in" without asking who it was. Even though Calumet was a bearded giant, and Mr. Gifford, with his look of an unhugged hermit, made a mean grumble while he worked, they were treated with the easy courtesy of lords welcoming guests. By the end of the week, Calumet found it was actually Mr. Gifford's company that put him most at unease: his inattention to detail, his tendency to stand to the side and give commands rather than help. The two of them would invariably end the day on poor terms, heading opposite ways once the service elevator took them back to the second floor and spreading rumors about each other. That is why, Calumet explained to me, the server never truly envies those he serves, though he may pretend to. The chasm of difference between them is so great that neither side can actually imagine it being crossed, freeing them to regard each other with the comfort of strangers seen through a telescope. The server learns this last. Whom he in fact despises are those right by his side, whose smaller distance from him he can understand, have a measure for, and one day even traverse with a hock of spit.

Madame Lupont was happy about the pairing. Even when Mr. Terry recovered from his mysterious illness with the renewed vigor of two men, she kept the arrangement as it was. Calumet, with his dogged way of finishing tasks, like a mule, was getting the storm windows done in record time. He heard word that Mr. Gifford had complained to Madame Lupont about wanting his old partner back, whose tempo of life better suited his own, but she refused to ruffle a Fit that worked. They were almost done; Mr. Gifford could endure. And in fact all was not right with Mr. Terry. He had reentered the world of the living on a sudden whim, sitting upright in his bed one midnight and clapping. Now he no longer slept at all, had lost the color in his face, and had a clarity of vision that unnerved those to whom he spoke. She assigned him to laundry. What's *more* is that Calumet was well liked and had garnered good reports—on three separate occasions Madame Lupont had had a resident ask after the tall young fellow with the tragic air, to see how he was. So much *so* that by the end of October, all the storm windows finally installed, there was already a new entry in the schedule for Calumet, this one a special request. She met with him separately after the Sunday meeting and explained, sounding confused herself: someone had requested him as a typist.

It was the man from before; Calumet returned to the eighteenth floor. Stepping in for the second time, he noticed the place properly. The door opened onto a hallway from which he could go either left or right. The walls were wood paneled and lined with framed prints of old concert programs. He went right and entered a room of Persian rugs, crimson drapes, and leather seats. A massive window looked out onto a dizzying scape of Polis and on the gramophone a staticky woman was singing about love. The man, brown like teak, strode over from the bookshelf to shake Calumet's hand. Up close Calumet could smell the pomade in his straightened black mane, see the sharp angles of his cheeks and the trimmed hairs lining his nostrils. He gestured to where Calumet should take his spot behind the desk, which was no longer strewn with papers. Still holding his hand, he said, "I remember you had a good ear," looking him over with limp eyes. He wore soft slippers, gray, creased trousers, and a high-necked naval sweater stiffened by his poise. "It's best we begin."

Sir Artem Borand was a novelist of some acclaim to whom fortune had not been too kind. Bad memories had been taking lodge in his soul for some time now and even the happier ones he no longer revisited. On that first day he gave Calumet a quick show of the typewriter's quirks, set him up with a glass of lemon water, and began to dictate. "A storm is about to hit and rations are low," he said of the plot. He spoke slowly, but in two different voices, as if in conversation with himself: a rich velvet like that of a sultry woman, and a light soprano like that of a girl. Calumet, whose typing had not improved one bit since that hasty runaway letter, did not dare ask what was for what. The desk itself was perpendicular to the big window but off to the side, such that in order for him to look out at the view it was necessary to lean forward. Straight ahead on the other side of the room was the bookshelf covering the wall, and to his right, in grand position before the window, was a long sofa, a chaise longue, and two small stands of nautical instruments. Even in the morning sun the room seemed more to glow than shine, as if lit by unseen candles. Sir Borand walked around on light toes as he spoke; he had the high arches of a ballerina and paused for minutes between sentences. That lasted until lunch, for which he offered Calumet a slice of shepherd's pie from the kitchen, and, for himself, inhaled a pinch of snuff from a leather pouch in his pocket. He sparked up. "Away, darkness!" he snapped, apropos of nothing. "Man the bulwarks, you cowards, face the wind, hark! We will not go down like this!" and other such proclamations. He plodded in a long counterclockwise oval, and on passing Calumet's desk it occurred to him to check his work, resting a hand on his shoulder and reading intently. "I never said any of that," said Sir Borand, as if accused. He had Calumet throw it away and began again in an entirely new plot direction. Calumet wasn't exactly one to stand up for himself. In fact, he was a little bit awed. Sir Borand was prowling the room with the charged steps of a fighter in the final round. He darted, he dodged, he spoke directly to old grievances as if they were right before him. Calumet saw he was in the company of some other man, whose green eyes were brighter, whose mane of hair was more magnificent, and in the effort to keep up he took to typing furiously, sinking into the hunch that marks him to this day.

"Slow down just a little," Calumet said in the evening, stretching his palms. "I'm not getting it all." Sir Artem Borand, already dripping at the nose, took another pinch of snuff before he answered from his erect spot by the big window. "Young man," he said, with all the gravitas of a deathbed confessional, "there is no further filling of a cup once it has reached its brim." But Calumet could not figure out what that meant.

In Sir Artem Borand's mouth, all of the English language liquified into molten ore for use along the ramparts against the siege of life. He had a mind addled by time spent at sea and now used words like *scalawag* in total seriousness. He kept Calumet there from morning until evening while dictating the novel, which centered around an erratic young genius spending time at sea, and then at times switching without warning to sad rants about all the misfortunes life had laid upon him. A bad knee that shivered when it rained; the rising prices of Polis, designed to ruin him; the pregnant wife who had run out on him fourteen years ago with only the occasional word to let him know his offspring was being raised with neither his memory nor his name. "Yes, this is what they do to you," he said on that day, blowing his drippy nose into a kerchief. Now he lived in that grand old suite with his partner, Ms. Fiorina, a slim Italian who would return in the evening with dinner and kiss him on the forehead. She wore practical clothes and the same pair of knee-high boots every day. Her shoulders slouched. It was apparent straightaway that she was necessary for whatever semblance of order there was in that place, for the only parts of the household Calumet saw Sir Borand use with any proficiency were the microwave to heat up lunch, and the bathroom. Ms. Fiorina straightened chairs, checked mail, gave the rooms an air of lightness. And (wonder of all wonders) she would have Calumet come sit with them both around the granite island in the kitchen, to eat from broad plates and discuss how the day's writing had gone. These summaries on the part of Sir Borand were as helter-skelter as the dictations themselves, but she simply nodded along proudly. "You see how she treats me like a child," he would say, though continue to talk. "This is the price for living too long, you come full circle." After, the three would return to the drawing room, where Sir Borand poured brandy and muttered his way through a last few nautical commands before nodding off on the chaise longue. "He misses his wife," Ms. Fiorina said to Calumet. Her face was shiny and smooth, with no footholds for jealousy's frowns. She leaned over from the sofa and stroked Sir Borand's head. "Some people are so cruel." Outside, autumn had bloomed into canopies of orange. Polis was a twinkling symphony of lights. Calumet could go now. But he must be back in the morning.

Day after day Calumet left that place drunk on words, unable to sleep, heart pounding to return. He'd collect himself out on the landing with deep breaths, and call the service elevator only after staring at the button for a long time. The ride down to the staff quarters seemed a plummet into an underground nest. He was struck by its narrow tunnels, its noise, the rough jargon cobbled together from every kind of alley-slang there ever was. For the first time he recognized a blue haze that colored the air, and developed a cough. His brain grew foggy during games of dice and he started to lose money. The only people to whom he could complain were Bones and Wisp, which he did by means of tactless comparison. "You should see in Artem's place, there is a picture on the wall signed by a laureate," he would say, or "Artem said the other day that poets are the only people worth trusting," to which they mostly nodded and tried to change the subject. He lost his appetite for trifles. Impatience took over his dreams. Occasionally at first, but by midway through November he no longer turned up at President's room to eat, explaining that he had had something already and needed to iron his shirts. Maybe next time, perhaps. But crabs in a bucket take poorly to those who try to climb out, and Calumet's talk of being too busy for President was seen as a boast. President himself came by one night to see what the matter was. "Brother Legs," he woke him up by saying, "I have heard the worst of things. Is it true? You have let yourself become the instrument of your own destruction? Let me tell you a little something about pyramids, my brother, you see, though it may not look like it to the unopened eye, it is the brick at the bottom that..." Once Mr. Gifford spread the word that Calumet was snacking on shrimp and caviar up on one of the top floors (bitter, that man, mean as a troll beneath a bridge), it grew worse. In the showers one morning two loudmouths on either side of him had a conversation with each other—

"Have you heard, Thirdrail?"

"What's that, Westwind?"

"Somebody, and I only just heard, somebody thinks they got a big swinging dick."

"You're lying."

"I'd never. The biggest and swingiest."

"That's quite a thing."

"I heard it myself."

"What you think he's going to do with that?"

"If I were him..."

"Uh-huh?"

"...between you and me..."

"Speak on it!"

"...I'd be sure to measure before swinging it around is all."

"That's good advice!"

"Because one thing you'd hate to happen is to think you got the big guns..."

"...when you really don't have squat!"

"Embarrassing, isn't it?"

—which by that afternoon had transformed into a story about Calumet having been caught hunched over, abusing himself. Even newcomers to the Rudolph, when being shown the ropes by their cohorts, were made to understand a few basics: that a plastic bag was enough to fool the smoke detectors, that dice tournaments were on Fridays, and that Madame Lupont was tough but fair, except in the case of that tall fellow over there who has blackmailed his way into special treatment, and who is only so tall so as to better poke his nose in the air. Wisp's pink slip arrived by the end of the month and he was replaced by a mouth-breathing gossip who quickly fell into step. Things were made no better when Calumet one day misused a fancy word he'd heard. He said after the Sunday meeting: "It's getting so cold I'm flabbergasted!," and all through the courtyard a great cackle lasted for minutes. So swift was the rising tide of ill feeling that Calumet began looking for ways to prolong his hours on the eighteenth floor. Whereas he had previously been content to sit passively behind the desk and type, now he began to roam during breaks and ask about things, such as the naval instruments on the stands. This had the unexpected effect of deepening Sir Artem Borand's madness, as if the tools awoke the vestiges of ongoing battles. Of the astrolabe he said, "Pyotr the Blighted would have snatched that from my grasp were I not the quicker man!" The touching of a rusted compass caused him to shake Calumet by the wrists and say, "Give that to me! It still works." And when Calumet read out the names of a now-dead crew engraved onto the side of a flask, Sir Artem Borand embarked on a long, gruesome tale involving dagger fights and cannibalism. It was doing the trick, for Sir Borand soon worked himself up into a fire that could not be extinguished even by Ms. Fiorina's arrival, but Calumet was not sure the extra ranting after dinner was worth the tormented look in his eyes. So instead, once his bravery mounted, Calumet one evening stopped typing and in a voice that crept gently across the silence asked, "Can you tell me about your child, Sir Borand?" Sir Borand startled as if caught naked. He faced Calumet as if he were a stranger. Then a dam in him broke and he retrieved a thick journal from the book-shelf just in time to collapse onto the sofa and call Calumet to his side.

It was a book of pen-sketched portraits of children's faces. Over the years Sir Borand had imagined every possible ren-dition of what the estranged child could look like, working from a picture of his wife he had glued to the inside cover—a Spanish-blood woman named Margery. The sketches were sometimes of boys, sometimes of girls, ranging from light brown to dark. One of them had his icy eyes and her reddish hair, a sharp chin and big lips; while another was pudgy in the face, tired-looking but with the beatific smile of a saint. He really had no idea. The earlier drawings were slack, cartoonish, but he had improved with time and now they each had their own history, names, invented personalities that he recalled at once. At each new page, Calumet would gasp and say, "But they are all so beautiful…" A funny thing happened after that: Sir Borand dictated incremental changes in the appearance of his novel's hero. He grew taller, adopted a sad air, walked as if in slow motion. Exactly what lines were being blurred, it was hard to tell, but they both knew without saying. Side by side they would traverse the drawing room, past the sofa where they traced the outlines of the portraits with their fingers, the desk where Calumet was writing himself into existence one day at a time, growing braver, touching shoulders, and, if you don't mind me saying so myself, Slide, that made me grow close to him without realizing. I would ask him, Sir Borand, were they really so cruel, banishing you from the island just for gazing upon the empress's feet…? He would say, Young Calumet, it was even worse! They sent their assassins to pursue me for years… I would say, Please, Sir Artem, tell me more, how many were the fish on that Arctic night…? He, swirling the ice in his glass, leaning on me, would say, They glittered like stars legion… I, unable to stop, would say, Artem, she'll come back, she'll bring your child one day, you'll see… He'd say, I know, I know, his eyes wet, that hand on my elbow, my neck… Finally the day came. The hero in Sir Artem's novel met a novelist who needed help transcribing a novel. The novelist seduced him. Calumet looked up from the keys, his heart in his hands, begging for a touch…

"I became his lover. He fixed it with Madame Lupont, you see, he was a bit influential, I mean, he fixed it with her that I could go up there even earlier than usual, and I brought him breakfast too. A bagel shop just up Avenue XIX, that's what he liked, there'd be an order already waiting for him as soon as they opened—I'd walk inside and the woman knew my name, they were expecting me, I mean. There'd be two in the bag they gave me, he always ordered one for me, too, and I'd walk back to the Rudolph, I could see my breath the air was so cold, and go up to his place just as Ms. Fiorina was leaving. She worked as an archivist, or at a library, it was something like that. We'd practically pass each other in the hallway. She'd go and I'd wait for Artem in the drawing room, just like always. He was so prim in the morning, so neat. He ate his bagel by cutting it into smaller bites with a knife. Then he would read to me and sometimes I typed. It was like bowing before a waltz. I felt cold, but hot too. By the afternoon, there'd be no typing, none of the rants, we stayed in his room, you understand. We called it our bower. The skin on his back was soft. My head fit in the crook of his neck, even though I had to curl. I could have died there. On evenings after work, Ms. Fiorina volunteered at an animal shelter. We'd be dressed again by the time she walked in the door, cat hairs clinging to her coat. Artem had a sense for when she would return. Oh, but it wasn't so scandalous as all that, Ms. Fiorina knew what it was. I knew she knew because she began to kiss us both on the forehead, right here, isn't that strange? She had a way about her. I believe it was a part of the arrangement between them; she always slept in a separate room. I wanted to say something, perhaps to apologize, I don't know. Later I found out, and you know I am not one to talk, but later I found out he had once helped her out of some sort of trouble with traffickers. There was a debt between them somewhere. He was a good man. We made an odd threesome, eating dinners in the kitchen, watching the winter strip the trees. I mixed eggnog on the stove and served it in mugs. She would show me old maps she had brought home while Artem put records on to play and kept a hand on my back. It was the very height of my happiness. I should have died there. Ah, have I shocked you, Slide?"

Time passed. The manuscript was soon forgotten (if it had even been a manuscript at all) and Calumet was given free rein to go up there as he pleased, no knocking necessary. Sir Artem Borand had bought him a pair of house slippers to change into, and Calumet brought along a little bag of more comfortable clothes. Should he be missing anything, he knew just where in the closets to find it. The winter was mild and never brought life to a halt. They began to take short excursions—into the neighborhood at first, a Turkish café serving baklava and strong coffee, walks in the botanical gardens—which soon became more daring in their scope: a concert by a brass-horn band in one of the Downtown piazzas, where they sat near the front and lay a blanket across their laps; a ride in a cable car from the peak of Millennium Mount down to the jetties, then dinner on the private boat of a friend. Sir Borand ran in a circle of frustrated intellectuals who always knew better, with vicious minds they could never manage to make use of. More than a few of them were accompanied by a man or woman many years their junior. By silent agreement, none of the young companions spoke to each other or locked eyes, not even on the night Pietro Jacaranda (a fancy blue-blooded historian with a habit of hosting old-style balls) taught everyone a line dance that involved the continual switching of partners. When leaving the Rudolph, Sir Artem Borand and Calumet took the elevator all the way down to the garage and into a tinted-window car, to save Calumet from the spectacle of being seen by his coworkers. Still, there were those manning the gate, who seemed to look beyond the darkened glass and onto his face, which he hid. Indeed, trouble was afoot in the lower regions. Besieged by jealous complaints, Madame Lupont tried explaining to Calumet that his labor was needed elsewhere in the building and that he would be moved next week to pool cleaning. "I don't run a democracy here," she said, "but we can't have anyone turning into a lord either." He waited until they were lying in bed to tell Sir Borand: "They're switching me to pool duty. I won't be able to come up here anymore." Sir Borand sat up. "Zounds! The beasts! Blasted savages! They would take this from me too?" He pressed a few buttons on his phone and the next day Calumet quit his job at the Rudolph and moved all his things up to the eighteenth floor, condemning him to a fate of bitter looks and prank calls full of slurs. Ms. Fiorina helped ease the transition by encouraging Calumet to head to the bedroom when Sir Borand did, instead of waiting around, pretending to sleep on the sofa, as he'd been doing. When Calumet told her all the nasty things he knew his mother would say, were she to find out, Ms. Fiorina said, "Yes. People are cruel. They want you to chase happiness, but only chase. They think it will run out and there will be none left for them." She kept her smile, but on the day he saw her in a towel headed to the shower, he noticed three long scars lining her back. He did not admit as much aloud to himself, yet in his heart of hearts he knew they were now a family. It was winter. It was spring. Then a knock came on the door.

I'd been needing to pee for a bit now and kept having to cross and re-cross my legs. Every time I did, the cat made a game of pouncing at my ankles. Strange cat. It hadn't napped once in all that time, what kind of a cat doesn't nap? Dawn was coming. Outside it was still dark, but quiet in the particular way of morning. Calumet had finished all the pistachios and fallen into a pause while itching the underside of his chin. I realized I'd been breathing in, but not out.

"Well?" I said. "Who was at the door?"

"Do you need to use the bathroom?" Calumet asked.

"I'll be fine."

"You've been fidgeting."

"I'll pee after, stop talking about it."

He ran a forefinger in a circle on his desk. A nearby book titled *Lighter Than Air* lay open and facedown, a picture of a hot air balloon on its cover. It looked old and reread, they all did. He cracked his forefinger's knuckle.

"I wouldn't usually have opened that door, you know. He didn't like me to. But it had rained earlier that day and Artem's knee was acting up. It must have been April. On the other side were two teenage girls. They were identical. They wore sweatshirts and sunglasses but you could tell they were identical. They each had a large suitcase in hand. I knew what it was as soon as I saw them. They were his daughters and they had come to ruin him."

"Daughters?"

"Yes."

"Plural? From the old wife? Was she there?"

"Twins. Yes. No."

"That's wild!"

"Oh, it's much worse than that." He leaned forward, growing desperate. "It happened just the same. We looked at each other for a long time. They asked if an Artem Borand was there, and what choice did I have but to take them to him? I thought

I could blame his knee and say he was not up for guests right then. But I didn't do that. My old instincts took over, I said Right This Way, like I was a servant again. Oh, Slide, that walk down the hall was a purgatory of a thousand steps. Sometimes I think I am still walking it and the rest of my life is an imagining between footfalls. I was panicking, bargaining with fate, hoping for an excuse. What we had there, Artem and me, it was balanced so delicately. Any ruffle of the wind was going to topple it downhill. I knew, I knew. They stayed a little bit behind me and kept whispering. By the time we got to the drawing room I had aged a century. Artem had only had a few sniffs for that day, I'd been getting him to slow down, but he was hazy already. I told him he had visitors and he looked up from the puzzle—we were doing a jigsaw—he looked up from the puzzle and waved them over to shake their hands like they were anybody. What a fucking fool. He enjoyed having guests. He couldn't tell who they were because they did not match his drawings, his drawings were his children. He had a magnifying glass in one hand and the other hand he used to shake theirs, one at a time, all pleasant-like. He did not know, but I knew. 'How may I help you young ladies?' He said something stupid like that. The one in front, she was wearing gray, she was the one they had agreed would talk first. She mumbled, I remember they were nervous. They were so small. *Come again? Speak up!* Oh, my fool, my fool. I shouldn't have opened that door. The one behind took over, the one in white, just the same, she said, 'Margery sent us.' Artem had a shock like he'd slipped through a sheet of ice. The girl said, 'She sent us, she said it would be okay,' and pulled off her hood and her shades."

Here the man Calumet straightened his shoulders for the first time in a decade and looked at me with the last embers of heat burning in his eyes. "And I say to you, Slide, with every ounce of truth within me, that one in white, she was the very same as the one who again appeared tonight to cause so much harm. It was a face with nothing good in it. It was pure ruin and scandal. It was Monica Iñes."

"Whaaat."

Calumet the boy standing to the side as the terror of realization creeps across Artem's face; Calumet the man, erect as an obelisk, speaking through clenched teeth and flicking pistachio shells. Calumet, all his eggs in that eighteenth-floor basket, his throat closing as Sir Borand's arms open toward the twins. Calumet the hermit, holed up amongst old books and a cat. He was looking at me but really looking at the past. I could see he was still in that drawing room, twenty-four years old, watching the currents of Artem's love change course without warning: "Oh, my blood, my blood, how I have dreamt of you..."

Noting the stretch of sunlight across the sky, he told me the rest as quickly and unceremoniously as it had happened. Margery Iñes, the invisible wife to whom Sir Borand was technically still married, was in the throes of a chronic cough emptying out her lungs. It sounded like there were medical bills. She had set the two girls on a bus to Point James with instructions on how to find their father and to let him know where she was only on the condition that he first accept them in his arms. They had a letter saying as much. The girls, Monica and Marissa, had heard all about him, his great mind, his noble personage. They were both so happy to finally meet him. Sir Borand cried and cried. But it was

Monica Iñes who made herself comfortable right away, peeking into all the rooms and handing her luggage to Calumet. Marissa, a shier soul, kept their father's company and
offered her shoulder. She said, "Alright, alright," and cried
too. It was quite uncomfortable, made worse by Sir Borand's
introduction of Calumet only as "a young gentleman." By
that night Calumet knew better than to sleep anywhere other than the sofa, and he made himself scarce the next day,
walking around Point James in aimless circles. By the end of
the week Monica and Marissa Iñes had moved all their things
from the nearby hotel where they'd been staying and, at the
insistence of their father, took pride of place at his side all
around town. He was like a child set loose. He organized a
continuous stream of events to have them meet every person
in his life and kept bursting into tears at the slightest prov-
ocation. Here they were! The children he'd always known
would come back! Yes, there were two of them instead of
one, but that only goes to show that life can sometimes repay
all its pain with double the joy. Though Calumet still came
along to each of these debuts, it seemed more in the capacity of an assistant. Monica Iñes in particular delighted in
asking him to hold things for her, or pick up snacks around
the corner. She seemed to take something like offense at his
absurd height, commenting on it with such regularity that a
note of mockery soon emerged. "You really are that tall," she
would say to him, almost as a question. And if ever Calumet
tried to sneak a word in alone with Sir Borand, she would
soon appear with a suspicious look and new commands. For
all of Artem's delights, Calumet still recognized in his eyes
the frenzied mania of a man who no longer knew what to do.
He felt something should be said of the torment Sir Borand

had had to endure for so many years, the book of sad drawings, the nights of weeping. Where was that to go? Had it
disappeared just because these two had shown up with an
old letter and good promises? And what of the mother? The
wife? Could he be sure of all this? Those were not Calumet's
exact words, but he tried bringing up something of the sort
to Sir Borand on the afternoon when he finally got a moment. Monica and Marissa Iñes were off with Ms. Fiorina
checking out private academies to resume their schooling.
It was the first pause since the wild rush of their arrival.
"Artem," Calumet began, holding his hand, "about the girls,
your daughters... They're quite nice, they're lovely, and I...
Well, but I... a part of me was wondering... with no offense
intended, of course..." Sir Borand stiffened. He said, "Yes?"
in the threatening tone of a dreamer who does not want to
be woken up. That was as far as Calumet got. After that,
no one had to say as much for him to know he should be
going. They no longer fooled around; the pet names disappeared. First he lost his room in Sir Borand's heart and then
the one out front by the sofa, where every morning Monica
Iñes threw Calumet's bedding into a corner and complained
about clutter. That is how they treat you, Slide, even after so
long. You empty your veins for them and they say, *Get a mop,
you are staining the upholstery.* They do it with no ceremony.
They want you to pack your things and be quick about it.
At the end, what are you left with? Some books you'll never
read, memories full of thorns. They give you a final hug and
an old kitten brought back from the shelter and one day you
find you have left the Rudolph after all, with hardly a dollar
in your pocket, not a friend in the entire world, and nothing
to sniff at but the phlegm in your nose.

Opening Hours

Something was wrong with that cat. It had stopped mid-stride, tail upright, one paw hovering in the air, and was looking intently toward the door. Calumet noticed, too, and stood up at once.

"Eustace is awake," he said. "You cannot be here." He began to rummage through his books on the floor.

"Wait. Wait! What about after that?" I said.

"After?"

"When you left the Rudolph. There's a whole nine years left, man!"

"After that, nothing. It never got better than that. There is no after. You have to go, Slide."

"I *know* I have to go. I'm the one who *said* I have to go."

Shaking one of the books, he found what he was looking for. A piece of paper folded twice in half fell to the ground. He snatched it up and stuffed it into my pants pocket.

"Make straight for the door and do not let Eustace see you. I will distract him. The trains will be working now. Go. I've set you up an appointment with Osman the Throned, Tuesday morning at ten, on Lumquist Street."

"What on *earth*?" I was saying as he scooted the cat beneath the bed. "You set something up? Like with a broker or something?"

"Yes. A real estate agent. He will help you in your search, but you must not waste his time."

"The *Throned*? What kind of a name is that? And why didn't you *say* so, Calumet!" Geez-oh-geez: one thing that stresses me out is surprise appointments without any *details*.

"There was no time." He stepped toward the door. "Now, I have noticed that you avoid talking about where you are from. Do not stop doing that, but do not assume it is some

kind of a power either. Remember, Slide: they love no one.
Keep everything to yourself and Polis may not have the chance
to use it against you. Remember: Osman. Be there by ten. Buy
a padlock for your suitcase. You must go."

Then he bid the cat stay put and burst open the door, ushering
me through. I had my suitcase in hand and hustled down the
hall, past my old room and Eustace's bright inferno with but a
split-second glimpse of him rising from his bed, looking like
his own ghost. "What!" he began to shout. Behind me, Calumet made a sharp left and entered to soothe him, using his
height to block the doorway and giving me a last push on the
back to make sure I made it. "What! What! What!" Eustace
was shouting. "How dare he! What kind of nerve!" I fiddled
with the front door and threw it open, dashing for the staircase
with a final wave to the fugitive woman peeking around the
corner and ran down down down, through the lobby, outside,
into the new day of fresh heat.

But once there I saw it was no regular morning, even though the
sun was the usual bully. There were too many people, almost all
of them walking in the same direction. They took quick steps
and tittered to each other anxiously. I had barely a moment to
get my bearings before I found myself bumped along by a line
of grannies chattering: *It's open, it's open! The subway, that is.* Old
handbags swung wildly from their shoulders. Already was I half
a block away from the corner where I'd joined the crowd. Looking around I saw my woman from the deli, many teenagers on
skateboards, a teller from the bank where I'd opened an account,
all of them *hustling*. Oh man, it was quite a thing! Every foot had
somewhere to go. Somebody had what sounded like a trumpet

and was playing it loudly. And just a couple blocks later the crowd had thickened by some dozens, stretching from sidewalk to sidewalk and stifling all the cars! And I saw Philomena, and Agatha, and Willa too: Eustace's old dates (still a bit stunned), all headed the same way. And folks who didn't know were poking their heads from windows and shouting, *What's that down there?* and someone would have to shout up to them, *Haven't you heard? The trains are open, dummy, it's true. The first one leaves soon, we're not kidding.* And some of them would run down from their windows, *Oh shit!*, to join us outside with half-buttoned shirts and worried aunties warning, *Be careful!* from the doorways. And others were pouring in from everywhere else, little side alleys I'd never noticed before, leaving the driver's seats of cars with the engine still running! I swear, it was really crazy. I had to hug my suitcase close to my chest with two arms because the road was so packed. And we passed the barbershop and Rex and Reginald were right there opening up for the day and I said, *Rex and Reginald, this is it, I'm leaving like I said I would!* And Rex and Reginald turned around and said, *So long, New Boy! You know the hard time we gave you didn't mean anything, just to toughen you up a bit, you'll need it, take care! Hya hya hya!* And I said, *Yes, I know, it's alright, and you two weren't that bad either, I've met worse, but get a third ceiling fan, okay?*, then the procession moved on and people were throwing confetti from windows and waving adieu to loved ones. *We're going to the subway!* we were all saying. And those who suddenly changed their minds for whatever reason and tried holding on to a lamppost to pull themselves aside, announcing, *Wait! I have an appointment in the afternoon. I can't go anywhere*, were still swept along for it was too late and the current was too strong and there to my left was Soup-Eye climbing some scaffolding with another orphan friend to get a good view. He called to me, *Hey, Slide! I'm sorry I took your socks, you were right, it's a stupid thing to do, I'm going to do better!*, and right as I was pushed on I said, *You're a good kid, Soup-Eye, you're going to make a family very happy one day.* And gosh it was some strange luck I was having because after that was the girl on the tiny bike drinking water from a large bottle and going, *Aah*, until she saw me and said, *I used the money selling your shoes to buy a case of water bottles on the internet, also, what happened to your face?* Then she waved me on toward the subway, straight ahead, and suddenly I realized I was nervous because now the subway was a real thing and I would have to buy a ticket for the subway and I didn't know what the subway fares were, and people were noticing on my face that this would be my first ride on the subway, and that even though one day the subway wouldn't even be that big of a deal, that day wasn't today and even strangers were saying to me, *Goodbye! Stay cool, remember to hydrate! Farewell! Be careful, young traveler, this is Polis, don't forget!* And I said, *Thank you! I will! I know!* And at the subway itself, all the wooden partitions had been removed and the DO NOT ENTER signs and orange tape and befuddled protesters were all gone, and there it was revealed: nothing to speak of for all this waiting but some plain gray steps, a couple ads for the new movie, a rumbling underneath, and that dark, steaming tunnel into which, ten-by-ten, we all poured, jostling pushing swarming herding, krill swallowed whole into the open gullet of an endless whale. Adieu, adieu, we go to the subway. And that, the two of you, is how I got started on this whole mess in the first place.

"Alright, Slide. Settle down. This is good stuff, but why don't you take a breath? We're not going anywhere, if that's what you're worried about."

(And as for the one named Eustace Rose-Peters? Many months
later I heard word that he'd saved enough money for that tummy
tuck, after all, the operation overseen by a celebrity surgeon
from Austria and filmed as part of an ongoing reality show.
It went almost perfectly, except for a minor complication involving the anesthesia, which caused him to wake up midway through and gurgle his mother's name. From behind the
bright shine of lights the voice of a producer could be heard
whispering, *This is gold.* After the procedure he started going by E and took to referencing that particular episode as a
means of introduction. He resumed eating solid foods, mostly
prunes, and when it grew cold he refused to cover up his hard-
earned body in sweaters, so was often seen jogging through
the snow wearing nothing but shorts, without which he would
have been camouflaged. A quick bout of pneumonia had its
way with him, taking his voice with it on the way out, and,
out of necessity, he developed a habit of listening. One day
on the internet he met a nice girl named Brigid, who wrote
code for digital billboards and made bread on weekends. Her
figure was plump, her look shy. She was eternally pale. He had
her over for a dinner of lasagna that next Sunday and during
a tour listed the dimensions of one of the rooms as if it was

up for lease. She moved in. They bored a hole in the wall between them and had loud sex. Afterward, he braided her hair. They loved each other. He spent the lamplit nights guarding her sleep, staring at the moon, thinking of poems, and going through her phone. That is how he discovered the Swede, an enormous Nordic man whose nude pictures filled an entire hidden album. But the images were a couple years old, and E could find no evidence of the man lingering in Brigid's gaze. Still, it bothered him. He took to making vigorous love to her at a moment's notice, hoping to pound all memory of the Swede from her mind. Brigid was soon lost in a cloud of orgasms and glowed in the obvious way of the well satisfied. Other men found her attractive. Afraid, and never once willing to voice what truly bothered him, E could only further compound his predicament as each of them grew more healthful by the day, trapped in a spiral of beauty he could never have imagined. "What is it, love?" she asked on a tear-filled night in his arms. "It's nothing, it's nothing," he said. "It's just what I've always wanted.")

DOWNTOWN WEST

(in which a place of wellness turns out to be not-so-well
and—following a mad guide's dilemma—
a dark decision is contemplated before an unturned knob)

The mission would be this: I was to go into Polis and find a place to live. Not just any somewhere to eat sleep defecate and wait for the Reaper in a grim carousel of repeating days, mind you, but to *live*. Where the floor underneath was a fertile ground for the planting of a soul. Somewhere to anchor myself against the winds of life, an end to all drifting, to wait out harsh tides and take stock of my cargo of hopes. Where, even if seven separate bandits stole my bike on each new day of the week, still I could walk back there, to my apartment, and kick my feet up until tomorrow. Where after a day of cutting hair I could scrub beneath my fingernails in my own sink and tweeze my cuticles free of ingrown stubs. Or if, as was happening while we descended those subway steps, there were too many of us pressed together, bumping, buying tickets in a frenzy and squeezing past turnstiles, too much heavy breathing, knocking of elbows amongst the dull *ding* of the train's doors sliding open, a tumult of shoves in which I somehow ended up crushed into a seat amongst a multitude of face-height crotches pressed around me, the *rackety-jank-jank* of it setting off in a slow sway… then still I could return home to my apartment and raise a drawbridge against the noise of existence and do a full cartwheel before turning on the shower. Yes! Yes, that was it. I could invite Calumet over for a cappuccino and put out a saucer of milk for the cat. More than just four walls and a mailbox. There'd need to be room for decorum too. Peace of mind, class, *sophistication*. Things of that nature.

I'll admit it was a dubious proposition. Most of what I believed, I believed through hearsay, or glimpses of the insides of magazines. It seemed all of life was but a horizon to be grasped at over circuitous miles. You see, you two, for someone like me who's never had anything, Tomorrow is the slot on the table where we place all bets. That's why you'll hardly ever see me strolling down memory lane with my head in my ass like some dope! Even though I'm here telling you this stuff right now, I'm just making an exception. Polis is where those of us came who were willing to test time, to haggle with the stars and barter destinies. Down in that train, I had a powerful sense that the person I was about to become was waiting at any next stop—an unwavering anticipation tinged not with the fidgety heat of suspense but rather with a happy resignation. I mean, all I'd needed was a little *push*. After all, how many others had I already heard of who had stumbled into fortune just by knocking on the right one of Polis's doors? Had there not been that man in Petit Julienne, fresh from the Balkans and with a cleft lip, too, who bought himself an entire duplex by selling vitamins from a mail-order catalog? Were there not those panhandling newlyweds who'd saved a man's life, except that this man was no ordinary man but instead a clever man who had in return introduced the newlyweds to loopholes in the law through which they qualified for a low-rate mortgage? Plus there were those spin-the-wheel game shows where they just *gave* you an apartment if you knew a bit of trivia. I bet I could get onto one of those. How about all the accidental heirs who'd befriended the right old countess a couple weeks before her death? Half the houses in Haverford had residents from those exact circumstances, I'd heard, and those people had started with nothing but the letters in their name! Me, at least I had a little more than that. I had my leather suitcase full of essentials, savings from giving haircuts kept safe behind a debit card, a quarter century of life, a couple things I didn't want to talk about, a number for Monica Iñes, an appointment with a real estate agent, and—ah! I had almost forgotten— that piece of paper from the man Calumet, folded twice over and yellow with age. I took it out right there on the train and opened it, squeezing a little elbow room from amongst the people squished next to me... Oh goodness *gracious*, Calumet. This isn't how I thought you'd been spending your time...

A Map of Polis

The whole thing was a map of Polis torn from page 815 of some unimaginable tome, and on which he'd doodled in an array of inks. He'd doodled on it so much you could hardly *see* the original, except for a few spots where I could tell it had been labeled in Latin or something. So intricately wrought were its labyrinthine details that I felt a mild vertigo in the pit of my stomach, as if viewing the whole world from the eye of a mad cartographer. I mean, you really had to see it... It featured all the basics, of course—the central palm of the island and its four fingers jutting upward (Point James, where everything was fancy; Middleton, where it was shit; Petit Julienne, where it was dangerous; Haverford, full of country estates); the alpha- betized streets from Aberforth, at the top, to Zumickis, at the bottom; the island-long Avenues I through XX, from east to west—the stuff everyone knows. Where it *really* got crazy was in those markings Calumet had added in the cramped scrawl I recognized from the notes he'd slipped beneath my door. He'd labeled some neighborhoods and left out others, included footnotes, grave admonitions of no real sense. *Bad beach, salt for wounds*, one of them said, with an arrow pointing to a spot along Haverford's shore. *Vultures*, said another, this one in Downtown. Where in the surrounding water the original map had illustrations of ancient sea monsters, Calumet had drawn chewed-up limbs between their jaws. In Point James there was a lonely purple dot with *Rudolph* written underneath it, next to a drawing of two smiling figures holding hands, one tall, the other short. I tracked this strange geography with a squinted eye while the train swayed, wondering at his haphazard warnings even as I finally found the Downtown dot labeled *Osman, 924 Lumquist, Emergencies*—the name of the real estate agent I had an appointment with! That's how I would decide what stop to get off at to look for a nearby hotel. By then the razor-bumped fidgeter next to me was nudging me in the ribs because the map was a little in his face: "I brought my own reading material here, bub." When I tucked it back into my pocket and rose to check the subway map, a quick teenager wearing headphones slipped into my seat right away. Geez, what a load of sharks. Stop by stop, that exuberant procession from Middleton had been replaced by an unimpressed, coffee-wielding crowd avoiding each other's eyes, seemingly as tired in the morning as at the end of the day. From the darkness beyond the window, a parallel train veered close to ours, illuminating its own disgruntled crowd, as if we were in twin submarines with their portholes aligned. It had been an uncomfortable seat, anyway. Although, I'm not gonna lie, standing like that and holding my suitcase to boot, that was about the time I realized I still hadn't peed since last night...

As a matter of fact, needing to pee was about the only thing on my *mind* by the time I got off at Jucond Station, a stop

Downtown on the Magenta Line where there were hotels nearby, according to the lady standing next to me whom I'd asked, about the only nice person on that whole damn subway car. Exiting the train, I barely had a moment to catch my bearings before the swarm of commuters waiting on the platform was pushing me aside. Nurses, executives, students on their way to school—they all barged into that train like a sweaty stampede. "You have it all remembered where to go?" the lady's bobbing head asked from the other side of the shoving crowd—she'd gotten off there as well for an interview at a scholarly journal, I'd asked her all about it. Me I had to stand almost on my tiptoes to keep seeing her, making it even harder to squeeze my bladder shut. "Yes, of course!" "Okay, take care. Good luck with your apartment," she said, before being swallowed up.

But I *didn't* have it all remembered. Making my way toward the stairs at the other end of the platform where the crowd eventually spit me out, then to the buzzing mezzanine where yet more people were lined up for tickets as a busker in a tuxedo played a noisy violin, and finally onto the long escalator lurching its way upward, I could feel just about every last *step* of those directions getting wiped away by the agitation in my crotch. I started skipping stairs two at a time is how badly I needed to go, using my suitcase to wedge anyone out the way who was on the wrong side of the escalator. "Excuse me... coming through... on your left." Plus it didn't help that my face was starting to throb everywhere that cheat Eustace had punched it. Near the top, an automated voice over the PA warned that we were Approaching the Exit and to Please Mind Your Step, which I tried to do, but I've never been good with the timing of those things, so instead I ended up nearly falling on my face as I tumbled aboveground into that onslaught of a million buildings. Geeez-uuus! They extended block after block in either direction like a valley of silver walls, gleaming at full attention in the morning sun. It seemed so unlikely that there would be so many that I first thought it a kind of trick of mirrors, or one of those mirages you see while trying to cross a desert. Glass spires and steel totems, black obelisks, stone monoliths, side by side by side as far as I could see. And goddamn were they tall! I was getting dizzy on the *ground* just looking up at them. Well, at least one of them had to be a hotel where I could check in to a room and pee. I set off into the morning bustle. Some people were going here, some were going there. Office commuters with important briefcases and sinewy women with phones to their ears. Cars and buses sounded their horns in the street where a traffic warden was blowing his lungs out through a measly whistle. I headed over to a vendor selling hot dogs from an aluminum cart and tapped him on the shoulder.

"You know where the hotels are around here, by chance?" I asked him.

"Hey, not so fast!"

"What the hell is this?"

"Get to the back, buddy!"

Geez-us: there was a whole bunch of people waiting in line and they thought I was skipping.

"Oh no, I'm not skipping," I reassured them. "I need to find a hotel is all. Say, sir, someone recommended me this area. Which way would you say I go?"

"Sorry, bossman, I can get you in a second," the vendor said as he slathered a fat one with relish.

"Bullshit!" said a coiffed secretary in a yellow pantsuit.

"This look like a hotel to you?" said an old geezer with an oxygen tank.

"What happened to your face?" said a uniformed schoolboy wearing sunglasses.

"It's plenty other weenie carts that don't got lines if you can't wait!"

Boy were they being some hard-asses.

"I don't *want* a weenie!" I had to wave the hand not holding the suitcase and say. "Who even *eats* weenies this early in the morning? What's *wrong* with everyone?"

Although I had to admit: smelling those peppery hot dogs was making me realize I hadn't had anything to eat since that shit family dinner last night.

"Rule's a rule, bub," said the vendor, a balding workhorse with a bulldog's slack face. "Can't help the streets if you ain't buying the meats!"

Great, he was one of those vendors with stupid slogans to attract customers. In fact, right then he began shouting, "Weenies! Weenies! Get your hot weenies!" as a half dozen women carrying yoga mats exited a nearby gym. Me I dug in my pocket for some spare change, slammed it onto the cart, grabbed a hot dog, and dashed away from those psychos as fast as I could. "Hey!" "He took one!" "Bring back that weenie!" "That one was going to be mine!" "I'm sorry, it's really an emergency!" I shouted.

Half a block later I'd eaten most of it already. Yuck. Its insides were so wet and salty, they made me need to pee even *more*. I threw the rest away in a trash can and dodged a line of teenagers on scooters whizzing by playing music from their backpacks. The chattering of jackhammers, the warble of cathedral bells, the groaning arm of a garbage truck—all around me the morning was coming to life. Near the next corner, two bowing Buddhist monks behind a brass pot were ringing bells for spare change. I figured if anyone was going to be helpful it would be a Buddhist monk for sure, but right as I was walking over to them, an employee from the store they were in front of came outside and started shooing them away with a bucket of water. She had a warty red face and kept saying, "Enough! Enough!" as she splashed their feet. Everyone walking by just cut around them and kept going. The monks rang their bells *ding-a-ling-a-ling* even as they were chased. The warden continued to blow his whistle *tweet tweet*. Five more times I had to move out of the way for people bumping by, *Excuse me, Pardon, Coming through, young man*. It was really a lot. My suitcase to my chest, I shuffled from awning to awning with the tiny steps of a full bladder, past Red Sherbet, offering a special on new flavors; past Faraday's Emporium, where seated women with extended legs considered new shoes in the light. Then around the next corner I saw them lined up at last: one sparkling marquee after the next with the names of hotels. What a jackpot! Their tongues of red carpet wagged out onto the sidewalk as if to gobble me up. Me I headed toward them with a surge of satisfaction, already imagining the professionally cleaned bathroom, the soft white sheets laundered with floral detergents. The nearest one was a slim golden tower where a haughty concierge stood out front with her hands behind her back: the Faraday Hotel.

"Good morning, ma'am," I said as I got to her. "I am interested in checking in to a room for a short stay until I find a place of my own. In the meantime, however, may I avail myself of the restroom?"

I was doing all I could to maintain proper decorum despite

the awful pressure that made it hard to so much as *inhale* too fast. She looked me up and looked me down, then told me:

"I'm sorry, we're all full at the moment. May I suggest the Portersmouth some doors down?" I stormed off to the Portersmouth, sleek and elegant, with automatic doors. In *that* one I got only as far as the metallic lobby before a white-gloved butler escorted me out with the regrettable news that they were booked until January! Wow oh wow. They thought I was some dope but I knew what was up. I went on: at the YZ Hotel they said *No Availability*; at the Chatworth too; as at the Mashead Inn, Cleverton House, Langrum Towers, and the Althura.

At Redison Suites the desk attendant agreed to check me in; he was a fuzz-faced newbie fumbling over his keyboard; I made upstairs and down a hallway of doors before the elevator opened behind me and he reappeared, alongside his manager charging after me.

"You! Stop! What's this about?" the manager was waving my credit card and saying. "You think you're slick?"

"I beg your pardon?" I tried saying.

"This card don't work that you gave us!"

"What! That's impossible." I was holding up my suitcase like a shield as they closed the gap between us. "I'm sure it's simply a matter of your employee here screwing it up. I'm sorry to say, but he's a bit incompetent."

"Hey!"

"It don't *work*, kid," said the manager. Geez, he had so much sugary cologne on it made my eyes sting. His suit was of a cheap, baggy cut, too, like from a secondhand warehouse. You take a close look at things and they're *never* as nice as you'd thought.

"As a patron of your establishment, I'd appreciate some le-
niency in the matter. Perhaps if I could accompany you downstairs once I make use of—"

"Ain't no patron if you ain't paying. The card's a dud! You
look like a ruffian. You think I won't call the authorities? Get
out of here before something happens to you…!"

Polis was allowing me no quarter for relief and everyone was in
on it. Every last one of those hotels was actually a dead end in disguise, hoping I would wet myself. I was starting to fear the worst.

"Please!" I was still saying as I was ushered out that last
one. "It really is an emergency, you have to understand!"

"I'm sorry, my brother, but there's nothing I can do," the
security guard said with a grip on my elbow. "No one's going
to give you a room around here, you know."

He plopped me out the back exit where there was less of a
chance their fancy customers would see me, and the Russians
offering illegal taxi rides swarmed me at once.

"Taxi?"

"Taxi?"

"Good man, taxi for you?"

"Cheap ride."

"Taxi?"

"Taxicab?"

All six of them had hairy, grabby hands and cigarette smoke
for breath.

"No, thank you! Move, please."

I elbowed my way through them to find that the side street
I'd been dumped out onto was a winding, tree-lined way
with a row of shops facing a length of conjoined town houses.
Uniformed waiters were giving their restaurant tables the first

wipes of the day, while elderly neighbors fanned themselves on their balconies. Polis's incredible towers loomed all around as if to hem in the small dot of a neighborhood with an impenetrable fence. JOSERMAN STREET read the sign on the corner. I didn't know if there was some sort of a record for holding in your pee, but I was definitely a contender. There had to at least be some kind of a park farther down where I could get it over with. Heading along the sidewalk, I passed the narrow town houses with their small gardens, the old-timers in the street huddled over the open hood of a rusted jalopy. It was a dense neighborhood overrun by pedestrians squeezing between traffic-jammed cars. Still no park, but around halfway I spotted something pretty funny happening on the other side of the street. It was this one lady out on a stoop yelling at another lady, who was marching off with a heap of clothes in her arms.

"You never heard about human rights?" the lady with the clothes was yelling. "This is some bullshit! You think I won't talk? My brother-in-law's about to be a judge!"

"Well, you call him then!" said the lady on the stoop while waving a teacup. "See if I care. You get out of here, you understand?"

Geez, what a scene. Most the neighborhood was out on their stoops just to see what was happening, and the group of old-timers fixing the car had taken off their straw hats as they looked on. Also, for some reason, out of all the houses on the block, that was the only one with about one *hundred* pigeons crowding the upper ledges. It definitely looked like someone was being kicked out, though. Me I crossed right over as they were going at it some more.

"I know news people, too, lady! I know all kinds of people. It'll be problems for the both of you!"

"I don't care if you know Jim and Jean and the whole of Channel Six! Scram!"

"Hey, lady, not that I'm intruding or anything, but I couldn't help but overhear you may have a room newly available." I was on the other side of the low garden fence, waving. "Perhaps I may inquire as to the rate and use the bathroom, in no particular order."

"Huh?" She whipped her attention to me. "You say what now?"

"A room!" The pressure of the pee had me on the verge of shouting. "I see that you must have a vacancy."

"Vacancy? Oh no, that little *jezebel* over there was supposed to be the help. If only she weren't such a *thief*!"

"I never touched a thing in that place, Yvette!"

Wow, the two of them were still really trying to yell at each other, even though the girl with the clothes was practically a block away by now. As they got going again, some of the old-timers were saying, *Mmm mm mm*, and another neighbor leaning out a window yelled, *That's some mouth that child's got, Yvette...*

"Pleeez," shouted someone else, "you arr going to wake zee babee!"

"The help?" I piped up again. "What kind of help we talking about here? She clean up and stuff like that? Because that's just what I happen to do. In fact, you need help getting rid of her, ma'am? Watch."

Leaving my suitcase, I rushed over to the woman on the street, a redhead with long eyelashes, and started shooing her along.

"Alright, you heard the lady, beat it is what she said." She was in one hell of a huff, that redhead. I mean, she'd even spilled some of her *panties* on the sidewalk. "I'm going to have to ask you to vacate the premises, ma'am. These your panties? Here, looks like you dropped some."

"Who the hell are you! Freak! Don't touch those."

She spilled half the rest of the clothes trying to grab the panties from my hand.

"Look, look, she's spilling them panties!"

"Help her pick up them other panties, kid!"

"How terrible!"

Damn, it really was a whole show for the neighborhood.

"Come on now," I went on. "Let's pick those up then."

"This is intimidation!"

"Uh-huh, uh-huh, tell it to the judge. Hurry up, please."

Oh Lord. It was one sad sight, seeing someone getting kicked out with all their clothes spilling everywhere. Ordinarily I could have related, but I wasn't in a position to be understanding right now. Everyone around was still going, *Look! He's getting her to leave*, or *I was about to step in myself*...

"Great," I finished up. "And don't you come back, you hear?"

"You supposed to be the tough guy? Some tough guy! I'll show up with some real tough guys."

"Yes, yes, I'm sure. Cross that street now... One step at a time, there's a good girl... That's it— Ah-ah-ah! You were doing just fine... Go on now... Righty-o."

Then I returned to the town house, grabbed my suitcase, and climbed the stoop steps to where the lady still was.

"See? Helping already. And you'll need a replacement for her now, I bet."

Up close I saw she had thick purple lips and a brown flat face warped by oversize spectacles. She wore a flimsy polka-dot dress and a matching head wrap. Past her shoulder, I got a peek inside and saw what *definitely* had to be a bathroom door out of the three along the dim vestibule, though I kept having to lean from side to side for how much she was shaking her head.

"You try and you try to help people but some of them can't be and that's your own fault..." She also had extremely large breasts. "...terrible energy, that girl..." I'm not trying to sound a certain *way* or anything, it's just that I'm not sure her breasts were supposed to be that large. "...and a Scorpio moon, you know? Pity. Always trouble, those ones..." It might have been something medical. "What happened to your face, child?"

"That? Oh, it's nothing. You need to see the other guy, to tell you the truth. Now, about that room we were discussing."

"Room? Oh no, we got sick people in here, child. You'd need to be qualified. There are hotels around the corner if you'd like to try that. Have a good day."

"Wait!"

She'd been closing the door but I'd jammed it with my suitcase.

"Sir!"

Now those nosy neighbors from before were starting to go, *Oh, what's this one, now?* and *Everything alright there, Yvette?*

"Sick people, you say? I can help with sick people," I said.

"Remove your suitcase, please!"

"I'm serious, ask me anything. Just about my whole time in the orphanage all I did was take care of sick people. I was the best at it out of everyone."

A hesitant, plaintive look rearranged her flat features, those big, mopey eyes blinking behind her glasses. "You an orphan, child?"

"Yes, it's a sensitive subject," I said, "but we were raised by a bunch of nuns and some of them were sick. Neck pains? Anyone

PAY AS YOU GO

in there have neck pains? It's my specialty is all I'm saying."

"You don't look like no orphan, child."

"How's an *orphan* supposed to look? You want me to be dusty or something? Geeez-uuus. Why don't you let me in there and we can talk numbers. My fee is quite low."

With my suitcase wedge I pried open the door and stepped inside. I was in a dim foyer with dark wood paneling, worn rugs, and cutesy wallpaper. Right in front was one of those staircases that wrap around so you can see all the floors above by looking up the center, but me I was already two steps headed to those doors. I tried the door straight in front: it was just a big kitchen. I opened the next one onto an ornate room with many, many chairs and about a half dozen *more* geezers I could tell had been watching out the window too. I'm not kidding, it was a bigger place than you would've thought at first glance. I closed that door.

"Hey! Slow down, now! What was your name, dear?"

I told her my name.

"Well, Mr. Slide, you are being very unusual, you know."

Then I knew it was the one under the stairs, because she'd situated herself to block me from it, giving me the ol' up-down.

"Listen, lady, I'm pretty sure that's a bathroom behind you. I can practically smell it. You gonna let me use it or what?"

"Who's that?" I heard another voice come from upstairs.

"Says he's looking for work."

"He say what now?"

I couldn't wait for them to have that chitchat. I faked her left, then went right, slipping past her and leaving my suitcase in the hall. "Wait!" she said, trying to grab me.

I opened the door and there I saw it: a toilet with a porcelain sheen and an open, waiting mouth. My goodness. I was trembling with weakness now that the end was in sight. Dropping my pants I shuffled toward it, pushing my underwear to the side and gripping my spurting penis as it let loose just in time. Ooh. Aah. I was peeing. I sighed and shuddered, going stupid with relief. It was such a long piss that I felt myself growing dizzy, hunching a little given the slope of the ceiling beneath the stairs. The lady was somewhere behind me shouting back to the voice upstairs and freaking out—I hadn't even closed the door—"...yes, I don't know! No, he's still here! I'm looking at him right now but I can't do anything...!" Then I flushed, washed my hands, and noticed there was a small sofa in there too. I mean, it was seriously a nice bathroom. That looked like a good place to lie down, if only for a little. Quivering all over, I braced myself against the wall to steady my way downward, only vaguely aware of the onlookers who must have followed me inside and were whispering: "Yvette, who is this?" "Careful! Don't step on his suitcase." "Oh my, he doesn't look good..." What happened next wasn't that I fainted (I'm not someone who faints); it's just that when I closed my eyes to take a lie-down—I was so tremendously tired, it really had been a long night, you must understand—I simply didn't open them again for a very long time.

"I'm not being ironical here or anything, but I do really need to use the bathroom right now as well."

"This is only a short break. You might have to wait for the longer one."

"Really? Even if I'm fast?"

"Standard practice. You wouldn't make it back in time."

"Fine."

"We can get you some water if you need."

"Water? That's about the opposite *of what I need!"*

"Ah. Of course."

"I mean, geez, why would you even suggest *water at a time like this?"*

"Pretend we never said it."

"You trying to make me have an accident *here or something?"*

"Sorry. We thought you might need it, is all. You know, it's our line of work, of course, so perhaps we should expect it, but we've never quite seen anyone talk so much..."

THE COUSINS DE SANVILLE

I slept until evening, dreaming of leopards, and awoke not knowing a thing. For a second I thought I'd ended up in one of those hospital beds I'd sworn never to remember. But sitting upright helped me re-anchor myself to the world, and I found my senses one by one through the haze of dusk. I was in a cool, dark room with a standing fan. I had a dry mouth and a heavy head, a light throb behind my eyes. To my right was a window with a lowered blind that let through tiny motes of light, and from somewhere above came the soft clink of a wind chime. *Gosh* did it hurt being awake. I could hardly get to thinking for how groggy I was. It felt like I'd run through about three brick walls, then stared at the sun for good measure. Someone I used to know would always say I didn't have the consti*tution* to be a drinker, as if it was science or something, and I would always say back, *No one* has the constitution to be a drinker, that's what the headaches are for. He'd usually change the subject. When I lay back down, the throbbing flowed from one side of my head to the other, causing the room to spin slightly. I knew it was the same house as before from the faint cooing of pigeons and the cloak of potpourri draped over the dusty air. That lady must have agreed to let me stay after all. I would have to resume our earlier discussion once I got my bearings. From beyond the walls around me I could hear the *pitter-patter* of footsteps, the groans of the wood floor, and every now and then the howl of a dog. They were those high, long howls dogs usually make when several of them are all howling together, except this was for sure only one dog. *Awoooooooooo.*

I kept expecting my eyes to adjust to the light coming through the blinds, but I couldn't make out anything but shapes. What was the time? Was the light orange because the sun was setting or because of streetlights? I didn't want to look at my phone screen's glare, and I wasn't going to stand up yet. I tried placing the time of day from the sounds of the cars outside, but I didn't know what you were supposed to listen for in something like that. They sounded about regular. For a while all I did was lie in the dark room and nurse my aching head.

When I did eventually get up, I noticed that my shoes had been taken off and the socks on my feet were fresh and soft. One of the dark shapes was my suitcase sitting neatly against the wall with my sneakers on top of it. When I covered my mouth to yawn, my palm came back with an oily smear and I held it up to my nose to give a sniff: ointment! Or some sort of salve. I felt more of it spread across the bruised parts of my face, where Eustace had struck me. Damn, someone must really have been taking care of me while I'd been napping! Then again, they could have done something suspicious too. After all, who *knew* how long I'd been lying there totally exposed? Alright, now I had to know the time. Only when I checked my phone did I see I still had up Monica Iñes's phone number from when I'd saved it earlier. I thought of Monica Iñes. I thought of Calumet. Geez, that had been some story he'd told me. I wasn't a statistician but the odds of that kind of bad luck happening to one person had to be slim. What I couldn't figure out was if he was implying I shouldn't talk to Monica Iñes anymore. That would be a shame—we'd really been enjoying each other's company until everything went sour. Plus I hadn't had a chance to ask her about any other apartments she might know of. And you know what? I technically had only heard Calumet's side of things, which wasn't being fair to her. It had been a sad story, yes, but it wasn't necessarily a reason to cut her off before we'd gotten a chance to know each other *and* when she hadn't done anything wrong to me. I had to be fair to everyone. So I texted her *Hey,* then felt pretty embarrassed about it. The time was 7:13.

I tugged open the blind and startled off a bunch of the pigeons on the ledge. From there I had a view of the same street I'd walked up earlier, Joserman Street, and its chattering sidewalks. Diners were having supper al fresco beneath strings of white lights while laughing neighbors on either side of garden fences caught each other up on gossip. Now this was more like it! In Middleton, you'd *never* see people eating outside, unless they were chewing on shitty sandwiches while walking. The window slid only halfway open no matter how much I tried to move it, but I stuck my head out all the same and inhaled the fresh night. *Aah!* "Yvette around?" a hand-holding couple called up to me from the sidewalk. "Don't know who that is!" I piped right back. Behind me I heard the door to the room open and pulled my head inside to find a wrinkled blackman wrapped in two shawls poking his nose in.

"Ah, good-eve. Recovered from your faint, I see."

"*Faint?*" I said, holding my hands up. "No, no, no. I definitely wouldn't say that, mister, I'd had a long night was the only thing."

"That's the spirit!" he said, opening the door some more. He had a small, cheery face complicated by fidgety eyes, and entered on his tiptoes as if inspecting the ground for booby traps. In the hand not clinching the shawls was a portable TV tuned to the news.

"So you're the new help then? I heard the whole fiasco. Wonderful. That last girl had an attitude. Do you have anything with which to write, my boy?"

"You're telling *me*!" I said, checking out my face in the bureau mirror now that the room had a bit more light from the hallway. Damn, I was seriously beat up. "She just about threatened to have me killed is what."

"A pencil, perhaps?"

"Afraid not, sir. But, say, something I should ask you, how much were they paying her, anyway?"

"I can't say I know."

"I just need to make sure I negotiate a fair fee is all. That lady from earlier around?"

"The cousins are here, yes, but I would like you to note a few things before you talk to them. It'll be easier coming from me."

Geez. He was really insistent.

"Listen, why don't you just tell me and I'll remember. It's no point me writing things down when I haven't negotiated my fee yet. I may decide to take my talents somewhere else, for all I know. Don't you agree?"

"Yes, that's reasonable, I suppose."

"Tell me what it is and I'll see what I can do."

The news report on his TV was going on about how gas leaks are more common than you might expect, and the dog from before started howling again. Something must have been seriously bothering it for it to be howling alone. Plus right about then a mechanical whirring started sounding from within the walls.

"Well," he began, "for one thing, when making the tea, please don't do mine too hot. Everyone around here has a habit of making mine too hot."

"Uh-huh."

"As for laundry, I must insist, the scented powders can irritate my armpits and the unscented ones hardly do a thing. I've found that an improvised mix of vinegar, alkaline salts, and toothpaste is best when it comes to my clothing. You can find them all in the pantry, of course..."

Now that he had my attention, I could see he was really going for it. He went on a little more about things like his preferred choice of citrus, what steps to avoid along the staircase so the creaking wouldn't wake him up at night. Lord almighty, what a proper kook.

"... and be careful with that window I see you have opened," he wrapped up by saying. "We're expecting rain, you know."

I looked back out the window and there wasn't a cloud in sight.

But before I could say anything else a second set of footsteps came thumping down the hall and the woman from earlier appeared in the doorway in a new dress of blue-and-brown stripes, nudging him out the way with sharp elbows.

"Alright, Mr. Borsnitch. Shoo, shoo! No bothering Mr. Slide."

"Yvette! I was only introducing myself."

"Now's not the time, Mr. Borsnitch."

"Remind him about the tea, please!" he whined as she moved him out the way some more. She bustled over to a section of the wall that the whirring sound had been coming from and slid open a panel just as a dumbwaiter finished making its way up. Wow: I'd never actually seen one of those before. She reached inside and extracted a loaded tray.

Behind her, a tall, reedy woman with tangled hair and watery eyes was cutting her way in front of the old guy with a bit of exasperation herself. "Yes, we all know. Now give us some space. The kid's been beaten up, apparently."

"Wait, I wasn't exactly beaten up!" I was trying to clarify even as Mr. Borsnitch was edged out the room. I'm telling you, you let other people talk for you and they really get the whole *story* confused. "You need to see the other guy. What's everyone doing around here, starting *rumors* or something?"

"Of course, Mr. Slide." The short one had settled the tray on a nightstand and was fiddling with mugs of tea as her breasts sloshed around beneath her dress. One of the mugs she handed to me after adding three shakes of powder from a small vial. "This one's for you then, drink up, it'll help with the swelling."

"That's alright, I'm more of a coffee guy myself."

She tipped it up to my lips. "You should really have some."

I took a sip. It was hot, fruity, and very delicious. My muscles felt instantaneously relaxed, as if from a massage.

"Hey, what's in this?"

"Gorsham's root and honey," said the tall one as she rolled up the sleeves of her dress. "And some ginger, since you stink of alcohol. Alright, let's have a look at you now."

She took a rough grip of my chin and turned my face back and forth in the light—"Hey!"—then squeezed the length of my biceps as if testing livestock.

"He's not very strong, Yvette."

"He doesn't need to be, Toussaint."

"And he doesn't look like an orphan."

"He says that's just assuming."

"Let's have him cut the cards."

Next to the china on the tray was a deck of large cards with patterned backs that she plucked up and laid flat on her palm.

"Cut."

I looked them over like they were an invitation to my own funeral. "Whoa, whoa. Let's slow down here. I don't want to know when I'm going to die or anything like that."

"Cut the cards."

I pinched a measly few and cut the deck. The remaining ones she started turning over faceup onto the bed. There was a prince holding five goblets, an owl with three eyes, a tower on fire, and a man riding a chariot off a cliff, all arranged in a cross.

"You see?" the tall one said to the shorter one, with the tried, triumphant air of someone putting an argument to rest. "You *see*!"

Yvette was shaking her head as she looked them over herself.

"Yes, you were right."

"Is *this* what you want?"

"Wait! Right about what? What's wrong? What're those things *saying*?" I'd nudged my way between them for a closer look. I wasn't an expert, but you just about *never* want anyone shaking their heads so much when discussing your fortune. "Why's that building on fire? That have to do with my apartment? And who's the guy going off the cliff? That supposed to be me? Can I get a second *opinion*?"

They shuffled out into the hall to murmur in low tones while moving their hands.

"... but perhaps we should try a man instead..."

"... another one of your projects..."

"... the girls always give trouble..."

"... we need to start locking the door..."

"... really think it'd be a good change..."

"... why I even put up with this..."

"Hey!" I joined them in the hallway, seriously freaking out. Those cards were putting my new situation at risk before it so much as began. "Listen, ladies, I can see I have to reassure you. Why don't we talk about this properly, alright?"

"Alright, Mr. Slide." Yvette placed her hands on her hips. "Well, me and my cousin Toussaint here have been considering, and she agrees that it's most unusual, of course. But I was saying to her, Toussaint, we're just in no spot. We're in no spot to be turning anyone down, Toussaint. There's so much to do around here and we need the help."

"Of course. That's what *I've* been saying." We were in the wan light of the cloudy chandeliers dangling overhead. Me I was taking in the vaulted ceilings and the ornate rugs, the multitude of oak doors and the rim of cherrywood banisters spiraling though the floors. It was some kind of a place—I could definitely see myself staying there for a bit. "I'll tell you what, let's not even worry about that fee. Let me have this room a couple of days until I find my own place, and maybe throw in some breakfast or something along the way. Then I'll pick up some of those chores around the house. You feel me? You scratch my back and I'll make it a win-win."

The tall one, Toussaint, scoffed. "Fee?" she said.

I held up my hands to calm her down. "Yeh yeh, like I said, let's just forget about it."

"We are in such a tight spot, is the only thing…," Yvette was saying distractedly.

I could see it was Toussaint's decision, Yvette and I both looking to her for a verdict. Past both their shoulders, in the room across the hall, Mr. Borsnitch was eavesdropping through the crack in his door.

"You said you're looking for somewhere else to stay?" Toussaint finally said.

"Yup! It's nothing to worry about. I got an appointment tomorrow morning and everything. I'd say a week tops and I'll be out of here."

She finished her consideration with a solemn nod. "Alright. One week is fine. Come back after your appointment and you'll get started."

Phew! What a *relief*. "Thank you! You won't regret it and that's my guarantee."

"Mhm. And no fighting while you're here, Mr. Slide," concluded Yvette as she retrieved her tray from my new room. "Some of the other guests can be sensitive."

They gave me a quick tour of the house and my chores, introduced themselves properly as Yvette and Toussaint de Sanville, and in the morning I went to my meeting with Osman the Throned after all.

A CONSULTATION

His office was in a plain brown building on Lumquist between VIII and IX, in a stretch of similarly plain brown buildings of no real distinction beyond the stores occupying their ground floors. I got there at 9:48, bright and early with a couple minutes to spare just to be sure. Earlier, Yvette de Sanville had pulled me into the kitchen on my way out the door and applied new dabs of ointment to my face. "It's no point you looking like a hooligan everywhere you go, Mr. Slide," she said, before returning to the pots she had going on the fire. Out back I could see a couple construction workers eating breakfast around the patio table. "You're not wrong, Yvette!" I said. "That's me then, I'm off. As they say, it's the early bird that gets first serve!" Outside it was a clear, brilliant day with a sheen of white radiance, a warm, brisk wind stirring the morning bustle of the sidewalks. The sky was such an expectant blue I thought I might waft up into it from giddy delight. Well, I was out of Middleton and it wasn't even a joke! Some people insist on pinching themselves at moments such as these, but for me that was time better spent getting a head start on the future. I walked and walked and walked south along Avenue XVI, amongst the incredible towers, even past some of those same hotels where they'd been real assholes to me. The joke was definitely on them now. The day was hot but not Middleton hot. I swear, Middleton had the worst of everything. Out here it was clear that the residential buildings were done to proper regulations where not a single one of them would have broken fire escapes, or shitty paint jobs that made you choke at night. At the corner of Julworth Street I fell into step with three blue-suited executives on their way to some meeting. That one made me pick up my pace! This was the way people in Polis walked when they had somewhere to *be*. Whoever this Osman guy was, he had to see that I arrived to things punctually and that my socks coordinating with my belt was no accident. Me I'd decided on khaki pants, a good white shirt, black shoes clicking at the heels. It's not to say I'd never had an *appointment* before or anything like that, but some of them you want to take a little more seriously. I would be cool and relaxed, though not aloof. I would speak in full sentences so he knew I was someone worth helping. A feeling of confidence grew. Hell, I even whistled a tune! The blocks went by in a haze of ordered names, first Juniper Street, where bespectacled university students were making their way to classes; then Latchman Street, where a TV crew was filming something, Lovelace and its endless stretch of construction, Low, Loyals, Lubin…

At 924 Lumquist, I entered through a revolving door and signed in with a security guard who pointed me to the middle elevator, where I got in with a couple others. I rode up to the twelfth floor, the doors sliding open to a glare of hard tiles, a common area with snacks, men in suspenders walking and talking in the hallways, and women in pale blouses pointing out things in folders. Everyone was going, "Shoot me that file," or "We'll set something up," or "Let's circle back once we've touched base." Walking down the hall, I read the various company names embossed on the frosted panes—VERIDIAN SOLUTIONS; HART & HOLLY DESIGNS; MACROPLEX LLC; TRITON, PERTH & PERKINS, ATTORNEYS—until I found OTT REAL ESTATE, gave it a buzz, and, after a quick click, pushed the door open into a bright waiting area with a rim of orange chairs. Behind the desk was an androgynous receptionist chewing gum, who right away asked if I had an appointment.

"Indeed I do," I said, closing the door behind me. "I should be down for ten o'clock."

"Oh, that one you? Didn't have a number for ya. Gimme a sec."

I stood in place while the receptionist pushed a button on the phone. Dispersed on the chairs were a few others seated beneath framed pictures of glossy interiors. The receptionist's desk was placed almost like a barrier to the room just beyond it, from which you could hear a telephone's ring go on without answer.

Hanging up, the receptionist yelled instead: "Hey, Osman! Your ten o'clock's here!"

A voice shouted back: "Well, let him wait already!"

"He said he'll be a few," said the receptionist. "Have a seat."

Geez, that was one way of doing it. I picked a seat near the corner of the room. From beyond the door I could hear the voice wrapping up a chat.

While I was waiting I began to have some doubts. It's good to be early, but you shouldn't appear desperate either. What I really wanted was a casual balance. Actually, I should've been a minute or two *late*, even, though with a passing apology of having run into someone I knew or having checked out an apartment beforehand. Taking a look at some of the others waiting, I couldn't help but notice their anxious, fidgety airs. They looked like one desperate bunch. Even sitting *down*, some of them still had the forward-leaning postures of sprinters about to start a race, as if they were behind on life and hoping to catch up—the guy in a fast-food uniform typing desperately on his phone; the skinny, furious couple conducting a whispered argument. "Look, we can always get a refund," the man was saying to the woman, who looked green in the face. "They'll be gone by now," she weakly replied. I definitely hoped I didn't look like any of them myself. The slender, anxious type right next to me had a wrapped present in his lap and was constantly checking his watch. The box was so large it could have been some sort of appliance, like for a housewarming. "Housewarming you're on your way to?" I asked him, just to make some chitchat. He looked at me, then looked back at his watch, ignoring me. What a snob. It wasn't like it had been an unreasonable guess, given where we were. The thing was, though, his shoes were really nice. They were some sort of leather brogues with tassels and could have been handmade. I looked at my shoes: they'd gotten a little dirty already. Damn, I was feeling like an impostor again. Oh geez, don't even let me tell you, most of what I've ever done in my *life* is feel like an impostor. Perhaps there was still some time to go get my shoes polished at that shoeshine across the street that I'd noticed on my way in. I could even tell the receptionist I'd remembered I had an important phone call and had to step outside for a little, then return with the shined shoes.

"Whoops! Silly me! Almost forgot I have a call I need to hop on," I stood up from my chair and said. The couple thought I meant them and paused their quarrel. They were so skinny they might as well have been on one seat.

"What's that, dude?" said the receptionist.

I stepped a little closer, going, "My own fault, I'm always forgetting my calls."

"Huh?"

"This one won't be too long."

"You're stepping outside?"

"Don't worry. It's just a quick call about one of my investments, usual stuff, back before you know it."

"But that's you right now, dude."

"Oh…"

And indeed, the door behind was just then opening, an old lady in pearls making her way out with laughing promises to the voice inside to be in touch. The receptionist waved me through.

On the other side of a wide desk sat a handsome middle-aged man with bushy eyebrows, big dark eyes, and the rugged beard of an Arabian castaway. He was finishing up typing something on an old computer as I made my way in.

"Alright, alright, come on then," he said, in a bit of a sharp tone. "Slide, correct? You're a little early, aren't you?"

"Why thank you." I closed the other door. "I pride myself on punctuality in all matters."

"So I see, so I see."

The office had a cramped industrial feel with its concrete floors and teetering stacks of paper everywhere, some as high as his head. There were panels of rough fluorescent light, a rusty filing cabinet with two printers stacked on top of each other. As soon as he finished whatever he'd been doing, with a final clack on the keyboard, one of the printers began to wheeze out a couple pages. He stapled them together, then lowered his arms out of sight to push at something, and, with a brisk churn, glided smoothly around the desk to where I was and extended a hand. He was in a wheelchair. That's when I saw that beneath his boxy suit jacket he had on extremely slim pants. Behind him hung a ponytail so long it reached past the wheelchair's handles.

"Please, have a seat."

He indicated two chairs, a black and a gray. Sitting in the black one, I crossed my legs, flexing my fingers from what had been an extremely powerful handshake. It definitely could have been a nicer office, though. The only neat things were the rows of photographs of apartment interiors and certificates of excellence lining three of the walls; the fourth had a window with the blinds drawn. Most of the room's space seemed reserved for the wheelchair to maneuver around his splintered desk topped with the computer, three telephones, a cactus, and more papers. In fact, he was sliding one of these papers toward me as he resettled behind the desk and began to speak.

"A couple things to fill out so I can put you on file. Tell me something, there still a lady outside selling bug spray?"

"Pardon?" I said, scooting my chair closer. "No, I didn't see that. What do you mean?"

"Been a lady in front of the building trying to sell bug spray. A real nutjob." He wheeled over to the window to take a peek out the blind and sip from a flask in his jacket pocket, returning once satisfied. "Alright, that's good. Probably moved on. Can't just be selling bug spray everywhere. How's it outside? You enduring the weather?"

"It's pretty alright," I said. "I've just been having to shower a lot is all."

"A little hygiene never hurt anyone, my friend." He threw his head back and laughed a mighty laugh. He had scraggly, disjointed teeth.

"Yes, yes, you're right. I'm not some slob or anything like that. It's just my towel is never fully dry from the first shower by the time I have to take the second."

"Let me get you a pen for that."

He opened a drawer and searched around. Only then did I look properly at the paper on my lap, which turned out to be some sort of form. There was a line for my name, and lines for my date of birth, current occupation, current address, past address, a whole lot of etceteras. And that was just on one *side*. Geez-us. No one had told me it was going to be some sort of inquisition. Osman handed me a pen.

"You need me to turn up the air condition?" he asked.

"That's alright."

"So, Slide. You have come to me with a need. I'm your guy. I'd be lying if I said otherwise. How long have you been in Polis?"

As he talked, I started on the form, glancing up only occasionally from my lap.

"I would say a couple months, though it's mostly been in Middleton, unfortunately. Which also reminds me, Calumet sends his best wishes and hopes you are well. I was very grateful to him for setting this up."

"Who?"

One of the phones on his desk rang.

"Hello?... Ah! How's it going?... That's good. What can I do for you? Yes. Yes. No... Come again?... What?... Listen, why's it so staticky on your line?... Try changing rooms then... A little... Alright, you were saying what now?... On Maldridge and X?... Okay, I have some bad news and it's not really mine to tell but the proprietor offed himself a couple months ago and the bank's been holding up the assets since... Mhm. Mhm... I'll send your condolences... Yes, I agree, a true diamond... Archie, you know my feelings on this already, a four is beyond your needs at the moment. Now, the units on Corsicund are still on the market, quiet as kept, and I can get us a viewing for this weekend... That's calling in a favor, Archie... Mhm. I see. I see... I'll tell you what, Archibald. I'm in a meeting right now and this is getting rude of me. Let's pick this back up during coffee tomorrow, sound alright?... I agree... It's not impossible... What?... You're staticking again... The what?... Oh. I'm afraid the details there get a bit gruesome. Do a search online if you're curious but I wouldn't be eating anything while you do. I tell you, Archie, you never know what's going on with some people." He hung up. "Dani!

What I tell you about letting that guy through!"

"He said it was urgent!" yelled the receptionist with such pitch and volume I had to check if the *door* wasn't still open. They really liked yelling in that office, I'm not kidding.

Osman grumbled and returned his attention to me, taking another sip from his flask.

"How's that form coming?"

"I'm getting there," I said, which wasn't true at all. I'd gotten distracted by his phone call, and by the odd shock of him not knowing Calumet after all. Maybe Calumet had only heard of him from someone else? It felt like I'd entered a prank show and not been told. Only a few lines were done.

He waved a hand. "All of it's not important anyway. So tell me something, Slide, what kind of place are you looking for? You like that one on the wall? I saw you looking." He pointed to one of the pictures, gliding himself closer to better indicate. It was of a brightly lit living room with glossy wooden floors and flowers in a vase. Two friends sat on a sofa laughing in slanted beams of sunlight.

"Oh yeh, it's seriously nice," I said.

He tapped the picture twice with his finger. "Closed on it last month for a heck of a steal. Should be illegal how good of a steal it was. Lady on the left runs a lollipop business. Organic and all that. How about this one? It's a one-bedroom." He went to the other side of the room to get to another picture— a wall of exposed brick, a color-coordinated kitchenette, and the bedroom up in a loft. Halfway along the ladder to the loft was a pretty girl in a billowing dress. "Is this something that interests you?"

"Yes. That interests me quite a lot," I said, more than a little excited.

"I can imagine. Something like this would do you nicely."

He went on, whizzing over to several more photographs along the walls, each of a more idyllic scene than the last, unpinning a few to form a collage on his desk. I was halfway out my seat as I traced his zigzag progress.

"We're building a picture here," he eventually said. "Sure you don't want me to turn up the air?"

"Oh, I'm completely fine. Don't worry about me."

"And you're good on water?"

"Yup yup. No problem."

"Excellent."

Back behind his desk, he arranged the pictures so they were upside down for him but right side up for me.

"Tell me about your vision, Slide."

"My vision?" I asked. "I've never gotten it checked but it's never been a problem either."

He laughed his incredible laugh. Then he pointed to his temple.

"More like your third eye, if you get my drift. What do you see when you see where you'll be living?"

"Oh, my *vision*," I said. "Yikes, that wasn't too bright of me!"

"An easy mistake."

I looked over the photographs as I thought. One was of a refurbished studio with wooden floors and in-unit laundry. That one looked nice. But then so did another one with a private backyard and louvered windows painted blue. I was having difficulty: my vision was pretty flexible. The thing was, it was more of a *feeling*. Finally I answered:

"Okay, I have this friend, the one I mentioned, he owns a cat. It's a strange cat. I'd like to be able to serve the cat some milk when my friend comes to visit me. In a saucer. The cat will drink its milk from the saucer while my friend and I are having cappuccinos." I paused to gather my thoughts. I really wasn't doing a good job. "It doesn't have to be cappuccinos, actually. Regular coffee is fine."

Osman was already nodding. "Got it. Somewhere pet friendly." He removed a few photos from the desk.

"No, wait, I mean… it won't be *my* pet, you could put those pictures back, it'll only be when my friend comes to visit. You know what I mean? I just want to make sure the cat is fine for a few hours and that I have some soup on the stove or something. Sorry, this sounds a lot better in my head. Look, people will take their shoes off when they come to visit me. I'll have some art. Somewhere like that. I don't know, I'm confusing this whole thing, aren't I?"

He tried out an understanding look.

"It's okay. That's why we're here. To build a picture. I'll tell you what, let's do this another way. You tell me more about yourself first and we can go from there. How's that form coming?"

I looked down at the form. I'd still done only a few lines. Noticing as much, he said, "Get through it. I have some emails to send anyway." Almost at once he began clacking away on the computer keyboard.

I shook the pen hard and continued, now in a hurry. Educational background, marital status, income, blood type. All these *questions*. At the bottom of the other side was the worst one: a space to leave the name and number of a previous landlord, as a reference. I thought of Eustace. That wouldn't do. I would've put a number for Calumet but he didn't have a phone. Maybe I could put Eustace's number but tell Osman to ask for Calumet?

Hell, it might even jog his memory. No, too risky. All it would take was Osman mentioning what it was regarding and Eustace would be sure to sabotage me. That could be the one of the few parts I left blank. When I finally handed Osman the form he looked it over and said, "You left half of it blank."

"Yes, well, I don't have any references, for instance," I said, "but I am available for an interview should the question of my character ever arise."

Suddenly his face got suspicious.

"No references?" he asked.

"That's correct."

"You're looking to purchase your first home, is that it?"

"*Purchase?*" Dammit. "I believe we've been having a misunderstanding. I'm trying to rent somewhere is the thing."

"Rent?" His eyebrows tried reaching for each other. "I see." He looked at the form again. "And educational background is blank too..."

"Yes. It's all a long story."

"But you are a... hairstylist?"

"That's correct."

"And you only wrote down your first name," he said with finality.

Setting aside the form, he steepled his fingers. When the phone rang again, he lifted it off the receiver and hung up. He looked at me for a long time.

"Ah, I see," Osman eventually said. He took a sip from his flask.

"You see?"

"Yes. I understand. I must be looking dense today."

"Huh?"

An apologetic nod shook his ponytail. "It's not your fault.

Some days I wake up looking dense and I'm the last one to find out. What's it today? Tuesday? Must be one of those days."

"Osman, wait, it's definitely not anything like that."

He was already wheeling himself away from and around his desk to start escorting me to the door. "You're not to blame. I'd do the same if I felt I had an idiot facing me. Slide, I want to thank you for your time, however—"

"Wait!" I said, clutching at his shoulder as he passed me. "Don't go escorting me out if that's what you're about to do. There's a real good explanation for all of this, Osman, I swear, give me a second and I'll walk you through it."

Oh no! I slapped the hand clutching his shoulder to my mouth. I hadn't meant to bring up walking, given his condition and everything. Geez, the situation was going from bad to worse faster than I could keep track of. He didn't seem to mind, though.

"Is that so?" He stopped and angled his wheels toward me and propped a lazy elbow on the wheelchair's back. It looked like he really was on a throne after all. "Go on then."

Me I fidgeted. I hemmed and hawed. For a split second I wondered if it was too late to take him up on that glass of water, but I could tell I'd reached about the end of his patience. Man oh man. I guess I really had to talk. These parts were always the most difficult.

"Well," I began, "the truth, Osman, is that I'm an amnesiac. I got a serious case of amnesia sometime ago and now I don't remember anything."

"Am*nesia*?" he said.

"Yeh," I said. "Of the head."

Scooting my own chair over, I propped my elbows on his desk.

"It's embarrassing to talk about, trust me, I know, but if I talked about anything else it wouldn't be the truth—it would be me lying to you. I woke up one day in a back alley of garbage dumps, next to a shattered vase. I had a scorching hot headache that wouldn't go away, and what was worse, I didn't *know* anything. Nada. Squat. A white wall where all my memories should have been. Alright, I knew my name and how to give a haircut, things of that nature. But not any of the other stuff. I waited a couple minutes for the rest to start coming back, like what's supposed to happen, but an *hour* went by and it was still zilch. That then turned into days. You should have seen me, Osman, going up-and-down, trying to figure things out. I'd stop by the police station to see if they had my fingerprints on file, but I must not have gotten into any trouble before, because there was nothing on me. At the hospital the docs and nurses thought I was a maniac and wouldn't take me seriously, and *those* people are supposed to be professionals. Oh Lord, I could go on. You ever had amnesia, Osman? No? Not even a little bit? That's good, I wouldn't recommend it to anyone. The worst part is how *paranoid* you can end up becoming if you aren't careful. It's a real risk. Sometimes you can get to feeling like everything you're doing, you might have done it before, except you have no way of knowing. It's a serious trip, *especially* when it comes to something like looking for an apartment, that much's for sure. Hell, I might have even been *born* in Polis for all I know. Luckily, I'm not someone like that, I'm not a paranoid, so I haven't let it get to me too much. I'm a pretty stable guy. Anyway, the only stuff I'm certain of for sure is what I mentioned on the form. So you can see why it's a little sparse, is the thing."

*   *   *

I leaned back. Osman's face had grown as inscrutable as a night sea, his hand making a dry rustle as it rippled through his beard. It was so quiet in there you could hear the ticking of a clock—if there had been a clock...

"Ah, c'mon, Osman, give the kid a chance, won't ya!"

Geeez-*uuus*: that receptionist was some kind of eavesdropper!

"Goddammit, Dani!"

"I'm just saying, Osman, you never be giving people a chance or nothing. That's one sad story the kid just told ya."

"Dani! You need more things to do out there? This is grown business!"

Wheeling back to his desk, he picked up my form again, no doubt to throw it away, except that in giving it a second glance, something strange happened. He had it pinched between his fingers when his eyes did a double-take, first flickering away dismissively, then flickering back with sudden interest. He squinted.

"Says here you're staying on Joserman Street?" he asked me. "Seventeen twenty-four?"

"Only until I find my apartment, of course."

He stared a second longer. Returning to his computer, he typed a few things. Then his sudden smile bloomed across his face again.

"Got some units in mind that might match your needs. You're in luck, my friend! An exception won't hurt."

"Oh man! Really?"

"Really." He pulled his smile even tighter. "We'll keep it between us, alright? Can't be risking my reputation on rentals. You'll be my exception, understood?"

"Of course! Mum's the word, you have my guarantee."

Gathering myself, I stood up at once; I didn't want to spend a second longer waiting for him to change his mind again.

"You want to know the worst part, Osman? I still have that headache is the thing. It's softer, but it's still there."

"Yes, yes, yes. Shame. Okay, no sense delaying. You filled out your phone number, at least, so expect to hear from me. Let's talk again soon and I'll show you a few units. In the meantime, some homework for you: let's work on that vision, alright? This has been a revealing consultation, sir. Very revealing. Don't slam the door, please."

Out in front the couple was gone and the man with the present just about barged by me to get in there next. There were also two-three others who'd just come. On my way to the exit, the receptionist held me up for a moment.

"Hey. That Calumet fella. He tall?"

"Yes!"

The receptionist nodded.

"Odd fella."

OSMAN THE THRONED

We met up again two days later. I'd awoken to a pair of buzzing text messages from him, the first with the good news that he'd lined up some viewings of places he felt might match my profile, and the second an instruction to meet him at such-and-such bistro at such-and-such time. I bought a monthlong SubPass and got over there pronto to find him at a small outdoor table wrapping up a call on a tiny flip phone. He hung up once he saw me approaching and explained it to me like this:

"Alright, kid. This is how it's going to work. I'm a busy man and don't really have the time. But you're lucky some space freed up in my schedule. I'll show you a couple places if ever I'm not doing something else, and you don't know what you're looking for, so there can't be too many complaints. My fee will be twelve percent of the year's rent, that's industry standard. A lot of people out here have gone up to fifteen and those are what we call crooks. You'll see that I'm traditional. Coffee?"

We were near the corner of Moriat & XVIII, in a homey neighborhood of bookshops and bakeries, the street's ends cordoned off for a farmers market. Instead of a boxy suit jacket he had on a boxy untucked shirt with blue and white stripes and wrinkled chinos.

Me I nodded along the whole time he was speaking:

"Oh, for sure, Osman! And may I reiterate my appreciation for your services once more. It's like everyone says: if you want something done right, find an expert. I'm fine on the coffee, though."

He gave me a pitying look, then took a sip from the flask in his jacket. Geez, he really liked to hit the booze no matter the time of day. "Come on then." And he boosted himself off.

That day he only had time for two viewings before appointments with other clients, close enough to where we were to knock them out within the hour. The first was on West Lilliberth Street between Avenues XVII and XVIII, right where they have those ice sculptures in the winter. We made it through the foot traffic real light and breezy, Osman's maneuvering slowed hardly at all by the families in coordinated outfits considering glistening produce in the early light, or by having to occasionally wave to some passerby he knew. A farmer selling jars of honey shouted to ask him if he'd heard back about the cul-de-sac, followed by two ladies eating sorbet who wanted to know a good time to have him over to review the latest paperwork. "Patience, Patrick! Soon, Julia! Don't I always say?" Osman shouted right back. At the building in question he fished a massive ring of keys from his pocket and selected a small brass one with which to open the door at the top of the ramp, and then, once we'd ridden the elevator up to the ninth floor, another one to open unit 9C. "Laundry's in the basement. No parking spots but you don't look like you drive. Fifteen hundred with amenities, that's just so you know. Okay, I'll do the honors." The olive door swung open with the soft creak of a secret, releasing a rush of air-conditioned air. I could hardly believe it! It was my first viewing...

It was a plain, midsize one-bedroom, with cream walls and no furnishings. Walking about its sunlit expanse, I made note of its airy bedroom, though it was too small for a queen bed, and its pleasant view of neighboring rooftop gardens, though it was marred by scratched windows. I felt first one way and then the other about every last thing. It had high ceilings but cramped closet space, a newly outfitted kitchen but a rusty bathroom, wood flooring but linoleum counters. The whole thing took me about four minutes to check out, as I snapped a few pictures on my phone and sent them to Monica Iñes to ask what she thought. It was a decent start, and definitely something to consider.

"This is definitely something to consider, Osman," I rejoined him in the front room and said. "Although, I've been mulling over what we were saying about my vision. That was a shit job I did last time. Look, I was wondering, you ever heard of these things called antechambers, Osman? It's like a smaller room before you get to the real room. It's not like I *have* to have one of those, per se, but that's the kind of feel I'm going for, you know?"

"Ah, I see, yes, an antechamber," he said, finishing another swig from his flask with a few dribbles into his beard. "You're a man with standards, aren't you? I've noticed things about you. An antechamber! That's good. You won't just go for anything. Good to know! Fine. Forget we came here. Let's get you somewhere else…"

On our way to the next one he really got going, picking up an accelerated pace of chatter like a locomotive kicking into gear. He shared various tidbits about this building and that, using his chin to indicate since his hands were occupied. The glass-walled penthouse secretly owned by Uzbek oligarchs and the rent-controlled loft due on the market any day now. The steals in that tower, the traps in the other. As I went around with him, Polis began to seem like nothing but quick steals and easy deals. I'm not going to lie: it had me feeling pretty positive. "See that one over there? Triplex, six bedrooms, hot tub too. Owner used to forge famous documents and sell them to museums. Had a good thing going but then got her dates wrong on one of her forgeries and they sent her off to Quandry. So she's not the owner anymore. Shame! Poor insulation, though." As for our next stop, it was an enormous two-bedroom in a doorman building on West Nelson, with oodles of sunlight, room enough to jump, all kinds of amenities, like a washer-dryer combo and whatnot—except there were about a *dozen* other people in there walking about inspecting everything.

"Who're all these other *people*, Osman?"

"It's an open house, kid. Go get a soda," he wheeled off while saying.

Geeez-uuus. I hadn't known I'd be walking into some sort of live competition. All those others were in whispering pairs, rubbing their fingers along surfaces to check for dust and going over numbers. That one made me want to check everything out in a hurry in case someone else snatched it up right then. Me I elbowed my way into the main room to get a better look at the color-coordinated sofas, the set dining table, the bookshelves full of books I might want to end up reading. I saw three chitchatting women about to enter the bigger bedroom, but I cut in front of them to take a bounce on the bed first. It was a good bed. Hell, I even got that soda like Osman said, from a metal tub in the kitchen, where an acned guy was having a chat with a slender, droopy one.

"... think so. Now I'm being told only until next month when they switch me."

"So you're thinking around here then?"

"Or maybe up in P Jewel? I don't know. It depends on what they say."

"Oof! PJ is rough—"

"One of you thinking of getting this place?" I cut in to ask.

"Hm?" said the droopy one. "Oh! Yes, well, it's on my list. Lovely location, isn't it?"

"For sure, for sure, a swell location. But, say, don't you think you're both a bit too tall for some of the furniture, though?" I added. They both had a couple inches on me, especially the droopy one.

"Excuse me?" said the guy with acne.

"I mean, I just tried out the bed myself, and neither of you would fit."

"Well, I mean, that's just the staging, of course. I'd be bringing my own."

"*Staging?*" I practically yelled.

"Oh my."

"You mean it doesn't come with any of this stuff?"

"It's been nice meeting you," said the droopy one, and led the other guy off.

I scooched over to Osman right where he was by the fire escape catching a signal.

"Osman, were you aware that—"

But he was already cutting me off with a finger in the air, attending half to me, half to the tiny flip phone buzzing in his hand. "I know what you're about to say, Slide, practically a steal, but I have some bad news, I just shook hands on it with that brunette over there by the radiator. Not much we can do. It's a nasty business, but she had her paperwork ready. That's our time for now, I'm afraid. And remember what I said about keeping this between us. Alright, I have to get this. Hello? Who's that, Frank? Son of a bitch, where have you been! Listen, I have some excellent news for you about that unit around Battery. Don't you go anywhere, you rascal, I'm headed over right now...!"

One day he squeezed me in for a tour of a renovated one-bedroom, resplendent with exposed brick and rustic beams, only to tell me there'd been about six murders on the block already that year, with a seventh due soon; on another it was a perfectly located sublet with a washer-dryer combo but that had been so eroded by termites the *floors* were liable to give out. Me I was avoiding any rash decisions, my hands forever on my hips like a man of options.

"It's like my real estate agent was saying, I'm someone with standards, he wasn't wrong about that," I was explaining to Yvette de Sanville while helping her prepare that Sunday afternoon's tray. We were down in the kitchen as she flitted amongst the cupboards plucking this thing and that while I held the tray in my hands. "I can't just be jumping at the first place I see, you know? We're talking about my *home*, after all. So anyway, like I was saying, I'll need one more week, if that's alright."

The kettle went off and she poured some of the water into a porcelain teapot.

"One more week is fine, Mr. Slide. Square it up with Toussaint." Placing everything onto my tray, she slid open the dumbwaiter's panel for me to set it inside and pressed a button for it to start going up. "Okay, come along, and no accidents today, please..."

"Al*right* already!"

Now that it'd been a week, I was starting to get the hang of those chores the cousins wanted me to do, but geez-us: it definitely hadn't been what I was expecting. Those two were trying to run a madhouse in a hurricane. They lived like a pair of busy bees in that weird, odd hive of four sprawling floors, too many rooms, a rotation of sick visitors always in need of something. For just about anything you could think of that was *wrong* with someone, they knew some sort of tea that could fix it, which they spent most of their days brewing in the kitchen. I swear, I'd never known there were so many things you could make *tea* out of, but it just goes to show. One of my first mornings had featured a stern tour with Toussaint of the dusty pantry on the second floor, where they kept shelves of medicinal ingredients in murky glass jars.

PAY AS YOU GO

"This is slippery elm," she'd held one up and said, a pale, bloated root floating in amber goo, "good for constipation and skin rashes. Mr. Yeltsin needs two teaspoons in a cup of the distilled water from beneath the sink when he stops by. Don't stir."

"What happens if I stir?" I'd said, plucking another jar from the shelf, a pink, granular paste with the lid screwed on tight. She plucked it back from me.

"This is not going to work with your questions. Moving on. Here we have smoked ginger, lemon balm, and marshmallow root. They're analgesics, so you'll be needing them often. That one is nitric powder, you'll notice the scent. Put a pinch under Mrs. Wenmore's tongue once a week and make sure she swallows. If she doesn't, tell her I'll come see her..."

Me they had me wear a dusty old smock so I wouldn't ruin my clothes while chopping up ingredients, and I had to lend a hand attending to the guests. Down in that kitchen it was a calamity of brass pans and screaming kettles, Yvette's breasts sweating through her dress as she flitted amongst the cupboards, going: Measure this; Fetch that; Quick, Mr. Slide, get the door, it must be Mr. So-and-So...! For instance, take some of those old-timers I'd passed in the street, tinkering beneath the hoods of vintage cars like a team of greasy surgeons. They were bearded blackmen, laid off from the plants, with dry, hacking coughs from a lifetime of inhaling fumes. Well, I would be the one to fix them a tray of saltwater tea with raw ginger root and carry it all the way outside to where they'd be huddled around a blue convertible with grim, serious looks. Each of them would pick up a small china cup with their knobby, cracked hands and slosh the contents down in one go before hollering for more. *Plus* they wouldn't let it drop that I wasn't the old girl:

"What happened to the old girl?"

"We saw what you did to Pamela!"

"She made our teas better than whatever this is."

"You aren't exactly easy on the eyes, daddy-o."

"*Sheesh*, I'm her re*place*ment, alright? You guys are seriously stressing me out. Also I heard she had an attitude. Hurry up and give me those back, I need to be washing them..."

Meanwhile, in the parlor would be about six neighborhood aunties slathered in jewels, who'd come to gossip and play cards amongst the elaborate old tables. *They* needed fresh leaves of cat's claw in lukewarm water to help with their arthritis, plus a constantly refilled plate of saltine crackers and jam. "Be a sweetie and see if there's any chocolate too," one of them, Mrs. Clementine, always liked to ask, with a pinch on my ass as soon as I turned around. "Ouch!" They were long-nailed and girlish and yellow-toothed and divorced, and had an ongoing bridge rivalry with some of the waiters across the street who'd come to play after their shifts. I mean, it was *that* kind of place. If it wasn't the postman knocking on the door for something to relieve his backaches, then it was the local apothecary owner coming to drop off a new batch of roots for the pantry. Every evening around six a ragtag bunch of hobos would arrive through the backyard fence and settle around the patio table to start sorting the cans they'd picked up during the day. Which, I don't mean to sound a certain *way* or anything, it's just that they were a bunch of hobos—three guys and a lady-hobo, in thick, rugged clothes and clunky boots held together by tape, sorting their cans from one garbage bag to another with the happy cheer of workers along an assembly line.

"Hey there, Slick!" one of them, Mikey the Albino, always called out to me. "How about some of that what-you-call-it for these rashes we got?"

"Yeh, Slick!"

"Some of that scarlet bush!"

"Come on, how about it?"

"Can everyone *wait* a minute? I'm not even sure which one that is!"

In the town house next door lived a Frenchwoman with a baby she brought over whenever she couldn't get it to stop crying, practically thrusting it into Toussaint's arms for her to do something. "Pleeez! Eet weel not cahlm down seence eets bath!" *That* one would mean I'd have to heat up a saucepan of unpasteurized milk, ginseng, and agave, plus throw away a swollen, shitty diaper, while Toussaint got to stand around cradling the baby in her arms and making silly noises. "Aah, I don't know how you do eet," the mother would say, an arm over her eyes, from the parlor sofa onto which she'd collapsed.

Calming the baby, that was about the nicest you'd ever see Toussaint. That and around this one dog. She didn't like dogs, but she did like this one dog, owned by another neighbor, a widower who'd been in the military, and who stopped by every time he was passing the building to see if anything needed fixing, as if reporting for duty. He was a portly stalwart with russet hair and angular motions, a mean scoop of an underbite. Lieutenant Chesney. I knew right away that I liked him, because he was about the only person you could get Toussaint to talk to, since she liked petting the dog. He'd enter through the patio gate and march past the hobos sorting their cans, then go poking around to see what work there was. "How's that knocking we heard in the pipes upstairs?" he might ask Toussaint, or "Had a can of paint lying around if you'd like to tackle those walls finally," he might say to Yvette, or, like when he'd stumbled upon me the first time:

"Need a little elbow grease?" I'd looked up from what I'd been doing, scrubbing one of the black cast iron pots the cousins used to boil roots, and saw him standing at-ease by the refrigerator.

"*Do* I?" I dropped the brush. "I'm like a one-man show around this place. Here, you have to make sure you're getting at the muck down in those creases."

He took over, rolling up his sleeves and snapping on the rubber gloves I gave him while I took a moment to pat the dog at his feet. It was a nice dog. It was a dalmatian. I would have to ask Lieutenant Chesney if I could take it for a walk sometime.

"Copy that," he said, scrubbing the pot with his sharp, brutal strokes. *Geez* was he an intense guy. You could tell it bothered him that he was no longer in the military because he was always finding a way to use an acronym when it wasn't really necessary, like DIY to explain that he'd done something himself.

I swear, there were so many people in-out-and-about the house all day, it took me a while to figure out who was actually *staying* there in the rooms. As it turned out, there were really only two. One of them was that guy Borsnitch I'd met on the first day, with the room across the hall from mine, who would turn out to be some sort of hypochondriac. I'm not kidding, if ever there was a place to be a hypochondriac, it was *definitely* that house. Borsnitch, he wore thick shawls all day so sweat would flush out his pores, and he didn't like shaking hands in case you'd recently been outside. He'd arrived at the house one day to spend the night while his apartment on Garrith Street was being fumigated for bedbugs, apparently, but that had been about eight years ago. Now, with his wary expression and that portable TV always switched to the news, he made a daylong haunting of the house's floors like a ghost with unsettled concerns. What really killed you was how *nice* he was.

"Oh, hullo, Slide! Tried any black knuckle in your tea yet?" he asked me one morning when I opened the bathroom door to find him soaking in the tub. The water was extremely pink and fizzing as if carbonated.

"No, not yet, Mr. Borsnitch, I haven't had a moment, to tell you the truth."

"It's quite rejuvenative. Flushes you out. Many people have parasites they don't know about," he said, twiddling a foil antenna to catch the latest headline. He kept a running tally of all the murders for the week, as well as of the many cancer-causing foods you might be eating for dinner. He had gotten it into his head that it was always about to rain, possibly tomorrow, no matter the endless drought still parching the streets, and he went about trying to warn you every chance he got.

"I'd recommend against too much quarreling with Mr. Borsnitch, Mr. Slide" was most of what Yvette had to say about him on that same Sunday afternoon that marked the end of my first full week. We continued our way upstairs past the library, where two of the old-timers had opened the windows to feed the pigeons. "He's set in his ways at this point and there isn't much to be done. It's because of what happened with his wife."

"You don't have to keep calling me 'mister,'" I said, still a couple steps behind her. "It's not like I have a degree or anything."

"It's particularly bad if he's watching Jim and Jean," she continued. "They come on at nine, child, but then they have another one in the evening too. That's where most of his nutty ideas come from."

"Those the ones on the billboards?"

"Yes. I know they're quite popular and whatnot, but if you ask me, they're a hot load of nonsense. Always stirring up trouble. You give me a wish for this place, Mr. Slide, it would be to get those two off the air," which, just so we are clear here, were her words and not mine...

As for the other boarder, she was a sick woman the cousins were taking care of, up on the fourth floor, in the deepest slumber I'd ever seen. Yvette and I made it to the top floor at last, and into a dim room of heavy incense where the woman slept amongst a multitude of thick cushions. She was dark, hairless, and incredibly muscular, like a statue hewn from obsidian. Even from the doorway could you hear her ragged, shallow pants, like those of a monster in a lair.

"This is Rosa," Yvette had whispered during my first time up there, earlier in the week. "She used to be a boxer, Mr. Slide. Then she went to Quandry for something."

"Quandry?"

"The prison, Mr. Slide."

"Damn. I hate to tell you, Yvette, but she doesn't look too good at all."

"We know. We're just hoping she gets better soon. The specialists all left scratching their heads, but we give her a hot puree of willow root and hibiscus leaves to keep her toxins down, and once a week you'll help me move her limbs so she doesn't atrophy too bad. Sometimes we get her to say a few words, so she must be hearing everything, we think. She doesn't have anyone but us..."

That Sunday, though, she wasn't too chatty. With unusual quietness, Yvette slid open the dumbwaiter panel on the wall, where our tray from the kitchen was waiting, and began preparing the medicine. Using a mortar and pestle, she ground the roots and added the hot water from the teapot to make a thin tincture. Me I had to hold up Rosa's smooth head—hot to the touch like a stone left in the sun—so Yvette could pour sips of the concoction into her slightly parted lips. With every few drops Rosa made the *oooi*ng sounds of a calf and softly gurgled before swallowing on reflex. Heaven above. I don't think I'd ever seen anyone that sick before. Yvette's face had sunk into the deep worry it always did when we were up there. It made me realize she was old. A loud thump-and-crash reverberated up through the dumbwaiter, followed by the din of an argument between the old-timers. Yvette sighed.

"It's an old house we got here, Mr. Slide," she said, "and, child, if old troubles don't come with it. Some mornings I hear its joints croaking and think, Yup, this is it, it's about to all fall down." She fed Rosa another sip. "I ever tell you it was abandoned when we found it? We had to convince the squatter hiding in the rooms to let us have it, so we could transform it into a house of culture. Ha! That had always been my dream. I was going to have one of those salons where all them artists and inventive types came to discuss important issues. I was a girl. When we found it I had to plead with my cousin—Toussaint, can't you see it's a sign? So what if the timber swells when it rains and it's bugs in the attic? We'll get new wood. The spiders will leave once we shake them out. Well, that's what we did, child. Except afterward we found we didn't know any actors, or painters, or any such types. We knew a couple invalids with fevers, and knockabouts who couldn't sleep. What were we going to do? Sit here by ourselves in the dust? So this is my new dream. And, Mr. Slide, it is a better one, though I couldn't have known. I guess we should have let the squatter stay after all."

She finished up by dabbing Rosa's head of sweat and raising her own mug of tea to her lips. What she put in hers, I wasn't quite sure.

"Finding a home is a tough business," she said. "I'm glad you're not worrying. These things take time."

I lowered Rosa's head back to the cushion as slow as I could. "Oh, no way, Yvette. I'm definitely in good hands. This guy Osman's a real professional."

She coughed up a mouthful of tea, spilling it onto her dress.

"Careful! You don't want to burn her!"

"I'm sorry, bad swallow."

"I'll clean that up. You alright, Yvette?"

"I'm fine. But I need to go see what that ruckus is about."

The commotion from the library had only gotten louder— they could be really cantankerous, the old-timers.

"One more week is fine," she said on her hasty way out. "Time, it all takes time. It'll get better."

But it didn't get better! Those next couple days I met with Osman bright and early without fail and we set about touring Downtown with a refreshed list of options. One after the next it was something with each of them.

It would be a two-bedroom condo on the western end of Tilton Street, described beforehand as an "open floorplan," which turned out to mean there was simply a bathtub, right there, next to the bed like it wasn't anything! "Osman, do you even know how un*sani*tary this must be?" "That's a classic feature, kid. Got a lot of people out here would kill for a little something like this!" Or, if not that, then the studio on Upton & XV with slanted floors, and which was next to an aboveground stretch of train tracks, such that it shook about whenever one went charging by. Osman had to set the brakes on his wheels to keep from sliding around like a loose marble;

I couldn't imagine myself having any dreams in there that didn't involve some sort of stampede. There was the moldy one. The haunted one. The one across the hall from a vicious couple having a tremendous argument and threatening to set fire to everything. The low-ceilinged trap, the dive reeking of disinfectant. The one where the mice had their own territory and the cockroaches another. One of them was in the Franco Quarter, where there'd been all those Norman settlers a long time ago and yes, fine, it was very historic, and the plazas and terraces were exactly like I'd imagined, and I even chucked a good-luck coin into one of the fountains along the way, but that didn't stop the apartment from being on the first floor of a rickety tenement and exposed to an alley of foot traffic. I couldn't have been there for more than twelve *minutes*, but it was enough for two different tour groups to make stops by the window and peer inside, taking pictures like we were on display.

"Now for the architects amongst you," the tour guide was saying, "you'll notice an engraving of a bulldog on a few of these bricks. Many attribute this crest to Count Devernouy, who, one hundred and twelve years ago..."

"Any way we can lower a blind or something?" I asked the current tenants, who were showing me around.

"Lower a blind?" said the girl.

"When the Quarter is outside?" said the boy.

"Why, that's half the fun!" they said together.

They were two giggling blonds of unusual fitness. I had the feeling they were exhibitionists. They probably had sex with the blinds pulled up and let people take pictures for tips. If I moved in there, audiences would expect me to do the same.

"What now? Yes, well, you aren't exactly a millionaire, kid.

Give it a second look, why don't you?" Osman told me over the phone. He was waiting for me out on the sidewalk, since the building didn't have a ramp.

Out there, Osman navigated Polis's streets like a lemur through a forest, and he never stopped for directions not even once. There seemed not to be a single block on which he didn't know a piece of ancient history, or at the very least some spicy gossip to scintillate the ears—the building over there that had had the assassination, this neighborhood where the Poles used to live before they closed the cannery, that decrepit park on our right, where all those women you see on the corner aren't exactly waiting for the bus, if you know what I mean, Slide... He wore his boxy shirts untucked at the waist and his shoes were pristine only from never having touched the sidewalk. That black beard tangled its rough way across his face like a knotted fisherman's net. As for the little flip phone of his, he must have given the number to everyone he'd ever met, for I swear, no sooner would one of his loud calls end than a new one would begin, as if on the other end there extended a queue of infinite length. Going about Polis with him, you had to be as ready for what you were *supposed* to be doing as for what you actually did—his detours and errands, the run-ins with people he knew. "Hey, Osman," the pastry makers on Rita Street East said from the other end of spotless displays of apricot tarts, "Chef's been asking for you, heard there's movement on that villa in North Battery, that true?" "Osman," rang the voice from an open manhole near Westbury & XX, "bad news about the sewage in some of these condos." "Osman, we're thinking of selling," said the bejeweled divorcée he'd once helped close on a classic six in Point James, and "Osman, the children are always asking for you!" said the well-to-do couple we bumped into while picking up his dry cleaning. He had an in with some construction workers in Easthalen to preview the new penthouses first and was owed a favor by a legal executor trying to get a Haverford estate off her hands.

All along, he maintained a fascination with my current living arrangement, often mocking me for what he called my "voluntary indentureship."

"So let me get this straight, Slide. They having you scrub the toilets where you're staying? What else they got you on your hands and knees for?"

"Come on, Osman! I told you already, it's not anything like that."

"Ha! What's it like then?"

"I mean, it's boring. I chop up some vegetables, I help them make some teas. Things of that nature. There's some sick people there is all."

"Sick people? Teas? They running a hospital? You some kind of nurse?"

"I wouldn't say all *that*. It's more of a hospice, if anything. You can come by to see it if ever you want, Osman."

"That's quite alright, kid."

In fact, for all his popularity, he remained weirdly insistent that *our* working arrangement be kept private, and that I not mention it to anyone at all. Me I didn't see what difference it made, with us going about every part of town together anyway. You don't worry about that, he'd cut me off and say. Osman he was always cutting me off. The apartment tours he'd join me on were little more than hasty sprints during which he'd zoom from room to room, then fix me with an amused look to gauge my response, as if pleased by my growing desperation after each shit place. He'd take a long swig from his flask before considering another key from the large ring he kept hooked to his belt, and beat me to the exit at a swift speed. There could be something a little mean about him, I'm not going to lie.

The worst were the rooms without windows. These pitiful cells were found behind the most inconspicuous of doors and introduced by their lessors with a cheer that did not match the circumstances, as if they were showing me a patch of garden instead of a hole in the ground. They had walls and little else. Some books on a shelf. A fan, perhaps. Mostly a scent of madness. No amount of bright paint could cover up their desolation, and sometimes, if I listened just right, I was sure I could hear the combined screams of all their previous residents. One of them had a framed picture of a sunset where a window should have been, which seemed to me a kind of gross mockery, like a taxidermied animal. Osman gestured eagerly to a dim corner, where a row of electrical sockets lay in wait as a consolation prize, but me I never stepped past the doorway. I couldn't pry my gaze from the sole lamp fighting off waves of irreversible darkness. It probably had to stay on the entire time. To tell you the truth, the whole thing was making me want to cry.

A DELIVERY

My friends, my days were going by with not-too-much to show for them. Every morning I headed out from the town house with a belly full of gusto and every evening I returned flatter than an old balloon. Walking back along Joserman Street's sidewalks, I'd delay for slow, sorrowful moments to peek into the glowing windows where contented professionals with loosened ties poured the glasses of wine that were the day's reward, or to stare with jealous eyes at the groups of dining friends laughing gaily beneath strings of white lights. The effort of so much envy was leaving me weary and sickened. I'd climb the town house's steps in a feverish state, then stomp around doing my chores in so dark a mood that just about anyone could see I needed some cheering up.

"Pah!"

"Lift your head up, Slick!"

"You're on the right track!"

"It makes it that much sweeter when you find the right place at last!"

That last one was from Mikey the Albino.

"But how much *longer?* I don't think I need that much sweetness, if it's what I'm waiting for, a regular amount is fine," I told him. I was pacing out on the back patio where the four of them usually sorted their cans—Mikey the Albino, Horace, Lance, and Mildred the lady-hobo—although today I'd gotten them to chop up some roots from the pantry for me instead. "Careful with that one, Horace, it needs to be cut horizontally, remember? Here, let Mildred show you."

He slid his cutting board over to Mildred, who'd gotten through about five whole roots already. She was the best of all of them, Mildred.

"My fingers supposed to be turning all purple like this, Slick?"

"Don't be such a baby, Horace, it's only some violetshade. Rinse with an alkaline soap after and it'll come right out. I wouldn't recommend touching your face, though."

He stripped off those fingerless gloves they all had and held his hands out and away from him like they were about to explode.

"You got to trust us, Slick," Mikey the Albino went on pontificating. "We know all about this stuff."

"Got apartments everywhere you look in this place!" said Mildred.

"Lance there had a wicked one once! Didn't you, Lance?"

"I most certainly did."

"Tell him then!"

"It was some place, Slick."

"We're talking big-screen TV and everything. Boy, that was some place, Lance."

"It most certainly was."

"Shame what happened, though."

"Geez-us," I was still saying, "never mind, it's like I'm misunderstood. I need more than just a TV after everything I've been through, no offense or anything."

"None taken, Slick."

At their feet were the funny cardboard signs they used to ask for money during the day—TOO UGLY TO PROSTITUTE or CRIME DIDN'T PAY AFTER ALL. The military neighbor, Lieutenant Chesney, arrived right then, clean-shaven and with the dalmatian at his heels.

"Lieutenant! Good news," I said, taking a perch on the table. "I know you are always looking for things to do, and Yvette has requested that we all chip in to chop up these roots…"

Sometimes I texted Monica Iñes with an update. *All good on my end!* I'd say. *What's new with you?* By then our thread was thirty-three messages long, all of them from me. Sometimes I turned on my electric clippers for no reason and wondered what Rex and Reginald were doing. Were they getting to that hard-to-reach part beneath the sink when they swept the floor?

Or was that just being ignored without me around? Also, who had they found to replace me? Some dope, I bet. I even thought of Eustace, who I assumed was in front of the TV, jiggling to exercise videos. Thinking of Calumet, I didn't do so much. Every time I surveyed his map it felt like a bunch of sad predictions I was doomed to fulfill: *Booby traps... Look twice... Asbestos...* And to think my troubles in that place were just getting started.

It must have been October, five weeks into my stay and not an ounce luckier, when one afternoon Toussaint de Sanville appeared in Rosa's room to say I'd have to start making deliveries.

"You're going to have to start doing some deliveries."

"Yikes!"

Her sudden voice caused me to drop Rosa's limp head onto the cushions with a floppy thud. I spun around to see her shuffling her deck of strange cards—the same ones from before. *Flllt* thwap. *Flllt* thwap.

"Yvette has become too busy."

Me I could have caught flies in my *mouth* it was open so wide.

"Something wrong?" she asked.

"It's just, something like that will really cut into my *time*, Toussaint. I thought we had an arrangement worked out already!"

"Yes," Toussaint said. "An arrangement for a week."

"What, are we being *literal* around here?"

Turning back to Rosa with a huff, I picked her head up again and continued tipping the rest of the tea into her mouth.

"I mean, you guys are really getting a deal out of this situation, I'll have you know. If my labor were any cheaper it'd be *illegal*."

She didn't say anything for a few long seconds, still shuffling the cards. It was uncomfortable having her right there, so close behind me. Eventually I turned back around to find her wet, brooding eyes still observing me, as if I'd said nothing at all. *Flllt* thwap.

"How long you say you was at that orphanage for, boy?"

"Oh. *That?*"

"Mhm."

"Why you want to know about that?"

Flllt thwap.

"Umm... you know... it's hard to say. We tended to be in and out a lot."

"Mhm."

"Because... well, the way it worked... sometimes a family might pick you up for a while but then bring you back if they changed their mind."

Flllt thwap.

"So it makes it hard to add up..."

She continued her cold survey. I wasn't really done with Rosa (it was one of the days I was supposed to move her arms around too), but I started packing up the tray anyway, just to get out of there. I swear, I'd never seen anyone so sick before. It didn't matter what you said or did in there, she'd keep panting away with no difference. Between her and Toussaint, who looked like a drowned mermaid with that tangled hair and those watery eyes, I was getting some serious heebie-jeebies.

"You'll start tomorrow," Toussaint said.

Well, she wasn't kidding: the next morning she sent me out the door with a kick on the ass and a bag of sloshing glass bottles to drop off around town.

Not good kid, Osman scolded me by text when I had to re-schedule. *It's already a lot of favors I'm having to call in to find somewhere in your budget.*

I know, Osman, just push it back a day, alright? I've got a couple errands and can explain later!

In my pocket was Toussaint's handwritten list of addresses that would take me as far north as Gangary Street, dropping off treatments for a bunch of patients I hadn't so much as *heard* of before. Oh my. These were the true freaks, too hobbled by mysterious illnesses to make it to Joserman Street them-selves, or too vain as well. One apartment was a household of emaciated drag queens in neon wigs, passing the days with the comfort of opioids, their dull black eyes on the lookout for death. In another, a pair of conjoined twins grown immo-bile from the insatiable appetites that sometimes led them to consume even the clippings of their own nails. Jittery para-noids, bedridden invalids, demented geriatrics who'd ask me for my name on the way in then call the police for help on my way out. Going about on those sad tours, I started wondering if Polis was simply a stockpile of pathetic fates waiting to be doled out, and to spend time avoiding your lot would only worsen the inevitable blow... On the top floor of a Harold Street tower I waited a full twelve minutes for the dragging sound of footsteps to make it from the other end of that pa-latial apartment so crammed with trinkets it seemed like a museum, if not for someone still living in it: a bespectacled blackman somehow no older than *me*, yet so near the verge of blindness he had to rub his hands all over my face just to try telling who it was.

"Who's that? Come closer now. Right on then. Oh! You're not the old girl! What happened to the old girl...?"

*   *   *

At least on one of the mornings it was only a single bottle Toussaint had for me, a murky green tincture to be delivered to 232 Torrick Street, and that she had apparently prepared herself.

"Let yourself in when you get there. It should be unlocked."

"Alright, alright, got it. And I appreciate it just being just one today, Toussaint, I've really been busting my ass trying to get these done. Torrick Street is a bit far, huh? I'll call a cab. Don't worry, I won't bill you for it."

I was a little intrigued, to tell you the truth. Toussaint just about *never* made any of the teas herself. The few that she did took her nearly a full day of delicate slicing, soft simmering, a stirring of the pot so meticulous that its contents hardly moved.

But she'd been shaking her head the whole time. "This one cannot be rattled about. You are going to have to walk."

"What? That'll take me like an *hour*, Toussaint."

"Mhm."

Right then you could hear the Frenchwoman with the baby arriving through the front door and calling for help.

"And take Borsnitch with you," she added on her way to her. "He needs air."

Well! I've never had to herd a cat before, but I swear, this was about as close as you could get.

"… alright then, Mr. Borsnitch, there you go. One step at a time now. Great, that's the stuff."

"Righty-o! I say, perhaps a stop at this shop to ask after a restroom then?"

"But you just *used* the restroom, Mr. Borsnitch. You didn't get it all out or something? You'll be alright."

"Ah, correct you are! Very well then. Onward. Lovely air we're having!"

We were only as far as Newton Street, after half an hour of walking, and with no picking up of the speed. To make matters worse, we were approaching some sort of parade that was holding up traffic. Borsnitch he had on a waxy green raincoat over his usual shawls, a wool hat, and rubber galoshes up to his knees. His TV was going in and out of static as it picked up moments of signal along the crowded sidewalks.

"I say there, Slide, here's a lovely park. I used to be a champion draughts player, you know? Perhaps a stop here?"

"Maybe on the way back, Mr. Borsnitch."

"Yes, yes, on the way back. Jim and Jean did a feature here once with all the draughts champions, but I was a little unwell that day."

I swear, it was like Toussaint had made me take him to make *sure* I'd walk slow. Every few steps I'd have to turn and check that he hadn't wandered off. Me I had one hand holding the glass bottle and the other my phone, messaging Osman.

Bad move kid. The market waits for no one! Recommend you take that unit on West Vivian, he'd just written.

I thought of the one he meant: a mildewed railroad apartment thirty minutes' walk from all the subways.

That one was shit, Osman.

I really think it's for the best.

He'd been getting even more flippant as of late, every next unit more dismal than the last.

The parade turned out to be a protest and I almost lost Borsnitch forever trying to cut through the throng of marchers banging drums.

"Borsnitch? Mr. Borsnitch! Hey, are you seeing me?"

One of the marchers going by said, "My brother, you are headed the wrong way, we need every voice," while three others tried handing me the same pamphlet at the same time.

"Not right now, please. I'm looking for someone."

"Every voice, my brother, come on, it's this way!"

Geez. Stuff like that is the exact reason I got out of Middleton. Finally I saw Borsnitch's wrinkled little head bobbing amongst the sea of protesters and fished him out onto the other side of the street.

"Slide, I think this is about the evictions at the docks. Have you heard? Jim and Jean did a lovely exposé. Perhaps we should head back with them..."

I began to tune him out. We went by Northram Street, Oppenheim, Othelier, and Putnam. The farther we went, the less patient I got—I was *definitely* shaking up whatever was inside that bottle. *It's a lot of pressure you're putting me under*, I was saying to Osman. *I think we definitely need to do some rediscussing of my vision.*

We were having an argument.

Osman sent: *Look, kid, don't annoy me.* Then he sent: *Do you know how busy I am?* And a minute later: *Perhaps you should seek another arrangement.*

"Ooh ooh that looks like the dance club I used to go to. Slide, do you think we could..."

"Mr. Borsnitch!" I spun around. "Not! Now!"

That's when I saw he was nervous. I mean, there I'd been thinking he was being all cheery about everything, but now that I looked, he was clutching his TV like a float ring while his eyes darted to the sky to check for oncoming clouds.

"I used to be a good dancer is all." Oh Lord.

"I'll tell you what, Mr. Borsnitch," I held him by the palm

and said, "we'll stop by every one of these on the way back from where we're going. It's just a couple more blocks."

His hand was clammy and trembling, like a small, damp animal, but it relaxed a little in mine.

All the rest of the way I had one hand holding his, the other the bottle, as well as the phone crooked between my ear and shoulder, on the line with Osman. I'm not kidding, I must have looked like some sort of crazy person, dragging that old man along and yelling into my neck.

"... So what, you're just going to drop me when the going gets tough? That's how it is? You're some professional, Osman. Some professional indeed!"

"Don't you talk to me about professionalism, kid! The Vivian unit will do you just fine."

"Are you trying to *play* with me, Osman? You think there aren't other real estate agents in this place!" We'd just walked by a lamppost papered with flyers for just about everything. "I could snatch up any one of these flyers I'm seeing all the time and find a place just fine. I figured I'd give you a *chance* was the only thing."

"Alright, alright, let's calm down a little!" I could practically *hear* him smiling. "Listen, there is something I've had in mind for you, actually. Let me get to this other call and then I'll—"

"No you don't! You stay right here until we sort this out...!"

In fact, I was still on the phone yelling at him when Borsnitch and I finally got to 232 Torrick Street, an industrial slab of a building in a squalid neighborhood of warehouses and soot-covered children playing amongst the rubble. I'd seen stuff like *that* before. I would've definitely told Borsnitch to tuck that TV beneath his raincoat if I wasn't so occupied already. "… something you've had in mind? You better start telling me…!" Going up the ramp, I freed a hand to open the front door, then counted off the unit numbers along the smoke-stenched hall, giving 1B a quick knock before opening it anyway. Yuck. Whosever place this was, they were some sort of a slob—even the vestibule had a calamity of shoes, bulging garbage bags, and stacks of magazines I had to lead Borsnitch around as if winding through a maze. A yucky medicinal odor of creams and stale pills filled the air.

"Hello? I'm here for your delivery," I shouted, even as Osman was trying to calm me, going: "Okay, you're a little antsy, I can tell, let's discuss something…" Except: something weird was happening… "wasn't going to bring this up until the time was right, you see…" as I tugged Borsnitch farther down the hall… "in Polis it takes patience to find what works…" it was like I was hearing double… "Call my office tomorrow and let's schedule a—"

But he stopped short as I turned the corner, and into the latest shock of my life.

It was Osman the Throned. He sat on a ruddy brown recliner in the middle of a squalid room of junk like a forlorn king amongst ruins. All around him were the yellowing newspapers, scattered pill bottles, unwashed dishware, mounds of clothes, speckled bars of soap, strewn dresser drawers, disposable coffee cups, and stagnant, musty air that are the hoarder's true signs. Plus on just about every available surface was a bunch of dead potted cactuses. His legs appeared thin and sallow without any pants to cover them, and his phone was still pressed to his ear as his face slowly matched mine in a look of total confusion.

"Os-Osman...," I began.

"Kid! What the— Shit!"

He propped himself up some more, squinting to confirm it was really me.

"Shit shit shit shit!"

"Geez, I must have the wrong address or something," I said from where I was. It felt like I'd stepped into a dream, except it was someone else's. I swear, I'd never seen so many dead cactuses in all my life. I didn't even know cactuses *could* die, but he'd managed it somehow.

"What did you *do*, kid?"

I was still hearing double because of the phone, so I hung up. Behind me, Old Mr. Borsnitch was already asking how long we'd have to stay here. A place like this must have been his worst nightmare.

"What's that in your hand? Answer me!"

"Just something I'm supposed to be dropping off somewhere around here, Osman. Hey, listen, this is some sort of mix-up—"

"You told them!" he suddenly yelled. "You told them you're working with me! That supposed to be my tea? You get that from the pantry? They say I'm supposed to drink that? Huh!"

"I think he means the cousins, Slide."

"I *realize*, Mr. Borsnitch."

"He does seem a little familiar, actually."

"Mr. Borsnitch, it's really not a good time."

"What the fuck did I tell you, kid?"

"Geez, Osman, slow down. I'm not sure what we're talking about."

"Lies!"

His mood was getting worse and worse yet. He was shifting his weight to reach for his wheelchair.

"They know. They *must* know! They sent you here to show me they know..."

But he reached too hard the next time—more of a lunge—and instead of getting a good grip on the wheelchair's arm, he tumbled to the floor as it went rolling off a few feet into a hill of wrinkled shirts.

"Look out!"

Geeez-uuus! He must not have had the brakes set. Down on the ground like that, he looked so feeble it was hard to watch.

"Alright, Osman." I made my way around the junk and cactuses. "Let me help. I'm super confused. Why didn't you say you knew the cousins? Here, how about you hold your tea and I'll give you a lift."

"Get away from me!" He snatched the bottle from my hand and dashed it against the wall in an explosion of green drops.

"Dammit! It was really hard getting that over here."

"I gave you a simple instruction. It was the only thing. And to think I've been wasting my time on you. That was my end of the bar— Don't you touch those!"

Borsnitch had been privately breaking off chunks of cactus bark and pocketing them in his raincoat. "Some of these can be quite potent with the right preparation, you know," he said meekly.

"Hush, old man!"

"Hey, don't talk to him like that!"

"You shut up too!"

Osman began making his own way to the wheelchair. He did it backward along the gross linoleum, his thick arms holding his hips up as he waddled his way through the squalor. Once he got to the wheelchair, he fiddled with the brakes, then climbed up to its seat, finally lifting his legs into the stirrups. The whole thing had left him huffing and frantic, slightly sweaty on every patch of skin. It hadn't even been that far. The effort must have exhausted him of some of his anger, though, for when next he spoke, it was with the desperation of a gambler weighing his options.

"Wait, wait—there could still be time," it suddenly occurred to him. "Yes, kid. Slide!" He wheeled over and grabbed me by the elbow with a trembling hand. "I need you to be honest. What did you tell them? What did you tell the cousins?"

"Ouch, Osman! Easy. I don't know, maybe I might have mentioned you. I didn't know you meant them when you said to keep things private."

"What the hell do you think 'private' *means*, kid?"

"Like from a rival real estate agent who'd want to take my business or something."

"Nobody wants your damn business."

He took to wheeling from cactus to cactus, breaking off bits of bark and muttering.

"It can still work— Wait, Slide—there's something you must do. It's not too late..."

Mr. Borsnitch was shuffling around looking for a signal on his TV. Osman's phone began to cry from the recliner like a baby startled awake by the commotion. Stopping what he was doing, he rolled over to check who it was, looking back-and-forth between it and me, torn.

He was still sputtering, "I must... But, Slide... Please, you can help..." Then he closed his eyes for two deep, recomposing breaths, and I could see the veil of his usual bluster falling over him again.

"You couldn't keep a simple secret, kid," he said, pressing a trembling finger to his temple. "I have to get this."

"Osman..."

"Please go."

And on our way out, you could hear his voice booming from that junk-filled apartment: "Abraham! My man! Are we going to talk numbers at last or do you just like spending time with me…"

A LOVELY APARTMENT

For days after, Osman could not be reached at all. I would call him five times in a row, then get a response by text three hours later: *A bit held up.* When I replied, my messages would bounce back undelivered. One time I went so far as to stop by his office, only to find that receptionist, Dani, watering plants in the waiting room. "Don't know what to tell ya, dude. He hasn't been around." Left on my own, I had no choice but to resort to those flyers after all, peeling off the first batch I saw taped to a mailbox and giving the numbers a ring. That kicked off three disheartening days of misleading pictures and overpriced sublets, a tour of a spare back room so sweltering that fingers of tar dangled from the ceiling…

As for Toussaint, I could get as much out of her as from a sphinx in a bad mood.

"What the hell was *that* about?" I said as soon as I'd gotten back from the delivery. "You know that guy was my real estate agent, Toussaint? He really didn't appreciate being surprised like that, I would have you know. Is there something anyone here wants to *tell* me?"

But she'd brushed me off with a flippant hand, going, "I don't keep track of everyone," before loading me up with a rake and a garbage bag to start scraping leaves from the back patio.

Yvette, on the other hand, just about freaked out when she heard I'd been over there.

"You did *what*? Toussaint sent you *where*? Oh no, child, oh no, why she go and do that!"

"That's what *I've* been saying," I said.

"Oh no no no, this'll be some trouble now, child. I'll have to explain to you later, let me have a word with her and then I'll answer whatever you want to know," she said with a re-assuring pat on the back, but afterward was gone on errands every waking hour of the following days and I couldn't track her down—no matter the number of times I dashed out of bed early to try catching her quick shadow flitting down the stairs.

"Wait! I thought we were supposed to talk...?"

I was getting hemmed in by suspicions, harassed by worries, increasingly paranoid every hour that went by. It wasn't that anyone had *lied* to me, exactly—they just hadn't told the truth either. More and more I grew preoccupied by a sense of im-pending disaster, and the noise of that crowded house became the tumult of a babbling swarm, like so many voices trapped in purgatory. I couldn't put up with Borsnitch's doom-and-*gloom* anymore, the chatter of the hobos crushing cans, the stomping in the vestibule all day long, the pigeons' cawing, the Frenchwoman's baby crying, the offers from Lieutenant Chesney to fix every last thing, or even the silent, brooding presence of Rosa on the top floor, who had begun to appear in my dreams, mouthing inaudible warnings. For the first time ever I began to imagine that house as a sort of pestilential nexus, and that it did not so much attract all those invalids as create them—it seemed the whole *point* of being there was to suffer from ailments and never recover. This was around the time I took to asking some of the aunties how they were doing when I handed them their tea in the parlor.

"Say, Mrs. Applebaum, I was only wondering," I whispered while handing her a cup, "how's your fever been going?" She was a high-cheekboned battle-ax in big, thick furs she never took off.

"Coming along, darling, coming along," she played a card and said.

"*Still?*" I asked. "I mean, didn't you have a fever like a *month* ago?"

"Oh, that one went away. I got another one, I'm afraid. Quiet now, we have some money on the line for this one."

I left them to it, moving on to another who'd just arrived through the front door.

"Mrs. Potfuller," I blocked her and said, still speaking *quietly*, you understand, "how are your warts? What happened to them?"

She bristled; she was a thin-haired neurotic who talked shit about the others when they weren't around. "They've moved," she said, lifting her arm so I could see the fresh set beneath her armpit.

"*Moved?*"

"Yes, it's common with my condition. You are being rude, you know."

"Have any of y'all ever been to a pharmacy?" I suddenly asked the room, startling them from their card games, their endless crochets, their swirling cups of tea settling between sips. "I mean, there are *pharmacies* you can go to for some of these things, you know. It doesn't have to always be here."

None of them budged. They had the dull, compliant eyes of zoo animals who think their cage is the entire world. That one made me get out of there for the next six hours, walking with my hands in my pockets amongst the twilight markets, the tireless billboards slathering the night in neon options...

But Osman *did* reappear in the end, with a curt text the next morning telling me to meet him at 44 Vulpine Row, unit 201 at ten o'clock. Well, me I leaped out that house right away and took a taxi so there'd be no chance of delays, pulling up in a neighborhood of artisan shops and broad-canopied trees turning gold for the fall. Neighbors raking mounds of leaves waved hello as I walked up the garden path to a glimmering white tower. There were sunflowers in the window boxes, and in the lobby three laughing residents patted a dog with ivory teeth. Osman was already upstairs when I got there. There'd been no ramp out front or elevator inside, so I didn't know how, but there he was beside an upstairs door, waiting for me. He wore an ironed blue shirt and flat-front chinos, and on his lap there rested a briefcase. As I drew closer down the mahogany-lined hall, I noticed a triumphant expression within the grove of his beard, which he seemed to have combed.

"Osman!" Holy *moly*, you go without seeing someone a couple days and you start to worry something's happened to them. "Oh *man* is it good to see you!"

"Good morning, Slide," he said when I was close. "Here, I brought you a coffee." It was from the High Ground, the one shop that always had a line. I took a sip and an awesome swell of good feeling radiated through me.

"No wonder they're always so busy," I said. He laughed— a hearty, genuine laugh like the one I'd first heard in his office. "Listen, Osman, about the other day—"

"Please!"

"No, I mean it, listen. I'm just saying, I could have done better with keeping things private. I need to watch my mouth more and that's the real truth."

"Mention it no more, Slide. I should have been more honest myself. I'm very glad you had the time to meet with me today."

From his belt he unhooked his ring of keys and offered me a shiny silver one so I could open the door. I could hardly believe it—he'd never let me use the keys before.

"What's this…"

"Go ahead, Slide," he said.

I held the key against the weight of all the others and slid it with ease into the lock, turning.

Clean, unadorned walls in the off-white shade of sliced apples. Long cedar planks with glistening coats of polish. Parallel closets right as you entered, and, straight ahead, windows as clear and wide and lovely as still pools. It was a true one-bedroom and not some studio. In the living room alone there was enough space to do three cartwheels in a *row* if you wanted, and even in the kitchen you could probably manage a split. A dishwasher. A new fridge. A washer-dryer combo tucked into yet another closet. The bedroom was in the corner, with perpendicular windows looking out onto Vulpine Row and the nearby museum, and the black-and-white tiles in the en suite bathroom were softly illuminated by the skylight above. The whole place had the held-breath perfection of a thing that had been kept waiting; I had the sense he'd known about it all along. Osman sat expectant in the living room once I'd finished my dumbfounded tour.

"It's fifteen hundred a month. That includes amenities. That includes internet. Parking is in the basement, where there are storage units too. The exterminators come once a month to spray, so there are no rats. Groceries, restaurants, parks, they're all around the corner. The super lives downstairs and there's never been a break-in. All the trains come here. Is this something that interests you, Slide?"

I spilled some coffee on the ground I was waving my arm around so much, going: "*Interests* me? What is that, rhetorical? Of *course* this interests me!"

"I had hoped so."

Our voices were echoing in the empty space.

"And, Osman," I went on, "are you serious about the price? Maybe it's a typographical error. You sure that's what it says?"

"It's fifteen hundred," he said again. Another beam of a smile.

"Wow oh wow oh wow."

I marched around. I leaned on the windowsill. I needed a seat but there weren't any chairs. It would have to be furnished. I already had in mind a faux leather couch I'd seen in a store display around Chancellor Plaza, and the hobos said they knew someone who made African-style stools. Oh man: I should have asked them about pricing. Alright, perhaps I should compromise. I could pass on the couch for the time being and cut a deal with the hobos for those stools. I didn't need a lot, two was fine for now. Plus there would have to be a bed. I couldn't believe it. And the timing was so right! Osman had come through after all.

"I really can't believe this," I said out loud, tugging at one of the windows to see if it opened smoothly. It opened smoothly. The giggles of happy children poured into the apartment. "Osman, you've truly outdone yourself."

"It's what I do!" he said and smiled. "Everything I do is what I *can* do. So you see, Slide, I *cannot* outdo myself. It would be impossible!" *There* was the guy I knew. With that last one he swept his arms out as if offering me the world. I'd say it was like old times, except we hadn't known each other that long.

"Man oh man, Osman. I'm not gonna lie, you had me a little worried back there."

"These things take time, Slide."

I'd been having my doubts before, but if you added it up, I'd started my search only about a month and a half ago, and now here I was about to bring it to an end.

"You like the place, Slide?" Osman then asked.

I said I did.

"And I have been helpful to you?"

I said he had.

"That's good, that's good." He joined me at the window. Gazing across Avenue IV, we watched a line of newly arrived tourists get off a tour bus and ascend the stairs of the museum, where an exhibit on suits of armor had just opened. They were in autumn browns and burnt oranges, crimson scarves wrapped around their necks. The children we'd been hearing were in an adjoining backyard jumping into piles of leaves. "Here, I've brought you something." Clicking open the briefcase in his lap, he riffled through various papers and took out a stapled stack. It was a lease. I knew by the winning manner with which he offered it. Setting my coffee on the sill and flipping through the first few pages, I saw the multiple lines where, were I to sign, a tenantship of one year would begin as soon as next week. My heart was banging against the bars of my ribs as if for release. Oh holy hell! Heaven and below! I mean, what on earth...

"Osman..."

"I really panicked the other day, kid. Shouldn't have said some of those things. You accept my apology?"

Me I was nodding like a maniac. "Of course, Osman! Let's let bygone water go under the bridge."

"Excellent. That makes me happy to hear." He let a moment pass as I went through some more pages. I'm not going to lie, some of the stuff was pretty complicated, but reading phrases like "constitutes the only agreement forthwith" had a reassuring effect on me. Eventually he resumed, "You see, Slide, there is something I need your help with."

"Sure. What's up?"

"I have lived a good life, Slide, and I do not have any regrets about what happened to me. But I cannot sit back and accept what they are getting away with."

I turned to look at him and saw the hollows under his eyes deepening.

"The cousins and I have our history, kid. I should have told you. I was a different man before I met them, and since then, precious things have been taken from me."

"Osman, you mean like to do with... with your legs and stuff?"

For a moment he seemed to consider my suggestion. Then, nodding slightly, he said, "Sure," and lowered his gaze to the open briefcase.

"Oh wow. You know, I *knew* something was up about that place, I'd been starting to suspect it." I slapped a hand to my forehead. I could already imagine it: Osman must've wasted *years* going to them for help instead of doing something simple like scheduling a surgery. "You should see some of the other people they have there as patients."

"When you go home I want you to do something for me. Here." He dug out something else from the briefcase, a bundle of dried bark I could only assume was from the cactuses crowding his living room. "Give this to the other cousin. Use hot water that is not boiling, a pinch of granulated salt, leave it to steep for twelve min—"

"What the hell!" I was looking at the bundle like it was a stick of dynamite. "You want me to do *what*? Osman, I'm not sure either of them would want to drink whatever this is. They're pretty particular."

"No, Slide. Not them. The other one. The one sleeping upstairs."

"*Rosa?*"

He nodded, a little surprised. "They told you her name. Yes. Rosa. And you must give this to her."

Osman's shoulders sloped downward in surrender, and although the noise he attempted to make at first seemed a laugh, it settled into a clearing of his throat. I realized he was sad.

"There are things you do not know, and I should not involve you. But she is not safe, and this is all that I can do now that we are out of time. Once you have done this, we will move ahead with the signing. In the meantime there'll be nothing more to show you." He took the lease back. My hands felt empty without it. "This is what you are looking for. It can be yours, too, but you must do what I ask first."

"What will this stuff even *do*, Osman?" I was starting to panic a little. "I don't know about giving anything to her, Osman, she's really sick. They have her on a strict regimen and everything, trust me, I'm the one who's been taking care of her. Ooh, there's something fishy here. There's definitely something fishy afoot, and I don't like it. Let me look at those papers again."

But he had already shut the briefcase and was wheeling toward the door. I saw it in his eyes: that look I must have had in my own: the distressed hope of reaching for what you want most and fearing you may topple it in the process. Though he still smiled, now it seemed more like the revealing of clenched teeth.

"And, Slide, don't bother calling until you have done this. As you know, I am a busy man."

He opened the door and gestured that I might leave. His beard blotted out half his face. Geez did he look sad. Forlorn and terrible, like a ghoul with nothing left. Also selfish. For the first time ever I considered kicking over his chair. Yes, I'm not afraid to admit it: I wanted to kick over his chair. That's what I thought I was about to do as I neared the doorway. Instead, I trudged out that apartment as if evicted from paradise, flinching as he shut the door behind me. I dragged my feet toward the staircase. How he eventually got out of the building himself, I really don't know. It's not like I ever saw him again.

A CHAT WITH THE COUSINS

So it was that very afternoon that I found myself climbing the stairs to the town house's top floor, stumbling like a sun-scorched nomad toward a mirage. I had on soft socks to silence my steps, a shaky tray in my hands. Visions of that last apartment had haunted me the rest of the day: of me walking around its sunlit expanse. Of me cleaning the wainscoting with a handheld vacuum. Of me and Monica Iñes putting the morning coffee to brew while our windowsill plants flowered in the spring...

*   *   *

My heart was aflutter, my palms clammy with anticipation. To tell you the truth, I wasn't too sure of my intentions once I got up to the sickroom. There on the tray, amongst every-thing else, was the bundle of dried bark Osman had given me. But oh *geez*: I didn't like the thought of it at all. What if it ended up making her worse? In fact, what if that was what he *wanted*? It could be the perfect kind of revenge for the cousins not helping him out with his legs. Suddenly I was seeing it in paranoid clarity: he'd spent the preceding weeks drumming up my despair with shitty apartments until I was willing to do anything for a good one. But I wasn't so desperate for a place that I'd be willing to *poison* someone, I was pretty sure. Even when I'd gotten home just now, I'd had to take a long shower, then confront myself nude in the mirror to see who I really was. I hadn't noticed anything. The afternoon was loud and bustling with traffic and people downstairs shuffling about. All the while I tried to remember if Yvette and Toussaint had mentioned that Rosa was also their cousin and I'd simply missed it, or perhaps Osman had just made it up to confuse me. Although I didn't see why he would. How come *I* had end-ed up being the one feeling my way around in the dark while everyone else seemed to know better? I wasn't sure whom to believe anymore. You have to understand, I mean: I felt like I was down to my last resort. I got to the fourth floor, shadowy and humid as usual. All the house's scents had wafted up in a thick cloud. Me I placed the tray on the stand next to Rosa's door and fiddled with its contents. All I had to do was go in and give her the regular medicine, business as usual, and leave without any shenanigans. Yes, that was why I was up there. That was all I was going to do. I thought I could hear her breathing behind the door, a hallucination suddenly so loud it clouded my hearing. Oh man oh man. I walked away. I came back. My skin erupted in an itchy heat. "This is crazy," I said to myself. "You're being crazy right now and you definitely know it." But then there was my vision again, the same one as ever, of the other life I could be living if only I was in that new apartment, with the sounds of children's laughter as they tumbled in the leaves. I clenched my jaw, my fingers trembling as I reached for the doorknob, taking a grip, turning, I mean, after all, maybe I would only give her a little bit...

But oh, my friends, I'll never know what I would have done in there, no matter if I relived it a thousand times. Because just at that moment I heard a voice from above call my name: "Mr. Slide, is that you?" I yelped and spun around, spooked, spotting down at the hallway's dim end a ladder lowered from a trapdoor in the ceiling. Holy shit. I'd never even noticed it before. Tucking Osman's bundle of dried bark into my pocket, I walked over to the foot of the ladder and looked up at a faded patch of sky. "Come up here, dear." I climbed up rung by rung into the afternoon air, where I found Yvette and Toussaint folding rows of dresses from the rooftop's drying lines with the slow nonchalance of having been there all along. Damn. I'd always wondered where they put their clothes to dry...

"We were just coming to look for you, child. Go on, grab a basket and help us with these."

It was a rectangular rooftop, with plastic grass and lawn chairs, separated from the adjoining rooftops by low brick walls. Rows of pigeons sat cooing along the edge, looking out over the neighborhood. Four rusty poles held up the pair of lines the cousins were plucking dresses from before folding and laying them in plastic baskets near their feet. Yvette had a green one with sequins she was making into a neat square, while Toussaint you could hardly see from behind a veil of billowing cloth. Yvette slid me an extra basket with her foot.

Instead I flew off the handle almost at once:

"Listen, Yvette," I waved about saying, "I don't know what kind of a racket you two are running here, but it's some fishy business afoot and I definitely don't like it. What was that stunt about, sending me over to Osman's? And where have *you* been these past few days? I mean, you two not telling me about any of this stuff, it's put me in a seriously tricky spot is the thing."

I was pretty angry. I was upset about my dire situation, about the house's air of sickness, about all the work they were always having me do. But more than anything it was from feeling plain ol' manipulated by every last person I spoke to. I swear, there's no one angrier than a pawn that doesn't know what direction he's supposed to be facing, take it from me.

But Yvette was already shaking her head *tut-tut-tut* like a concerned auntie.

"I hear you, child. That must have been some shock going over there. And you know I said to Toussaint, Toussaint, why'd you go and send him? You're always making things complicated."

"He needed his treatment," said Toussaint from the other side of the dresses—all you could see was her hair. "Isn't that why we hired the boy?"

"Always making it complicated," Yvette repeated.

"Well, I can just about guarantee you he didn't appreciate it. Geez, Yvette, and he's something of a hoarder too. People like that can be very private."

"What he say to you, Mr. Slide?"

"Listen"—I held my hands up—"I don't want to get myself in the middle of things, but he wasn't too happy with his treatment when I went over there. Whatever it is between you guys, I can move out of here right away as soon as it's cleared up."

"He say anything else?"

"Anything else like what?"

"That's what I'm asking you."

She fixed me with a cool, implacable stare usually more at home on Toussaint's harsh face. In my pocket, small thorns from the cactus bark poked into my thigh.

"No. That was it."

To show my good intentions, I started folding some dresses after all, starting with a mustard gown with long sleeves.

Yvette's gaze lingered on me a moment or two longer, but she finally resumed folding with a hectic swaying of her breasts.

"Mr. Salam is a good man, Mr. Slide," she said, "with a natural eye for real estate. Yet he is troubled. We have not been honest. Yes, we've known him for some time. I could have told you earlier, but it would've only been trouble if he'd known you were staying here. I was trying to help, you understand."

"I don't see what difference it makes," said Toussaint. "He needed his treatment, and it was getting late. Were you going to be the one to go over there?"

Yvette didn't say anything back, but instead stared at her feet, lost in thought. After a moment, she turned to me with a melancholic smile.

"Mr. Slide, remember I told you I used to have my dreams? There were things I wanted too. Well, back then, I would say to Toussaint, Why don't we expand this place? It's not too late. We could take out a second mortgage and buy the unit next door. Or maybe just plant a larger garden. We had a little change from selling medicines, and I knew it could do something, though I wasn't sure what. So we called in an expert to help us decide and that is how we met him."

"Yes, some expert," cut in Toussaint. "He arrived like a big shot, running his mouth, back when he could walk, poking into all the rooms and telling us what to do. I would find him on hands and knees in places no one had invited him, asking me questions about the house's permits, or having loud phone calls in the backyard. The bastard. You could see in his eyes what evil calculations were afoot to pry it from us. Well, we'd already had those battles."

"He had a vision of his own, child. He wanted us to sell and I didn't like it. I would say to him, Mr. Salam, can't you see we are poor girls? This is what little we have. What would we even do if we sold? We would have full pockets and nowhere to go. Let us have our little place where we get to care for others, at least. He wouldn't hear it. He kept harassing us with offers, inviting over buyers to march through our home like some sort of parade. *Mmm mmm mmm.* Yet, well, it goes to show, Mr. Slide, you never know who you're going to need in the end. Because you see, when the weather changed that fall, Osman picked up a nasty fever, and required some of our help after all."

"I was the one to mix that one. I used ginger leaves, cayenne, mint puree to soothe the throat, lavender, and the sap of a black pine. I gave it to him to drink three times a day after meals, and instructed him to sleep before an open window."

"It worked well."

"It worked perfectly. In four days the fever had disappeared completely."

Together they were making quick work of their portion of the dresses, with a unified rhythm. In the wan light of that gray evening, their lips took on a rich violent shade, like coagulated blood. Whereas me I was moving slow, the wind numbing my fingers.

"But, Slide," added Toussaint de Sanville, calling me by my name for the first time maybe ever, "would you believe the bastard blamed us for what happened next?"

"It's so sad, child."

"It turned out that fever was only one symptom of a much more serious illness. A fungus making its way from his lungs to his spine."

"No one knew at first, how could we, but soon he was having trouble walking, falling over often and losing coordination."

"He would stub his toes on sharp edges—"

"—and not know until someone else pointed out the bleeding."

"It's bad luck, but it's no one's fault. He lost his legs. He lost his clients. He lost the place he used to have on Intiya Street since there was no way for him to get up to it, and he had to move to somewhere with better facilities. For a while things were still fine between us, except that when all the doctors couldn't do anything, soon we heard that cripple was going around blaming us for his condition. When we had tried to help him!"

"It really is sad."

"Ingrates all around."

"We went to see him ourselves, Mr. Slide, when he moved to that boardinghouse you went to. We came in peace—"

"—that was your idea—"

"—to let him know it needn't be like this between us. It was bad enough what happened to him without him having to go about trying to make it worse. I told him, Put an end to these rumors, Osman. Hell, I even said I'd refer new clients to him to show there was no hard feelings! But, Mr. Slide, it was worse than I'd expected. Some notion had made its way into his head that we could cure him as well. Oh my heart. He spent that entire visit apologizing and saying he'd change his ways. I'm talking about groveling. He was so desperate, Mr. Slide, and we felt so sad, you understand why we wanted to try. That's what we've been doing all this time—poor Toussaint, she loses sleep trying to figure out something that could work for him, you know. It's been no success, but we have only tried to help him."

"Can you believe such a thing?" Toussaint de Sanville said. "You hear some of these knocks on our door sometimes and you would swear we had the answers to all of eternity's questions. How many disoriented louts? How many roaming good-for-nothings with their ass in their hands? I for one am tired. We're nurses who couldn't cut it, caring for sick nobodies, and that is all. We're not miracle workers."

Their baskets were full. To compress the dresses in hers, Yvette was sitting on the pile and bouncing, a flat palm turned upward as she looked to the sky. Toussaint, meanwhile, had hoisted hers to her hip and was making her way to the trapdoor. I was still lost in my doubts, succumbing to an awful dread matched by the suddenly darkening sky.

"But but but—" I blurted on seeing them leaving, "what does this mean for *me*? I don't get it. Slow *down*..."

They were brushing past me like I wasn't even there. Yvette went down the ladder first, to be handed the baskets, followed by Toussaint, whose descending head lingered long enough to say, "You've overstayed your week, so it's only fair that you do more around here. It's what's necessary for running a house like this. My cousin agrees, though she won't say as much. What Osman wants cannot be given, not by us, or by anyone. So we cannot help you. And hurry up with the folding before it gets too late. I don't like the look of those clouds."

And that was when the sun disappeared behind a weeping gray curtain and could not be found for days.

PHYLLIS

(in which an impromptu deluge makes for a wet labyrinth
and—after a dreamless intermission from life—
a captive guest rows to pick up the pieces)

The rains that Mr. Borsnitch had been predicting arrived after all, in those first days of November. Not some light pitter-patter like the kind for quenching flowers, but a wet cataclysm that drowned half the world. I mean, I don't need to tell *you* two anything about it, of course. After all, if not for what happened, I probably would have never laid eyes on you in the first place. But for those of us who couldn't yet imagine what was even happening... well, time itself might as well have been splitting into Before-and-After right in front of our eyes.

PHYLLIS

What happened was that a herd of lost clouds came drifting to land in the middle of the day, too heavy to go anywhere after drinking from the ocean. I noticed them blotting out the sky like spilled ink as I was up there folding those dresses in a hurry. For the next half hour they silently brooded over the horizon, casting Polis in the gray shade of their worries. Meanwhile, a sticky heat filled the air and muffled every sound. The pigeons saw their noise was going nowhere and gave up cooing. As if to replace them, a banshee wind from the east came screaming through the streets, loud as the ghosts of three thousand women. To further warn everyone, the sky cleared its throat in long rumbles of thunder and the clouds began to drool a cold drizzle. Then: on a whim: they burst. Me I made it inside right in time to keep those dresses I'd just gotten done with from getting wet, closing the trapdoor behind a volley of piercing drops and leaving the basket at the foot of the ladder.

From there I headed to my room, half intending to start my packing (I didn't yet know it was about to be a catastrophe), but instead found myself following the storm's progress, transfixed like a witness to the apocalypse. It rained for thirty-three hours, took a break, then rained for sixteen more. It was a horrendous storm.

First things to go were those same pigeons from the ledge, which you could soon see tossing about in hopeless gusts, only to get sucked up forever into a tornado of feathers. After that (a true sign of disaster) the knockabouts left. I made it downstairs in time to catch them opening useless umbrellas from the stand and streaming out the front door like ants from a flooded nest, going, *Oh my Lord, would you look at that, I have to be getting back if it's going to be this serious.* The feverish waiters, the phlegmatic louses, they couldn't have gotten out of there faster. One of the old-timers who had come by motorcycle tried getting it going in all that wind but gave it up for dead after it twice toppled over. Those of us who were left formed an impromptu troupe, moving from window to window, pressing our noses against them in disbelief. "This is seriously *crazy*!" I said out loud. "You're telling *us*!" said the rest of them. By then the drops were the size of marbles and twice as loud, falling *clack clack clack* against the glass. The horizon was losing its shape behind sheets of rain. An hour later it had disappeared completely. The fail-safes were failing. The drains couldn't drain fast enough and the roads were beginning to clog. First with water, then with frustrated traffic that exhausted itself by honking. Seeing no hope, the drivers were getting out their cars and wading through the water with their pants up to their ankles. Only then did the Frenchwoman with the baby remember she had left her own car windows down and, in a fit of desperation—drenched from having crossed the rooftops—came pleading for someone to go wind them up for her. "Pleeez! Any-vahn! It ees a new ve-hee-cahl!" she said, rocking the baby and describing what the car looked like...

Me and Mikey the Albino were the ones to have to step out into that howling world with plastic bags over our shoes. My cheeks stung with rain; invisible things were gliding between my legs. The wind was so loud I couldn't hear what Mikey was saying—with his colorless skin, he looked like a bloated body waiting to be washed up somewhere. We passed the bent-over trees, the tossed-about trash cans, the people huddled for dear life beneath the stingiest of awnings. At one point a crack of lightning tore the sky in two and I yelped, squeezing my eyes shut and waiting to be electrocuted. When we got to her car, it was done for, of course, its insides soaked, which is always the way these things go. "Lance used to have him one of these, too, Slick!" "Al*right*, Mikey, read the *room*, why don't you...!" Rolling up the windows was about as useful a precaution as a breathing hole in a casket, but we did it anyway. When, on the way back, a family of drowned raccoons washed by, a cold shiver wrapped itself around my spine and could not be thawed, no matter the number of blankets I swaddled myself in as soon as I was back inside. That would turn out to be one of the last moments you could have gone outside without knowing how to swim. Soon, rivers slithered around the corners with the malevolence of snakes. Back indoors, a network of leaks was springing along the ceilings no matter the floor. That sent us scrambling for every last pot pan bucket and cup in the house, setting them underneath the drops *pa-tink pa-tink* *pa-tink.* The linen closet was emptied of all its towels for use as mops. As if to show how silly we were being, a deluge of brown water came pouring through the doors and submerged the first floor. Yvette and Toussaint were able to just-in-time grab some foodstuffs from the kitchen and ferry them to safety using their dresses as hampers. At one point a sudden *krakow* caused us all to jump, which we only later learned was the cry of an oak in a nearby park surrendering its life. The lightning was so constant it was hard to tell when the sun had set. Weather advisories flashed on our phones every six minutes in blaring beeps—*severe flooding, thunder strikes, stay indoors if you live between here and here*—and on Borsnitch's TV the news was all doom-and-gloom. One correspondent (in case you needed any more proof) had been sent out in nothing but a poncho to stand at the edge of the wharf as massive waves tried to consume him. You could hardly hear his blown-out voice over the crash and boom: "... levels of precipitation... highly un-characteristic... couldn't have seen this coming... back to you, Jim and Jean...," as a blue-and-white chyron scrolled along underneath—SUPERSTORM PHYLLIS. It didn't look like I'd be going anywhere, after all.

That was the first day. On the second, the power went out. We *heard* it happen more than anything: the high whine of electricity suddenly quieting. I was recruited with everyone else to rummage box by box through the junk on the land-ings looking for candles, equipped with a sputtering flash-light of little use in those darkened halls that appeared to me like the catacombs of a submerged palace. Geez-us were there some silly knickknacks in those boxes—rubber stamps, emp-ty perfume bottles, coffee beans, foreign coins, dried markers, an etcetera of etceteras—but we finally managed to gather enough candles to last the night. At night the looters came. We saw them emerge from the water itself, shady types certainly from somewhere else, immune to discomfort and with eyes for opportunity. In pairs or trios they paddled toward the most vulnerable of the shops to take their fill, smashing the windows with nothing but their elbows. The wig shop was pillaged of every last one of its pieces, and of almost as much interest were the jewelry stores. TVs were going for nothing at all, held high overhead in a waddling retreat. In the windows across the way, the poking heads of an audience watched like sentinels along a valley. Many of us hissed, or shone our flashlights upon the looters, but the bandits flinched only momentarily, as if stung, then quickly recovered their shamelessness. Old Mr. Borsnitch, who really couldn't stand such a thing, emerged suddenly from his usual haze of timidity to deliver a thundering lecture from the balcony. What a *voice* it turned out he had: *You wretches! Hounds! No-gooders, all of you! Do you know what you are stealing? You think it is only a new camera that you hold in your arms, but what you are taking is the Fabric! Of! Society! It is what lets us live jammed up here in this box and not tear each other to shreds! You cut it out from underneath us, and soon we will have no choice but to become brutes like you...* One thief in particular seemed quite moved, for he stopped where he was, up to his chest in water, and looked directly into the light that Borsnitch was pointing at them as he responded: "Grandfather, I know, I understand, and you must forgive me. But I have been struck more times than I have cheeks left to turn. Must I count for you the days I entered these shops only to be greeted by a detective on my heels? What kind of a fool would I be to sit at home now and twiddle my thumbs? How is it my job not to hit back? You are like my father's father, but this Polis where we live—isn't it obvious? It is no sanctuary...," which to me by then sounded like the very best of arguments.

When the rains paused in the morning, things were no better. The clouds still hung, debating further malice. In the stagnant pools, mosquitoes quickly proliferated. All there was left for us to do was head to the higher floors and note the waterlogged damage: the alleyways of flotsam, the puffed-up carcasses of dogs, rats paddling against the current, the shrieks (barely audible) of a man looking for help, cars washed up into mounds, a lamppost stuck in the upper branches of two trees. "You see? You *see?*" Mr. Borsnitch kept saying once we returned from our survey, indicating his proof. Yes, Mr. Borsnitch, you were right, we see, we said.

We were: me, two of the hobos, Mr. Borsnitch, one of the aunties, a deliveryman, and Yvette and Toussaint de Sanville. Everyone who'd either had nowhere better to go once the rains began or who had ended up stuck faster than they realized. The deliveryman was of the second type, a sour-faced Pakistani who had shown up two days ago with an order of samosas for the auntie's craving, then discovered the water was too high to use his bicycle by the time she'd found change for a tip. During the rain he'd chased a signal through the rooms with his phone held overhead like a prophet awaiting a sign. Now his phone was dead, as were everyone's, and he sat stewing in annoyance on a footstool in the library, reading the newspaper from two days ago and occasionally glancing at his watch.

*   *   *

Things had slowed. With the bottom floor submerged, we were relegated to the second and third, of which the library was the nexus. The military neighbor, Lieutenant Chesney, was receiving updates from a shortwave radio he'd powered up, and would come over the rooftops every now and then to give a situation report. Downtown was underwater, emergency personnel were on their way, it would be a couple days.

"It's a hairy situation, ma'am," he was explaining to Yvette. "Finger-pointing every way you look. The Municipal Council says it's the Sewerage and Sanitation Authority's responsibility, SSA is pointing to the Land and Water Division, LWD is pointing to Emergency Disaster Response, EDR says its PHF, who's blaming GRO, of course, who are pointing right back at MC. Not to mention those boys over at Engineering. My recommendation? Sit tight, look sharp."

He'd brought along a propane tank and portable stove, too, which he handed over. Disaster had made him newly useful and you could tell he was enjoying it. At his side was the dalmatian, also with a serious look.

"Thank you," said Yvette, unusually curt, then shooed him off before he could continue. She walked past us eavesdroppers to rejoin Toussaint in the second-floor pantry, where they were rationing the recovered foodstuffs. Back in the library there was not much to do other than play the occasional card game or listen to tiresome stories from the auntie about all the nasty habits of her late second husband. It was Wednesday, I think. Between the pots to collect rainwater and the saucers holding candles, there was little room left to walk. When we opened the windows for a breeze, it grew cold and stank of garbage. When we closed them, it was hot and stank of sweat.

*   *   *

That evening for dinner, several cans of black beans had to be heated up and I was required to figure out how to operate the propane tank and stove.

"I don't know how to *do* that," I whimpered.

"You'll have to figure it out," said Yvette and Toussaint. After our talk on the roof it was obvious they had no qualms left about further exploiting me, yelling my name for every odds-and-ends task. But I was at a loss until the deliveryman offered his help—he used to go camping, he explained, and knew what to do. He and I settled in the telephone closet and fiddled with the equipment by candlelight. As we worked, Yvette and Toussaint could be heard in the pantry discussing something in murmurs. Every now and then one of them would emerge to wordlessly go upstairs, then come back down again to the pantry to keep murmuring.

"Sounds like something's wrong," the deliveryman said. His sleeves were rolled up to his elbows as he worked.

I said, "I'm sure it's nothing. There's enough food here to last through another storm."

He shook his head. "Something's wrong," he said.

Perhaps. As the night grew quieter, the sounds of Yvette and Toussaint's continued rummaging could be heard everywhere in the house. We had gotten the gas tank connected and heated up the cans (directly on the stovetop, since all the pots were in use), but they ate not even a bite as they walked about. They greeted Lieutenant Chesney's radio updates with tight-jawed tension, shooing him off time and again when he had nothing but bad news. Geez-us, they were seriously out of sorts. Toussaint was the one to fetch me many hours later from where I was sleeping curled up in a corner of the library, since the cot in my room was soaked.

"Slide, this way, please." She led me to the pantry.

There, every shelf had been emptied, in no real order, onto the floor. Yvette stood with creases of worry along her flat face. On seeing me, she stopped wringing her hands and grabbed one of mine. A flashlight lit the ceiling.

"Hello, Mr. Slide. We have done some reconsidering and would like to change our position. We were a bit harsh. There's no harm in us reaching out to Osman for you, if that's something that would help." The leap of my heart made my throat seize up almost at once.

"What?" I managed to sputter. Then: "You're serious? Oh, wow, I'd really given up."

She made a forced laugh *ha ha ha*. "Never give up! We're reasonable people. Now all we need is a slight favor and we can call it even. As you must understand," she went on in a hurry, "the flooding's made it hard for anyone to come or go. I'm sure we're all suffering. Nonetheless, certain necessities cannot be abandoned for the care of our guests." The rate of her speech was leaving out the gaps for me to say anything. "Mr. Langley is up there in age and cannot be expected to leave his home in this weather. Clearly you understand all this."

"I'm not sure I follow...," I said. Langley was the owner of the apothecary they got some of their roots and herbs delivered from, a slow-moving man with dreamy eyes and a rusty bicycle.

"We're going to need you to go out, Slide," Toussaint interrupted. "There are things we need. Ingredients."

"*What?*" I said.

"Mr. Slide," said Yvette.

"But it's *crazy* outside. I already almost *died* once. Are you being serious?"

Toussaint said, "It is only to Langley's shop. Write down this address."

"I'm not writing down shit!" I said. "Do you know what I saw in the water today? Not that I can be sure from our height, but it looked like an alligator. Who *knows* what kind of crazy shit is in there."

"Mr. Slide," said Yvette again.

"Don't Mr. *Slide* me," I said. "You two are joking, right? I'm being joked with." Toussaint was staring at me with gritted teeth as if readying herself to strike. "It's bad enough all the other shit you've done to me. Now I'm supposed to go out there again? For some *things*? What kind of *things* are we even talking about?"

Toussaint snapped, "Listen, you penniless cur. You mooch, you lout. You come here like a vagrant with your pockets turned out, run your mouth every quiet moment of the day, make it a fuss to try to get a dollar out of you, and on top of all that, on top of *all that*—"

"No, no, no, Toussaint, no. It's alright. Mr. Slide is a little tense is all. We're all stressed because of the close quarters. Aren't you stressed, Mr. Slide? Come, how about some tea. You know you've hardly had any, and it's really a shame. I made this one for you. Here, drink up."

Yvette revealed it seemingly from nowhere, using a magician's flourish: a mug of steamy tea with a bitter scent. They must've prepared it beforehand. In the close confines of the pantry, she didn't have far to reach to hold it under my nose.

"But I really don't want to, Yvette. It's dangerous out there..."

"We understand, Mr. Slide. How about only a sip? Okay? Good, that's it now, a sip will be alright. I promise."

I took a sip, the first I'd had since the one on the day I arrived. It was hard not to, with it so close under my nose. It tasted both sweet and bitter, too syrupy, like melted sap. A warm, smooth feeling draped over my senses.

"Isn't that better, Mr. Slide? It's alright, we had some ourselves."

I took a longer sip, then I got to thinking that, as a matter of fact, it wasn't as if I was any worse for wear for having gone outside once already, it was only water, after all... I sipped... plus the rains had stopped too... Getting wherever I had to go wouldn't be so bad; if anything, I would swim... In fact, someone I used to know always said I would have made a good swimmer if only I had applied myself...

But right as Yvette was readying to pour more tea down my throat there came a *thump thump thump* through the dumb-waiter, and in her resulting shock Yvette jumped and dropped the mug. It fell and shattered. They both turned. It had come from upstairs. Yvette's eyes opened wide. "Toussaint," she said in a whining plea. Her hands were shaking and—I could hardly believe it—she seemed afraid. We were frozen in place until one more *thump* jolted them into action, Toussaint first, heading up the stairs in huge strides, Yvette following, and (I hadn't been told to stay put) me at the end, all the way to the fourth floor, where without much delay they opened that middle door onto the darkened, muggy space. Right at once a dense cloud of perfume made its escape. It smelled like every kind of leftover incense had been lit all together. Toussaint shone the one good flashlight into the room's center, where amongst the tangle of cushions I saw something I thought I'd never see: Rosa de Sanville was waking up.

ROSA

In the ring of light her figure looked more like the absence of someone than someone itself, a black space left for a body to fill in. She was nearly upright, nude, on trembling legs, and had been rearing up to full height when the flashlight's glare had struck her in place. One arm clung to a dresser for balance, the other was shielding her eyes.

"Light," she hissed. Toussaint switched the light off. We were in total darkness. No moonlight came through the drawn shades.

"Ceiling," corrected Rosa.

Toussaint responded, "The power went out. There's been a big storm."

She considered this awhile with ragged breaths. "Light," she said again, this time a resolution. Toussaint switched the flashlight back on. Rosa moved only to angle her face away from the beam. No one made a sound as she thought. Looking down at her right leg, she used her free hand to grip it by the thigh and raise-and-lower it to the ground, *thump thump thump*, the same sound that had a few moments ago alerted us. "Leg's asleep," she said, still staring at the thing.

As if on cue, Yvette bustled forward, kicking cushions aside, but Rosa recoiled at her approach, almost in a panic, and stumbled away. The sleeping leg buckled and caused her to fall back amongst the cushions, only to continue her scrambling retreat with her arms. Yvette stopped. Rosa was panting panting panting like an animal cornered.

"It's okay, cousin," Yvette said. "Let's just get you to the bathroom. It's right there, okay? Come, let me help you." She moved forward delicately, extending her small hand. Rosa only gritted her teeth and stood back up by herself, quivering against the wall for support. Her head was darting around with two pitch-black eyes. Yet, stubborn as she was, it was clear she wasn't going anywhere without some help, and a second attempt to retreat saw her fall once more. Yvette kept on creeping toward her in nervous steps, making cooing sounds. Rosa's breaths slowed into deep shudders. She twice shrugged off Yvette before having to accept the arm placed around her waist.

"I have you, cousin."

Together they began moving toward the door, Toussaint angling the light so they could see where they were going. At Rosa's every step, Yvette nodded and rattled off a stream of encouragements, "We're so glad you're up, there's so much to fill you in on. Cousin, you were really out for a minute that time! How are you feeling? Are you feeling okay..." I don't know how much of it Rosa heard. Her sole focus was on the floor, where her feet were making the stumbling progress of a fawn. Only once she was at the doorway did she lift her gaze across Toussaint's face and across mine. Our eyes met for a flicker. In hers I recognized the endless gaze of mirrored hallways. In mine she must have seen nothing impressive. She lowered her head and kept it moving.

"Who's that?" I heard her ask.

Thusly she spoke, in hardly two syllables, her voice a whisper eroded by neglect. Sleep had done a number on her faculties, leaving a residual crust she was slow to chip away. In the bathroom she coughed reservoirs of sticky phlegm into the sink with pauses to guzzle water from the faucet. No matter how many times she rubbed mucus from the corners of her eyes, a moment or two later she found she had to do it again.

"You're bleeding," she told Yvette while looking at her ankles. Shards of the shattered mug had cut her feet and no one had noticed.

Yvette said, "Oh, you know me, clumsy as always! It being so dark and all, I was just... we were only—"

"A window broke," finished Toussaint.

"A window broke!" said Yvette.

They were both keeping a strange distance from her, not too close, but not far either, as if timing an explosion they would have to contain. Now, with the edges of the sink to hold on to, Rosa had cast off Yvette's arm and was looking at the cousins. She raised her hand to yawn. Dark, she was so dark. Toussaint had set the flashlight on its base to shine at the ceiling such that shadows traveled upward across their faces, but on hers there was no real difference. She then cracked every one of her joints. This took six minutes. Anyone walking by might have thought a whole roll of bubble wrap was being popped. "Clothes," she said once she was done. I felt that was for me to go fetch a folded dress from where I'd left them, in a closet along the hall, but no sooner had I taken a step than Yvette was again jumping up.

"Allow me!" she said, and disappeared. Soon we could hear her rummaging around. Rosa de Sanville leaned on the sink and swung her leg *thump thump* again. Satisfied, she tested it with her weight for the first time and stood at full height. She was taller than Yvette and shorter than Toussaint. Yet it was Toussaint de Sanville who stiffened when Rosa looked at her.

"Your hair's different," Rosa said. Yvette returned with a white dress.

It took us some time but eventually we got her to the library, where the deliveryman was awake, playing a game of solitaire. She shrugged off Yvette's help again and leaned on the chairs instead, one by one. In her progress through the room her body seemed to sometimes flicker invisible in the darkness between the candles. Finally she made it to the red divan near the balcony, settling upon it with grave finality. The old auntie, Mr. Borsnitch—everyone had woken up. The deliveryman sidled over to me. "What you think this is then?" he asked through the dust mask he'd been using to cover his mouth. "Me?" I said. "Why're you asking me? They're the ones you want to be—" But on looking over my shoulder to point out Yvette and Toussaint, I found nothing there but the faint trail of their musk. I couldn't believe it! I checked over my other shoulder just to be certain, then along the stairs, but it didn't make a difference. They were gone. Only then did a burst of raw emotion swell through the stupor that had been clouding my senses since those sips of tea. Once again I was walking a thin line between ill humor and confusion. The deliveryman was still asking me questions, but I could hardly pay attention. Rosa, who had folded her legs beneath her, was now looking at her hands and flexing her fingers. Only Mr. Borsnitch dared interrupt the awful tension of that wet, dark night. "Rosa," he said tremulously, "how have you been?" She startled, but settled upon seeing who it was. "Hello, Jerome," she said hoarsely. "I have not been well."

For the rest of the night's hours she stayed right there, alternating between a static calm and—should anyone move at all—a quick, flinching alarm in which her nostrils flared and she breathed *foom foom foom*. Near her on the ground was someone's unfinished can of beans from dinner, which she picked up and devoured in mouthfuls with her hands. Without being asked, Mr. Borsnitch fetched the rest of the beans from the stovetop in the telephone closet and gingerly placed them near her on the ground. These she also finished. If she ever closed her eyes to sleep (you would have thought she'd had her *fill* by now), it was only for the flimsiest kind, springing up like a cat at any slight motion. She went in-and-out like that, beneath a mist of drizzle from the open balcony, and awoke the next morning with patches of skin visible through the damp cotton of her dress. We had hardly slept a wink ourselves, given her presence in the room like a panther at rest. No amount of prodding could get Mr. Borsnitch to tell us anything more than her name, Rosa, and that she had been sick, though a brow-furrowing look of anger had replaced all other expressions on his worried face. The deliveryman (this guy was seriously fed up, I'm not kidding) was in a corner on his own, sizing us up like we were a team of maniacs. Rosa stood into the day with a renewed strength and, after once again cracking her joints, set about on a mission no one could decipher. She sorted through old clothes in some of the boxes along the hall and walked around the town house touching things as if fitting together the pieces of a puzzle. At least she was a little calmer and could be approached without startling. When Lieutenant Chesney came by with his morning update, it was to Rosa de Sanville he reported, after recovering from the shock of seeing her amongst the living.

"Ma'am," he kept on saying, "what a relief, Rosa. We had you MIA, ma'am. What a relief."

"It's nice to see you, too, Lieutenant."

From him she learned the full desperation of our situation, that the death toll was rising, that it might still be days before we could go anywhere. Any helicopters seen overhead were not to be relied upon, for they had instructions to prioritize the truly distressed regions farther north.

"Lieutenant," she soon said, "accept my apologies, but as you must understand, I have a few more questions."

"Ma'am, of course."

She went with him to a separate room, where they talked for much longer. When he was done, Lieutenant Chesney left Rosa there and found Mr. Borsnitch, to have a private word on the third floor. *Geez-us* everyone was having private words. Clearly the old-timers knew her from before and were making something of it. The rest of us were left to suspicions and conjectures, hasty whispers in the hallways between rooms: "... definitely some sort of coma," Mikey the Albino was saying to the auntie with his usual confidence. "Happened to my brother-in-law. He lived a whole life as a priest in his sleep and woke up a Catholic." "You think so?" said the auntie, fingering the large jewels on her many rings. "Ooh but heavens, her eyes, so dark. No different from that lout of a husband I had, that's desperation for you and trust me on that." "Funny luck that she slept through all that thunder only to wake up now," said the delivery man, with a bit of paranoia... Me I could hardly participate at all, drifting through these chats in a daze. I could only ponder those last few months with a rising sense of outrage toward Yvette and Toussaint de Sanville. For their part, those two spent the rest of the day making themselves scarce, heard only when darting along the fourth floor to grab something before scurrying back through the trapdoor to whichever neighboring building they were hiding in. No matter how much I tried timing it, I was always too far away when I heard them, spotting them only as they zoomed *tap tap tap* up the ladder. "Wait!" I yelled uselessly. "You liars!" I felt a red anger mixed with three kinds of confusion, injury, and the vile traces of vengeance with which all sad endings begin. I couldn't stop thinking of all the hot teas with which they'd had me drown Rosa's murmurs in her sleep. The guilt must have been lying heavily on my features, for if ever Rosa looked my way, it was only to say, "What's wrong with you?" as she carried on with her inexplicable business.

She tossed and dug about in the hallways' boxes. She found a pair of rubber boots that she thumped around in throughout the afternoon. Every potted herb she came across growing on a windowsill, she chucked over the ledge down into the black water below. If she ate, then it was directly from a can, and she drank nothing but faucet water after first letting it run. Sometimes a bolt of confusion seemed to strike her and she'd address whoever was nearby with the simplest of inquiries, such as what month it was. Our curiosity slowly gave way to the unease of bystanders, though no one could quite say why. But to see someone so lost in the midst of life, fumbling about like an infant on a ledge—it was enough to freak anyone out. Soon we were drifting to our separate ends of the house to avoid her, and even each other, finding damp, quiet corners in which to wait out the bad news.

So it happened that, in the evening, it was Rosa de Sanville who came to *me* and set in motion the next part of my Polis destiny. I was up on the rooftop hoping to catch Yvette and Toussaint and observing the latest development in the storm's fallout:

ropes strung from building to building for various uses. They extended like the strands of a web between floors of differing heights. Some had been made into pulley systems and outfitted with buckets, for people on one end to put things in the bucket and pull until it reached the people on the other end, who'd send something back. Dry clothes, candles, boxes of crackers— I only knew what some of them sent because they'd shout and ask what the other had to offer first. A few of the other ropes had been turned into zip lines, mostly by wild kids, using belts for the rigging and squealing through the air as they slid down, watching their own reflections in the water. Once they made it to the other end, they had to go up some floors in the new building so they were high enough to take another zip line back to where they began. Gosh, where were people's parents? Someone was going to hurt themselves. Anyway, that is what I was doing when I felt her presence behind me and spun around.

She was in another new dress, this one also white, the clunky rubber boots almost to her knees.

"You have been staying in the room underneath me," she said.

I said, "Yes."

"My cousins offered you?"

"Yes."

"And you have been taking care of me?"

"Something like that."

She blinked.

"They told me you were sick," I added.

"And my cousins. They have not been honest with you?"

I hesitated. I really was sore about it.

She spoke again: "Do you know who I am?"

I nodded. "You were a boxer. Then you went to prison." I wanted to shock her into leaving me alone. Instead she regarded me steadily with that face of hers like a portrait of a thousand shadows.

"Yes," she said.

The water glistened in the diffuse light. Polis had become an enormous mirror interrupted by buildings. Slowly, she took something out of her dress pocket: the bundle of dried cactus bark Osman had given me.

"What the hell!" I said, panicking. I hadn't so much as *touched* it since the pants I'd put it in had gotten soaked going to close the car window. "Listen, I can explain that," I was trying to say. I had half an instinct to back away from her if it wouldn't have meant falling off the roof.

But she had already undone the twine and popped a piece into her mouth in the time it took me to raise a useless hand and yell, "No! Wait!"

She chewed and swallowed. I stood as still as I could, waiting for her to topple over dead. Instead, a sudden spark illuminated her eyes. She swallowed a deep breath that shivered its way out in a sweet relief, then looked around at the world with the bewildered gaze of a newcomer. I couldn't believe it. She joined me where I was, standing uncomfortably close to the roof's edge.

"You may not understand this, but you are in danger here. If you stay any longer my cousins will undo you. It is worse now that I am awake. Do you follow?" Her voice had lowered to a whisper. My throat was so choked up I could only nod.

"Good," she said. "I have heard you in my sleep, through the dumbwaiter, and know of your struggle to find a place to live. It will not happen here. Tomorrow morning I am leaving.

If you are packed, you can come with me. What questions you have, I would save for then. Do not drink any more tea."

That night I stayed in my room, curled up on the floor because the bed was still wet. Mr. Borsnitch came by to warn me about catching pneumonia, but I told him I'd be alright. I wanted to tell him goodbye, too, to tell everyone goodbye, but I knew without being warned that I should shut up about it. I can't say I slept that well. In the morning I was ready like Rosa said, my suitcase packed yet again, eyes heavy from a night spent climbing endless staircases in my dreams.

She entered with a large garbage bag that I assumed held her life's belongings and headed straight for my window. It was dawn and the clouds were a little lighter, though unmoving. She gripped the underside of the half-open window and strained to pull it up further. *Don't bother,* I was on the verge of saying, *I've tried that plenty already,* but I'd hardly gotten a word out when with a slow creak the window lifted all the way. "Oh," I said instead. She stuck her head out, looked left, looked right. In quick, shrill bursts, she whistled. She was in the same clothes as yesterday. Soon after, someone whistled back.

"Are you ready?" she turned to me and said. I had my suitcase by its handle and a cap on my head. "Yes." From the garbage bag she uncoiled a makeshift rope of bedsheets knotted together, handing me one end. "Tie this somewhere secure." Looking around, I decided on the handle to the door through which she had just entered. I made a solid knot then joined her by the window to see where she was unspooling the rest of its length. Directly below us was a wide raft of no homemade variety. It was neon orange, inflatable, and with all kinds of knobs and contraptions along the side. Standing in its middle was the military neighbor in camouflage fatigues. He had a long paddle, which he used to move the raft closer to where Rosa's rope eventually ended, just above the water's surface. He grabbed it and whistled again. Rosa gave the rope two tugs. It seemed taut. "I'll go first," she said, before securing her garbage bag and releasing it out the window. Crouching on the sill, she eased herself out backward, unsteadily at the start, but after tightening her two-fisted grip on the sheets, she quickly kicked off the ledge and rappelled her way down. She landed with a small jump on the raft, causing it to bob and dip, and water to splash over the sides as the military neighbor steadied it again. Looking up to where I was, she waved me downward. "Come on," she said, and the two of them waited. But me I thought that whole thing was fucking crazy.

I was only three floors up, and considering the height of the water it was probably more like two and a quarter, but none of that reassured me even a little bit. It took an awful amount of coaxing for me to send down so much as my *suitcase*, which I pitched too far and threw straight into the water. "My electronics!" I shrieked. "Shhh!" said Rosa. They paddled paddled paddled to where it was barely floating, salvaged it, and paddled back to under the window. "If you are coming, you have to do it now," said Rosa. I could tell I was annoying her. I raised a foot onto the ledge and envisioned my death. But the moment I turned around and caught sight of the dark interior from which I'd emerged, all my doubts were erased. Positioned like that, I saw the room in stark relief. Its thin cot. Its lone mirror that had watched me grow frazzled. I thought of all the false

promises I had endured, and with two gulps I eased myself off
the ledge. Beyond the window it was a cold, slimy day. My
shoes were slippery on the brick wall. I lowered myself past the
third floor, past the second, refusing to look down until the time
came for me to jump. Water swished below in a restless whisper.
Rosa and Lieutenant Chesney had cleared a space on the raft for
me to land. "Now," said Rosa. I did it with a held breath: a big
push off the wall and through the blue air. I thought of plum-
meting waterfalls, of pancaked roadkill, of all the rash decisions
I'd ever made. My back hit the plastic with a resounding *thwap*.
Finding my feet again, I gasped as if electrocuted, delirious with
bravery. "I did it! Rosa, did you see? That was wild. From all the
way up there. Wow. Gosh, I was really on some stuntman shit,
wasn't I?" "Yes, Slide, I saw. You did well."

We dropped off Lieutenant Chesney at his building's backside
where the trash was normally collected, by a fire escape jutting
into the water. He grabbed a rung with one hand and with the
other wrapped Rosa in an embrace. "Look sharp," he said. To me
he offered a crisp salute, then hoisted himself up and out, flashing
a thumbs-up once on the landing where his dog's spotted face
was waiting, and disappeared inside. Rosa now held the oar. To
paddle, she pulled twice on one side then twice on the other, her
hands set shoulders' width apart, her legs in a sumo-wide stance
for balance. We crossed Avenue XVII through a hodgepodge of
submerged cars. A slow, creeping wind lingered as if lost, ruffling
the reflections in the gray water. The world was quiet. Distant
echoes of distant sounds indicated no direction. We passed few
others—shifty faces peering from lightless windows, who seemed
to disperse into nothing as soon as they were seen. Where the mist
ended and the clouds began I could not tell. Solitary herons would

dart upon the water and scoop up a struggling fish. Where are we going, Rosa, I wanted to know. East, she always said.

For the entire day our progress was slow and the sun absent. The raft was an old, troublesome thing held together by nylon thread, musty, in need of constant pit stops to replace lost air through tubes on either end. We made our way along the alleys and backroads that Rosa de Sanville knew by heart, despite the unrecognizable waterscape in which street signs had been torn from their posts, or were otherwise invisible beneath the depths. What little she said came in momentary bursts that were impossible to predict. Sometimes a half hour would pass with her offering only a comment on the rain; at other times she would launch into full diatribes. Who could say what motivated her. If she responded to anything I asked, it was only much later on. I had the feeling that my presence behind her was incidental, and if not for the few times we had to rely on each other to overcome some obstacle, I might well have slipped into the water without her noticing. The only other sounds were the whistles of onlookers, the *splish-splash* of the water, the rumble of our hungry bellies. So it was Rosa de Sanville, guided by whims, who spoke out loud, and me, for once, who kept my mouth shut. She began by responding to my earlier moment of meanness back on the rooftop...

Rosa upon the Water

"I found the house when it was nothing but brambles and the notices for demolition kept sunlight from the windows. I made a nest of old newspapers, and stole cold french fries from the trash out back the eateries. I was happy. Then my cousins found me and said they could help. What help could I need? I'm a hermit eating french fries. They said they would buy potatoes and make me warm french fries. So, alright, I ate their warm french fries. They moved in and cleared away the brambles, and invited over everyone so it was noisy for years. I said I liked it better when it was quiet and that they should go now. Then they told me I was not well and to drink from this. Well, that was the end of everything. Now I'm a madwoman on a raft," Rosa would say.

"My childhood wasn't some buffet, either. Growing up in Petit Julienne, if you couldn't run, learn to fight. If you couldn't fight, fight anyway. As a girl I stumbled into the gym lost on my way to somewhere else and they strapped me up with gloves before I could even give my name and threw me in there with a trembling pup. I swung about terrified and knocked her out cold. The men cheered. It was the first time anyone had been proud of me. They trained me up and put me through the circuits, rigged bouts and underground tournaments. I wasn't some savant, or one of those prodigies, but you had to be willing to lose teeth if you stepped in there with me, and I could take my blows to the head like it was a whiff of wind. Then when my coach convinced me to put cement in my gloves I knocked one of them into a coma and was sent away for six years. Everyone forgot about me. That's how it is. They say the prison is what makes an animal out of you, but I have never felt that way. Being an animal is what gets you there in the first place. The prison is where that animal goes to die," she'd say.

We drifted by the waterlogged gardens, the submerged shops, the wading vagrants robbed of everything yet again. At a junction, a tall yellow building with a flat face had many windows, each with someone leaning out on their elbows. They waved for Rosa to stop, which she did by dragging the oar. They were all of such good cheer I thought them related. "Where's that you's going to down there?" one of them shouted. Rosa de Sanville made a sweeping hand. "Just over there." "Dry over that way?" another one asked. "We believe so, yes." "Hey, is you hearing this? Lady on the raft said it's dry over in Battery." "She didn't say Battery, Franky, stop overexaggerating." "She did *too* say Battery, she said it with her hand, what you think *this* means?" "Well, of course it's gonna be dry in Battery, it's uphill." "Then why didn't none of *yous* know that before the lady said it…" "Look, we're wasting time. Give them a message for Tony before they sail away." "Oh!" "True!" "That's a good idea." They had another quarrel about the message for Tony. Some changed windows to better talk to each other face to face. Finally the one who'd spoken first did so again: "Hey, you twos," he said, "if you see Tony, tell him we don't need the tires no more."

"Everyone in the prison is guilty of the same crime, the crime of being in prison. Murderers, fraudsters, politicians, drug runners, dog drowners, schoolteachers who once let a boy touch their breast, it did not matter. Your being there meant something indelible was wrong with you, if not before, then certainly now. No amount of scrubbing could remove such a stain so no kind of scrubbing was tried," said Rosa de Sanville.

"But you would hear of Melanie Supergirl, who had her whole case overturned and took the ferry home the next day. Of Dyan Schecherhorn, who wrote a letter to the warden every Sunday and softened his heart. We remember their names. Stories of their sort, ones that trafficked in hope, were the first type of torture. Over on Quandry Island, the night we learned to forget such hope was the night we had our first proper sleep, which is still not to say peacefully. Recognizing something does not necessarily free you from it. You are simply better able to describe your cage if someone were to ask. That's what I think, at least. Out in the yard, which we called the Bay, we were allowed to: walk, talk, gather in groups of five, or play catch with a tennis ball. Never run. For a while there were larger balls, like basketballs, but one day Bethy Big Wop found a way to overinflate one to the point that it was like a rock and she sought out Pretty Hunter by the fountains and smashed it into her temple. Pretty Hunter fell. Bethy had grown up in a family of horse breeders in Haverford. Their specialty was an Arabian Andalusian bloodline from which three stallions had won major derbies. She and her brothers had all broken their fingers in the mouths of horses. Big Wop straddled Pretty's chest. She slammed her again and again with the basketball. Pretty Hunter lost the features of her face; she snotted up blood; she made a sound like mooing; she looked fetal; she raised her hand only one time. We watched the whole thing from afar, careful not to gather too close and exceed a group of five. Of course the guards were coming, unsheathing their batons. 'Big Wop!' we said. 'That's enough.'"

"So there were only tennis balls," she later added.

I lost count of the confused fish, of the overturned cars becoming homes for tadpoles. The raided stores. The leaning lampposts and tangled wires. The messages for help scrawled on redbrick walls. The sullen rooftops where blackmen with shotguns kept warning eyes on all who approached. And I would try saying to her:

"*Geez*, Rosa, that's seriously sad, it's awful, I mean. That's about as tough a time as I think I've heard," shaking my head to show I really meant it, even as my belly grumbled from a day's worth of hunger. "I mean, I've had some rough stuff myself, if that helps at all…" And so I told her of Middleton's awful trap and hellish heat. Of its dead ends and thirsty gangs. Of how I'd felt life's walls constricting around me like a cell of my own until I'd escaped, only to end up walking up, down, and around chasing phantoms.

We rowed past the dead traffic lights. Fragrant patches where spilled gasoline had turned the water iridescent. Dislodged doors topped by facedown souls you had to hope were only asleep.

"Not to say any of this is on the same *scale* or anything, Rosa, I'm just hoping to relate is all. The thing with me is, I've never stumbled on an empty house in all my life, and trust me I've tried. There was always someone in it already."

And Rosa de Sanville said: "Is that so?"

"When the cousins moved in they cleared away the brambles and swept the floors and laid mattresses in the rooms where anyone could pay money to stay. Soon they were rich. They gathered a hopeless clientele, infantilized by strange medicines, and spent lavishly on antiques. Then their appetites grew. They called in appraisers, a crew to redo the floors, sought out advisers to help draft their plans for expansion into a new building. To afford that they would have had to take out a mortgage on the first one. Except it was not their building, it was mine. Me. I had found it. Now they would make me into another one of their patients? I was stubborn."

*   *   *

"By then I'd begun having problems. Fighting in the ring, I hadn't exactly been careful, and at Quandry it only got worse, having to fend off barbarians every time you sat down to eat. Anyway, the point is, all those blows to the head were starting to catch up."

"For me it started as a pressure toward the back of the skull one morning that refused to go away. Then a ringing in my ears that I mistook for unanswered telephones. Soon my cousins were pointing it out to me: that I was losing my place in sentences without noticing. I would catch them waiting for me to finish saying something I didn't remember having started, asking them, 'What?' 'You did it again,' one might say. I snapped; I was angering easily. 'Don't lie! That's enough, you two, and you will leave my home at once!' Such outbursts irritated them, for suddenly it would appear to their patients that they were not the ones in control. But I did worry. I had heard of those fighters who'd risked too much in the ring and later had difficulty telling their left foot from their right, or who called to report break-ins when they encountered their own reflections. Oh, but what to do? What to do?" Rosa asked.

Sometimes the whirlpool gape of an open manhole threatened to suck us into its depths if not for her quick action, lashing the raft to a lamppost with a loop of rope and tugging us away one sinewy pull at a time. Sometimes an arc of birds along the featureless sky was the secret calculus by which she determined which street to turn down next. Our clothes were soaked, my body shivering. There was no way of knowing when it was lunchtime for sure, but I guessed as much by the awful rumbling in my belly. I slumped over, woozy, unable to keep scooping out water with the empty paint can we'd found earlier. "Holy hell... no breakfast... so hungry..." She said nothing, kept paddling, and an hour later begged a slab of meat off some bearded geezers in fishing boats. We had come upon them somewhere along Mariner Street, floating right there with lines in the water, a half dozen geezers in waxed ponchos spread across an assortment of boats.

"The boy alright?"

"He hasn't eaten."

"Haven't got much more than this."

"That'll be fine."

They threw her the meat, which she caught and gave to me, gray, cold, with that thin coat of slime meat grows when left out. It wasn't even fish. But my blinding hunger had me opening my mouth before I could think twice. *Chomp chomp*—I bit in. *Oh no*: I knew the horrified truth as soon as I swallowed: it was the best damn meat I'd ever had. I took another bite before the first one was done so I wouldn't have to wait, then another after that, and another again. "What in all hell!" I yelled with a full mouth. "So that's really how it is? No pepper or seasoning or even a bit of salt?" Geeez-uuus was I eating the hell out of that old meat! *Chomp chomp chomp.* Big chunks of it were filling my throat, my chest, my belly, frothing around in a pool of sour gasses. There's nothing like some rancid mystery meat when you're starving to make you realize how much you've been wasting your time lining up for artisanal sandwiches. "Geez-us have I been wasting my ti—" I started to yell, but nearly choked on some of the meat and had to cough for my life. Damn, you can't even have an *epiph*any nowadays without choking. Thinking that last bit over made me laugh *ha ha*! Then I thought about it again and went *ha ha ha ha*! Then I gave it an extra once-over and was breaking down, clutching my sides like a madman, spraying bits of chewed-up meat everywhere, going *ha ha ha ha ha ha ha*...!

"Caught anything good here?" Rosa was asking them.

"Couple eels."

"I began to take incredible naps from which I would awaken having not realized I'd fallen asleep. Sometimes they lasted so long I'd confuse dusk and dawn, and, rising to the noise of the house, I'd be unsure whether I was in the same clothes as when I'd fallen asleep. Time was going slow-then-fast like a bead of water that gathers before falling. More sleep, in a tangle of dreams I could not tell apart from life. If I was awake, it was only to walk through a gray haze, interrupted by occasional moments of extreme lucidity in which I could recall the moment of my own birth. I became aware of my body in an objective way, and sometimes had the impression that, if I wanted to, I could swap mine with someone else's. The fibers connecting me to myself were loosening. From that interminable fog, the image of the girls' faces would sometimes solidify as they tipped hot teas down my lips. 'There, there, cousin,' they always said. 'It will get better.' Weakened as I was, I could do nothing but listen as their appraisers came traipsing through to discuss my house's fate, never entering the room I was in, since the girls told them it was full of junk. Well, one of them did anyway, one afternoon when they weren't looking. Oh, Osman, I remember you, how your shadow in the doorway blocked the hallway's rough light. You were supposed to be my savior."

*   *   *

And: as we sailed along: a spotting of sights from that life after the prison. The benches she'd slept on and the delis that would let her use the toilet. The halfway house, now boarded up, from which she was kicked out after they caught a whiff of the vodka she guzzled like a potion against wretchedness. In the winter twenty of them would huddle overnight in the train cars where they had to let the men rob them of everything if they wanted to stay for the warmth. Once the animal inside you dies, all you are left with is a zombie, she'd admonish while conducting a grim inventory of shattered windows. Odd jobs: collecting grease, mopping floors. When she pointed out the bakery whose doors she had held open for change—until gathering enough to, only once, step inside and buy a white chocolate eclair—I was sorry to tell her it was now a bank. That one made her sit for a rare moment of rest, holding her head, muttering, You fall asleep for one day...

"That is how Osman found me, a zombie clinging to life's last strands. At first I feared he would dismiss me as just another invalid they had lying around. I called to him, weak and hoarse as they had made me, only for a glass of water that first time. He closed the door with an embarrassed apology. Out on the other side, I was sure he was convincing himself to leave well enough alone, and to not mind other people's business. I heard him walk away. But he came back with the water."

"Day by day he showed up to talk business with the girls but soon I knew he could save me. If they were not around, or were at least far away, he'd come to my room. I could sense he was conflicted. They had read his fortune and predicted riches for him as long as he helped them, and he knew enough to know he shouldn't cross them. But I would ask him for water. For french fries. For certain herbs in the pantry that lent me the strength to sit upright, for a couple hours at least…"

"I told him how the house was mine, how every moment of wakefulness was now an extraordinary effort, how the prison inspections where they looked up your insides left a shame that never went away. He loved me. We made a plan. He would convince the cousins to sell instead and find a buyer who would let me stay. In the meantime he kept smuggling jars up from the pantry in search of the ingredients that would return me to health. We were unlucky. One made me blind for several hours. Another sent me to such high peaks of understanding that I was paralyzed with ecstasy. He would grow frustrated. Sometimes it was all I could do to convince him not to carry me out of there himself in the dead of night, but I would not leave my house. So he regaled me with stories of other houses, lofts in Point James and cottages in Haverford, of east-angled windows so large they welcomed each day in a festival of light, of the meals we could have together there, if only I would allow him. Oh, Osman, I would say, my prince, don't you see this is my last stop on the road… When the girls found out what he was up to, they took away his legs, then sent me back to that other prison forever. One of endless terrain, devoid of walls, with no gates and no locks, where the only escape would have been to let go and allow the lightless pit to claim me forever."

*   *   *

The path we navigated that day was as doubtful as that murky water, and my mind littered with second-guesses and too-late realizations. I did what I could to safeguard my remaining hopes against her onslaught of awful tales, but in such battles it is always the steady that have their way. Rosa de Sanville might have spoken from a place of morbid resignation, but it was a resignation thoroughly convinced in its morbidity. I didn't have the *mettle* to refute her is what I mean. I witnessed the buildings where I had once ventured in search of somewhere to rest my head and suddenly found the whole thing laughable. What *room* would have even been left when already every window was filled by those soggy eyes looking out at us in mute surrender? It had been a world of booby traps all along; the rain had only washed away the leaves. I felt all kinds of forgotten, tossed about, certain only of the endlessness of her misfortunes. And if it seems today that I somehow survived that most merciless of surveys, then please understand, the two of you, that it wasn't without my fair share of bruises...

"Cowards!" shouted Rosa de Sanville. "This place is nothing but cowards. A land of ambushes and burglaries, where all the honest pistols can be counted on one hand—the rest wait for your back, or while you sleep. I would hear those two at night plotting further evils and call out from the deaf hallways of slumber. How many more sad stories did I have to lie there and sop up like a spongy paralytic? Too many. No one has ever left that house except by escape, or from having been cast out when they closed in on the truth. And if you think they are the only ones, then let me tell you this: Francesca Bolo was known as the cruelest amongst us on Quandry Island, a puller of strings, whose chief pleasure in life was to abuse others in plain sight. We were neighbors. *She* had been the one to tell Big Wop that Pretty Hunter had called in the recent hit on one of their horses, and to help her inflate the basketball. A prostitute mother, a father who drank—she had tawny eyes and rigid bones. In another life she might have been a beauty. In this one she was a three-time arsonist with rashes around her neck. The fire that sent her there had been a twelve-hour blaze at the heart of Millennium Park that had claimed the lives of a teenage couple camping for the weekend, their bodies found in the uppermost branches of a sequoia tree, waiting for help. Bolo had an in with a fancy lawyer who eventually had her certified as insane so she could be transferred to a psych ward. When the ward closed for lack of funding she was let out, alongside the rest of them. They're all out here, somewhere."

"And as for you, Slide, you have attempted Polis with all your longings but you have not done so with courage, no conviction. The truth is that no one is given a home here. Not the old, not the clever, not the newly minted with their fat pockets. Those who manage to stay are those who carve a chunk from its flesh, then burrow into the resulting hole.

"To do this you need teeth, and an appetite for blood. At the very least you must give up your airs. I have seen nothing good come of the ones who sit around waiting for the right chance to fall into their laps. In this I include myself. Polis may sometimes appear like a land of fate, but what it is is a ship adrift at sea, with no compass and a mutinous crew. Nothing is in charge here. The rules are made after the fact, always in retrospect. The only guaranteed successes are those that are already gone, which so many of us still cling to as a sign of what's to come. It's a bad mistake. Everything gets to be fate when it's happened already.

"If you are not willing to endure such a thing then do as many others have done and pack up and go elsewhere. Claim a need for space and cleaner air. I have heard there are parts of the world where you can live for a year on what would last us only a month. Perhaps these places exist. I am not one to say. In any case, we will be here, maintaining the struggle.

"The struggle has one benefit and it is this: if it becomes all you know, then it no longer feels like a struggle. Get to this point and it will not matter where you lay your head at night, nor on which dotted line you sign your name. You will have learned how to endure, as an animal does, which is the best kind of ignorance Polis can offer. And who knows? Maybe one day you will look up from it and find you are somewhere comfortable after all. This is as far as I can take you."

We had alighted upon the edge of a massive park of thick trees, which I recognized from hearsay. The water wasn't quite shallow but it wasn't deep either, more a sort of swamp. Far away, rising from the center of the park—Millennium Park— was a hill covered in white shapes. It was late and their glowing dots of light poked through the evening. Rosa de Sanville had stopped the tattered raft short of the land to avoid scraping its underside on the brambles that poked up all around us. I put on a brave face like it didn't matter at all that we were parting ways. As I got out, she handed me my suitcase, which I held over my head. The water was cold, icky, up to my thighs. She was already rowing off without a word. But I suddenly couldn't stand it.

"Rosa!" I shouted. "What now? I don't understand. What am I supposed to do? Where are *you* going...?"

She rejoined the shadows as she paddled.

"Slide, boy. You never listen, do you?"

"Geez, there isn't anything we can do about these lights, is there?"

"You're hot?"

"Well, that's an understatement! If it wasn't for this makeup I'd be running rivers."

"There's not much we can do, unfortunately."

"Aren't we on break now? How 'bout we cut some of them for a little."

"Sure. That should be fine. Hey, Stage Two, can we turn a few of these lights off?"

"Phew."

"Better?"

"Definitely."

"How're you holding up, Slide?"

"It's still a little weird, I have to say, seeing the two of you in real life."

"People always say that."

"Sure. I hope you didn't think I was making fun when I mentioned y'all earlier."

"It's alright."

"It's just that you really were that important to him, is the thing."

"We know. It happens."

"Alright."

"Ready?"

"Sure."

"Alright, here come the lights."

"Ai-yai-yai."

MILLENNIUM
MOUNT

(in which wounds fester, giants abound,
and, from the sky, a pair of pundits arrives
in search of sad stories)

A Hike

Well, it was some kind of an ordeal, getting through that park. Before me lay a dense, unyielding thicket with no path to speak of, and glancing left-then-right into its depths was no help at all. I spent many minutes in a terrible ponderance, shivering in the night air, the black water reaching for my hips. Invisible mosquitoes were everywhere, their tiny whines flocking now that I had come. When I did begin to walk, thick, sticky mud pulled at my shoes. With every step I had to tug my foot back out of it. Holding my suitcase aloft made it harder to balance, plus all but impossible to swat at the insects flitting by my ears. Without power, Polis's buildings behind me were as bleak and faceless as the rows of an endless morgue. That one made me keep my eyes straight, gazing instead toward the park in which every tragic ending I could think of seemed to be waiting for me. That's life. If it wasn't going to be one thing, it would end up being another. The sky was so dark I couldn't see its clouds. The earth was so dark I couldn't see its shadows.

I knew I had to make it to the hill of lights, but on entering the trees it was almost like I forgot. They were these sturdy black trees, a little sparse at first, though clumping into walls all around the farther I waded toward dry land. Within minutes, whatever light I could see before was blotted out by a lid of branches. Alright alright, it's all okay, nothing to worry about here—that's what I was telling myself. Some kind of creature was making a constant *hisssss*. It made no difference if my eyes were open or closed. I was splashing my way through tangles of submerged shrubs, hoping the slope of the hill would eventually lift me out of the water. So far it was marsh and more marsh. Every inch forward was a prodding about, as if with antennae. At one point I stumbled into a hidden pool and fell, swallowing a mouthful of brackish water and bits of sediment. After that my clothes clung heavily to my skin; I had a sudden need to scratch all over my legs. There might have been parasites in there, but I wasn't an expert. A metal something that was blocking my way and too heavy to move forced me to double back, and while doing so, I stepped on my own shoelace and nearly fell again. Quick little legs ran down the back of my neck—if I yelled it was only swallowed up by the unseen trees. So when the ground began to harden beneath me at last and I realized I had made my way onto a footpath, I kept any celebration to myself. I followed the trail until the ground slanted upward and raised me out of the water. I gave my arms a rest from holding the suitcase, then bent over to tie my shoes.

Onward I went through that grove of shadows, the image of the hill in my mind's eye my only guide. I hardly knew my progress in so uniform a blindness. *Heavens* was it hard to see in there. I was starting to feel too-alert, electric, tuned in all-the-way with the senses I had left. *Come over here, boy, let me learn you something.* I spun around. Walking through those woods like that, I was getting to thinking about everyone who'd ever doubted me, all the lies I'd ever been told. The dark was becoming a featureless canvas on which memory could do its bidding. *Right this way, I'm in my room.* For instance, there was this guy I used to know, he was my grandfather, he always used to say my problem was I'd been sabotaged. *Your problem, boy, is you've been sabotaged! No one raised you right!* I mean, how is *that* a kind of a thing to say? Especially when he was the one left doing the *raising*. Some things are true only because you've said them, but they were lies just before. The flapping of wings, the wet plops of my feet, the hiss of hidden insects, leaves either rustling or whispering my name—every sound made my ears twitch like prey. I might have been going this way, or I might have been going the other, I really couldn't be sure. Anyway, don't try telling stuff like *that* to certain people, you'd just be wasting your time. I don't even want to talk about it, to tell you the truth. Sometimes he'd sell off the first couple things he could get his hands on for some change to spend at his man on the corner, but it'd take you a while to recognize what the things had been. Like, I used to have this xylophone. It wasn't the best xylophone in the world or anything, but I knew a few jingles to play on it. Except once when I was older I went looking for it and all the keys were missing. I mean, every, single, one—it was just a wooden block left behind with a pair of rubber-tipped sticks. *That's good copper you had lying around, boy!* he said. *Who are you, the queen of the world?* "That's not the point!" Damn: all of a sudden I was yelling out loud in those woods. Something off to my side scurried away at the sound of my voice. "It's not just the queen of the world who gets to keep her stuff. It can be the rest of us too." *Pah. More drivel. Same as ever, I see.* "Shut up!" *Where are you now? Lost, I bet.* I was plunging farther still into the smells of wet bough and rotten moss. Dark things with pinpoints for eyes were moving in the trees. I heard his mean footsteps coming down the stairs after one of his sleepless nights spent arguing on the phone. The dungeon of my imagination had been flung open without the sun to keep watch. "You don't get to do that," I said, and I meant it. You don't get to go around selling all the copper you find because you think no one can do anything about it. Not the copper, not the bicycle pedals, the motors for my toy cars, the night-lights. Not the screws from the bed frame so that the mattress had to be put on the floor, or the graduation rings, the razor blades, the alarm clocks, the cuff links for my one good shirt, the remote for the TV. I stopped where I was and dropped to my haunches. The swamp water was chilling my clothes and that was the reason I was shaking. "I'm not some coward." Geez, I was having some serious tremors. My clothes were really damp. Something must have flown into my eyes, too, since I was having to wipe them a lot all of a sudden. All that ever happened to me was bad luck and cold clothes, and I was tired of it. And as a matter of fact, I was lying just now, it *was* the best damn xylophone in the world. And he had been the one to teach me the jingles on it. So if some of us who you see out here are not musicians, it's only because those we loved the most once took back the keys. *Wipe your face, boy, what's the matter with you...*

Up ahead a beam of light was moving amongst the trees. Whoever was holding it, they were still far enough uphill that I didn't think they'd heard me. I started thinking quickly as the light swayed in rhythm with their footsteps. I wasn't sure whether to hide or not. They could have been dangerous, or easily frightened. The thought of scaring them scared me. I didn't have long to make up my mind, since they were coming downhill quickly. Alright. Oh shit. I got off the trail and hid behind a tree trunk. You never want to meet someone in the dark, for the first time.

*   *   *

I'd taken long enough to decide that they'd heard me moving
into the bushes. "Hello?" they said. It was a man's voice. The
beam waved left and right. It settled on a patch of greenery
near me, casting awesome shadows against the night. They
were really something, those trees, their bark black and wet,
like stones. "Hello?" he said again. "There's nothing there.
I know nothing's there." Geez people were seriously talking
to themselves in these woods, I swear. He waved the beam a
few more times as he reassured himself. But something about
the moment made him not want to progress any farther toward where he'd been going, and suddenly the beam turned
around and started returning uphill. My heart sped up: he was
going to the lights! This was my chance. I didn't move right
away, but once there was enough of a distance between us
I stepped back onto the trail and started following his beam
where I could see it ahead. Still having to carry my suitcase
meant I needed to hustle if I wanted to keep up, and soon
I was making noise for real. "Motherfuck!" I heard him saying
up ahead. He started to scramble. It turned out having someone else to scare was actually calming me down. I didn't know
how much strength I had left, but I was using all of it to keep
pace with him. In the dim light ahead I could see that the
trail had lots of forks and branches, and I realized I'd probably
taken some wrong ones before. He ran and ran and I ran too.
Suddenly the trees were thinning again and I could see ahead
of me where the land was clear. The flashlight was going, going, gone, but I emerged at last onto an open stretch, back
beneath the sky. Of course I hadn't been that far. Which is the
way these things go, mostly.

CAMP

Who saw me arrive? No one saw me arrive. Out beyond the
trees was an encampment of white tents as far as the eye could
see, many rows deep and bumping busy too. They were arranged with their backs to the woods and wound up the
mountain in an enormous spiral. Lines of hard-to-see figures
moved amongst them in the dark. Me stepping out into the
open, I drew about as much attention as an extra grain of sand
in the desert—out of the corner of my eye I could even spot a
few someones emerging from farther down in the woods with
rolls of toilet paper in their hands. Others dead ahead were
shuffling between tents by the light of dim, sickly lanterns
that made them seem ghostly. I crossed the thin strip of field
between the last tree and the first tent and entered the fray
as any old someone. Oh, it was a whole world of squalor in
there. Right at once was I struck by the odor of ten thousand
armpits. The air held the agitation of too many bodies without
room to move. The first ones I encountered were some dirty
men swaddled up to here in blankets, hawking mucus onto the
black grass that footsteps had crushed into mud. As I stepped
over their legs one of them reached up to me with his misera-
ble fingers, as if climbing out of a nightmare, saying, "What's
in that suitcase?" I slipped around the next tent onto another
pathway. But each new corner only revealed some other sorry
sight. A skeletal pair digging a hole; balding girls scratching at their heads; cold families blowing into their hands just
to stay warm; figures, certainly thieves, barging into tents
with brusque, discourteous movements. Everyone wore mis-
matched clothes and wrong-sized boots. What light there was
came from the chemical glow of the lanterns in which every

face seemed gaunt, or as if it had glass beads for eyes. "What are you looking at?" "Water?" "How about that suitcase?" "Have you seen this boy? He's about yea high." "Water, please, only a drop..."—all chatter was of the hopeless variety. Upon the walls of one tent, projected from the inside, was the shadow of a man positioned behind the shadow of a woman and thrusting. A couple perverts were gathered outside listening to the grunts and wagging their dry tongues, it was really nasty. I didn't know where I was going, only that there had to be something the rows of tents were all facing if their backs were to the woods. What a dark night it was. What a heavy suitcase I had. As I was moving on, one of those perverts even started to complain: "Hey, Barty, hurry up! It's been seven minutes already and some of us are dying here..."

My hunch was right, for soon I came to a wider dirt path on the other side of which were more tents. It was a sort of hapless thoroughfare with no real direction; some people were going this way and others going that. I went left, which by the looks of it would lead me up along the spiral toward the hilltop, clutching my suitcase to my chest even closer than I had when I first left Middleton, for if things had been bad walking through the tents, they were certainly worse along that awful road. I passed the wounded in bloody bandages and the infirm with festering legs. The frail, the disheveled, the frozen-over zombies dozing where they could. Parents looking for children; children looking lost; mangy dogs flinching beneath blows; scuffles and arguments; untraceable voices calling for help; rogues, scoundrels, ruffians with no upbringing taking shoes off the sleeping; more pleading, mud-covered things reaching for my palms; the scents of gauze and of iodine, of piss vomit tears oozing from puddles; mourning women singing forlorn hymns to the sky; owls picking through trash everywhere you looked; roaches, worms, horseflies, and mice; tents slashed in half, stretches of blue tarpaulin on which a few cross-legged someones had spread the last of their lives' belongings while holding up signs: WILL TRADE FOR ANTIBIOTICS, LOST EVERY-THING, ANY LITTLE BIT HELPS. On better days it might have been a market of cheerful sounds and vivacious spirit. But on that night, instead of the haggler's grin or the hawker's shout, in every direction that I dared turn, only the deadened eyes of tragedy and a dribble of murmurs behind unbrushed teeth. I almost wanted to go back into the woods...

There were along this road many soldiers in green fatigues whose job it clearly was to instill order amongst the mess and to do so in the most officious of styles. I noticed them in pairs sprinkled through the crowd, tall and healthy, gripping long rifles they pointed toward the ground. I'd never seen such long rifles before. The soldiers were finding all kinds of uses for them besides pulling the trigger, like as batons to whack people in the ribs who were causing a scene, or as battering rams to break down a conjoined tent someone had made by stitching a few together. "Safety hazard" was all they said, while the sorry soul cried and looked at his palms. By now I was a good distance from where I'd arrived. Even when all people had was a *question* for the soldiers, they kept on gripping their rifles, as if expecting a trick. A pair to my right was dealing with a man in Sufi garb holding a child under the arms and waving it in their faces. Not that I could hear what was being said, but from the way the soldiers' mouths were moving, I knew they weren't being too helpful. Sometimes you can tell by the way someone's mouth moves if they're being helpful or not. I noticed more and more soldiers the farther along the path I went, until I had to slow to a stop where everyone was clearing the way for four of them marching downhill. They were in square formation, the two up front motioning for people to move (with their rifles, naturally) and the two behind looking about serenely, as if from a great height. Clearing a space in the tight confines made for much jostling, and some people ended up standing on the blue tarps without saying sorry for whoever's things they knocked aside. The soldiers stopped not far from where I was, and one of them in the back took a paper from his jacket to refer to as he spoke.

"Alright, folks, listen up. Couple orders of business from Command. Effective immediately, E-Med Two will now be accepting any nonemergency situations. That includes your *fe*vers, your *pois*on *i*vy, your painkillers, your diar*rhea*, your *in*sect repellent, your *com*mon *colds*. Let's keep it *sim*ple: if you're not going *blue*, go to *two*. All current or new emergency situations, you'll keep reporting to E-Med One."

He had a funny way of speaking, nasal and droning, except for odd moments of emphasis. Everyone in the crowd had glazed looks listening to him, they were really tuned out.

"*Sec*ondly," he went on, "there are now *qui*nine tablets for use in *drink*ing water. Allotment is two tablets per indi*vid*ual per *day*, not to be used in more than one *li*ter of *wa*ter at a *time*. Make sure to bring your card with you. Questions so *far*?"

No questions.

"Good. Next is *this*: following last night's *in*cident, we're calling for a mora*to*rium on all *fires* not in Section E."

"What!"

"Are you kidding?"

"The hell!"

"Why's that?"

"What section is this we're in then?"

"This is Section C," he said. He'd straightened his back even more in response to the crowd's sudden awakening.

"Why's that?" repeated someone. "Why's that the rule?"

"Fires are to be built in Section E only and under supervision. This comes from up top. We need to preserve the park."

"Man, fuck this park."

"Hear! Hear!"

"The wood's all damp anyway."

"That's not what you told Napakakos."

"How's this Section C? Last week it was Section A."

The nasally soldier looked up from the sheet. He was a swarthy man with bulbous shoulders. "Need I re*mind* you, ma'am, that none of us were *here* one week *ago*," the soldier said.

"The hell you mean? I've been here my whole life it feels like. Shrub over there is where I had my first kiss." Well, there were a few chuckles at that, even one of the up-front soldiers had to clench a grin from his face. People were looking to see who had said it but I didn't have a good vantage.

"Funny. *Again* that's E-Med Two for non*emerg*ency is*sues*. Look for the green cross. Cut it with the fires, everyone. Come see us for *quin*ine in Head Tent. If there's nothing—"

"Hey, what happened to the lady then?"

"Yeh! How's that lady from yesterday doing?"

"This fire stuff is bullshit! Yesterday you told Napakakos something different."

"Yeh! You're switching what you said because he isn't here."

"Why can't we get back on the Lilypads?"

You could tell he was trying to be patient but his hand was thinking about his rifle.

"All de*ci*sions are ar*rived* at upon after extensive re*view.* No indi*vid*ual has any bearing on them," he said.

"You lie, sir!"

"We're going to tell Napakakos and you know it!"

The soldier folded the paper back up and looked about ready to move on. "Unless Napakakos has promised you some sort of afterlife, you would all do well to calm down," he said, and gripped his rifle at last.

That hushed the crowd for a bit. But once the four of them started marching again, following a short *yip* from the one in charge, more questions sprang up behind their backs:

"Is it true the power's back in Point James?"

"What about the lice? How do we handle the lice?"

"So we'll just freeze without the fires then?"

"Any dry blankets?"

"Some of these tents have mold, did you know that?"

"Just tell us if the lady's alright, will you? She looked in a bad way..."

From the platter of options he answered just one as they kept on downhill:

"Sham*poo* for lice is also on its *way.*"

It was a real grumble of complaints after they marched off, although you could tell people were also a little disappointed they were gone. It had been something to *do*, after all. Without the soldiers around to focus their discontent, the crowd was slowly returning to a sluggish state of waiting. Only a few die-hards remained, talking things over in muttering circles. And even they, as I walked on by, seemed more to be mustering the habits of outrage without any of its zest, complaining in tired, uninspired ways, I mean, I mean, you would think they could have *at least* told us about the lady...

One or two such groups were trying to rally momentum around their threat of reporting the soldiers to someone named Napakakos. But their efforts were dwindling as fast as they'd begun, and I could hardly hear what was being said through my own yawns. I was tired. Clearly I would need to find a tent if I was going to rest, and my guess was that the soldiers were in charge of that too. Approaching one of them didn't seem like a good idea, given all I'd observed so far. Then again, the alternative would be to go around asking some of these people, who were clearly a touchy bunch. There had to be some sort of compromise. I saw a man and a woman in the midst of what looked like a barter. I thought maybe she was the one who'd made the joke about the shrub, given that they were near the direction the voice had come from. Whoever that was had a sense of humor at least. I made my way over and interrupted, asking if she had made the joke about the shrub. She looked at me. "Come again?" Crooked in one arm was a sleeping baby in a stained, sagging diaper, and her foot was propped up on a large battery on the ground. I asked again, thinking they'd misheard, but it was clear by the way she was looking at me that she hadn't. She had bright orange hair and raised eyebrows. "Why would I have made that joke?" she asked. That's the damn thing with people. They always make you feel ridiculous when all you want is a straight answer and I was getting tired of it. "You could have just given me a straight answer. No need to make me feel ridiculous." I didn't snap, but it wasn't quiet either. The guy next to her said something about me going away. A muscular man who'd been trying to rally a group came by and asked if anyone wanted to come with him to see Napakakos. It looked like he was down to last resorts. "How about you, guy?" he asked. "Come with, why don't you?" I shook my head. "I'm trying to get a tent," I explained. "I don't need trouble." He nodded as if he'd known it all along and sauntered off. The woman moved the baby to her other arm and bounced to keep it from crying in its brown, shitty diaper. What a place to be a baby in. I hoped it wasn't getting traumatized for later in life. I could sense the guy from before was about to tell me to scram again, so I picked up my suitcase and headed off before he could. Freed of distractions, he got back to what he'd been doing, trying to convince the lady to give him the battery: "Ava, let's focus here, you can't be hustling me all night now. A kettle's a fair trade and that's being generous. What good's that thing going to do you anyway?" "All I'm asking is that I see what else you have first, Tim, it can't be that difficult...," Ava was saying.

I was about twenty steps away when the muscular man reappeared at my side. "You know, I've been thinking of that problem you asked me for help with earlier, about needing a tent. The funny thing is, Napakakos is probably your guy for that as well. How about it? I can take you." He was a dark blackman with a blank oval face and blond-dyed beard and hair. For warmth he wore two tracksuits one on top the other and a green headband, which only drew attention to how large of a head it was. Funny-looking guy. But he was about as close to a lead as I had, so I told him okay and even accepted his offer to carry my suitcase just so I could take a break. Getting to stretch my arms overhead was an awesome kind of relief.

He led me through the tents. While walking he started in on some chitchat about owing me an apology, about how he wouldn't normally have pushed in on my business like he'd done, it's just that he was helpful by nature was the problem, plus he'd heard me dealing with those others due to his good ears. "In school a specialist measured our hearing and said I was off the charts. What he did, he played all these tones and asked if I could hear them, and when I could hear them all he showed me on the chart where I was off it. It was a test for our ears. Everyone did it but mine were the best." He was having such an easy time carrying my suitcase that sometimes *he* was the one waiting for *me* to catch up. The kind of muscles he had, they almost came as a surprise, since from his wrists to his elbows he was still skinny, and his legs were like stilts. I could see them because he'd rolled up the pants legs of his tracksuit. We were on the side of the camp closer to the hill's top, and the slope of the land offered a view of the tents behind us. It was seriously a lot of tents, forming a sort of hive. We had to start and stop for people going in the other direction or overtaking us. "You're going to like Peter," he went on, taking a right between two graffiti-marked tents. "He and I have become something like partners around here. I'd even heard of him a little before the evacuation, so you can imagine my surprise. I said, 'Well, how 'bout that, if it isn't Peter Napakakos just like they said.' We hit it off pretty alright. Now people might wanna say, *Roger J, this is a hell of a time to be making friends, can't you see it's a disaster going on?* Well, to them I might say back, *What better time to be making friends?* You feel me? What *better* time?" He spoke quickly but without excitement, in a rush to get to the end of what he was saying, as if reading from an invisible text. With his dark, pimpled face, fringed on all ends by that ridiculous yellow hair, he bore a resemblance to a sunflower that I couldn't unsee once I thought of it. As we passed a pair of young boys in sweaters going the other way, he asked them if they knew anything more about the eggs they'd found but they shook their heads *uh-uh* as they kept going. He said to me: "Yesterday they found eggs, three red ones. Pretty sure they're turtles but we won't know until they hatch. Wish I could tell them what kind but I need to brush up on my turtles. I used to know them all."

We arrived at a sort of breakaway where the path ended in a bunching of seven-eight tents around an open space, like a cul-de-sac. It's not like we were at the *end* of the tents or anything—there were still a lot more continuing behind and all around—it was just a cul-de-sac in the middle of everything. In the open space were many men. Two of them sat off to the side curling weights in a makeshift gym, but most were stooped in a circle around a patch of dirt, craning their necks to look at something in the center. Whatever it was was causing them to shout and cajole with an air of festivity quite different from the night's otherwise morbid tone. *Go!* they yelled, or *That's it! Get 'em!* As we closed in across the mushy ground I noticed they were seriously muscular too. I mean, I'd been impressed by the first guy's muscles just a second ago, but after seeing these others, he was clearly no comparison. All the dozen of them were thick with sinews and so broad in the shoulders they had to turn sideways for everyone to have a view inside the circle, where a scorpion and a millipede were facing off in a ring of matchboxes. I had to stand on tiptoes myself once we breached their bubble of heat. The scorpion was shiny black, the millipede an odd blue with angry pincers on one end. To light the ring, one of the men with a scalp full of tattoos was holding a lantern over the center and with his other hand was using a stick to prod the scorpion and millipede toward each other. Another, having noticed us with a bored glance, muttered to my guide:

"Those better not be swinging hands I'm seeing, Roger J."

"What you mean?" Roger J said. He had rested my suitcase beside the huddle.

"I mean that I'm looking at your hands and they're swinging," said the man. "If your hands can swing, it means they're empty. But yours aren't supposed to be empty, Roger J. Your hands are supposed to have berries in them. Like you said."

"I was carrying this guy's suitcase."

"Are there berries in the suitcase, Roger J." It wasn't really a question. He'd turned away from the fight so as to better communicate his annoyance.

"Can't say I know that for sure," said Roger J.

"Is his name Berry then? Because you were supposed to bring back berries. You, pal, is your name Berry?"

"No," I said.

"His name's not Berry, Roger J," he said, refocusing on the ring where the others were still carousing. "You didn't bring back even a single berry. These are simple things."

You wouldn't have known by looking at Roger J, who was as plain and sunny as before, that he was the cause of all that disappointment.

"This guy was trying to find you, Pete."

"What am I? Lost? What's he want to find me for?"

"I didn't really ask."

I was about to explain myself when the scorpion struck a sudden blow to the millipede, holding it by the claw and stabbing with its tail. That made the one with the tattooed scalp cheer like a fanatic. "That's it! Get it! Get in that ass!" The millipede wriggled free of the claw and scampered around to regather itself.

"Relax, Ug, it's not over," said someone else from amongst the roars and yells.

"So what're we going to do about this, Roger J?" said Peter Napakakos. "What's Siren over there supposed to do without the conditioner, huh? Mr. Woodsman, right? Mr. Resourceful, aren't you?"

Some of the men chuckled, the sound in their chests like that of oxen snorting.

Roger J snapped his fingers and pointed upward, as if to a light bulb. "Actually! I do remember spotting some lingonberries on the way back. Those would work even better than what I was looking for at first."

"Mhm."

"It's my bad, Pete. I got sidetracked because this guy asked me for help finding you."

"Mhm."

"Okay, I'll go get those lingonberries right now. You crush them into a paste and rub it in overnight and Siren will be fine in no time. You hear me, Siren? You'll be fine in no time."

A man on the other end of the circle gave him a thumbs-up without looking away. He was an enormous light blackman wearing a shower cap. As a matter of fact, a lot of them had their heads covered.

"You do that, Roger J," said Napakakos.

"Pete, there was this other thing too. It's something Corporal said. Now he's saying no fires except for Section E. Plus no word on the lady. People are angry for real, they were about to head over here but I said I'd talk to you myself."

"Corporal said what now?" asked one of the others.

"No fires except for Section E."

"The cocksucker."

"Yeh yeh. That's what I said," said Roger J.

"He say why?" asked Napakakos.

"Not a single reason, Pete."

Napakakos seemed to consider. "Guess we'll have to negotiate then."

"That's what I told everyone. I said, 'Peter Napakakos will negotiate, don't even worry.' Alright, that's me then. I'm off to get those berries. Sit tight, Siren. I won't be long."

He left through the tents with a private nodding of his head, as if he'd been convinced of a good idea, a bouncy pep in his gait like someone in low gravity.

"I'm starting to think a lot of things about that guy," Napakakos said once Roger J was gone.

"He's alright," someone said.

"Why not let everyone be alright then."

It was the millipede's last stand and it wasn't doing too hot. It had tried wrapping all around the scorpion like a constrictor but was getting stung all the same. Going by this one guy's look of frustration, I figured it was his millipede and that the scorpion belonged to the man with the tattooed scalp who was laughing at him, going: "Oh, we're really getting in that ass now!"

"So, pal. You were looking for me. What can I help you with?" said Peter Napakakos. He sounded more pleasant now that it was just me, though he still wasn't looking my way.

I explained myself, that I'd only just gotten here and had noticed the disorder. That I needed a tent, and was told I was better off coming to him than trying to get help from the soldiers.

"You just got here? How would you have just gotten here?"
he asked.

"Someone brought me over. I was farther west, but we rowed
all day."

"You rowed all day *here*?"

"Yeh."

"Sure. And then what? You climb up Millennium Mount?"

"I did just now."

That made half of them look up to notice me for the first
time, my thin frame with mud up to the waist. I counted
plenty of muscle-bound necks, some bulging trapezoids, a few
more heads covered with shower caps.

"Impressive," one of them said.

I stood there awkwardly. I might have said *thank you*, I don't
know.

Then they turned back for some final cries of encouragement—the scorpion was taking full advantage now, stinging and
stinging the millipede, which had curled up into a flat circle.

"Ha! Ha! Yup! Just like we practiced!" the tattooed scalp
was saying.

"Bullshit, Ug. Fuck out of here talking about practice."

"Worry about your mans, then. You worry about yours."

The millipede was finished. They prodded it with the stick
to make sure, then everyone rose at once. Geez were they muscular, in tracksuits of various dark colors. From their pockets
they pulled out cans of tuna and began swapping them around
by a logic I couldn't quite follow. The one who owned the scorpion ended up with the most, cackling the whole time. Some,
instantly bored, went off to the tents, and the guy with the
millipede started scratching at his shower cap and kicking the
matchboxes like a sore loser. Peter Napakakos passed around a

can opener for everyone. I'm not your biggest tuna fan, but the smell of something to eat was making me salivate.

"Any extra cans?" I ventured asking.

"What?" said Napakakos. "This isn't a charity, pal."

The sore loser wasn't handling things well, I swear. He was getting into it a little with the tattooed-scalp man, complaining about the scorpion while the latter leered and laughed. Next he went over to the guys at the makeshift gym and yelled at them, then came over to Napakakos.

"Boss, that was Roger J here a second ago?"

"It was," said Peter Napakakos.

"Well, what's he doing, huh? Thought he was gonna get rid of the lice. I'm fucking going nuts here." He scratched at his shower cap to show his point. He was a ruddy-faced Slav looking wild in the eyes.

"They like loser blood!" called the tattooed-scalp man. This one was squat, with a barrel for a chest, a hooded brow, and the wide mouth of a shark. When he leered I saw his top-row teeth were filed to points. "You got *losing* written all over your face, Monsoon, you oughta accept your lot. It'll make it easier."

"Boss," said Monsoon, trying to ignore him, "when Roger J's back tell him I want to see him."

He marched off, still getting laughed at, kicking whatever he could. *Geez-us* was he a sore loser. He was about the sorest loser I'd ever seen. Peter Napakakos finished his can by tipping the last bits of tuna into his mouth and slurping the juice. Then he must have remembered I was still there.

"Well, I don't know what to tell you, pal. We don't have any extra tents in our tents."

With that he strolled away. People were lazing out front of their tents. Without the heat of the huddled bodies, the night was growing cold again, and in a great vista from where I stood, Polis was dim in its long sleep. A silent line of bats flew overhead.

That night I slept wrapped up in an extra tarp I found lying around, wearing my driest pieces of clothing layered one on top the other. Two pairs of socks so as not to shiver too bad. It was me and three others, in a cup of earth where I'd stumbled on them, nestled like eggs. They didn't complain or anything, when I joined.

A Cure for Lice

Going about camp the next morning, I picked up on a few things. Firstly, almost everyone there on the mountain was from farther uptown, where the flooding had seriously destroyed things. The soldiers had brought them over in convoys of amphibious vehicles, nicknamed Lilypads, as part of a mission from the Department of Intra-Military and Civilian Affairs. The first day, it had been a whole lot of gratitude on the part of the evacuees, apparently, especially when so many others they'd passed along the way were spending the storm as facedown corpses in the water. Everyone had cried, given thanks, hugged strangers they'd only just met. But now it had been some days and the gratitude had run its course. People were growing *antsy*. They wanted to know what would become of the lives they'd left behind, and just how many more decrees the soldiers planned on sending downhill. Weakened as they were (by despair and empty stomachs), they hadn't risen up in a wave of revolt just yet. Instead, the mood in the air was of a feeble, dangerous beast saving the last of its energies for a parting strike. It seemed all it would take was the right toe being stepped upon for a desperate riot to wipe the entire encampment off the face of the mountain, if only for something to do. Anyway. That's most of what I picked up on, from walking around.

I had awoken with the jolt of a sudden purpose, having done the work of planning in a dream I couldn't remember. All about was the *clack-clack-clack* of people shaking the chemical lanterns from last night to recharge them for the next one. My suitcase I left in the care of one of my sleepy neighbors (a mustachioed Hispanic with a rattling cough) after taking from it the unopened toiletry kit that I now had in one of my pockets. With no suitcase, I could move quickly, and there was a lot to do.

I first went to the blue-tarp market, walking a little hunched over to better look for what I wanted. Now, with daylight coming through the clouds, it was possible to see, though it also had the effect of further revealing the true wretched state of everyone around. As the morning warmed, a collection of stenches filled the air—of marinated vomit, of urine coagulating in puddles. Finally on one of the spreads I saw something useful: four button-up pajama tops of soft cotton. The person selling them was an itching woman crouching with her butt on her heels; she, too, had a sign requesting ANTIBIOTICS, which probably explained why she still had so much stuff left over. Who was going to have anti*biotics*? I held up the pajamas and told her I wanted them. She pointed to the sign and peeled down her lower lip to show me the inside covered in cold sores.

Instead I took the toiletry kit from my pocket. "How about this?" I asked. She shook her head and said: "What's that gonna do me?" I opened it and rummaged through the contents, which were each in a neat pocket. A pair of grooming scissors, a bar of soap, a sleeping mask, lip balm, a mini toothbrush and toothpaste. Last was a small bottle of antiseptic mouthwash. "If you rinse and gargle with this, it'll help," I told her. "Believe me, it's the best. Who has antibiotics? No one has antibiotics." Her face had grown considerate while I'd been going through the things. "I'm getting that whole pack?" she asked. "No," I said. "Just the mouthwash. You didn't want the whole pack." She didn't like that, I could tell she was about to feel swindled. I said, "I can include the toothbrush, too, but that's it," which made her feel better. "Fine," she said. So we swapped.

The grooming scissors were small and hard to hold but sharp for having never been used. Popping down behind one of the tents, I put them to use cutting up the pajama tops into squares. Still, my progress was slow. While I worked, a group of five kids came to see what I was doing. One of them asked, "Can I try?" She had a trail of snot running out her nose and into her mouth, which she kept licking at like it was candy. I said sure, though they would have to do something for me first. "I need talcum powder," I said. "Do you know what that is?" Only two of them did, another girl and a boy, who had to explain to the rest using exploding hands and comparisons to flour. Once they all understood, I said, "Okay, good. I need some talcum powder. Whoever comes back with it first gets to help me." They took off in three separate directions, two pairs plus a straggler, a scabby boy with knock-knees. While they were gone a drizzle fell for two minutes, then stopped. They took so long I could have finished cutting everything, but I didn't want there to be nothing for them to do when they came back, so I paused. I realized what the problem was going to be only a minute before they returned: with no way to know who won, they were *all* going to come back with talcum powder. That's what happened: the boy and girl who'd known what it was (you could tell they were the sharp ones), followed by the scabby boy and then by the shy girl, who had lost track of her partner, the snotty girl. All in all it was two squeeze bottles of powder plus a plastic bag tied in a knot, I don't even know how they found it. It would have been a big argument between them if I hadn't calmed the whole thing by saying there was enough work to go around. They took turns, one of them cutting while the other three said how to do it better. At one point a green helicopter passed overhead, causing them all to freeze where they were and look upward in wonder. The snotty girl never came back.

Finding the woman with the orange hair, whose name I remembered was Ava, was the day's most arduous task, made even worse by hunger striking me with a sudden wallop to the gut. I still hadn't eaten since yesterday. Sometimes when you've been hungry long enough you can forget it for a time, but it'll always come back to remind you—it's the story of my life. I rinsed the squares of cloth in a pond by the trees, left them to dry on a broad stone, and headed uphill. For food I had only one option: to take the spiral path to the top of Millennium Mount, where the soldiers were administering the refugee efforts from a hexagon of central tents named Section E. These ones were olive green and looming, outfitted with humming generators. There was a wide building in the middle with a sign saying HIKERS' LODGE, then some metal scaffolding on top of that, from which the lines of a cable car extended all the way over the woods and down toward Polis. Around the rim of the plateau was a series of periscopes, but they cost a quarter to use and no one was using them. I mean, it would've been really *crazy* to use the periscopes at a time like this. It was from the Hikers' Lodge that the soldiers were doling out paper bowls of soup with rolls of bread. The line was long and slow, made of men and women still reliving the horrors of evacuation. While waiting, I was asking them: Ava, Ava, have you seen Ava? She has orange hair. No one had seen her. I might have had no luck at all if not for another moment of complication when I finally got to the front of the line an hour later: I didn't have a ration card. "What do you mean you lost it?" the soldier behind the table asked. He had on a hairnet and latex gloves. "I gave it to my friend to hold on to yesterday," I said, "except now I can't find her. Can you help? Her name's Ava." He told me to stand to the side and asked the soldier next to him to look up the name. He flipped through a few pages in a large notebook. Five more people were served their soup in the meantime and I was getting woozy. I asked if I could have some soup anyway and the soldiers said no.

"Why don't you just give the kid some soup," someone in the line said. "It's not like it's any good."

"Can't you see he's suffering?"

"What're we really trying to do here?"

"It's our tax money paying for all this gunk, you know."

A rabble was starting up. People were never too far from starting a rabble in that place, I swear. Sensing a thick situation, the soldier gave me some soup with no complaint, which practically frustrated everyone who might've preferred a fracas instead. I drank it all at once—hot, salty, three slivers of cabbage slipping down my throat. When I was done, the one behind the notebook said, "Here we go. Ava Riffin. She's in Section B. Bring your card later or there'll be no more of this nonsense."

Nearly an hour later I found her in a tent with red stains, just like a man I'd asked along the way had said. There was a *whack-whack*ing sound coming from the inside, and when I twice hollered her name, she came out holding a rock in one hand, a boot over the other. Half a nail jutted from the boot's heel. She was thick waisted and full cheeked, wearing a jacket and hiking pants. She looked me over without an ounce of rec- ognition. "Do you still have that baby?" I said. I was holding the cut-up cloth and the talcum powder. "You were from yesterday," she said. "Did you find a tent?" "No. Look, I have something to help the baby. Is it here?" On the lip of tent that covered the ground, I laid down the squares of cloth and began to sprinkle one with powder. I had eight in all, although only half had dried properly in the time spent on the stone. By now the day had taken on a stale yellow glow. She must have been *curious* at least, Ava, seeing what I was doing, for when I was done she weighed something in her head before opening the tent's flap to lead me to the baby in the back. We approached on hands and knees, past three sleeping bags and mounds of damp things. The baby lay swaddled in a blanket. It had pudgy legs, swollen eyes from a life spent sleeping. Beneath the blanket it had on nothing at all, just plain naked all over. The skin of its lower regions looked tender with a rash. It was a girl. "May I?" I said.

I laid the powdered cloth next to it. Following my lead, she lifted the baby and placed its lower half on the cloth. Its slow limbs extended like unfurling petals. I took one of the damp

squares and started wiping its body. "These are clean," I told
Ava. "I used soap." The baby cooed and twitched. Geez-*us* was
it little. I applied talcum powder to its legs, butt, and crotch.
Then I made three folds of the cloth, one around each side of
the waist and one rising up to fold over the front, where its
legs poked out. Turning it over, I made folds on the other side
and tucked the flaps in around the waist. I turned it back. Only
then did I stall and plumb my memory for the knot Toussaint
de Sanville used when the Frenchwoman would come in one of
her panics. When I remembered, I made tight knots on each
hip, tugging to make sure the diaper would not come undone.
The size was exactly right. Ava during this time said nothing, breathing in the ragged way of a bystander witnessing a
rescue. Suddenly she kissed me on my cheek, my cheek, my
chin, my nose. A light dew covered our skin despite the cold
outside. She was holding me by the wrists. "Thank you. I can't
even." A wind bulged one of the tent's walls toward us. Still
close, caressing my palm, she asked how she could ever repay
me. My heart sped at the chance. "Actually," I said, "I was
hoping I could have that battery I saw you with…"

That afternoon when I returned to the cul-de-sac the giants were
more scattered about. Some were here adjusting the tethers of a
tent, others were there laughing at a story, and about four were
over by the makeshift gym, including Peter Napakakos. The
gym's bench was a thick plank of wood supported by two cinder
blocks, on which the man with the tattooed scalp lay shirtless,
holding a cloth bag of rocks over his head. He was going at it,
busting out sweaty reps while one of the shower-cap guys counted
for him. Napakakos sat on a three-legged stool, fiddling with
an accordion. Upon seeing me approach, he put on an amused,

magnanimous look, as if readying to sign an autograph. But it was one of them in the shower caps I had come to talk to.

"I can get rid of your lice," I said, and tapped his enormous shoulder. He kept on with the counting even while looking at me... twenty-one... twenty-two... twenty-three. It was the light blackman whose name was Siren. "Did Roger J find the berries?" I asked. "I bet he didn't."

"Who's this?" said the other, the sore loser.

"He was looking for a tent," said Peter Napakakos.

"Did *you* find the berries then?" Siren asked once the tattooed man was done with his set. The latter sat up and was toweling his smooth head of sweat.

"I don't know anything about berries," I said.

"My man, let me ask you something. You ever hear of manners?" said the tattooed one. I shouldn't have been surprised by this, but he had tattoos all over his chest and back too.

"So did the shampoo come then?" asked the sore loser.

"No," I said. "It's madness on top the hill. Come, let me show you."

I bent to unbuckle the straps of my suitcase. But I must have moved too quickly, for suddenly they spooked, said *Whoa Whoa Whoa*, and the sore loser, Monsoon, pinned my arms behind my back and lifted me off the ground while another slammed his foot onto my suitcase. My *goodness* were they strong! My legs were dangling in the air with no chance.

"My man, you never heard of *manners*?" repeated the tattooed one. "Boss, who the fuck is this guy? Huh? Someone want to answer me?"

Peter Napakakos still looked as if a mild diversion was being put on for his entertainment. The accordion in his hands wheezed a tired chord. "He's alright, Ug."

"So now people are alright again all of a sudden."

"Put him down, Monsoon. Let's see what it is."

I was put down, my heart fluttering like a bird set free. It really wouldn't have been anything for them to have snapped me in half.

"Go on then," said Napakakos.

I unbuckled the straps of my suitcase and flipped it open slowly, squatting to lift the battery out. It was about as big as a small boulder, the label illegible from scratches. Along its top were the two diodes for hooking it up to a car plus two regular sockets like what you'd find in a wall. From a knotted plastic bag I retrieved my favorite electric clippers, unwinding the cord then plugging it into the battery. But when I clicked it on nothing happened.

"What's all that?" said the tattooed one.

"Oh, I see," said Siren.

"This the guy that climbed up here?" said Monsoon.

I'd found what it was: on the battery's side was a red-and-black switch that I popped the other way then flicked the dial on my clippers again and this time it worked. Its small motor hummed like a handful of bees.

I moved the battery and clippers over to the bench and asked Siren to take a seat. He considered for a long moment. Then in his earthquake strides he came over and turned around to sit on the wood, which groaned beneath him.

"Siren! You about to let that man do that to your head?" said the bald one, the heat from his exercise causing him to steam. Meanwhile Monsoon was bent over ferreting around in my suitcase and Peter Napakakos had stood up from the stool.

"You think we'll be getting that shampoo, Ug?" Siren asked. The question floated in the air to reveal its own uselessness. Siren nodded. "Might as well."

"Any dry socks in here?" Monsoon asked.

"No. And please step away from my suitcase."

He bristled and ambled over to the space around Siren. Now it was a bit of a scene and others were coming over too.

Peter Napakakos let his accordion hang against his chest by the strap. I saw him appraising me with a smile so slight it required no effort. He said: "You know what you're doing there, pal?"

I snapped on the pair of latex gloves I'd swiped when the soldier serving soup wasn't looking.

"I used to be a barber," I said.

A BARBER IN THE MIDST

I worked tenderly, under the quiet gazes of Peter Napakakos and the gathering behemoths, who crossed their arms. Beneath Siren's shower cap was a thick head of curls packed tight. It was strong hair, full of luster, midnight black down to the roots. Plucking out its length brought it to his shoulders, and for all its smelliness, it did not have the dank odor of true neglect, as is sometimes the case. Someone watching said what I'd been thinking: "Nice tresses, pretty boy." They laughed like oxen. When I lowered my clippers the strands parted from the scalp as easily as the wisps of a spiderweb. I had almost forgotten the feeling, that of satisfying a deep itch. I shaved from back to front, going against the grain so I got very low. Each new row made me bolder, my hand steadier, moving around him on all sides since the bench couldn't swivel. He had a head shaped like an oblong egg; you never really know until you get down to it. On his scalp was a pattern of red dots where the tiny creatures clinging to his skin could be seen. I had to ask them not to *crowd* me so much is how fascinated people were. The lice would take off soon now that they were exposed to light, I explained. I swapped a different attachment onto the clippers, then held Siren by the crown and angled his head for the finishing touches. He was a good customer and did not stiffen his neck, like some of them do, or look into my eyes when I was in front of him, which makes it too intimate and uncomfortable. All in all, it took me about twenty-five minutes. I'd given him a bald fade with a line-up around the sides. "Siren! That's a good look for you, you fuck. You look like you finally got through puberty!" they said. At my feet the fallen locks lay curled on the grass like the springs of a gutted machine. I've never really forgotten that hair.

After that, I didn't have to worry as much that I'd get shooed away. "Alright, pal. You know a thing or two," Peter Napaka-kos said while watching me eat my fill from a can of tuna. He'd handed over two from his pocket like I'd asked. No sooner was I done with them both than I was requested to shave the heads of the other waiting giants, who one by one unveiled a variety of manes from beneath their hats and shower caps. "I'll get me one of those too," the one named Monsoon said, taking his seat on the stool. I played it a little coy, like I wasn't quite sure I could do any others. "You will let me sleep in a tent?" I countered when they insisted. Yes, yes, fine, you can share with Paramount... "And I want tuna in the morning too," I said. Oh, you're a tough sell, aren't you, skinnyboy? Okay, that's no problem either... I took my place behind Monsoon's head and clicked the clippers back on. "Hold still, please."

*   *   *

Word spread through the tents that a solution to the lice had arrived. By the time I finished shaving the heads of Monsoon, Charge, Two Piece, and Tank, a bevy of others had appeared to replace them, scratching at their scalps as they milled about waiting. At first, most were the giants from the cul-de-sac, who numbered twenty-three (though not all needed cuts) and were each bigger than the last. One of them named Harpoon wanted something fancy when he sat down: "Give me a faux-hawk on the left and a French taper on the right side with two paths as well." Oh boy, that would have been a tough one. He was one of those pretty boys under regular circumstances, it was obvious. "I wouldn't recommend that," I ended up saying. "The lice would still hide underneath." "What would you recommend then?" he said. I said I'd recommend a bald fade with a line-up around the sides. Same with the next guy: a bald fade with a line-up around the sides. In fact, that could go for everyone. It was a bald fade with a line-up around the sides or nothing at all. They didn't mind not having a choice; they were glad just to get rid of the *itching*, really. Soon regular-sized people from Section C were showing up, too, drawn by the hum of the clippers, saying, *What's this?*, *Oh my!*, *Now, that's one hell of an idea...!* The mud in the cul-de-sac was getting mushed up anew by their arrival. Whoever sat down kept sighing and saying thank you even as I worked, and afterward headed off to find someone they knew in Section B or D who could benefit from just such a service. It certainly didn't help slow things down when some of those same kids from earlier came stumbling upon the scene, their eyes widening, then flew off gossiping in every direction like an army of pigeons.

I suggested to Peter Napakakos that there be a piece of tarpaulin on the ground to catch fallen hair, for sanitary purposes.

The tarpaulin could be rolled up when there was too much hair and emptied into the woods with no problem. He considered it a brief while, then instructed an underling to go fetch one. Because I kept having to tell people to fix their posture or else it made my job hard, I also asked Napakakos if we could perhaps get a chair with a back instead of the bench. That one he didn't mind doing since it let them have the gym again. The new chair was one of those foldable types you see on the beach and it was just right; we placed it on top of the tarpaulin in the middle of the clearing, where the matchbox fighting pit had been. "Anything else, milord," he asked while fingering his accordion, still with his bewildering smile. As a matter of fact, I said, there *were* a few other things…

I requested a bottle of ethanol or methanol, it didn't matter which, so I could dab some onto a cloth and wipe people's heads down after to provide them with that good burn. I suspected it would kill the lice outright, too, though I wasn't sure. He found that from who-knows-where, I didn't even ask, ten minutes later. He even got me a bigger supply of latex gloves, plus a spray can of air to clean the clippers between cuts. When a fat man and a skinny one had an argument over which of them was supposed to be next in my chair, I made the inconvenience known to Peter Napakakos, who then told the man with the tattooed scalp to regulate a queue within the cul-de-sac. *That* man's name was Uglygod. He had a meanness about him that seemed his life's sole enjoyment. You could tell the only thing he wanted more than an orderly line was a disorderly one, so that he could move in upon the culprits with his pointed teeth, his skin covered in green-and-black images of horned angels. "What did I say? What did I *just* say?" he'd ask during his patrols. He'd even brought along the scorpion in its jar for use as a threat against those who strayed so much as a toe out of place, waving it before their eyes with a twisting hand on the lid…

At least there were no more arguments. But when I noticed soon after that some of Napakakos's henchmen were going up to those in line and, one by one, extracting some sort of fee, I brought it up with him during my next break:

"What are they doing? They taking people's money?"

"Something wrong with that?"

"*Wrong?*" I said. "I want to make sure I'm getting my *cut* is all. We have to split this."

"We are giving you tuna," he said.

"Tuna is not enough," I said.

"It was enough earlier."

"Yes, but it is later now and you've been gathering dollars all day. Some of those should be mine."

"We'll talk it over later. Slide."

The hardest thing to find was the mirror. Such rare treasures either had not made it to the camp at all, or else were being hoarded out of sight by a vain few. Suspecting the latter, Peter Napakakos went to find one himself, taking along Uglygod and another named Kid Vicious. In an hour they returned with purple knuckles and three mirrors. One they kept for the section that was their gym, gazing into it sideways as they continued their biceps curls. The other two were for use by my chair, so that when they were held up facing each other, someone in between could have a front-and-back view of my handiwork. I could hardly believe it. My barbershop was set up.

*   *   *

There was no way of knowing how much charge was left in the battery, so every time my clippers clicked back on I let out a private sigh of relief. I wasn't expecting to be *blamed* or anything if it died, but I didn't want to see what would happen if the show was over either. By later that afternoon the cul-de-sac was the place to be. Those awaiting cuts were making new acquaintances and those already cut were still hanging around. I'd say about thirty people. It wasn't always easy, you had a few patrons who'd get almost *traumatized* by their haircut, like this Guatemalan cat with cornrows ending in plaits on either side. The cornrows had long since frayed at the edges and were damp with days of sweat, a ripe home for parasites. But you should have seen him: I almost had to get him a *tissue* when I was done is how much he missed his hair. He even scooped up as many handfuls as he could from the tarpaulin and took them off with him, probably to make a pillow. People are freaks. He didn't look good bald, that's for sure, but we had to count all the lice dots on his scalp to remind him it was a health issue. A few others had come not for their hair at all but because they'd heard there was somewhere to plug in their phones to charge, but they were disabused of those notions right off the bat. "Nothing else goes in the battery," said Napakakos. A siege of complaints surrounded him. What about their electric lights? Their speakers for some music? He repeated with no change in tone: "Nothing else goes in the battery." That decided it. They went back to what they'd been doing, discussing the crisis and trading rumors, whispering a hunch that Polis was draining and we weren't being told.

Peter Napakakos next-to-never changed his tone and he remained unruffled in the midst of chaos. That he was a leader amongst men was written so plainly all over him that *his* muscles out of everyone's seemed merely cosmetic. Wherever he got his power from, it had little to do with the bags of rocks he lifted over his head. Despite the surrounding wretchedness, he and his crew had afforded themselves some tiny comforts to make the passing of the days not-so-bad. Apart from the gym, they had a stockpile of tuna stolen from a bodega before their evacuation, plus a portable camping stove to heat it up if anyone wanted, though they mostly ate it raw. When thirsty, they filtered water from the downhill puddles through thin T-shirts, so as not to rely on the soldiers. Known to those in the know as the Dread Merchants, they were a tough team from the heart of Petit Julienne, on a de facto vacation from rougher lives and not minding it at all. Their names were Uglygod, Siren, Monsoon, Kid Vicious, Two Piece, Tank, Blood Tooth, Charge, things like that. I didn't want to ask, but I was pretty sure they were gangsters. For entertainment they had the fighting pit—which had overseen the final moments of two dung beetles, a tarantula, a chameleon, twenty fire ants (those they allowed to battle as a team), and a blue millipede—and the accordion that Napakakos had traded for upon getting here, and on which he repeated the same handful of chords while singing hoarse arias from memory. A large weatherworn man with the curious aspect of a Mediterranean wanderer, he had hide-like skin immune to mosquitoes, high cheeks, and thick eyebrows on the rim of a low-set forehead, such that the space left for his eyes was somewhat compressed, which made them appear small. No matter the calamitous mood, he maintained throughout the day the amused, solitary air of a man out for an evening at the theater, even when licking his knuckles. Even when the soldiers came at dusk and spread a hush through everyone like we were doing something wrong...

This time there were three of them, quite young, one pointing his rifle toward the middle of the cul-de-sac. "No fires," he said. He was right: we had built a small one to fend off the cold, and for me to better see what I was doing. "You don't think that's unreasonable?" said Napakakos. A line of five giants formed at his sides, causing the soldiers to jitter and repeat themselves. The giants just stared. Napakakos and them were so relaxed you would've thought *they* were the ones with the rifles. What they lacked in weaponry they made up for in their improbable size it seemed no number of bullets could subdue. Then, in a spasm, one of the soldiers dashed for the fire to stomp it out directly with his boot, his eyes wild as if braving a den of lions. That he remained untouched was due only to the hand Napakakos held up to stay his men. The soldier returned to his group, swinging his rifle madly and yelling for everyone to stay back. We were still, the buzz of my electric clippers the only sound. They retreated like bullies in over their heads. Once at a safe-enough distance, they yelled a promise to report the incident to the folks up top, and to see that Napakakos was dealt with for insubordination, even though Peter Napakakos—and I'm not kidding here—he hadn't stopped smiling since they'd first shown up...

Amusement seemed his default mood; it was only when that guy Roger J was around that anything appeared to bother him. He turned up a little later when it was fully evening, Roger J did, and came right over to me:

"Yo. So I see you've gotten to know everyone. What did I tell you, huh? They're swell guys. I knew you'd like them."

I was trimming the hair of an old lady with the flu, working by an electric lantern Kid Vicious was holding up for me. The old lady was wrapped in five blankets and shivering.

"How's it going, Rog?" I said. I actually *did* want to thank him, but I had to focus.

"I've been alright, thanks for asking. Here and about, what can I say. Say, what make of razor is that you got there? I used to do a bit of grooming work myself. Although with me I did lock twisting. You ever done that? It's a bit of the opposite of what you're doing, it's when people are growing their hair instead, but I've dabbled in everything."

"Oh yeh, I know that."

Now he was over my shoulder.

"Right, right, I'd expect no less. Say, what kind of razor is that? You ever seen these foldable kinds they sell on Bertford? They're not too known, and the price is killer. I bet you I could—"

"Is that Roger J I'm hearing?"

Peter Napakakos had come out from his tent and was walking over.

"Oh, hey, Pete. This guy was just asking me for some advice on razors is all, talking shop. Glad to see he's fitting in. I told him y'all were going to be swell."

"Where are my berries, Roger J?" said Peter Napakakos. "All night and all day I'm waiting for Roger J and his berries and now here he is but I still don't see any."

Again, the flash of a bulb turned on behind Roger J's eyes.

"The berries!" He slapped his forehead. "I *knew* it was something. Oh man, I'm so disappointed. Pete, you need to hear what happened, Pete."

But Napakakos had made up his mind and it was clear to see. He wasn't smiling even a twinge.

"Alright, Roger J. And I've put some thought into this too. It's been a nice little tryout, this whole thing, but here's what we're going to do with these excuses you always have—"

"Pete, wait, I brought you something, Pete. Look, you're going to want to see this."

From a pocket in his tracksuit he lifted out something in his cupped palms and held it out to Napakakos. He opened his hands to reveal a small white turtle.

"It's a turtle, Pete. Born just this morning. These kids found the eggs two days ago, Pete, and now they've hatched. This guy knows. He was with me when we ran into the kids. Weren't you, guy?"

I nodded my head yes, too stunned. The turtle was soft and translucent, with a pair of slits for eyes. Through the gelatinous shell could you see its tiny red heart pumping furiously. We were all leaning in to look at it paddling its flippers in his palms—even the old lady, who went, My Goodness.

"It's a turtle, Pete," said Roger J.

"I know what it is, Roger J," said Peter Napakakos, but he, too, was leaning in and the edge in his voice was gone. He made a cup with his own hands for Roger J to release it into, then rested his large thumb on the turtle's back and stroked. It opened its mouth in a silent cry. We were pressed so close around it our heads touched.

"I was thinking you could use it for the fights, Pete," said Roger J.

Napakakos looked up. "Come again?"

"Like with the critters and them. Something to beat Ug's scorpion, ya know?"

"It's a turtle, Roger J! It's a baby!" said Napakakos. "What are you, sadistic?"

"You don't got to do it *now*, Pete," said Roger J, holding up his hands. "I'm just saying, when it's grown and all. When the shell comes in."

"You're a real sadistic kinda guy, you know that, Roger J?"

"Pete, Pete, Pete." He backed up. "It's a present, Pete. You can do anything you want with it. Whatever you desire it's alright by me. Pete, I got you a turtle."

Any good cheer he might've been on his way to earning was clearly out the window now, although it didn't look like Napakakos was going to continue with the scolding either. He called over Siren and told him to find the turtle a bowl to splash about in and some grass or whatever it was baby turtles ate. I used the time to finish up the old lady's bald fade and was lifting the beach chair for the tarpaulin to be rolled up and emptied into the woods. It had gotten full of hair again.

"Not so fast with that," Peter Napakakos said to the two giants lifting the tarp by the corners. "Bring that along. And you don't go anywhere either, Roger J. We're all going for a walk…"

He led us in a single-file line, as many as wanted to come, toward Section E and the top of the mountain. It was me and Roger J just behind him, carrying the tarpaulin full of hair and huffing to keep pace. We wove through the tents then got onto the spiral path going uphill. Behind us everyone else was going, *What's this?*, *Where are we going?*, *Boy, Napakakos sure looks on a mission, huh?* Section E, when we got to it, was a constellation of fires stretching across the plateau, like a reflection of the night sky if we could've seen it beyond the clouds. Each fire had a dozen or so souls huddled around it for warmth and a pair of soldiers looking on to supervise. Napakakos started with the nearest one, reaching into the tarpaulin for a handful of hair and throwing it into the flames. It caught with a quick sizzle and a puff of smoke. Wafting through the night almost at once came the acrid fumes. No sooner were the folks around that one pinching their noses, asking, *What the fuck?* because they really didn't know, than Napakakos had thrown a handful into the next fire, then another a couple steps on. He proceeded like that, the head of a snake of which the rest of us were the tail. Roger J, holding the other end of the tarpaulin, was nodding constantly, as if this whole thing were a scheme of his he was happy to see pulled off. *Napakakos, hey, what gives?, Look, we're getting poisoned here, Someone stop this!* Coughs and sputters were filling the night. Some of the supervising soldiers who'd only just caught on were making their way toward us, but Napakakos was swifter in navigating his way to the Hikers' Lodge. Off to its side was the largest blaze of them all, a bonfire with logs in a neat tower, surrounded on all sides by twenty-some lounging soldiers. They had been enjoying a funny story, when, upon noticing Napakakos's advance, they grabbed the rifles at their feet. Oh boy, my heart was starting to pound. "Stand down!" one of them said, taking aim. Napakakos kept on. "Napakakos...," I began to say. He paused only to take the tarpaulin from Roger J and me, then continued on with it slung over his shoulder, leaving the rest of us where we'd stalled. The soldiers had formed a phalanx to block his way and he barged into them. They began to hit him with their rifle butts and grab at his arms. He lowered his head to better endure their abuse; all he had to do was get close enough to their fire. When he had pushed through a few inches, he looked up and flung open the tarpaulin, releasing a cloud of hair. It was a stagnant night with no wind. The hair drifted down into the flames and caught with so many tiny hisses. Oh gosh, you didn't want to be there to smell *that*. It was worse than a bottle of hot milk uncorked after a month beneath a bed, worse than two mean skunks in a fight. Some of the soldiers who'd taken hold of him let go in order to pinch their noses. But it didn't stop a vicious few from grabbing him by the scruff of his neck and dragging him into the Hikers' Lodge, where a door opened and swallowed them inside... Alright, all the rest of you, nothing to see here, show's over, folks, and that's an order!

Some hours later he returned to the cul-de-sac and brushed by us where we were worrying, on his way to his tent. His clothes were torn and his limp slight. He said he needed to sleep, and offered not-much-else other than to add we could rebuild that fire from earlier if we wanted, as long as we kept it a safe distance from the tents and put it out before dawn. He said he had negotiated.

Two Helicopters

The next day was more of the same, the cul-de-sac serving as a site of brisk commerce, me cutting hair from sunup to sundown. Stretching into the overcast morning, I ate my can of tuna while taking in the view of Polis, still stagnant in its long rest. I had slept in a tent, as promised, next to the one named Paramount, who might have been the largest of them all. He was a humorless meathead, Irish-built, with arms like legs, who explained before dozing off that he would be farting all night to keep the tent warm. It was pretty awful and I don't want to get into it. Me I didn't complain, though. I was just glad to have a roof over my head and a battery at my side that I hugged like a doll. What a *battery*. There didn't seem to be an end to its charge, and I even forgot to worry about it throughout the day. Whatever secret my barbershop might have been before, it was now fully known about, and from Section A to E people were coming. While waiting they traded anecdotes from their drowned lives or various atrocities committed by the soldiers. Again, during lunch, I brought up with Peter Napakakos the issue of a fair split of the cash and he gave me one hell of a deal. I would get half of what the people paid, the remaining half he'd share with his crew. Half! Oh man. That was more than Rex and Reginald would have ever *dreamed* of giving me. I'll admit, I was a little suspicious at first—Napakakos seemed a bit spaced-out after last night's walloping. He stayed in his tent most of the day attending to the baby turtle, for which he played the accordion and had Kid Vicious go about digging up worms to feed it. Perhaps he was brain-damaged, but I wasn't going to jinx it. Uglygod waved it off when I mentioned as much during his workout. "Boss suffers from good moods sometimes. It'll pass." Well, maybe *that* was also why Roger J seemed more comfortable than ever hanging around all day, making himself of use where it wasn't really needed. He had remembered a few things about electric clippers that he needed to talk to me about, as well as some weight-training tips I could use if I wanted to get started. This guy. I was starting to figure him out. Everything you'd been through, he'd been through something worse, he was one of those people. You lost a tooth? No matter, he'd once lost two, these ones you're seeing here are replacements. With his junior muscles and his neon tracksuit, he seemed a bizarre facsimile of the others, as if he were a fan, or someone auditioning.

Also: he answered rhetorical questions. I said at one point, shivering, "Gosh, is it *cold* enough for you yet?" and he responded without a pause, "Funny you should feel that way, I'd say too cold, actually. If you watch you'll notice your breath starting to frost." Well, I couldn't do much there but laugh! Even if his eternally blank face didn't seem to know why... Uglygod and the others kept calling him over throughout the day with silly concerns, just to hear him rattle on about this-and-that, then chortle about it. Hey, hey, Roger J, tell us again about your ex-girlfriend the supermodel, you know the one, who proposed to you at midnight, we are forgetting the details... Oh man, it's like he was immune to embarrassment, Roger J was—he didn't even blush as he started explaining. But the giants must have liked him at least a little, since no one shooed him away despite all his nonsense. After all, there wasn't much else for anyone to do but stew in boredom, or sing a few songs in the evening when Peter Napakakos played his accordion around the fire we built.

But the day after that, the sun shone. I had had an inkling it might, for my night's dreams were littered with blue beaches too bright to look at, a sure sign of the clouds having cleared. Stepping out into the illuminated morning, I saw a few bravehearts staring right into it against their better judgment. We remembered it from the months of blistering heat that had preceded the storm. The time spent away had made it wan, more timid than its old self, but it was still the sun. Within its light we looked around bedazzled, imbued, seeing each other as if for the first time.

With the sun came heat and with the heat came a kind of fidgety energy that must have been the soldiers' worst nightmare. New types of discomfort were sprouting throughout the camp, such as bouts of fever and delirium. The gears of an awful restlessness were being lubricated by sweat—here-and-there were groups of schemers, sounds of rabbling, a story from Section D of a husband and wife wrangling in the mud until indistinguishable from each other. *Alright, you fucks*, people were saying to the soldiers, *enough of this now, we want to go home. Call back those boats that brought us here, why don't you, and let us get on. Look, we can see the roads are draining, we have been using the periscopes...*

If that was bad, it was only made worse by what happened in the middle of the day. We had gotten so used to the buzzing of helicopters that they'd become another of the camp's ignorable sounds, no different from the hooting of owls in the woods or the constant moans of some invalid with a fever. But although the *chopper-chopper-chopper* that started up after lunch sounded like any old thing at first, this chopping drew nearer and nearer, too close for comfort, and looking up at it we saw that the helicopter wasn't one of those olive military ones but a rich blue and red. It came lower yet, hovering close enough to bend some of the taller trees. In its open door a man could be seen holding a large video camera and panning it over the grounds below. The helicopter traveled up the Mount, inspiring a trail of people below to follow its progress. This was something crazy, there was no doubt about it. I picked up my battery and went with everyone uphill, following the path Uglygod and Siren made by muscling their way through. But soon the helicopter was too far ahead and there were too many people blocking the way for us to keep tracking it. We slowed to a shuffle and tried to see where it would land. Instead, it twice circled the top of Millennium Mount, as if considering, then came right back downhill and over our heads again. Some panicked aloud that it was leaving, but others (with a little more sense) said it was headed to the strip of field between the trees and the tents. That's where we ran, downhill now, just in time to see it slowly hover and land on the ground and the people inside disembark. The man with the camera got out first, walking backward to keep his shot trained on whatever was inside, followed right after by someone with a fluffy microphone at the end of an extendable pole. Next came a silver-haired gentleman with a compressed, hawkish face. Getting out of the camera's and microphone's way, he surveyed the land with his hands on his hips, as if to plant a flag, motioning for the other two to back up. All that done, the remaining passengers emerged, a man and a woman, extremely coiffed, adjusting microphones on their lapels. Stepping onto the mud, they smoothed wrinkles from their suits and flashed brilliant smiles. The pilot shut off the helicopter's blades such that I could hear the people in the crowd gasping and oohing and aahing. I had to stand on my battery to make sure I was seeing what I was seeing. From there it was unmistakable. Oh man, I could hardly believe it! Why, it was the two of *you*, obviously: Jim & Jean from the news...

Looking gravely into the camera, you began: "It's twelve fifteen on a Sunday and we have just touched down near the peak of Millennium Mount, one of many such sites set up to administer to flood evacuees. As you may have noticed from our overhead footage, it's a tightly packed scene here. Tents cover nearly every square inch of available land. With high ground having become a recent commodity, what higher ground is there than Millennium Mount?" you said, Jean.

And "Now, unlike some of the other volunteer efforts, we understand that Millennium Mount is an operation conducted by the Department of Intra-Military and Civilian Affairs, who also helped oversee the evacuation itself. Come with us for an inside look, in part three of our series *Survivors of Phyllis*," you said, Jim.

You were talking like you do on the news, except it was real life, what a trip! For that shot you stood with your backs to the crowd, facing the helicopter, but once done you turned around and started to make your way toward the tents. Right away were you intercepted by the soldiers, who had only just arrived in a huffing march from wherever they'd been. Shielding their faces from the camera, they blocked the way. We couldn't quite hear what was being said—something about protocol, procedure, license to operate—but in response, the man with the hawkish look produced a docket of papers from his jacket and pointed. The soldiers looked it over, scratching their heads; anyone could tell they definitely weren't lawyers. They told the crew to wait until someone else came, but the man with the silver hair refused. Cleared of all obstacles, you proceeded.

Like two furies you swept through the camp, upsetting all order. At the first sign of squalor you stuck a microphone in its face and asked for comment—a bandanna-wearing woman nursing a leg of flesh wounds. Well, it didn't take much to get *her* going: glad for an audience, she lit up in the eyes. She complained about the tenfold overcrowding and the latrine stench. The malnutrition, the damp, the holes in her tent through which the bugs were crawling—that is to say, the sorry state of affairs. "And look at this," she concluded, taking off the bandanna. "Had to get me head shaved for all tha fookin lice in them woods." Jim & Jean, you both nodded with great concern as the producer's steely gaze scoured the landscape. Next you went to the family of seven living one on top the other in a single tent and had the camera zoom in on a picture of their abandoned home, which the father kept in his wallet. You nabbed a shot of barefoot little girls playing catch with a rock, plus another of you, Jim, catching one of their throws, which you redid a couple times to get it right. There was a man with a fungus, a mother red-eyed from sobbing, two dogs fighting over a black bone. You interviewed the geriatrics with sallow skin about the quality of the food and asked the ones shivering the most how they felt about the cold. All the while a bevy of helpless soldiers looked on in frustration. A garrulous Croat with three teeth you let rant for minutes about what had happened with the fires, an indulgence that led others in the roving audience to ask for their own turns: *Jim, Jean, please, speak to me next, I have something to say too...* but the hawkish man would tell them to hush and not to mess with the audio. For the last shot, deep into the tent hive by now, you each held a baby in your arms, one black and one white, and cooed to them softly. "Follow us tomorrow as we continue our climb up the Mount and attempt to sit down with some of the men behind the operation," you said, then returned the babies. Seeing nothing else, you headed back to the field where you'd landed while signing autographs along the way. At the helicopter, you entered in the reverse order in which you'd exited, and the pilot took off at a steady enough pace for the cameraman to get a good shot of the field below, where all our heads were turned upward watching you depart like a chariot across the sky. And to even think it hadn't been forty minutes since the buzz of your arrival first sounded in our ears...

That night we could build as many fires as we wanted; in fact, the soldiers almost *encouraged* it. They were very friendly all of a sudden, and busy, too, a constant stream of them going up and down the hill trying to help anyone who needed it right away. They tidied the tarpaulin markets and adjusted sagging tents to stand more erect. As best as they could, they were neatening up the place, except now they were having to deal with a freshly cantankerous population that seemed to have smelled blood. *Man* were people getting uncooperative. The new thing they were doing was turning off the shake lanterns so that none of the soldiers could see who was throwing the little stones hitting the backs of their heads. That, plus some ruffians were going through the tents scattering garbage to make things worse, for tomorrow's cameras to see the truth. I wasn't nearby for this, but you didn't have to be to hear it anyway: the sound of a rifle finally going off *pow pow* two times. That one made our heads snap up quicker than a rabbit's at a hawk's cry, and caused me to mess up the bald fade on a teenager whose hair I'd been cutting. Rumor soon had it that they were only warning shots, fired in the air. But a while after that four soldiers came to see Peter Napakakos at the cul-de-sac. If they were the same four as those I'd seen on the first night, I couldn't be sure, but one of them was the nasal-voiced official whom they called Corporal. "Per*haps* there's somewhere *priv*ate we can *speak?*" he said from where he was received by Napakakos at the gym of rock bags. Napakakos's bruises from his recent beating had taken on darker hues, like spots, and he still hadn't done much since besides make up new songs for the accordion. But the look of mirth with which he surveyed life's happenings had not budged, and he rose from amongst the others without ceremony. "Right this way," he told him. The two of them entered his tent. A dozen minutes went by, then Corporal left.

I found out what that was only much later, probably after midnight if there had been any clocks. I wouldn't have discovered it at *all* had I not been awoken by a tremendous fart from Paramount that shook me out of slumber. I gasped awake, looking about. There Paramount was, still asleep. I swear, that man, there was for sure something wrong with his intestines. He farted about as much as a regular person snored, except louder. Everyone's diet was tuna, but with him it was as if a whole fish had died in his guts. I needed to breathe. Putting on my shoes, I stepped outside.

It was a thick, primordial night through which the crickets were screaming. The camp was still peppered with scattered commotions. But the cul-de-sac was strangely empty, even of the insomniac Kid Vicious, who was always doing push-ups. I saw a glow of shadows lining the inside of Napakakos's tent. I couldn't count, but there had to be *at least* eight people in there, sitting on their haunches, by the looks of it. Well, I crept on over, on tiptoes, toward the backside. From there, close to the maze should I have to dart off, I listened in on what was happening. Uglygod was in the middle of saying something:

"... them fucks, how many times we heard the like? North, they say. West, they say. Watch them go east and we're dumped in the ocean."

"Remember what happened with Racks and them," came Monsoon's voice.

"Racks and them it was the cops," said Napakakos.

"Same difference," said Uglygod.

"Soldiers and cops not the same."

"Yeh?" said Monsoon. "Explain the difference for me then."
No one answered.

"No need to get semantical about it," Uglygod went on.
"My point's made, you don't step into a snake's mouth because
it says it's got its teeth pulled. We keep waiting it out."

"Soldiers was how we came here, Ug." It was a voice I didn't
know well enough to tell for sure whose it was, either Tank's
or Two Piece's.

"I came here between a woman's legs and it's the way I'm
going out. Not in a silly trap."

"Yeh, you're a real motherfucker, aren't you, Ug?"

"Ha!"

"We always knew it was something, huh, Ug?"

"Someone's got to father you senseless fucks."

"Ha ha!"

The light flickered out. I got nervous they'd come outside
for a new one, so primed myself to run, but next there was the
sound of the lantern inside getting shaken and a minute later
it turned back on, though the light was weaker.

"Boss, I'm with Ug," Monsoon added. "It's the reasoning
I can't get with. It's a good thing we have going here, a cornered market. How often you come by a cornered market? Not
often. I'm no idiot, I know it's not going to last forever. But
that's all the more reason to stay to the end. We have the tuna,
we have the barber, it's our own economy. I'm no idiot, Boss."

"I see what you're saying there, Monsoon. Fiscal theory is
what you're talking about"—now it was Roger J speaking,
geez it was like everyone had been invited to this meeting but

me—"believe it or not I know some things about fiscal theory, I used to do a bit of reading when I helped run that book-store. What you're referencing is actually a textbook case of monopolistic—"

"Shut it, Roger J!" everyone said.

He shut up.

"It's just the *reasoning* I can't get with, Boss," repeated Monsoon.

"What you mean, the reasoning?" Siren now, of that I was certain. "We got the reasoning already."

"He's saying it doesn't make any damn sense," said Uglygod.

"Requires some reading between the lines is all," said Napakakos.

"What's it say between the lines then?"

"Says that bad behavior pays."

They laughed in their bovine way.

"You saw how it was today," continued Napakakos, "and that was without warning. When the crew returns tomorrow, people will be ready for them. It's happening already. Corporal knows we could make it real nasty around here if we wanted."

"So we stay and make it nasty then."

"For what? It'll only be for spite."

"Spite's good enough."

"Only sometimes," said Napakakos.

"Boss," said Uglygod, "what would we be going back to? Do we know? Last I saw of my block it was an aquarium. I'm no shark, Boss. Not like that, if you get my drift."

"Yes, you're a real comedian, Ug. He said that information will be provided for us."

"That information will be *provided* for us! Am I the only one hearing this? Siren, you can't be taking this seriously. Tell me that me and Monsoon aren't the only ones hearing this."

I'd figured out which shadow was Siren's, the one closest to me, and he seemed right then to have settled into the stillness of thinking. Uglygod's intensity was causing him to reconsider.

"It may be a ride straight to a cell," said Uglygod. "They can cook up charges along the way then say anything they want. What kind of fools are we? This is what happened to Racks and them boys and now look at them. Food through a tube! I'm no vegetable, Boss. We're supposed to walk into their lair and *then* they give us information?"

"That part is a little suspicious," Siren finally said. Uglygod was gaining ground.

"It's a good thing we have here, Boss. We can leave with the rest of everyone when the water's gone."

The flow of talk broke down for a bit as a chorus of low rabbling took its place. Smaller discussions were happening around the circle. They all quieted at the same time, probably at a signal from Napakakos. A small pause ensued.

Finally Tank or Two Piece asked, "What've you been feeding that thing anyway, Boss?"

"Worms."

"That's its diet?"

"Oh yeh, for sure, you've got a scoop-finned snapping turtle on your hands right there, or as we like to call it in the scientific community *Chelydra serpe—*"

"Alright, Roger J."

They were quiet again. The gnats biting my ankles were a mighty annoyance, but I didn't dare move an inch.

I heard some rustling. The angle of the shadows changed as the lantern must have been moved.

"I ever told y'all the one about the yogi?"

Uglygod groaned. "No, Boss. Why don't you tell us the one about the yogi then."

"So there's this great yogi, he's known all about." (Napakakos launched into the story straightaway.) "People come from everywhere to see him and they bring gifts of fruit too. This is in one of those old countries. Long, long ago. They ask the yogi things like the right time to copulate, how to wage wars, those kinds of things. Advice. One day a merchant comes to him with a problem concerning his daughter. Our merchant here plies a decent trade in preserved fruits despite their village being cut off by mountains. He's had to ride days just to get here. He explains to the yogi that a traveling king will be touring his way through the land and is to make an unexpected stop in their difficult village. All the noblemen will be presenting their daughters in a line for the king to pick from. Now, it's well known in the village by then that our merchant has a very beautiful daughter, and it has occurred to him that—"

"How beautiful are we talking here?" interrupted Monsoon.

"The most beautiful," chimed in Siren.

"How do *you* know? You never heard this one," Monsoon said.

"The daughter's *always* the most beautiful in these kinds of stories, you dope. Or else it's no point telling them."

"You don't *know*, though."

"He's right, Monsoon," said Two Piece or Tank. "Daughter's gotta be the most beautiful or else merchant's not going all that way. Boss, just tell him already."

"She was the most beautiful."

Monsoon settled into a disagreeable grumble and said, "Whatever, keep going."

"So what's the merchant's problem?" continued Peter Napakakos. "Merchant's problem is that the king who'll be coming through is only a minor king, without great riches, and our merchant only has the one daughter. I mean, what kind of a waste would it be to use up your one daughter on a minor king, you know? Who doesn't even have an army. This kid's his ticket, he's thinking. So he comes to the yogi and explains as much, wants to know what to do. Well, the yogi says to him, 'All that comes, comes again.' I want you to remember that. Yogi's been living on this same hill since he was a boy and he's never been wrong, he's been gifted from the start. The merchant understands. He knows there are plans to build a road connecting their village to the rest of the world. Soon there'll be all kinds of kings making their way through, serious ones, with armies galore. His daughter was a young wine that would only flourish over time. So he departs, leaving a gift of plums, and when the minor king comes to town some weeks later our merchant keeps his daughter hidden inside wearing long cloths and the king picks the child of a herder, a faint, demure girl known for the quality of her weaving. That's that.

"Anyhow, for the following years sandstorms battered the region and the road was never built. That daughter grew up to become a great burden upon the merchant's house, driving him almost to ruin with her expensive taste for dates and imported perfumes. Raised on delusions of a distant king coming over the mountain to marry her any day now, she rebuffed the local boys with terrible insults and bullied the girls into playing maidens of her court. Her beauty hardened into something harsh and impenetrable, like an armor, and no one who saw her remembered any longer the lithe nymphette who'd so frustrated the dreams of many a good husband. Finally she ran off, with a wandering musician playing the lute, leaving in her place a mark of shame upon the merchant's name that never faded. By then the yogi had died from choking on a seed and vengeance could not be exacted. You see, he'd been wrong. Sometimes things happen once. Everyone pack your fucking bags. We're going home."

The discussion was over. There was a bit of a tail end for others to explain to Monsoon what the story had meant, since he didn't get it, but for the most part it was over. He wasn't too bright, Monsoon. I didn't want to be there when they started to leave the tent for real, so I scampered back to Paramount's tent quick-quick and slipped inside that nasty furnace to return to my sleeping bag and close my eyes. He was still farting away. Lying like that, I could barely hear the soft movements of the giants as they first exited Napakakos's tent, then spread through the cul-de-sac to gather their things. I didn't even know why my eyes were closed, as if there were someone there to witness my act. I kept straining my ears to hear what exactly was happening, but with the noise of the crickets it was hard. And the giants were being very quiet. Every now and then would the wan glow of a lantern light waft along the tent wall like a subdued firefly. Something was making my heart beat hot. All of a sudden Paramount stopped his farting, as if awoken by an alarm, and I felt him shift his great bulk to first rise out of the sleeping bags (he had two of them stitched together with fishing nylon), rustle about, then leave the tent. When I opened my eyes, I saw he'd taken all his bags too. Oh wow. Well, I lay down like that, eyes fully open now that there was really no use pretending, waiting for something to happen I didn't know what. At one point I heard Uglygod launch into a complaint, only to be quieted at once by a wave of *shhh*s. Suddenly I was rising to my feet again. There was my heart, churning like a forge. Those bastards—they were really leaving. Shed of all pretenses, I stepped back into the night and marched right through the center of the cul-de-sac, past the various tents, past the makeshift gym Pewter and Hot Head were taking apart, across the blue tarpaulin where my barbershop chair still stood, through the wide mass of them walking this-way and that-way (shocked to see me, like I was something unplanned), and back to Napakakos's tent, the front this time, where I lifted the flap and stepped right in. "Napakakos," I said. "We need to talk."

It was my first time in there; the tent was empty save for the accordion, a dog bowl, and a worn hiker's bag into which Peter Napakakos was packing some last pieces of clothing. As I moved farther inside I saw that the turtle was in the dog bowl flipping about in an inch of water.

"Yes, Slide?"

"So you all are leaving, I see."

"Corporal would rather we were not here for the cameras tomorrow. I tend to agree."

"Back to Petit Julienne, I suppose?"

"That's the arrangement."

"Oh, alright, of course. I bet it is. I bet it really is."

I was running out of purpose already. I had my hands on my hips but that was about it.

"I bet you have a whole lot of things to get back to as well," I said, just to say something.

"There's business to attend to, yes. Have you ever been up that way?"

"No, I haven't."

"I didn't think so."

He was having to move about in more of a hunch given the tent's low ceiling, which together with his size gave him the air of a minotaur. Oh gosh was I angry.

"Well, what's been the whole *point* then, Napakakos, huh!" I yelled. "Of me cutting everyone's hair? What's the point if when it comes down to it you're all just going to leave like it's nothing?"

"Would you like to come then, Slide?"

"That's not what I'm saying!"

"You can also stay here."

"I know I can stay here, no one has to tell me that. You aren't even listening to what I'm saying."

He zipped one of the bag's compartments. "Explain to me then."

"Look it. I've made myself very valuable and there should be room for me, too, in Petit Julienne when you get there. It's no charity, you understand? I've helped out here even if it's only small. Yes, I'm coming. I can't go back to where I left. And I'm useful, is the point."

"Yes, you have been useful." He tested the bag's weight. "And if I say you can't come?"

"Fine. Do that then. Even that's better because it'll be something to argue about. Geez you gotta at least give a guy a chance to *argue*. You leave in the middle of the night and it's like it wasn't even anything. What are you, a bunch of shadows? You never heard of loyalty? *Geeez-uuus...*"

He was zipping up the remaining compartments now. Pleased with the job, he hoisted the bag over his shoulder and readied to go. "Coming with us is going to mean something different than you think it does."

"Oh man have I heard that before," I said. "You wouldn't believe, Peter, but I've definitely heard stuff like that before. I'm not asking for a whole bunch. I need somewhere to stay until I find my own place, and I'm sure there are barbershops around there too. That's it. It's not a whole bunch."

The only thing left was for him to pick up the turtle, which he tucked into one of the pockets of his tracksuit. His expression sank into an arrangement that was at once ponderous and, as always, amused, as if the punch line to a joke was escaping him. He put the accordion around his neck and fingered the usual keys. Then he said: "Consider this your invitation to come. You are welcome with us."

Ay, what a *relief*! I kept my straight face going, though. You don't want to give up leverage too early when you're bargaining.

"And somewhere to stay too," I said.

"Something can be worked out," said Peter Napakakos.

"What's that mean?"

"It means something can be worked out."

"Alright then."

I wasn't going to push it anymore. The tent was now bare but for the accordion's sounds. The giants outside were making more of a commotion since it was almost time. I turned to exit at the flap. But he had one more thing to say as my foot crossed the threshold:

"Oh, and Slide."

"Yeh?"

"Did you like the one about the yogi?"

Oh wow.

"Yes, I did," I said.

*   *   *

That was about the fastest I've ever packed. Faster than the rush following Eustace's assault, faster than the tremble of fear following dire warnings from Rosa de Sanville. Faster even than the awful sadness when I had left behind that old man, stupefied and raging, in that crumbling room where he'd lost everything. I packed the usual, plus the battery, which I wasn't even sure if I would need. I brought my suitcase to the clearing and waited with everyone as Uglygod took his sweet time muttering and piling a mound of bags onto his shoulders. "One second, one second," he kept on saying when they told him to hurry up. His last delay was in taking his jar with the scorpion to the edge of the trees and unscrewing the lid, freeing it. Randoms from other tents had caught on that the Dread Merchants were leaving and they wanted to know why, or at least how. They were creeping around the edges going, *What gives?*, *How's that?*, but Napakakos waved them off and told everyone not to answer. "Let's go," he said once Uglygod was ready. Like a team of mules we set off uphill, through that squalid camp in which the last traces of order were fading. All who saw us wanted to know more and some even took to following. Along the way Roger J caught up with us, carrying a bundle on a stick, and said thanks for passing by his tent. Napakakos grunted. Then we were back at the top of the hill and in Section E. This time, only we were allowed through the phalanx of soldiers lining the edge, the agitated mob behind us barred from following. *Napakakos*, they were saying, *where are you all going?*, Now *is when you would leave?*, *What's this, huh, special treatment...?* There was even a stone thrown, but Kid Vicious grabbed it out of the air and launched it right back into the crowd, which erupted in screams. Corporal and a small team met us on the other side. "Is this everyone?" "Yes."

"I thought there were more of you." "We have that effect." "Alright, Napakakos." Waiting on the roof of the Hikers' Lodge was a long green helicopter with two propellers. We had to hand our bags up to the soldiers on top, then climb a ladder. Uglygod didn't like that part at all. It was funny watching him try to climb with all his bags on, swatting away help. In the end two soldiers had to support the ladder at its base just so it didn't bend while he ascended it. On top of the roof we loaded ourselves into the helicopter through its lowered back flap, sitting strapped along the sides on metal foldout seats, our bags in trapdoor lockers under our feet. It was so big in there that all of us plus Corporal and an aide could fit with seats left over. I was near the front, between Peter Napakakos and Uglygod, facing Corporal. Corporal knocked on the glass pane separating us from the pilot's cockpit and gave her a signal to start it up. The blades got going with a steady purr and—slowly then suddenly—we wobbled into the air as if upon surging waves. But the flap door was still open! Oh man, it was really something. We were going higher and higher as the camp underneath shrank to white triangles. Here was the frustrated mob moving about like a swarm, there were the fires now burning without constraint. With a lurch we started moving laterally over the slope of the mountain and the black forest I had once trekked through. I saw that there was in fact a *series* of plateaus all along the way, and if I had only known, I would have had an easier time getting up. That's how it goes. The view was trees, trees, and more trees before ending abruptly in a street, Polis then spreading out below like a silent kingdom, still in total darkness. The buildings stood like imperious tombstones in a darkened graveyard for titans. But as we picked up speed something truly amazing happened. We were high like that, in the air, you know, when in a unified blaze the lights down below flashed back on. Oh man! It happened like *that*, instantly so bright I thought a great bomb had gone off. Our resulting gasps were loud enough to hear over the roar of the propellers. The grid of streets had come back alive in shining squares, brilliant and luminescent in a way I had forgotten. How long had it even been? "Looks like them boys over at ANC got their shit together," Corporal yelled to the pilot. The way he'd spoken sounded so familiar. I shouted and asked him if he knew Lieutenant Chesney. "Who?" he stuck a finger into his ear and said. "Chesney!" I yelled. "He was in the military! Lives on Joserman Street now!" "Don't know him," said Corporal, returning to the view. It was a beautiful view. I've never been that high up since. Throughout it all, only Uglygod remained inconsolable. The farther we flew, the deeper his face sank into a pout. From my other side Peter Napakakos reached across to punch him on the knee. "Snap out of it," he hollered. Uglygod righted himself. "Sorry, Boss," he said. "It's just, you get used to a place, you know?"

PETIT JULIENNE

(in which hope spreads its wings, an old foe
is thwarted, and—on a night gone sour—
a runny mouth sets the end in motion)

Something was worked out. That was to be the season of my great enterprising, of which the time on the mountain would prove but a harbinger of things to come. Nowadays, when I think of these months, it's still not without a warm touch in the heart, even with the way things ended up. Whatever. It's not supposed to always be sad, looking back on happy times, or else what was the point, even? Sometimes it can just be about the time. That's what remembering is really about, if you ask me: not just recalling the past, but forgetting the future too. Besides, it's not like there was anyone around to warn me when the soldiers first dropped us off.

Peter Napakakos Has Something to Show

They flew us to another park, this one a small square in the middle of Petit Julienne, a place I had never been. We unloaded and the giants looked around with the weariness of vacationers returning from a long sojourn. It wasn't some flooded-out ghost town like I'd been expecting. In fact there were people around to see us land, waving from the stacks of balconies on which plant pots had shattered in the helicopter's wind, or else holding on to their hats as we hovered over the ground. Unloading the bags was a brisk affair conducted without sentiment, after which Corporal gave Napakakos a curt nod, climbed back into the helicopter, and was off. When the last of its noise faded, the invisible thread binding our group together seemed to snap. We were in a wet square of grass with a rusty playground, surrounded by rubbernecking onlookers and alleys too narrow for cars. The streetlights were working again and gave off a harsh glare to which our eyes were not yet accustomed. Suddenly everyone was saying, Okay, I'm going this way, gotta check in on so-and-so, I'll see you all around, I'm sure, or Well, that was some trip, I'll never forget it, someone give me a hand lugging this over to Earltop Street, it's quite a walk... Half of them were gone in such a hurry you would've thought they had *appointments* or something, and when I saw I was in danger of getting left behind with nothing to do but spin on the merry-go-round, I was saying to them, "Wait, what about me? I'm coming with you just like we discussed..." "Sure, Barber, that's no problem, you can stick with Paramount over that way, he has the most space..." And I thought, Oh no! Not this again...

But it wasn't that long. Two weeks into my stay, Napakakos showed up in a bomber jacket and red scarf, to see me, primarily, though he took some minutes to check in on how Paramount was doing too. They hung in the narrow garden behind the unit and discussed what he was planting to replace the begonias ravaged by the storm, toeing the spongy soil with their boots. As things would have it, it had rained a little that morning, too, though not in any ridiculous way. Now with the drizzle over, the sun had come out to offer a clear, tepid light in which the garden shimmered. Paramount tottered back into the kitchen, from which I'd been watching. "Boss wants you," he said, holding the screen door open as I squeezed by.

"You've been surviving?" Napakakos asked me once I was outside.

I told him yes.

"And with Paramount, things are okay?"

I thought of the converted room where I was sleeping on a foldout couch, the window I had to keep open for fresh air, even if it was cold.

"Yes, it's okay," I said.

He swung open the back gate leading to the alleyways.

"Come. Let me show you something."

In that intervening fortnight I had watched the environs slowly come back to life as the last of the waters drained. Day by day, evacuees who'd been held up elsewhere returned to Petit Julienne on foot and saw to the work that was to be done. During my walks through the alleyways I would pass them, moving tenderly amongst the destruction like archaeologists overturning ruins. Some, seeing nothing to salvage in the ransacked shops, the low-floor apartments crammed with debris, gave the place up for dead and departed in a salty stream of tears, as if the trip back had been for nothing more than to close one of life's chapters. Those who decided to rebuild got started right away. All about, wherever you went, people were hammering, sawing, lifting, drilling, carrying, throwing, discarding, recycling, remaking the order of their neighborhoods one nail at a time. The place felt like one continuous work site, I swear. It was all I could do to keep from getting in the *way* in such tight confines, and sometimes if I came upon a huff-puffing crew of laborers hard at it, I might even try helping, as happened with a team of Korean men I saw installing a tin roof under the supervision of a sparsely bearded foreman with expressive hands. Joining their relay line, passing sheets of corrugated metal, I'd helped toss two-three sheets from one side to the other before I noticed they didn't seem too pleased about it. No one said anything, but when they decided to take a break all at the same time, I figured it was because of me, and as I walked away I caught on that *every*one around there was Korean. Oh man, I don't like to assume things about people but I'm no dope either. I went on my way and a few turns later everyone around *there* was Hungarian, just like that. There wasn't even a sign or anything. After that a couple Sicilian streets gave way to the blocks where the Romanian Hasids lived, followed by the Turks, the Sufis, the Polynesians, each of them lending me peculiar stares if it looked like I was doing anything more than passing through. I'm not going to lie: it was a little uncomfortable. But (as I was to find out) that is how it *was* in Petit Julienne, a dense sprawl of misshapen neighborhoods squeezed one next to the other like the pieces of a jigsaw puzzle. It was the part of Polis that was doomed to tension from the start, long ago, when settlers from the six corners of the world arrived and each made a claim of having been the first. The surrounding roads today being narrow, winding, and full of dead ends, much of the area could only be accessed on foot, through the labyrinth of pathways squeezed between buildings, and at any given turn you might end up amongst the Cameroonians here, the Scots over there, a white-painted patch of electronics stores run by the Cypriots where I took my phone for repairs since it hadn't been turning on after the flood. If any of the streets had names, it was just for fun, and oftentimes the divisions marking one territory from the next were invisible or made of quiet understandings, such as the times of day to not be around so-and-so if you couldn't speak Portuguese, or a clothesline of red socks signaling where the Serb homes ended and the Croat ones began. You really wouldn't know unless you knew. Napakakos and the others stuck to a neighborhood called Little Levant, one of the larger ones given how many kinds of people it had to contain, and they were something of the de facto dons within its expanse. As a matter of fact, that was another thing: you could just as easily identify a neighborhood by its corresponding gang. Sometimes it was easier.

"Look it, Barber," Uglygod told me, "it's time you learn your uniforms, alright? You see anyone wearing green bandannas, then you get out of there, that's the Locoperros. Those boys are Venezuelan, true savages, they'll cut your head off and forget that they did. You let us handle them if ever it's anything. Up that way it's the Valhallans, you'll see them around the theater. Stupid name if you ask me but don't tell them that to their face. They're descended from Vikings and they take it seriously. You follow? Alright, sometimes you may see some pygmy-looking motherfuckers with birds on their shoulders. Pay attention now: if they're parrots, then you're alright, that's the New Jackals and we have an understanding. But if they're canaries then you're looking at the Windbreakers and we don't get down with them. Head of their outfit is a chick called Thorn, big dyke bitch, slaughtered her way to the top—you wouldn't have heard about it in the news. The news doesn't come up here. Any suit-wearing fucks you hear talking German is definitely in Six Bricks. Want to know why they're called that? Well, so would about a half dozen ghosts who don't know what hit them. You getting my point? I know you ran into some crews in Middleton or wherever, but you might as well forget about that. Those are the junior leagues. You find yourself in a bad spot out here and you'll lose a lot more than your shoes. Don't let me hear any more complaints about you, alright?"

"Alright, Ug, no more mistakes, that's my word, cross my soul and hope to die."

We were in the hookah lounge Uglygod managed, in his office where the bass from downstairs thumped through the floor. He'd summoned me to talk after hearing from the boss of the Kaitons (the same expressive-handed Korean, a man named Purple, whom I'd mistaken for a foreman) that I was nosing around in business where I didn't belong. Exhaling the big puff of smoke he'd been holding in from his last pull on the hookah pipe next to him, he squinted at me as if finally zooming in for a proper look. It was our first time hanging together, just me and him.

"Where you from anyway, kid?" he asked, and as I got going saying, "Oh *man*, Ug, is *that* ever a long story, geez, well, okay, hmm, I guess the first thing you need to know about is this brain disease I contracted a couple years back, and when I awoke from the coma I could hardly—" he held up a hand. "You know what? Can it. I don't really care that much…"

That hookah lounge was one of two base camps from which the Dread Merchants administrated their dealings, along with a heavy-duty gym on the third floor of a rickety tower on Ezekiah Lane. Whether by coincidence or convenience, no one lived too far from the gym. Siren, for example, he was right next to it, in a two-bedroom he shared with his woman, who had waited out the storm at a friend's place farther downtown. As it turned out, a *lot* of them had women who'd waited out the storm at friends' places farther downtown, and who greeted the giants' collective return with varying degrees of apathy. Even Paramount was involved with a petite Argentine who reached his hip, and who had nagged her way into his heart.

"Who's this?" she asked when she first saw me on the couch.

"Boss says he's staying here for a bit," said Paramount.

She shook her head after dropping her bags. "Boss says, Boss says, Boss says. That's all I ever hear from all of you."

Paramount munched another forkful of kidney beans, his regular diet if there were things other than tuna available.

"What's this noise?" the woman said, looking out the window. "A little bit of rain and now everyone thinks they're in construction. They'll be at it for weeks, I'm sure. Honey, did you put the baking soda in the fridge? You know it's going to mold in there if you don't. Here's what too: we need to take these rugs out to air, I'm feeling they're still damp. Honey, why don't you get up and make things neater or is that your plan for the rest of the day? And tell your little friend he's not here for decoration either..."

Her flittering hands, her pale skin, her habit of hovering in Paramount's general vicinity, to which he was seemingly indifferent, brought to mind a heron on the back of a wildebeest, and the intensity of their strange reliance on each other was matched only by how suddenly they would need a reprieve. In the midst of one of her complaints ("Honey, what do you want to do with this fan? Throw it out, I suppose, you are always wasting things..."), Paramount would rise with the determination of a private decision and trudge out the front door, saying only that he was needed at one of the sites and would be back later. She'd spend the hours he was gone chatting on the phone with the others—Monsoon's wife, some nine years his senior; Tank's mistress, whose face was tattooed on his chest; a Turkish vamp named Yasmin, on whom Blood Tooth spent lavishly—trading complaints, laughing, and hanging up only when Paramount invariably returned with a look of resignation and a chocolate bonbon that she would tuck into the top of her bra, as if adding to a collection. Geez, they were bound up in a bad way, that's no kidding. People are strange. But it wasn't fully a lie what Paramount had said either: with so much damage to fix up, Napakakos and his giants were making themselves some quick dollars around the neighborhood. Soon it seemed there was hardly a lot in Little Levant where some strongman in a tracksuit wasn't carting wheelbarrows of debris to-and-from a dump, smashing down broken walls with a sledgehammer, reshingling the roofs of low buildings. It was to one such site that Peter Napakakos had led me by the end of our walk.

We were in an arms-wide alley of crumbling buildings, a number of Arabs selling grilled meats from pits out front while their stores were being fixed. The children running about beneath the crisscrossed lines of drying clothes stopped their games of tag to point out Napakakos (with a bit of awe) and imitate his walk. One of the buildings was a shoddy, nondescript stack of two floors, framed by thin lanes of garbage cans, and from which the chirping of many birds sounded from the second floor. We descended its exterior set of stairs to a basement unit with no pane in the frame of the sliding door and stepped through.

"What do you think?" Napakakos asked me.

I looked around. An assortment of senseless jetsam cluttered the floor—soggy leaves, plastic wrappers, rags, sneakers, sheets of old newspaper, shattered ceramics, a ruined yellow rug, empty drawers, mounds of silt in the corners. Every step I took into that dim room of low ceilings was met with the crunch of glass shards. On the walls were the traces of a mural depicting a family of rabbits having a picnic, the colors faded. There were small cubbyholes on one side, little tables turned over, and on the far end some posters with silly rhymes teaching basic manners.

"Looks like some sort of day care," I told Napakakos. He nodded yes. "Gosh," I said, "so people were really dropping their kids off in some basement? I mean, there's hardly any *sunlight* in here. What, they'd just have fluorescent lights to last them all day?"

I was seriously shaking my head. You keep kids away from sunlight all day and they're liable to turn into creeps, I've seen it happen.

"Will that be a problem for you?" asked Napakakos.

I didn't quite get his drift. For *me?* I made my eyebrows say. He pounded the wall with his fist and continued: "We're thinking of making this your shop. Two chairs, maybe three. It's a busy street and the traffic will be good. You can keep on with what you started at the camp."

What... Oh *man*! Oh *wow*! I wasn't believing what I was hearing. Right at once my heart had picked up its pace and the rush of blood was making my head tingle. Suddenly I was seeing the place with fresh eyes, where just a second ago it had been a washed-up dump. There could be a bookshelf here, a red couch there... but I couldn't get carried away.

"Interesting," I said.

Putting on a look that I was mulling something over, I hit Napakakos with a couple technical questions, what about renovations, is there a lease, what will the split be like, how long of a timeline are we talking here, things of that nature. I was thinking back to how foolishly excited I'd gotten at Osman the Throned's last viewing and didn't want to be a dupe again.

"I don't want there to be any surprises here," Napakakos answered. "You take this offer and you will be indebted to us, at least until you break even. I have seen such situations end poorly before, it's no use pretending. But there'll be no tricks. We get half of what comes in. Upkeep, maintenance, hiring a second barber, that all comes out of your half. Advertising too. Gallon will do your bookkeeping. Does this sound like something you want to do?"

"The place is yours already?" I asked.

"Don't worry about that part," he said.

I stepped that much farther across the leaves and muttered some numbers under my breath. Then I couldn't help it: I ended up smiling.

"Oh, what the heck, Napakakos! I know better than to bite a gift horse's hand. We have a deal!"

I could see he wanted to smile too. "Yes. It's something like that," he said.

CUTS SUPREME

November finally sped up and I'd taken out a new lease on life. In the mornings I rose early, dressed in warm, functional clothes to make the winding walk over to the basement and help with the work at hand. Napakakos had assigned a half dozen of his guys to do the renovations, and day by day we were clearing out the debris, stripping the walls, knocking out the old counters. Those six were all new to me, none of them having made the journey to Millennium Mount, a bit on the younger side and still on their way up the ranks. Shift, One Speed, Reverse, Crash, Backfire, Horsepower— they all had names like that. In addition to them there was oftentimes the older gentleman Gallon, who Peter Napakakos mentioned would be doing the books when the shop was all done but was the project foreman in the meantime. A squat man of Lebanese decent—with a thick black mustache on an otherwise shaved face, hairy arms, bowed legs, and an unflappable practicality—he was a bit of a figurehead amongst the giants, having overseen the daily running of the territory during Napakakos's absence. Perhaps he'd been a big muscle-head in his day as well, but now he carried the stately weight of a contented veteran. That man, I'm not kidding, he was incredibly handy. Gallon was the one to help me deliberate between swatches of paint for the walls and ceiling, as well as determine what I thought my electrical needs might be. When some of us kept getting in each other's way in the small confines, Gallon was the one to organize our workstations into a more harmonious arrangement, techniques learned from his days constructing the subway lines. The building's second floor, from which I'd heard all the chirping, turned out to belong to a bird-collecting widow with a real sad past, so Gallon made sure some of us went upstairs to wish her good morning in that tiny apartment where parrots with clipped wings walked all day amongst candlelit shrines to her departed husbands. He even recommended a second barber for me to hire: a distant cousin of his named Rufus who had run into some hard times. "He's a decent boy. A little on the slow side but he cuts alright. If you don't like him, tell him no deal. No one's promised him anything," he said during a lemonade break. Well, I liked the sound of that! I didn't want some hotshot coming in there and making me look like a chump again like with Rex and Reginald. In fact, to be truly sure, I started studying my book of haircuts to finally expand my repertoire. It was a beat-up edition I'd had on me forever, with step-by-step diagrams of various difficult cuts. I'd never really read it before. Now, though, come lunchtime, when the group of us made the walk over to Mummy Sylvia's—a family establishment in the West Indian part of town that served stewed meats on red-checkered tablecloths (the crew around there was known as the Bad Johns, they dressed in camouflage and held dogfights, Napakakos and them were on good terms)—I'd have the book open the whole time, angling my head away from spilling gravy on its pages. "Oy, Barber is really taking this seriously, is he not," the guys would say. "Look look, you would think he had a barber exam coming up, someone ask him a question and see if he can answer…!" Barber: that's what people were calling me. They were some real kidders, those guys. They'd heard all about what I'd done on the mountain and loved bringing it up. Me I liked them a lot. They never let me pay for lunch, saying instead they wanted free haircuts when the shop was open, and that I should put in a good word for them with Napakakos. They must've thought I was someone important. "I'll see what I can do," I liked to say, flashing winks. That cracked them up. Just about everything I did cracked them up. Back in the basement, the strength of good food had me fit and spry, lifting heavier things than I'd ever imagined. I felt new muscles in my back and my chest, in the length of my legs and the pockets of my neck, burning with purpose. In the early dark of those afternoons I'd leave in the very best of moods, covered in dust and dried sweat, taking deep swallows of the cold air on my way to wherever I was sleeping next…

The Paramount situation couldn't work out for long because his habits at sea level were even nastier than on the mountain. He had a small toilet that he guarded jealously and didn't like when I used, plus would lay damp, dirty clothes on top the radiator to stink up the entire place. That's how I came to find out that the Argentine didn't have a sense of smell, an oddity stemming back to complications during her premature birth. Geez, if anybody was ever going to love Paramount then it was definitely somebody without a sense of smell, that's for sure. I complained to Napakakos about the whole thing and it was decided I'd stay at Monsoon's place instead, it wasn't too much of a move. There I was responsible for making breakfast for Monsoon, his wife, and their two sons, earning my keep on the top bunk bed in the older one's room. He was a shy kid of nine, obsessed with squids, never looked you in the eyes. In school they were learning about plate tectonics and he told me all about it. But every morning while I was pouring them cereal Monsoon would ask him if I'd done any Funny Business over the night, right in front of everyone like I wasn't even there! "That man do any Funny Business to you?" he'd say, leaning into the kid's face and pointing at me. Gosh was that awkward. I mean, he always said no and everything, the kid did, but he'd *think* about it first. What he'd do was dig deeply in his nose as if the answer was inside, then eventually say: "No." The next morning, there Monsoon would be asking all over again. It was an uncomfortable five days before I got out of there too.

I stayed at Uglygod's for no more than a night given how loud the rock music was that he played at all hours; at Siren's for barely longer, because he had fierce dogs that followed me and growled; I even spent a week in the office of that third-floor gym where a bunch of them spent their days. The gym was a concrete garage with equipment salvaged from a cruise ship that sank in the Eastside Marina some years ago. Waking up there, I'd find five-six grunting giants already in the middle of their routines, screaming encouragement beneath awesome barbells. Returning later on was even worse—by early evening the gym was in full swing, with twenty more of them yelling and going at it. If I'd thought I was going to have peace of mind in there, I was clearly crazy. Even standing still for a few seconds would make someone think I was available to help: "My friend, Barber by the fountain, make yourself useful. Come hold my legs while I finish this set. I have a bet with Lantern to make it to twelve..."

Eventually Roger J put me onto a couple no-questions-asked-type lodgings, where as long as you slipped an envelope of cash through the mail slot of a nearby door, you wouldn't be bothered. I had my doubts right away but he kept hitting me with reassurances of this-person and that-person he knew who had stayed there no problem. "It's a sure thing, guy. Things like this don't get more sure, take what I'm telling you." He'd been popping by to check out the renovations whenever he was just-in-the-neighborhood to see if he could help, given all he knew about construction, of course. He wore his own tool belt and hard hat and kept his hands on his hips the whole time, nodding as if in approval. You should've heard him that first day: "Heard the good news. Pete called to tell me himself. You're going to do well here. You know I said to Pete, 'Pete, that barber guy's one guy to have faith in. Knew it as soon as we met. It's a good investment you're making here, Pete.' He couldn't help but agree." I hadn't seen him since the helicopter. He'd hang around for an hour or two, giving One Speed recommendations on how best to cut plywood, or occasionally unsheathing the hammer from his belt and tapping some spot on the floor for reasons none of us could determine...

Anyway. I went with him to check out the place. It was a two-story square building around a concrete courtyard in the part of Little Levant that was mostly Moroccan. A pretty blackwoman with a rattling cough showed us the available units, the most hospitable of which was a one-bedroom with a rod full of wire hangers running the length of the main room. The bathroom was a tight squeeze of shower-sink-toilet all pressed together. The bed was firm and clean. In the surrounding alleys there was a handful of affordable restaurants, a fish market on Sundays. It wasn't the best place I'd ever seen, and the eight hundred dollars I needed for the first four weeks I had to borrow from Napakakos, who added it to my expenses for the shop, but, on the Friday when I picked up a copy of the key and brought my things over, after I closed my door and lay my head down on that first cool night, my friends, there was no one else in there to make a single sound.

In my mind the shop was a vision. It would have a red leather couch waxed to perfection and vanity mirrors with golden lights. On one of the walls there'd be a mounted TV with action movies playing on a loop, plus four surround-sound speakers installed in the ceiling, Roger J having assured me of a bargain from a sound engineer he knew down on Rumbrew Street. I'd always thought the outdated stack of magazines found in every waiting room the worst kind of bore, so I started looking into fun board games people could play while seated on the red couch. I met Gallon's cousin Rufus, my potential co-barber, for an interview one afternoon, a ponytailed man of indeterminate youth, with the sad, handsome features of a down-on-his-luck prince. He was recovering from something, he wouldn't say what, that required him to chew a special kind of gum all day one piece after another. He also stuttered. But to manage it he spoke slowly, and with great paucity, which made what he said seemed well considered. "I have... that is to say... I have a n-n-number of years, beneath my belt... practi-practici-... learning, from cutting the hair of m-my brothers," he said, when I asked about his past experience. I decided to hire him. December had come beneath a cover of cold, cloudy skies, but me I couldn't have been sunnier. One by one we found all those shop furnishings I'd dreamed of, even the red couch, which Siren came across in the junkyard of a deaf retiree who collected paraphernalia from classic diners. I had bought a collection of new clippers and disinfectant sprays that I was already leaving at the shop now that most of the messy work was over. The walls had been renewed with coats of mauve paint, clean glass fitted into the sliding door, a layer of hardwood flooring snagged for free from one of the other renovations Napakakos was overseeing. The week before we were due to open, he came by the site himself to discuss two matters. The first was a gift, which he brought over with Uglygod's help: a pair of barber chairs. "You guys!" I said. They were a rich ultramarine, with chrome bases and armrests, smooth foot levers for lowering and raising the seat. The space on the floor for them had already been cleared of tools. I was the one to do the honors of drilling them into place through the hardwood while everyone cheered me on. "Looks good in here," grunted Uglygod, giving one of the chairs a spin. "We'll be making back our money after all." With those two in the room, the six underlings suddenly got quieter than

I'd ever seen them, with serious looks and a way of puffing out their chests when standing, as if the principal had walked into the classroom. To bring up the second matter, Napakakos unfolded from his pocket one of the flyers I'd been pasting around town, in the safe parts. CUTS SUPREME! it said. COME BY FOR OUR GRAND OPENING NEXT SATURDAY! 85 DEBRANDT WAY! $10 CUTS ALL DAY! REWARDS PROGRAM AVAILABLE! The particular one he held was light blue, but I'd done others in green and magenta as well. "Free cuts," he said. I asked him, "Come again?" "Free cuts on the first day. You take your time so it's not everybody that gets one, but it's more important we get people in here. Free cuts." He'd said it in the same tone each time, of correcting someone who'd mispronounced a word. I was thinking about it. Everyone's eyes were on me and I knew it was important how I answered. "I like your think-ing," I made sure to say first. "How about this: Free for the first thirty people? Otherwise there's no *urgency*, you know? We want them in here fast, of course…" The twinkle of mirth spread across his face. "We'll do that then," he said, and be-fore the day was over I was back at the printer getting new flyers made. To tell you the truth, I was even a little relieved. I hadn't realized how *tense* I'd been, worrying about all the kinds of haircuts I'd have to do. Now if the first ones were free, it would make it harder for people to complain if I screwed up. After all, it's like anyone who's been through life can tell you: you get what you pay for.

We opened to no disasters, on the Saturday morning of De-cember's first snow. A trail of red balloons led from the nearby alleyways to the shop, to match the red of the couch, which I'd arrived early to wax a final time. On the teeming Debrandt

Way, where the shops of the Tunisians sold succulent meats
and some auntie leaning out a window was always telling a
kid to slow down, we were the newest addition to that riot of
loud commerce. Rufus and I were waiting behind our chairs,
dressed in black shirts and pants, fun sneakers, and black
gloves too. The board games were laid out. The TV was on,
playing a kung fu kick-up about a man looking for vengeance.
It smelled of fresh paint, plus pine-scented air freshener. "It's
okay to be nervous," I told Rufus. "The important thing is not
to *panic*, okay? Panicking is a whole other thing altogether."
He was chewing his gum. Its *squish-squish-squish* was a metro-
nome counting down the seconds. Then, at nine o'clock, the
customers came. The first was a blackwoman with four teenage
boys, who each wanted cool new styles like what they'd seen
in this one music video. Well, we handled them right away,
without even a hiccup, giving it our best effort like Napakakos had said to do. On my little whiteboard affixed to the wall
I checked four boxes out of thirty. Already was there a griz-
zled, Greek-looking type waiting on the couch watching the
kung fu movie. For him it was something simple—he wanted
his beard neatened and his split ends groomed—and for the
old-timer after him it was just a buzz cut. Suddenly people
were coming. A grown woman with braces, chattering Ni-
gerians, cool kids with their faces in their phones. Everyone
who entered hung their coats on a row of convenient hooks to
the right of the doorway and dried the snow from their boots
on the rubber mat. They were holding up the flyers and saying, *Hello, now!*, *Good day to you!*, *This is Cuts Supreme, correct?*
"It is! It is! Come, try a board game while you wait!" The music was going. The motors of our clippers made a happy hum.
Rufus cut hair with the concentrated look of a man defusing a

bomb, and he always swept up around his station immediately
after. He was a little intense, and wasn't the best conversation-
alist, that I have to admit, but he did what people wanted and
responded right away if they had any adjustments. Me, all my
reading had paid off. It seemed that every tricky haircut I'd
spent a lifetime avoiding was suddenly required of me, and
I was stepping up to the challenge no-problem. All it took was
a little gumption. There sat in my chair another teenager who
wanted a spiderweb pattern centered at his crown; a slim, regal
man who required complicated tricks to disguise his bald spot;
a puffy-faced fellow with a crooked jaw that made it hard for
me to know how to angle his hairline. Check, check, check—
I was filling the boxes of those free cuts like it wasn't anything. Around lunch a couple joke-crackers stationed themselves on the end of the red couch, a wheezy guy and a tall
girl, who weren't there for haircuts but just to shoot the shit.
"Hey hey hey, tell me something, what they be teaching these
dudes in Villain School?" they said between laughs, as the
criminal mastermind on the TV was getting ready to push
the button. "How many villains done died from them long
speeches? They haven't updated the curriculum in Villain
School yet? Ha ha ha! Oh man, too much..." I couldn't believe
it! You don't really have a barbershop until you have a couple
shit-shooters who aren't there for the haircuts, it was crazy
I'd gotten mine so quickly. But a little after them there came
five serious Indian men whose arrival spread a hush through
the place. They wore chain-studded jackets and gloves in the
shape of claws. I knew who they were at once: the Q9s, from
up on Biskram Street by the firehouse. In fact, I'd seen one of
them scoping the work site from afar over the past few weeks,
as if planning a heist. "You the barber?" the head one asked

Rufus. Rufus swallowed his gum in a gulp and pointed to me. "That's me," I said. Gosh had it gotten quiet. The five customers on the couch weren't saying squat. "How many more you got?" asked another. I said, "This one on the chair, then three waiting. Names are on the board." They looked to the whiteboard, where people had added their names to a list. The closest amongst them wiped them all off with his clawed glove. "I'm not seeing anyone next." My *goodness* was it quiet, in, there. They moved farther into the room and broadened, as if spreading wings. Me: I must have been crazy. I must have been hopped up on confidence. I must have felt taller than a tall tree, and just as sturdy. Whatever the case, I right then turned off my clippers and I said it to them like this:

"That's not the way it's done in Cuts Supreme. In Cuts Supreme there is a list and that's what we go by. If you sirs can't abide by that, I'll have to ask you to leave."

As if waiting for just such a thing, they took seats on the red couch, making people make space for them, and getting comfortable. "We'll go next," they said again.

"Like *shit* you will!" Now I was annoyed. "You'll go home if anything! And if you don't like it, we can make it real hot up on Biskram Street too. Don't you think we won't!"

It was the first time I'd used *we* in this way. They looked at me anew. "Scram!" I said for emphasis. Slowly they stood, kicking a few things, trudging back up the stairs, cackling and saying they'd see to me later...

Well, that was some sort of celebration after! Everyone was clapping their hands and turning the music louder, boasting to each other, *Oh yes, didn't you know? This is a Napakakos joint, you're safe in here, I knew it all along.* Uglygod stopped by in the

evening along with Siren and one of Siren's dogs for help closing up and they'd heard about the whole thing, of course. Even
they were thumping me on the back a little and commending
me for a fine day's work. Geeez-uuus, I had to seriously try
not to blush. It was nothing, it was nothing, I kept on saying.
Which wasn't far from the truth. After all, it was just like
Uglygod himself had told me about that crew: a bunch of no-
name pickpockets who flinched if you looked them in the eye.
Ah! What a day! What a day! What a day.

COUNCIL

Those were the times. Once we switched to charging money my life's coffers began refilling at last. At first it mainly
went toward nothing more than payments owed to Napakakos
and them, but as the weeks wore on and our popularity grew,
I found my pockets growing fuller with a job well done. As
it turned out, there really hadn't been a good barber in that
part of Petit Julienne for a few years now. The last one had
apparently been an ambidextrous show-off with some nasty
ties to some Algerian warlords. One day in the midst of one of
his elaborate two-handed cuts they'd come in black masks to
snatch him into a van and that had been that. That's P Jewel
for you. Every evening at seven Uglygod and an underling
came by on black motorcycles to empty the safe, and they were
never more than a call away should anything happen. Nothing
did happen, though. There were a couple times when some
boys from Ghost Disciples or X-Block came waltzing down
the stairs to sit on the red couch, but it was always for a haircut, or to watch from the growing collection of action movies

on old DVDs that people were donating. The gangsters, they always wanted to watch these black-and-white noirs from decades ago, with their codes of honor, their rosily lit damsels, their scenes in smoky alleys where olden thugs in baggy suits slit throats on their way to the cabaret: *Ai-yai-yai, Barber, did you see how the star boy holds his knife? Now, that's technique, it's not done like that anymore, wind that back so we can get it again…!* If anything, I had to ask some of them not to come *by* so often, for sometimes if a mother and her two kids descended the stairs only to find a collection of scar-faced rogues whooping and cheering as yet another on-screen henchman was dispatched with the most stylistic of cruelty… well, that mother would take those kids right on out of there and not come back. It rubbed some of them the wrong way when I explained, but they got the drift and didn't make a big deal of it. After all, I was a protected guy now, and had to be respected.

Yes, my friends, it wasn't too bad being me. Now that I was a gangster I was a real man around town. The uncles knew to give me salutes when I passed them on the sidewalk and the aunties provided discounts should I stop by their shops. Little kids who wanted to be barbers, too, were making me colored-pencil drawings to put up on the wall. What free time I had was spent practicing my hand signs in the mirror or loitering with the boys out front Gallon's chicken wing spot where the secretaries walked by on their way from work. The shop was a squat blue cube at the junction of five roads so you really couldn't miss it, with a long railing out front where we sat and nibbled at the bones. A jovial, fat blackman, Maurice, ran the kitchen alongside a one-eyed son he was forever kissing on the cheek, and as for whatever they did back there, it must have been some sort of magic: "Maurice! You big fuck! You gonna have us biting our own fingers off one of these days, come here, you scientist, and whip up another batch, that's the spirit now...!" When we were out in the open air like that, gathered like a family of rough crows on a wire, you couldn't tell us anything even if you were brave. From the shop it wasn't too far of a walk to the garage where Reverse, One Speed, and the rest of them ran their hustle swapping shittier engine parts into any cars left for repairs to then sell the good ones, or, a little past that, the repurposed warehouse where Hot Head and his team brewed counterfeit liquors they sold to restaurants at a markup. I mean, I'd had an *inkling* before of how big an outfit the Dread Merchants were, but seeing the full extent of their dealings was another matter altogether. There seemed not to be a single illicit pot into which they had not dipped their fingers...

There were Pick-Axe, Swamp, and Baby, hustlers all three, they were joke-cracking blackmen with a rotation at the pool halls to swindle marks out of their dollars. There was Hassan the Goat, who ran poker games on the seventh floor of the Aimsley Projects, as well as his accomplice Bang Bang, hot on the heels of any tapped-out suckers, offering impossible repayment programs they'd spend their lives trying to manage. There were Olof and Chomsky, a nasty pair of bruisers, they'd break whoever's bones you needed them to for the price of a good meal; the Bedlam Boys, a collection of sly cousins—no new construction happened in Little Levant without a piece of the action coming their way; a round mountain of a woman named Diamanta, known for the exquisite quality of the currency she forged in a complicated basement setup guarded by her beefy, humorless sons. Five Lives was a sleek prowler of an Arab, with a moniker already four times modified for each near-death scrape he'd come out of barely breathing, and he kept a couple Downtown corner girls for you to take home if you'd like, though instead of undressing, those fatales would flash thirsty knives and snatch whatever jewelry the johns had in sight. A bearded recluse named Cannibal, you'd see him around full moons, he had about as much English in his head as a preschooler, and something about his ferocious gait, like that of a barely tamed devil, made even the meanest of villains give him a wide berth—exactly what *he* did, I didn't quite know. On weekends, down by the wharves, the one named Lantern (a sinewy statue, darker than dark, with bright, roaming eyes always on to the next thing) organized the motorbike races where if you really wanted to lose your money you'd bet against my man One Speed, who rode that black bike like a blind man with a death wish. Sometimes I'd get a midnight call because Kid Vicious had found a new place to throw up tags and grabbing my own can of spray paint I'd go meet him under some crumbling footbridge. He was the one that never slept, Kid Vicious, plus had a massive dent on the right side of his head, though I wasn't sure if that was why. We'd work to the music of a dead soprano he liked and he'd spray the same thing every time: the smiling hyena that was the Dread Merchants' insignia. (Whereas me all I'd write was BARBER WAS HERE, since I'm not what you would call an artist.) They were the bookkeepers, the debt collectors, landlords and evictors, the most inescapable of middlemen. They hosted dirty-movie screenings in the community center on Tuesdays, then organized bingo games for old ladies the night after that. In their employ was a veritable army of teens they were starting off small by having them steal bicycles, though a couple with bigger appetites could already be seen shadowing Monsoon during his stops around town to check on the rigged slot machines he lent out to bars. Those dogs of Siren's that had so terrorized me during my stay were but a sampling of a larger pack he rented to outdoor events as security against potential threats, threats that were all but guaranteed should the offer be refused. There was Genie who had a shop for fur coats and Blood Tooth who had one for purses. Ape's for printers and stationery supplies; Black Titan's for mattresses (though he wouldn't cut me a deal); Gully's for orthopedic shoes; Thorn's for lingerie; and so on and so forth, an etcetera of inventory as if from the most sprawling of grand bazaars. Which, as to how all *that* was possible, might well have remained a mystery for all my days...

One time I was brought along to see how it was done. How on those darkest of nights still in winter's hold, the Dread Merchants would set off on their bikes in search of bleak roads on which to lay ambush. How on so finding one they scattered themselves along its length and burrowed into pockets of shadow, shutting their engines off. How their breath would steam, the hairs on their arms rise to attention, their chatter assume the cryptic jargon of highwaymen. How they sat balanced and waited infinitely. How the lights of passing cars, had their drivers glanced aside for even a moment, would have illuminated of those faces not the faces of men, but of ghouls for whom pity had been tucked away somewhere distant and secured behind impenetrable locks, and of those eyes not eyes but corridors without end, and that they knew nothing of love nor of tomorrow, and that their shadows were but extensions of their reach, for the spirit of malice was within them and held sway over their hearts, and that there remained of fate's outcomes not a single one they were not willing to brave on that cold, pitiless night with no stars to witness...

"Hey, buddy, road's closed that way."

Uglygod had been the one to emerge from the dark and bring a stray truck to a halt by blocking its way with his bike. Me I was on the back of Hot Head's bike clenching him around the waist as the rest of us came out from our hiding spots and surrounded it.

"Turn down here, why don't you?"

Whatever misgivings the driver might have had, he was discouraged at once by the gleaming pistol Uglygod pulled from his waist and cocked at the chamber.

On all sides was the truck flanked and led turn by turn deeper into Petit Julienne's tangle like a mammoth corralled by ancient hunters into a marsh. Although he would end up being quite the apathetic type, the driver—a snarky know-it-all already rolling his eyes when he finally exited the truck's cab in the lot behind Charge's hardware store.

"Congrats. It's all insured anyway. Alright, don't rough me up too bad, I'm getting my picture taken tomorrow. Any of you have a smoke, by chance?"

They let him have a smoke then tied his hands, opening the back of the truck with the key they found in his pocket and keeping his wallet too.

"What the fuck are these?" Uglygod saw the merchandise and asked.

"Them's tripods," the driver said.

"*Tri*pods?" said Uglygod.

"Yeh, tripods. For cameras and them. What? You mean folks like you don't have much use for tripods?"

Uglygod cracked him across the cheek with the butt of his gun. *Geeez-uuus!* He wasn't going to look too sharp for his picture tomorrow, that was for sure. "Start unloading," Uglygod instructed everyone. "I guess we're in the tripod business now."

We formed a line and started unloading. I was between Hot Head and Crash, passing box after box, when, lumped up in the dirt, the driver called to me to ask for another cigarette. He must have singled me out as the smallest one. Already had a purple welt bloomed across his face, on the verge of bursting like an overripe plum. Me I was terrified in the best of ways, frightened as if meeting myself for the first time. The way he looked like that, all bruised and battered, it almost made me want to cry. But people were watching me and it wasn't a time to wet your pants. I swallowed it down.

"This isn't a charity, pal," I told him.

I knew things were official for real when Siren one day told me to pick myself up a pair of tracksuits from the Sport-O-Rama, one in black and the other in a color of my choosing. "No yellow, though," he clarified, tugging on the chains he was holding to walk two of his dogs, rigid pit bulls with pink snouts. We'd run into each other on Carmine Street where he'd been on his way to take them for a jog on the beach. In the park across from us a family barbecue was going on with a bouncy castle for kids. Now that it had been some months, his hair was regrowing into the luscious mane it had once been, though it still had a ways to go. I tried petting one of the pit bulls but it snapped at my fingers. "No yellow?" I said, putting my hand in my pocket. "I thought that situation with the Sweet Poisons had blown over, didn't Gallon have a sit-down with them to hash out new zones? From the paint shop to the synagogue, no?" (I admit: I was trying to impress him a little with my knowledge of things.) But it wasn't any of that: "Boss hates yellow," said Siren with a smirk. He thumped me on the back, then set off tugging against the dogs.

Well, I did like he said, that afternoon, as a matter of fact: a tracksuit in black and another in forest green, sharing an understanding look with the cashier ringing me up since he knew what it meant. Peeling them out of the fresh plastic right there, I held the tracksuits up to the light as if to ob-serve the embroidery on an enchanted tunic. If they weren't the best pieces of clothing I'd ever purchased, I didn't know what was. The green one I started wearing at once—at my barbershop while cutting hair, during walks through the park, or while considering slices of salmon at the Sunday fish market, where it elicited the small, respectful nods befitting a man of my station. Yes, it was winter, and more often than not I'd have to wear my thick coat over it so I didn't freeze, but the moment there was so much as a warm hour in the day, I'd toss aside those outer layers to reveal my true form. I even wore it around the house, like while moving in the boxes of furniture I'd had delivered. With my little extra coin, I'd decided to spruce the place up a bit. I'd already found a neat bookshelf that acted as a divider, and a Japanese rug to pull the room together. I was making a few trips from the central courtyard to my apartment, carrying up a new order of chairs, when the coughing blackwoman who'd given me my keys opened her door.

"Slide! My lucky boy, just in time. Come in and help me with these, why don't you?"

Her name was Mrs. Watts. She'd taken an interest in me after I'd helped her out with one of her scratch tickets, a stack of which she kept secured to her waistband with a paper clip.

"Oh, good day, Mrs. Watts. I still have a chair or two to bring up, but I suppose I can take a break," I said, stepping in from the cold. Her decor inside was done in a lot of lilac, cheap tchotchkes everywhere, and she had plastic coverings on the seats to keep them from ever getting stained. While I worked on the scratch tickets at the kitchen table she treated me to coconut bars and a mug of hot chocolate.

"I'm not getting anything, Mrs. Watts," I said a couple minutes later, to which she said, "You're alright, it'll come," and kept on at her crossword puzzle. The ticket I'd won for her that one time hadn't even been anything special, just enough to cover the cost of her past week's tickets, but from then on she thought I was lucky. She had a niece she wanted me to go on a date with, too, a lean, shivering woman who worked as a phlebotomist at the Mercy Carriage Hospital, and who never said so much as a word when I ran into her at the grocery store.

"I don't know, Mrs. Watts," I said, "it doesn't look like she has much of an interest."

"Nonsense." She peered over her glasses. "What are you talking about? It was her idea. That's not even her regular grocery, boy, she only goes because of you. Oh, she's always been hopeless, Slide. Hopeless."

She fell into a fit of coughs, dry and harsh, always with an odd sense of purpose, as if hawking up fur. Which in a way she was—she'd had some sort of surgery a couple years back and they'd left something in there. Now there was no money for her to fight the case, or go back for a second procedure.

"Bastards," Mrs. Watts would say, if ever the topic came up. "They ruined my high notes too."

As for the black tracksuit, that one I was required to wear to Council—monthly meetings held on the upper floor of Ugly-god's hookah lounge. The gathering in Napakakos's tent on the Mount had been but another makeshift replacement, it turned out. At the real thing, there was a dress code of all black and a password delivered in person by Tank some hours before, to be spoken following five knocks on the back door. Monsoon's reddened eyes would appear from behind a slid-ing grate and he'd have you enter backward while patting you down. Upstairs was a dimly lit semicircular room overlook-ing the lounge below through a two-way window that, to the customers downstairs, appeared as a mirror. On one end was a large fish tank and on the other a fully stocked bar. Variously assembled in fours or fives around the many round tables were the Dread Merchants, making a commotion. Oh *man* were they monstrous. They seemed larger than ever with their dark uniforms and raucous air of pirates having come ashore. Me I'd ended up with Paramount, Two Piece, a horse vulture of a man I'd never met before, and Roger J, of all people. Around the room, Hot Head and Five Lives were partnered in a card game against two of the Bedlam Boys, the giantess Diamanta was telling her table a story that had them thumping their sides, and the one named Cannibal was muttering to himself in a lone corner. Many were counting money. At a central table sat the higher-ups: Uglygod, Siren, and Gallon, along with Peter Napakakos, who seemed as removed from the night's happenings as an image of himself projected from somewhere far. Once we were settled, Siren would thump loudly on the table and, one by one, call for each giant to present an update on their dealings to the assembled group:

Wham wham wham. "Pick-Axe, what've you got for us?"

From their seats near the fish tank, Pick-Axe and his boys stood and gave a report of the goings-on at the dry cleaners, that things were smooth, business was a-booming, hardly a hiccup on any given day.

"There's this, though—two more run-ins with the stick-up kids around Catédral Monetal. Jacobin handled the second one but they sliced him pretty good around the ears, on account of which he's not here, sends his apologies. I have some guys getting names right now," he concluded.

Next, Hot Head reported that they were having a problem with mice getting into the counterfeit liquor tanks and put forth a request that they relocate to the spot on Altorf Street for the time being.

At this Uglygod cut in with a quick response: "Spot on Altorf is for Cage's project."

"Right, right, understood. But if we could only—"

"Answer's no. Get rid of the mice."

Next went Lantern, then Martyr, then Charge, then the vulture of a man at our table, who spoke only in Arabic and required translation from Two Piece. Roger J set off on a rambling account of the computer hacking operation he was in the process of getting off the ground that might have lasted all night if not for Siren slamming on the table again for him to wrap it up. Reverse and One Speed spoke of their garage, and a table whose every member wore gold chains spoke of a turf dispute with the Terror Boys up their way. Me when I was called I stood up straight and broad and went through it all just like Gallon had had me rehearse: Cuts Supreme was doing A-OK. This was the amount of money going in and this was the amount of money going out. Plus here were some projections for next month.

"Oh, another thing," I added, "half-price cuts for anyone in this room, for the next month only."

Everyone liked that last part, there were lots of table thumps in agreement.

"You worked out a good rate with that man Rufus?" asked Uglygod next.

"Yes," I said. "I think it's a fair share and he hasn't complained."

"No complaint doesn't mean it's fair. Make sure with him. That's family," said Uglygod.

"Alright, Ug."

I stood a little straighter.

"And any further incidents with the Q9s, Barber?" asked Siren.

"Nothing after that one time. They won't be coming back, if I had to guess."

"That's a good job you did with them," he admitted.

Beneath their steely exteriors I could sense something like pride stirring. They asked me a few more questions, things like what my rate was for kids, any ideas I had for getting more people in there, business stuff, then moved on to Lantern with a concluding thump. Throughout it all, Peter Napakakos maintained his distracted mood. I hadn't seen him in some time, come to think of it. He let Uglygod or Siren do the talking for nearly every concern, except for once piping up when a brawler named Bandage mentioned a complication with the trash collection in Little Levant.

"What's that now?" he suddenly said, as if awakening from a doze.

"Those municipal boys up there says it's some paperwork holdup, Boss," Bandage repeated more cautiously. "Been trying to duck out on their payments too. Nothing to worry about, Boss. I'll be straightening them out."

Napakakos kept on softly grazing his left-hand thumb across the tips of his fingers, as he'd been doing all evening. Why he should have chosen that report to ask about was a mystery to just about everyone.

"Oh, I see," he finally said.

But that peculiar mood occupied him still when, some hours later, the updates finally done, he posted up alone at the bar while everyone else kicked back. By then we were in full swing, clinking glasses and smoking up a storm, standing by the two-way glass to watch the patrons downstairs dance obliviously to synthy electronic music. People hardly even *noticed* him, I mean. Me I was feeling hopped up and alive, a real one of the boys since I hadn't screwed anything up. That was some kind of a meeting, huh? I was saying to everyone. And we do this every month? It's not so bad if you prepare accordingly...! One Speed was chuckling and Roger J was in the midst of another of his ridiculous yarns—"... you guys might want to write this down if it's of any interest to you, the stock market's no joke. Remember my stint down in the Financial Plaza? That's a business for you. I was managing twenty-three people, they'd promoted me pretty quick, and one day on the floor I got this call..."—when from the bar Peter Napakakos's rumble cut through the room.

"I ever told y'all the one about Ms. Urma?"

That hushed everyone up. Whatever jabbering remained trickled off with the last clatters of dice. All eyes fell upon him as he poured himself a small glass of something and surveyed the room with curious eyes. Many moments passed. Only the bass from downstairs carried on with its senseless thumping. No one answered.

"Some other time then," Peter Napakakos said at last, cracking a full-on smile before downing his drink in a gulp. He picked up his jacket from a hook along the wall and was gone down the stairs with light steps.

Right at once did the whole room breathe a worried sigh. In overlapping blabbers people were saying:

"... well, that's about as good a sign as any to get going..."

"... could tell he was in one of his moods, the way he was looking at me in there..."

"... been a while since he's brought that one up..."

"... couple years, if my count is right..."

"... you won't hear this from me too often, but if it's anything like last time then I'm out..."

"... and he had a full drink, too, did you notice..."

Uglygod in particular was finding himself in the middle of a scrum of such concerns and not looking too pleased about it. Me I was turning this-way that-way with more questions than I could bear.

"Wait, what is it? What's the big deal? Why's everyone so *dour* all of a sudden?" I was asking whoever would listen. No one would listen. "Tank? Hassan? Hey, somebody *talk* to me..."

"You don't want him mentioning Ms. Urma, kid" was all Tank said as he gathered his things.

"What's the *story*, though? Did something bad happen? Someone give me a synopsis at the very least."

"No one's heard the story, Barber," he nearly snapped at me, "'cept for maybe Ug an' them. But last time he brought it up, it's how KV ended up like that." He indicated the dent in Kid Vicious's skull.

Me I didn't get it. "No one's *heard* it?" I was trying to clarify. "Well, then what's the big deal? How come all the fuss? Geez everyone's acting real strange for such a nonissue, in that case…"

They were conferring with each other and ignoring me. The vulture said something in Arabic that made everyone nod even without Two Piece translating.

"You know, for someone who's been around awhile, you can still be quite dense," Paramount told me, in one of his rare interjections.

A NEAT MAN

One day in February there came into my shop a neat Persian man with a medical boot on his foot, who thus could be heard coming down the stairs one sideways clunk at a time. He was large and particular, in a camel hair coat and animal-hide gloves that he folded away so as to better lace his fingers over the knee of his crossed leg. No one paid him any mind as he waited on the couch, nodded along to conversation, and eventually decided to depart before a chair could open up, as sometimes happens.

The next week he came back at an even busier hour and took some time finding a seat, since the couch was particularly full.

"Rufus here can get you if you don't want to wait," I told him. "Otherwise I got four in front of you." "Oh no, I'll be fine, thank you," he said, finally taking a seat near the end of the couch without writing his name on the board. The others waiting were a uniformed firefighter there before his shift, two brothers in sports clothes, Mr. Horace the school principal, a couple Pakistanis playing chess, and one of the regulars who'd come on the first day to shoot the shit—Yusef. I went on with what I'd been doing, talking to Rufus about the best ways to cure a cold:

"Now, I'm no expert on this, but you boil some lemongrass in alkaline water, add some agave syrup and the juice of an overripe lime in there? Oh man! You're ready to go that next morning, take what I'm telling you."

"How you always know about some crazy cure to something, Barber?" asked Yusef, sounding impressed. He was a guy who talked with his arms and said things twice, out of the side of this mouth. In fact he said again: "Barber always be knowing some crazy cure to something."

I waved over my shoulder like it was nothing. "You pick up a couple things, you know? Anyway, Rufus, give your girlfriend a little mix like that and see if she doesn't get better. You hear me?"

"It seeeeems... w-w-worth a... try," said Rufus. Sometimes to fight his stutter he'd jerk his leg a little to kick the word out, and I always worried he'd screw up whatever cut he had at the moment. But it was fine because he was doing a bald shave.

Right then FatBoy entered with his garbage bag of batteries. "I got your batteries right here. Two-pack, four-pack, ten-pack. How much you need?" He held four big ones in his left hand, the other holding the garbage bag slung over his shoulder like a pillager's loot. You had to pretend you didn't see him or you'd be doomed. That's what everyone was doing, except for Mr. Horace, whose eye FatBoy had caught and was homing in on. "What can I do for you, Gramps? Clocks, toys, smoke detectors, I know you got 'em. Keep 'em powered up." Mr. Horace was looking around like a man thrown overboard, but we couldn't help him. "What you saying, Gramps?" said FatBoy, his belly closing in on him.

A thin, querulous voice piped up: "Might I ask where you got your inventory?"

It was the neat man. His rich, slicked-backed hair glistened softly in the vanity mirrors' lights, exposing a smooth forehead atop a face somewhat younger than his mannerly ways would at first have had you think. He had flat ears, no beard or mustache, and large, mobile eyebrows on the verge of touching. Every crease of his clothing seemed etched in place by a draftsman's pen. He had uncrossed his legs so as to lean ever-so-slightly forward.

But I'm not going to lie: a couple of us were already exchanging looks at his silly question. Asking someone like FatBoy where he got his batteries was like asking a man in a midnight alley where he got that axe—you'd rather not *know*, is the point. Yusef he couldn't help himself and started nudging the firefighter. "Yo! Did you hear that? He asked where FatBoy got his inventory! You heard him, what he asked?"

FatBoy answered, "I got the best retailers around, Duke. Inventory however you like it. You look like a man that takes care of himself, my brother. I bet you got an electric toothbrush you like to use. Keep it powered up. Inventory's all good, Duke."

"I simply hope it is not anything illegitimate, of course," said the neat man. We watched him like he was a child.

"How you gonna do me like that, Duke? I'm as legit as they come. First thing the doctor did was stamp me with a seal of approval. I'm one hundred percent, Duke. I'm grade A, my man!"

We couldn't hold it in anymore and everyone broke out laughing, starting with one of the Pakistanis playing chess. I think we were laughing at FatBoy, but we were a little bit laughing at the neat man too. That was the great thing about Cuts Supreme, there was always some show even better than the one on the TV.

The neat man must not have thought so, though, for a cloud of ill humor was darkening his face. He rode out our waves of laughter with the stoic air of a man walking against a wind. When we were done, we took up talking about the local gymnastics team that had been missing since the flood. FatBoy saw he wasn't getting any sales and waddled up the stairs. When it was finally the neat man's turn to sit in my chair, he decided against it again, and departed with clunking steps back into the cold outside.

He returned the next time much, much sooner and I knew it was something right away.

"Good morning, sir. I trust that you will put a copy of this notice somewhere on the premises, as well as provide a copy to the gentleman selling batteries the last time I was here."

It was early in the day and I was out front clearing the trash bags on the sidewalk. The little light making it past the horizon was the cold blue sort of winter mornings. I took the sheet of paper he was handing me, some kind of notice reading SALE OF UNAUTHORIZED GOODS PROHIBITED ON PREMISES in large print, with finer stipulations underneath. Me I didn't even get to the fine print.

"What's this about?" I asked him.

"A simple precaution. I am sure you do not want any untoward business taking place on your watch."

He tried a smile but it stayed at his lips without spreading to his eyes, which (on closer look) were the senseless black of a cave-dwelling creature's. He had on a gray houndstooth suit with navy stitching, a checkered shirt crisp with starch, and an immaculate loafer on the foot without the medical boot. Wherever he actually got his hair cut, they'd balanced the proportions of black and silver and *that* looked quite good, too, I had to admit. Now that we were standing near each other out in the open, it was clear how large he was, almost like one of the giants.

"You talking about FatBoy?" I said, hoisting another garbage bag toward the empty lot. It was yesterday's trash, which should've already been collected the night before, but they hadn't come. "Look, he's harmless, you just have to ignore him is all. The man's making a living, you know?"

"I see. Nonetheless, some things are beyond our control," he said with the regretful air of a funeral attendee.

His business done, he continued along the alley with the *clunk clunk clunk* of the medical boot. I was fishing for my keys to start opening up.

"Oh. Lest I forget." He'd returned as I was heading down the stairs and handed me another notice. "A copy for the gentleman."

Well, I definitely didn't put up that notice, or even *think* about giving one to FatBoy (who didn't stop by that day anyway), and by the time I got home that evening the whole thing had turned into another funny story to tell Judith Abernathy, the niece of Mrs. Watts the coughing blackwoman. Mrs. Watts had gone ahead and introduced us after all, with a knock on my door one weekend as I was assembling new furniture for my apartment. "Slide, someone I think you should meet," she'd said once I told her Come In. From behind her poked the head of a sleepy-looking woman with a constellation of moles across a honed, pinched face, and reddish-brown hair that she'd done in braids. Once she'd fully entered, I saw she was still in the hospital's green medical scrubs, which contrasted well with her complexion of a sun-drenched native of some hot locale. Mrs. Watts introduced us then cut a sly exit. Suddenly we were alone, me in my green tracksuit and her standing right there with her hands behind her back. I felt we were two dogs meant to be sniffing each other's behinds while Mrs. Watts looked on from some hidden vantage. Or at the very least bow-and-curtsy. To break the silence, Judith Abernathy said, "Would you like some help?" and took a crouch by the scattering of tools and parts crowding a section of the floor. "Sure," I said. That first time, I had been putting together a desk and doing a shitty job of it. Nothing in the instructions matched the reality of the situation. But she settled in amongst the mess and went about sorting things out with a firm determination. Soon we were making progress. We talked about the work before us, saying little more. When it was finished we tested the desk's strength on either end and tried out a few places in the room to put it, eventually settling on a section of the wall near the bed where I intended to put up some art. I joked that I'd need her help again when my new bookshelf came, which turned out not to be a joke at all.

So I was telling Judith Abernathy the whole thing while putting the final touches on a stand-alone cabinet, our fifth project together: about the neat man with his absurd notices; about FatBoy, the all-purpose kook, who treated batteries like the latest wonder of the world. "That's so funny," she said when I was done, although she didn't laugh. She was one of those people who said things were funny but didn't laugh. The evening was dark, her shoes were off, revealing her thin toe- nails painted in a robin's egg blue. She wore jeans and a loose T-shirt. "Some people think they have all the right," I said and laughed. "Okay, let's see how this holds." We got up togeth- er and hoisted the cabinet. It was of cheap green wood that smelled a little damp, no higher than your shoulder. We set it next to the stove. I took the groceries I'd been keeping in a row of plastic bags along the wall and loaded them one by one into the cabinet, then closed its double doors. "It looks nice," she said. And it really did. Wordlessly, we moved to the entrance and surveyed my apartment. The place had really come together. Now on the bed I had a maroon comforter folded halfway down, plus an assortment of throw pillows in various paisley patterns. On the desk were my laptop, papers, a cup of pens, and a small succulent plant, which Judith Ab- ernathy had recommended as a starter since they were hard to kill. My clothes were arranged on the bar from dark to light. A low, wide bookshelf served as a partition between where I slept and where the two chairs we'd assembled stood on the Japanese rug. And now, next to the stove, was the cabinet where I'd keep my groceries. I didn't know how to cook yet but Judith Abernathy said she'd teach me. We were standing on the feathery white welcome mat she'd bought me as a gift. HEARTHSTONE, it read.

"It's really come together," I said. Her hand grazed mine. It might have been a mistake, since she pulled it away and clasped it with the other one behind her back, her usual pose when she was thinking.

Finally she said, "Perhaps we can do something else next time?" Wow, she was really two steps ahead of me.

"You're really two steps ahead of me, Judith Abernathy. I was thinking the same thing." I headed over to my laptop. "Look, I've been considering ordering this coffee table I found. Check it out. Now, I know what you're going to say, I don't drink a lot of coffee, but the way I've seen these things work, it's more a kind of placeholder in the room, you know?" I was pulling up the online catalog but she was still standing in the doorway.

"That's not what I meant, Slide," she said.

"Oh?" I said. She stiffened her posture like a dignitary making an announcement.

"I meant," she said, "that perhaps we can do something else outside of here. Of this room." In a pair of hesitant jerks she started to cross her arms but then put them behind her back again. Judith Abernathy, sometimes she ended up doing half of two things instead of all of just one. "We could get some fresh air somewhere," she went on. "It has been some weeks, you know."

I closed my laptop. "You mean like a walk?" I said.

She said, "Slide…" In the low glow of the evening her eyes had widened to swallow more light. Her chest was going up-down up-down in big, quiet breaths she was trying to conceal. "Like a date, Slide," she finally said.

"Oh!" I said. "Oh, right!" Shit, suddenly I felt quite silly. "Of course. Right! That's my mistake. That sounds great, Judith Abernathy. What was I even thinking. Sign me up… I mean yes."

She was hesitant. "Are you sure you would like to?" she asked. I said, Yes, yes, of course, I was being dense before, when did she have in mind? Her shoulders eased. "Good. I am busy with exams for a while but we can do it after that. I'll let you know," she said, pulling up her socks as she readied to leave.

When next he appeared it was with two smaller gentlemen in similar immaculate garb, as if having reproduced, and he had a clipboard in hand too. The two others went about scouring the shop, looking closely at things, while he stayed close to my chair and maintained an innocuous rapport.

"What're *they* doing?" I wanted to know.

"A simple check, of no true concern, relax," he answered. He took his same seat on the very end of the red couch, even though it was a slow day and most of it was empty. "Now, I understand you go by Slide?"

"That's correct."

He wrote something down.

"And the name of your establishment?"

"You've been here before, haven't you? It's called Cuts Supreme, says so right outside."

I was being snappy because of those other two, who were currently sticking small measuring-type gadgets into each of the electrical sockets.

"And how long would you say Cuts Supreme has been in operation, Slide?"

"Since back in December. Hey, what's this all about?"

He finished what he was writing first.

"We keep a simple registry. Of no concern. And you are the sole proprietor of Cuts Supreme?"

"Pro*prietor*?" I asked.

"You own the establishment?" he clarified.

"That's a complicated question. Why're you asking all this?"

"I see," he said all the same. More writing on the clipboard. "There was a nursery here before, correct?"

"Yes, but that has nothing to do with me."

"The nursery I remember quite well," he reminisced. "I didn't even know it had gone. But isn't that always how it is in Polis? You blink and things change!"

What was this, small talk? One of his clones had finished measuring stuff and whispered something in his ear, at which he furrowed his brow and wrote something else. I was supposed to be working on this old blackman's afro but *geez* was I dis*tract*ed.

"Look, am I supposed to get a lawyer or something?" I said. "I don't feel comfortable here."

"No concern, no concern."

"Stop *saying* that. What's that you're writing, huh?"

He ignored that. He was looking around at the walls.

"Now, Slide, I do remember having given you an advisory against unauthorized sales. Might I see where you've put it?"

"It fell off."

The other underling had lowered the volume on my action movie so that it was suddenly possible to hear every scratch of the pen, the wet squelches of Rufus's gum while he waited in his chair for customers. He was having a slow day.

"I see."

He finished what he was writing in a few decisive strokes, then tore off the lower half of the page along a perforated edge. This he handed to me upon rising.

"Your wattage is too high," he said. "It's a fire hazard. You'll need to cease operations until it's adjusted."

"What!" I went over the sheet. It had a bunch of jargon and metrics I didn't understand. I swear, just about every time someone's handed me a sheet of paper here it's been something I didn't understand.

"It's an inexpensive procedure and can be done quickly from the circuit breaker outside. Any electrician should know how. Still, until then, the premises must be evacuated."

"I'm in the middle of a cut here," I tried saying. The old black-man's afro was trimmed on one side but the other half was still high. The whole thing looked like two plateaus. But already were the underlings turning off the TV and the vanity mirror lights.

"He can return once the wattage is fixed. Perhaps a hat can assist until then."

I couldn't believe it. They were really shutting everything down, one switch at a time. Like shepherd dogs, they positioned themselves at the room's corners and herded us toward the exit like dazed livestock. I was the last to proceed, still wanting to say something. From deeper in the stack of his clipboard's papers he pulled out another of the advisory warnings he'd first given me some days ago. This time he placed it on the door himself, adhering it with tape.

I made a frantic phone call to Uglygod quicker than quick and he showed up on his motorcycle in nine minutes flat. "Ug, it's some real crazy shit! This one guy, he kicked us out for the electricity." I'd told him before on the phone but had to say it again now that he was here. We were standing out there looking ridiculous—me, Rufus, the old blackman wearing a beanie— amongst the stinking mounds of trash that *still* hadn't been collected. Geez, what a bunch of slackers, the whole *street* stank to high heaven. Right at once Uglygod's eyes fixated on the notice the man had taped to the door. He descended the stairs and ripped it off, then came back up saying, "What's this?"

"That's what *I* was saying!" I said.

Along with him had come Reverse and One Speed, who were now scaling the pole to where the circuit breaker for the barbershop was.

"He sa-sa-saaaid, n-n-no... sales. Becaaauuse of F-F-F-Fat-Boy," Rufus chimed in. It wasn't a particularly warm day, so on top of stuttering he was shivering too, a truly sad story in his mouth.

Uglygod wasn't getting it and he was clearly annoyed. "What's all this I'm hearing? Is it the electricity or is it the sales?"

I told him *both*, the guy had been showing up for a few days but today was the only day when it became something. "And you didn't say anything?" said Uglygod. It only became something *today*, I explained again. He wasn't pleased. He thumped on the base of the pole that Reverse and One Speed were up and told them to adjust the wattage to what the jargon-filled sheet indicated, holding it in pinched disgust.

He returned to me. "This man," said Uglygod, "he dress like a fop?"

"A what?" I asked.

"A fop!" said Uglygod. "Overdone. Too much. Like he stepped out of a play. Monocles and shit. A fop."

"Oh! Yes, I suppose he *was* dressed well, although I've seen better. He had a medical boot on his foot too. He might have been Persian, but Indian isn't a bad guess either. Ug, to tell you the truth, I've always had a hard time telling betw—"

But he cut me off with a hawk of spit on the ground. *Tfloop.*
"Yat," he said.

YAT

From then on there were complications. The neat, official man
returned a few days later for but some brief minutes and extended a smooth, manicured hand. "I'm afraid I have yet to introduce myself. My name is Behzad Diego Solayman Yat. I am
your local representative of the Compliance in Practice Board.
Think of me as your eyes and ears." He flashed a laminated set
of credentials on which that whole name was printed in elaborate script. Nodding at the sliding door where the sign was up,
he stuck a quick meter into an available socket. "Glad to see
everything is up to standards here. Take care, Slide."

But once he picked up a scent, he never let it drop, for every three
days was he back with something else. Next turned out to be the
action movies playing on a loop, which were on bootleg DVDs
and sometimes flat-out covert recordings someone had made in
the cinema. "Need I remind you, Slide, that Section eight thirty-
six, subheading D states that the use of pirated copyrighted
material carries with it a fine of ten thousand dollars and/or
imprisonment of up to six months. Of course I trust it will
not come to that." So, alright: we turned off the action movies.
Someone brought an antenna to pick up local channels but all
we could get was you two, Jim & Jean, which didn't exactly
fit the mood. On a bumping, busy Saturday when the crowd
was stupendous and there was that spirit in the air like anything could happen, the vibe's fresh like that, shit-shooters

are laughing, there's a good argument going and everyone's chiming in, the type of days barbers *live* for, Yat showed up concerning the fire code. We were some eight people over capacity. "They'll have to go now, I'm afraid. After the incident with the marching band, we can't turn any more blind eyes," he said, tightening a strap on his boot. Figuring out which eight people had to go was a whole exercise in unfairness. In the end we had to stick with the list, meaning that the shit-shooters who came just to pass the time and never even wrote their *names* down were the ones to leave, taking with them the day's humor, which never returned. February announced itself with a thin film of sleet covering all of Petit Julienne and that morning someone coming down the stairs slipped and fell. It wasn't anything serious, a bump on the rump, and she still made it to Rufus's chair well enough to get her split ends done, but Yat heard of the incident nonetheless. We would have to shut the shop down until the stairs were outfitted with no-slip-grip padding. That was a whole day. I spent it mad as a prisoner, and just as bored, too, sending message after message to Uglygod asking what was happening. Then we had to shut the shop down for another day until we could demonstrate proof of a bio-sanitary hair disposal procedure, instead of throwing it out with the rest of the piling-up trash like we'd been doing. Then we had to shut the shop down to check for asbestos. Then we had to shut it down for noise complaints from an anonymous neighbor, in that packed alley of all places, where all day long irate customers haggled over swaths of multicolored cloth, or some heartbroken couple was having it out in the streets...

*   *   *

In the aftermath of each case Yat left a printed notice stating the new ordinance, adhering it himself with four strips of clear tape. Square by square, my walls were being eroded by an onslaught of jargon. It was sub-article this, mega-heading that, such-and-such in accordance with whatever protocol. I had the feeling he'd published them himself, on a monstrous printer deep in the caverns of whatever bureaucratic purgatory he worked in. But *where* exactly did Yat work? None of my customers seemed to know for sure. His Compliance in Practice Board was but one strand of a municipal web strung end to end across Polis, the various manifestations of which were as hard to remember by name as by function. For people like the riffraff in Petit Julienne, a man dressed like Yat was a man you kept clear of if there was so much as a single spot on your past. His manicured hands, his patterned suits, his slight, obsequious bow at the waist whenever he was speaking—they lent him the air of a cautious vampire waiting for dusk. Never again did he flash that official badge revealing his credentials, even when I asked. He seemed to come into Petit Julienne each time from somewhere else. Now the shop had been reduced to low music, no movies, a population no greater than seven at any point in time, *including* me and Rufus. Of that paltry sum, most were the dull schoolteachers or postal workers who never had anything interesting to say. The people I missed, I only ever ran into them during stops at the bodega, or one of the other locales to which they'd relocated to keep shooting the shit without missing a beat. That's people for you: they'll move on from you in an instant. And if I'd thought I was going to find any sympathetic ears at Gallon's chicken wing spot, then I had another thing coming, for no sooner would I try piping up with a sad gripe of my own than someone else would beat me to it. As it would turn out, the Dread Merchants had been having a pretty rough time of it...

At Hot Head's distillery three of Yat's underlings had shown up on a Tuesday afternoon with a warrant for inspection and not an ounce of patience. Those boys and them had stalled all they could, taking their time to find the key for the main door while others in the back dumped out vats of the cheap chemicals they'd purchased from a lab out in Middleton. They weren't fast enough. Citing such-and-such memoranda in accordance with whatever recent ruling, the underlings had picked the front lock and stormed in to catch them in the act. The chemicals were confiscated, all their pictures were snapped, and Hot Head was taken somewhere for questioning, from which he had yet to return. At the swap-and-sell garage where One Speed and them ran their hustle, one underling had posed as a customer using a vintage convertible, and feigned such ignorance of all things vehicular that they'd thought him a real rube. He left the car with them for a few days, and returned with an expert's eye that spotted their felonious handiwork at once, plus a large moving truck with which to seize their equipment. With some scent-sniffing dogs of the highest pedigree had another raided the greenhouse where Paramount grew illegal herbs, and without so much as a warning did two more track down Monsoon's gambling machines and pluck them from the bars, never to be seen again. As for the shops, some of the owners had gotten the word in advance and reduced their hours, or were operating by appointment only, lest there be any gaps in the day for one of the minions to slip past their doors and wreak havoc. Still, they'd find those wordy notices with the force of the law plastered to their front doors, listing all manner of infractions, alongside ultimatums to appear in court on short notice. And if that wasn't enough, the suspicion was that the municipal mix-up with the trash collectors Bandage had mentioned at Council was no mix-up after all. For, slowly but surely, if you took the time to look, it could not be denied: Little Levant was being choked by garbage. In a sort of reverse siege, where goods could still go in but not their refuse out, mounds of odorous bags were piling up on the sidewalks and staining the air with a pervading rot that clung to the skin. The hum of flies underscored the day; rats were becoming our bedmates. Which is all to say that it wasn't too happy of a mood at the chicken spot. The Dread Merchants were grim and glowering, crunching through bones like monsters of terrible appetite.

"Feel like it's raining to you?" Charge was asking no one in particular as he stomped back and forth out front. "'Cause from where I'm standing I cans abouts swear the world's been pissing in our faces."

"Thought we'd never see that bastard again," said Two Piece, spitting marrow.

"Roaches don't die," said Lantern, to which a dozen others muttered in surly agreement.

Time after time when Uglygod came to manage the safe I'd ask him who the hell *was* this guy, but he kept on stalling and asked why I wasn't hitting my quota. "My *quota*?" I said back. "Oh man, you gotta be kidding me, Ug. You've *seen* what's been going on here, what kind of a question is that?" He wasn't having it. "Don't get weepy on me, Barber. A quota's a quota. You not getting yours one way, then get it another," he said, slamming the safe door shut, spitting on another of Yat's notices on his way out. Finally, when Gallon came to do the books sometime into the month, I nagged him until, looking at me over his reading glasses, he sighed, put aside his papers, and said:

"Look, kid. It's one of the worst kinds of stories, the ones that manage to be sad without being interesting. Those boys and Yat go a long way back. You might have noticed yourself but he could even pass for one of them, were he to give up those ridiculous suits. There's a reason for that: Yat used to run with the crew. That's so far back now it's funny to say. He came from Middleton wearing nothing but rags and that look of duplicitous servility he still has on today. We set him up in the lottery hustle we used to operate with the Wing Chuns during the truce. Through Yat's efforts—he's a stubborn workaholic with no appetite for sleep—it grew from a piddling operation into a major revenue stream. He moved through the ranks quickly, impressing many, until if there was something important Napakakos needed done, it was as likely he turned to Yat as to anyone else. You have to understand, kid, we weren't always this big outfit. Coming up, the competition was stiff and some brutal things had to be done to consolidate turf. Having someone like Yat who was willing to act without remorse, well, it went a long way. So things were good, which, as they say, is the surest sign things will soon be bad. Yat became involved with a babymother of a Westside Shade, an Egyptian woman who served doughnuts at the supermarket. He'd been climbing the fire escape of the tenement where she lived with a narcoleptic aunt and the toddler. But whatever they did in their time together it left the woman with scratches along her back and rope burns on her wrists and the Shade was made to look ridiculous. Yat was snatched, interrogated for hours, then shot in the foot. He returned to us limping and irate. That same night, he said, we were to retaliate or it would be the death knell for all that the Dread Merchants had built. It might only be him today, but you let an affront like this go unchecked and soon there'd be no end to the humiliations any two-bit crew felt they could inflict upon us, he argued. He seemed more motivated by this rabid notion of honor than by the oozing wound already soaking the cathedral floor where we used to hold Council. Instead, the boys decided to disaffiliate him. Why'd they do that? Some would say fear of the Shades, or envy of the up-and-coming Yat, who seemed a nascent boss in his own right, but that's not within Napakakos. Peter has different problems. In fact, I was the one to recommend he be let go. I've seen men kill, but few like Yat, who do it not as the most terrible of duties but with an ardent desire to destroy life. The longer you court such creatures, the greater the chance you, too, will become unmoored by the raging storms they have instead of hearts. Better to let the wounded beast go. To say he was displeased is nothing. Still, he left without a single threat, departing P Jewel in the same innocuous manner in which he'd first come. We would try picking up news of him every now and then as a precaution, but it was as if he had disappeared. One day years later he returned dressed like an outrageous dandy, flashing a badge from such-and-such and with a pair of underlings at his heels. Heaven only knows how such a miracle was pulled off. That first time, he went after one of our dry cleaners, armed with his papers, and when we roughed him up a little to show it was no game, we found ourselves enmeshed in a series of court appearances where officials in black robes slapped us upside the head with statutes, a couple of us went away for unrelated charges newly discovered, and the dry cleaning remained out of operation for many, many months. We could hardly believe it—Yat had found the biggest outfit in town. He had matched our betrayal of him with one even greater, becoming the very fabric of the operation whose cruel indifference is the reason for the gangs in the first place. Now any harm to him brought with it the retribution of ten thousand attorneys, plus a couple officers to boot. That first experience savvied us up and we tightened the loose ends of our dealings. I even went to night classes at the Hochoy-Shucster Institute of Law to pore over legal texts that gave me headaches for days. What finally held Yat at bay was discovering at last where he lived: a rundown boardinghouse in the Phantom District, where he shared a bed with a contortionist. A couple late-night calls telling him what would happen to her were enough to have stayed him all this time. Something must have gone sour between them if he has now reappeared. I wasn't there when he came to your shop, Barber, but it's easy enough to predict what happened. He deduced you were affiliated and resumed the old assault. It's bad news. Yat, the boards, his regulations—these are powers of a different magnitude. He comes from Polis itself and answers to no other authority. That's why no one wants to tell you anything, they know you will try concocting some outrageous solution. With Yat, that won't work. I've been speaking to Napakakos about it but of course all he's done so far is grin like the whole world is a wind-up toy. Typical. In the meantime Yat will start working his tendrils into more areas, like before. He is the worst kind of bureaucrat—low-level and long-serving, motivated by frustration. As for the foot, I'm sure it's healed. That he still wears the boot now is more a sign of his enduring enmity toward us. Poor guy. He must have a closet full of right-sided shoes."

Well, that was nice to hear. But it didn't really help me much. Now I had not only a serious pencil-pusher hot on my trail, but a brutal one as well. My dreams after that featured mostly slow chases through tundric landscapes and I wasn't the one doing the chasing. Back in the shop, my mood grew skittish and tense. I was losing my patience for complicated cuts. With every clunk on the stairway did I look to the door as if expecting the reaper. Walking in on a trembling barber clutching his clippers like some sort of talisman always left clients a little unnerved. Rufus had picked up on my energy and was stuttering more. As for FatBoy, if I so much as *heard* him within an inch of the place I'd dash outside myself to shoo him away, brandishing my scissors so he knew I was serious. "Shoo! Scram, FatBoy, you see what the notices said...!" That one would set him off through the alleyway stalls like something hot had pricked him in the ass, his bandit's bag knocking over pots of hot soup that sizzled and froze on the icy ground. Ah. What a scene. That's bad business.

Perhaps Gallon was right that it would've been better to have been told nothing at all, for when next I saw Yat I couldn't shake the feeling that he knew that I knew. He descended into the shop after we'd just finished shaving the unwieldy manes of a pair of ruffians, strolling the hair-strewn floor like a dungeon master come to check on his captives. Without anyone having to tell me to do so, I swept him a path all the way to a seat on the red couch. Rufus (whom he really made nervous) picked up the speed with which he was chewing his gum.

"Another fine day, Slide?" Yat asked. I told him yes, fine as always, nothing to complain about. "With the changes it's not too bad?" he asked. Oh no, oh no, the changes were great, sorry for all that whining I'd done before but now I see how much better it is. "I'm happy to hear," said Yat.

He tried it again: that smile that refused to go anywhere near his cold, unflinching eyes. Today he had on a three-piece suit in an ochre-tinged brown, a starched cream shirt, and a burgundy tie clasped by a thin gold bar, cuff links, a huntsman's boot, and an oak-handled umbrella in anticipation of the forecasted sleet. "In these parts of town," he went on, "a lot of establishments believe they are beyond the law. I am glad to see you have come around."

There was no one lined up for a cut and no noise beyond the chatter coming in from the streets. The three of us might as well have been in a waiting room for some other appointment no one had told me about. That's when it happened: Rufus started to choke on his gum. I thought it was just another stutter at first and was waiting for him to spit out whatever he had to say, but next thing you knew he was pointing to his throat and going purple in the face.

"Rufus, are you choking?" I said. He kept on sputtering. I ran to his backside and gripped him around the waist, then squeezed squeezed squeezed around his midriff, until right when I thought it was about to be really sad in there, he coughed up the gum onto the front of his apron. He gasped and swallowed desperate breaths of air. *Geeez-uuus*, it was about the first time I'd saved someone's life. Through it all Yat had looked on as if it wouldn't have made a difference to him which way it turned out. In fact, the next thing he did was check his clipboard.

"That reminds me, Slide, I've been meaning to ask. Is there a first aid kit on the premises?"

He had to have been *kidding* me. He definitely knew there was no first aid kit.

"No," I said. He said, "Hmm," and wrote something down.

When our eyes locked, I gave him a desperate look, silently begging with all my heart.

"You will need to get one. And you and your partner must be certified in cardiopulmonary resuscitation."

"Can't it just be one of us?" I asked. I was already thinking I could fire Rufus and hire another barber who was certified already.

"No. It will have to be you too," he said, as if he'd read my thoughts. I hardly wanted to ask the next part.

"How long will this take?" I whimpered. He stood to get going.

"There's a free course given by the Sons of David Community Center on weekends. Four weeks. In the meantime, I'm going to have to shut the shop down..."

Thirteen days into that latest purgatory I again ran into those Q9s who'd stormed my shop on opening day. They'd ended up sitting a couple feet down from where I was, on the edge of the pier watching the Thai fisherwomen cast lines into the water. We recognized each other, although they weren't wearing their jackets or gloves or anything. They must've been off-duty. Finding me on my own like that, they could've done what they wanted. Instead they kept on dangling their feet over the edge and looking forlornly into the sea, as if contemplating alternatives to life. "How's it hanging, barber man?" one of them yelled. "It ain't shit," I yelled back. "Man," said another, "you're telling us."

A Decision Made

On the night of the next Council I was getting ready at my place, putting on my black tracksuit, when a heavy knock on the door revealed Monsoon on the other side.

He trudged in. "This where you been living?"

I told him yes. He looked around with a grunt. Me I'd been expecting Tank to come deliver the password.

"No Council today," said Monsoon. "Come with me."

"No *Council*?" I repeated, thinking, *Geez*, what in all hell, at this rate I'll never get a chance to sort out my problems... But he'd already exited and was headed for the stairs.

It was a cold, stagnant night still stinking of refuse. Monsoon had parked his bike in a shadow behind the building. He hopped on and pointed me to a low sidecar attached to its right. "I'm not with that funny business," he said when I tried to sit behind him. I got into the sidecar, my knees pressed almost to my chest for it being so cramped. He secured a helmet for himself, offering me nothing, and we set off through the constricted alleys near my building, then along the more forgiving ones as we wound our way north. The silver eye of a full moon lit the world in a wispy glow. Monsoon rode like a motorized bully, speeding up if someone was crossing the road ahead, feinting veers onto the sidewalks where late-night vendors were roasting chestnuts on spits. Low-down like that, I could hear little else but the blast of the engine rattling my ears. Even if I'd *tried* asking him where we were going, I doubt he would've heard me. He made a hopscotch path from one safe territory to another—the Dread Merchant blocks to those of the Bad Johns,

then of the New Jackals, the Red Sentries, the Cape Verdeans
(whose women tolerated no gangs in their neighborhood),
the Never Looks, the Last Jeopardies. Past a string of paper
lanterns, the streets suddenly emptied of people, as if dictated by martial law. Monsoon and I blared through that eerie
ghost of a town with no change in speed, the engine's roar
that much louder for all its desolate echoes returning from
every corner. He made eastward turns until the buildings
degraded in quality and, eventually, expanses of bare concrete took their place. In the argent sheen of the night we
might have been traversing the moon itself. I was only just
figuring out what was what when we arrived. The road ran
for half a mile until dead ahead there appeared what seemed
in the dark to be a series of black foothills, but if the wafting
stench of them didn't tell you what they were, then the sign
on the chain-link fence we soon pulled up to certainly did:
AVERY YARDS—RECYCLING & WASTE MANAGEMENT, E.P.J.
No sooner had Monsoon parked his bike alongside the many
others already there than were a half dozen shadowy figures
sliding the gate open to welcome us inside. I recognized
them as the teenagers that stole bicycles for the Dread Merchants. Instead of their usual hooded sweatshirts, they were
in fresh new tracksuits and serious moods, blue dust masks
covering the lower halves of their faces, though their eyes
still shone with responsibility. Monsoon handed me off to the
care of three of them, telling me, "Go on then," as I opened-
and-closed my mouth uselessly. He leaned against his bike
and wouldn't say anything more. I went with the teens. They
were two jocks and a colossus, gangly from ongoing growth
spurts, one of whom I recognized from his having once sat in
Rufus's chair. With a respectful prodding they led me past

the first parallel mounds of trash that marked the beginning of that nasty labyrinth. Holy *moly* did it smell bad in there! A fetid layer of universal rot served as the backdrop from which more acrid odors made sharp jabs down my nose—putrefied meats and soured milk, rotten feces as if from the diapers of seven thousand babies. Every mound was at least twice my height, sometimes spaced little more than shoulder width apart. In the ghostly light I could make out the wriggling maggots beginning life amongst the composting mush and the clouds of bulbous flies whose unified buzzing was the hum of a diabolical engine. Each step deepened my sense of venturing into the ghastly bowels of a dead leviathan, or Polis's reeking asshole. "Dude, it be stinkin' in this joint," said one of the teens, the colossus, once we'd been nine-ten minutes making our way along. "Quiet!" said one of the jocks. He must have been the leader. Me I was breathing in only as was necessary, flinching at every next sound as skittering things burrowed out of sight. We wound so far into that dreary apocalypse that I couldn't have pointed out the exit with as many tries as directions on a compass. Now the trash heaps to our sides were coalescing into the walls of a cramped corridor. We came to a junction of six paths, stalled for a moment, then took the third, whose turn revealed three silvery silhouettes in the distance, huge and looming like renegade shadows. For the first time it occurred to me to be nervous. But our increasing proximity soon showed them to be none other than Siren, Uglygod, and Peter Napakakos fiddling with walkie-talkies as if in any old place. The teens were whispering to each other to keep it cool as we closed the gap. Peter Napakakos alone was the one to speak upon my arrival.

"Hello, Slide," he said. "I'm glad you could make it."

*   *   *

Phew! I breathed out the latest breath I'd been holding against the stench and didn't even mind taking in another awful one just so I could get talking:

"Holy *shit*, Napakakos, have I been trying to find you! I wish I'd been told where I was *going* at least."

You spend a couple minutes walking through a stinking trash yard at night and you can get quite pessimistic, take it from me.

Napakakos gave his slight smile. "I try to get to everything in its time."

In the dark, it had taken me a while to notice he was holding something else in his hand, a slowly wriggling mass that turned out to be a turtle. Wow, it must have been the one Roger J had given him, except now it was as large as a phone book, with a thick, muddy shell and a mean beak curved into a scythe.

"That's fair enough, I suppose." I gave the teens a nod as they headed back whence they came. "When I heard there was no Council I was a little annoyed, but it's good to see everyone. Say, that thing's really grown up, hasn't it?"

Uglygod and Siren had dust masks covering their faces, too, so that my only hint to their mood was through their stoic eyes, in which the moon was multiplying itself fourfold. Napakakos alone had his face uncovered, as if noticing no difference in the quality of the air. The turtle in his hand paddled its stubby legs uselessly. Together they looked at me with the impassivity of beasts. This lasted awhile.

Suddenly Uglygod said, "I'm off to go do that thing, Boss," though he was still looking at me.

"That's fine," said Napakakos.

"Monsoon back there?" Siren asked me.

"Yes, I think so."

"Mhm."

The two of them checked that their walkie-talkies were all in sync and then left me on my own with Peter Napakakos, who was zipping the final inches of his tracksuit. I fought off a shiver. They really hadn't been in a talkative mood, those other two.

"I understand you've been having some troubles at the shop," said Napakakos. "Let's you and I take a walk, Slide."

"More?" I wasn't too happy at the thought of going farther still into that unpleasant maze. "Well, alright then."

Of the many litter-strewn paths branching out around us, he chose one leading deeper yet, though how anyone could know where to go at all in there I still wasn't quite sure. I matched his easy pace as we made our first turn and left the junction behind.

"Why don't you tell me about them then?" Peter Napaka-kos said.

"Huh?"

"The problems at the shop."

"Oh! Gosh, sorry, Napakakos." We navigated around a sleeping forklift. "Geez I could really write an encyclo*pedia* about it at this point..."

I told him everything, from Yat's first appearance to his last. As I spoke, he led us into a new degree of squalor, as if we had breached the next layer of hell. From atop the walls of trash, the cruel faces of cats tracked our progress while meowing the cries of abandoned infants. Seas of black rats would scamper out the way, only to reassemble in a flooded hurry once we passed. My friends, it was one awful hive. All the while Peter Napakakos nodded along to my account with deep concern, even showing surprise at various moments, as if hearing about them for the first time. It was a little weird.

"That's a hard way to do business" was all he said at the end.

"You're telling *me*!" I said, waving my hands a little. "We need to *do* something about this, Napakakos, this is my money we're talking about. *Our* money. Remember?"

He nodded. We passed layers of festering eggs, discarded toilets, butcher shop remains, trash-yard dogs having the time of their lives. At a junction of three paths, he chose the middle one, where the way was narrowest. "Times have changed since the flood," continued Peter Napakakos, giving the turtle a stroke along the central ridge of its shell. It opened its quiet mouth as if in delight. "It is like a different world out here. Rearranged. People are thinking the old agreements were washed away with everything else, and the effort of reminding them grows more tiresome every day."

It might have been me he was talking to, it might have been the putrid night itself. Whatever the case, a displeasure was knotting his features, making dark pockets around his eyes. Slimy puddles, choking aromas squeezing upon the air. And: up above: a spiral of buzzards drifting past the moon.

"Peter...," I ventured again.

He didn't hear me.

"Have I ever told you the one about Ms. Urma, Slide?" he said.

Oh no.

"Napakakos, if it's quite alright, I'd rather we—"

"No, Slide. It won't take long." He lowered the hand he'd held up to hush me. "Besides, it's about the only story I have to tell."

"Well, okay, then, Peter..."

He began directly, as if simply raising the volume on a muted track already running in his head...

*　　*　　*

"She lived above the shop where my father sold meats, with an adopted niece and mangy cats she kept on leashes. This was on Basilica Trace. She was a crazy old bat who left reused foil to dry on the veranda. Every afternoon while playing in the street I could spot her through the curtains talking to a mirror and combing her hair. The niece was sickly and rude. She'd pinch her nose whenever she walked by us and suffered sunburns even in the winter. Angelica Ehrman, that was her name. Nowadays she works night shifts at a burger joint and has a set of conjoined twins she visits at a center," said Peter Napakakos.

"Well, one day, before all that, Ms. Urma died in broad daylight. She had been walking those irritable cats, who always took their bondage as an unbearable shame, when they made a dash for freedom with a strength that yanked her to the ground. She hit her head on the curb and bled out in groaning agony. That was on Corsicund Street, by the twenty-four-hour arcade the Tamils used to run. I was not there to see it, though footage exists. But we did attend the funeral, which my father insisted we do out of propriety. He was a stiff, elemental man from the old country who did not have to alter his black style of dress so much as a button for the ceremony. We sat near the front, in a crumbling church with six others, from where I could see the open casket in which Ms. Urma had been laid in a dress of yellow lace. The priest was a known drunk who slaughtered prayers with a sloppy tongue and was often weeping for reasons unconnected. My father alone carried the casket from the altar to the tiny cemetery some blocks away, where we opened its lid to offer some final blessings, closed it, and then she was lowered into the earth.

You understand what I am saying to you, Slide?" He paused in his walking and turned toward me, so close our chests almost touched. "I saw them lower her into the earth. With these very two eyes."

"I understand."

"Good. So then how do you explain how, two years later, I spotted Ms. Urma again, walking about, breathing the same air meant only for you and me, who have never bled out on a sidewalk?"

I couldn't believe how crazy it was for him to be strolling down memory lane with his turtle while a world of decay breathed its awful fumes upon us. Gone was his sense of mirth, his lifetime twinkle. In their place was an accusatory stare that caused his thick eyebrows to touch, and in the presence of which I felt both apologetic and indignant, as if I were a messenger of bad news before an irate king. Except I hadn't *said* anything! As I was opening my mouth to maybe do so, he held up another hand.

"Hush. I don't need another one of your excuses." He set off again more determined than ever. "I saw her on a spring day at dusk, at a time when I was already having doubts, turning the corner into a dangerous alley infested with junkies. I was on my way back from track practice and weary from drills. But the jolt of seeing her long, frail hair and that unmistakable gait of a disdainful aristocrat imbued me with a terrified energy. I followed her. Around the corner she had not disappeared. There she was in her yellow dress, walking amongst the junkies whose knobbly limbs were like a tangle of roots. She was stepping over them and making her way somewhere. From shadow to shadow I followed. I wanted to see her face as much as I was frightened to do so. But how? I was a good distance behind and moving cautiously. Already I could tell the more alert junkies had stirred from their dozing and were considering kidnapping me for a minor ransom, as was done in those days. The sky was darkening with night's quick approach. She was headed toward a pink stuccoed building at the road's dead end and was almost there. I took off in a short sprint to get as close as I could and at the last second shouted her name. Ms. Urma! She spun around. It was her. There were the exact two moles on her cheeks that we would always mock as nipples in school. She looked the same as the last day I'd seen her alive and scolding her niece. Perhaps she had aged two years, but what difference does that make? We looked at each other the same as I look at you now, and then she sped away like someone caught. She dashed into that pink building and was zooming up the stairs. I was following without thinking when a junkie grabbed my ankle at last and I saw I had to get out of there, slipping out of my shoe just to escape. I made it home an hour later, drenched with fear, shook about in all kinds of ways."

The aim of our long stroll had come into sight at last. Dead ahead the path was obstructed by a jittering commotion of bodies. We were still too far for me to tell just whose were the many silhouettes wielding the probing beams of light slicing the dark, but it was safe to say I had my guesses. From his pocket Peter Napakakos took out a flashlight himself, and relayed a message of approach with a series of intermittent clicks.

"What I saw, Slide, was not a ghost, or some cooked-up figure from childhood. I saw her just the same as others at that moment were seeing her, though unfortunately they were drugged-out buffoons of no use as witnesses. I asked question after question but all my father or anyone else did by way of response was to say I was mistaken, or scold me for having

ventured down that street where so many little boys had met ig-
nominious ends. That event, coupled with so blatant a cover-up,
helped me at last to put into words what had been my suspicion
since birth: that the world was not as it seemed. There were rules
behind the rules and everyone had a part to play in the universe-
wide conspiracy with me as the target. And if my father could
lie to me about it, then so could anyone."

It was the Dread Merchants. They were numbered twenty-
something in all, garbed in black, gathered on either side of
the valley of trash like a royal guard awaiting its monarch.
At their feet (this part is what truly terrified me, my friends)
lay a multitude of bound captives that could only have been
Yat's minions. Oh, heaven and above! Those well-dressed pris-
oners sat tied at the wrists by harsh wires, offering useless
cries against the torrent of abuses raining upon them. First we
passed Paramount holding one of them in place by a fistful of
coiffed hair. Next was Kid Vicious pinning a dapper blackman
in a three-piece suit to the fetid floor with a boot on the back.
Hot Head (returned from wherever he'd been) slapping some
sense into two struggling fools in suspenders, Lantern pressing
a glimmering knife to a powdered throat, Swamp, Hassan the
Goat, Pick-Axe, One Speed, Reverse, Five Lives—they over-
saw their wriggling charges with the stoic glee of sportsmen
after a hunt. "Settle down, you cunt!" "That's it, punk, give
me a reason, why don't you?" "We've got a live one here!"
"How's it hanging, Boss?" To Peter Napakakos they offered
solemn welcoming nods, as if waiting for the word, but you
would have sworn he had noticed not-a-thing as he stepped
over the many limbs in his way.

"Well," he continued, "I got angry. I gave up on the rules
and resented anyone who I thought was in on it, which was

everyone. They told me I had to leave school for disobeying and I went right ahead and left home too. I got my first gig digging up coffins with a ragtag group of Dutchmen who smelted the jewelry inside. Slide, would you believe how many of them were already empty? That only made me more furious. Everyone I'd ever met was but an actor smiling and nodding along, then meeting in secret once my back was turned to plan the next scene. Even the dead weren't dead, merely offstage. I fell out with the Dutchmen because of such frustrations and spent a number of years knocking about Polis's worst corners. Somewhere in there I decided that if no one was going to cop to the charade, I would make that anger into my slave and refuse to let it rule me. That is how I freed myself. Along the way those you see here decided to follow, though I required it of no one. Some have come, others have gone. To me it is all the same."

He'd been perusing the roughed-up hostages as if walking the aisles of a grocery, shining his light into each of their flinching faces. Eventually he stopped at Cannibal's victim, handing Cannibal his light and crouching to grab that captive by the neck with his free hand, then hoisting him into a seated position on the rim of a discarded toilet. It was Yat. He was tied like a hog at the ankles and wrists, a stream of sweat drenching his skin and a look of total fury blotting his eyes. Maybe it was something nasty he would have been saying if not for the dingy rag clogging his mouth. They'd stripped him alone of his nice clothes till he was down to his underwear, his once-pristine hair hanging limp upon his forehead like a spread of soggy weeds. A poor man's beard was encroaching lower and lower along his neck, and in the shine of that sinister moon his skin had taken on the wan pallor of a ghost. The foot that had for so long been hidden in the medical boot turned out to be pale and misshapen, with a network of black veins sprouting from a single darkened spot, each toe capped by a thick, rotten nail on the verge of falling off. He didn't look good at all.

"Is this the man that's been bothering you, Slide?" Peter Napakakos shone the light in his face and asked.

"What the *hell*, Napakakos!" I was already shrieking.

I was jittery and strung-out, swallowing a sudden wave of nausea. Frozen like a buffoon, I could only watch as Peter Napakakos settled a fatherly hand on Yat's shoulder, at which Yat tossed about atop the toilet as if he were about to fall over, and might have, too, if not for Napakakos's steadying clench.

"I'm going to need you to answer me, pal."

"Yes," I whimpered.

"Come closer. I can't hear you."

I got closer. "Yes. That's him."

Napakakos nodded. "I thought so."

"Okay, this is too much!" I blurted out, looking around for help. The others along that cramped hall were craning their necks to watch. "Holy *shit*, I didn't know it would get like this. I'm trying to cut hair is the only thing. It looks like you're on top of the situation, though, Napakakos, so I can just be getting right on out of here if that's al—"

But he interrupted me by holding Yat's hand up to the turtle's mouth until, in a reflexive strike, it snapped shut on one of his fingers. The small, sickening pop of it rang in my ears. Lord almighty! Yat's eyes bulged as he let out a torrent of screams muffled only by his gag; for many long seconds he flailed around while the turtle held on. It wasn't a time to be vomiting but oh *man* did I almost. All in front and behind, the Dread Merchants were looking on with wicked approval.

"Geeez-uuus!" My voice was squeaky with shock. "Did you have to do that? What's the idea here?"

The turtle kept at it for a few seconds longer, letting go only when Napakakos stroked its spine. The stream of Yat's cries settled into a more steady moan punctuated by deep, ragged breaths, half his finger dangling limp from the knuckle. Regarding him with an ordinary dispassion, Napakakos said:

"In my employ I have always kept one soul who I hoped might free me from the prison of my suspicions. Who might, even as a single act, do something so out of keeping with the script that I would have no choice but to believe again in the simple chaos of the world, and that the rest of you are not automatons. They've all failed. Did I ever tell you that, Behzad?" He made Yat look at him directly by clenching his chin and lowering his own face to his. "That is why you had to go. You were a good monster, but that is all you were." Yat lurched to try headbutting him, to no avail. Releasing his chin, Peter Napakakos rose to his full height. "Now perhaps it is that nincompoop Roger J, though I am starting to doubt it. And sometimes I have felt it might even be you, Slide. Well, we are about to find out."

Slinking a heavy arm around my shoulders, he drew me in closer yet.

"So what do you say we do about this, pal?"

"*Do* about it?" I said.

"Mhm. We have invested a lot in your talents. Which is another way of saying you have cost us a lot of money. This right here is a problem you could have handled. You didn't. Fine. Here he is now, though, so something must be done. Or perhaps the full meaning of that outfit you have on was not explained to you."

He looked me right in the eyes, the tiniest of smiles again pulling at his lips. I felt the awful sense of a junction's approach, the fowl air between us thickening with implication.

I tried: "It's not *true* what you've been saying, Napakakos! That thing with Ms. Urma, those junkies. We're not just in some *make-believe* here, things have all kinds of consequen—" but for a second time he interrupted me by letting the turtle have at another of Yat's fingers.

More screams. A thrashing about like a fish on a boat's deck. That one made me back into the wall of waste, dislodging cockroaches that fell onto my head and down the neck of my tracksuit.

"Napakakos!" I screamed and tossed about in disgust. "Come on! What are we talking about? Untie him, why don't you! Yuck, get them off me!" I was still feeling the cockroach legs skittering on my skin even after I'd shaken them out. It was *gross*, the absolute worst, enough to vomit forever. Was the ground tilting or was it just me? Oh gosh, I must have been getting delirious.

One of Yat's subordinates tried making a break for it. He was a nebbishy geek in tweed who'd managed to unbind his own feet without notice then leap upright and dash into the night with his hands still tied. "Runner! We got a runner!" The overlapping beams of the Dread Merchants' lights fell upon his scurrying backside where he was tripping over wooden crates in his haste. Black Titan and Baby, who were nearest, set off after him with galloping strides, disappearing for only a moment around the corner before returning, dragging him by his loafers. Sludge smeared his cheek as he groaned at every gash along the ground's piercing debris. Even after he'd been returned to his spot (as if having gone nowhere) was he still trying to yell some last-ditch message to his cohorts, only to shut up for good once Black Titan stomped him on the throat. "Hush." Oh *geez*, oh *geez*, oh *geez*, my friends, there was no hope there for anyone at all!

The diversion had sparked the giants' impatience. Suddenly they were roughing up their own charges worse yet to keep them from getting any ideas, saying to Napakakos:

"Boss, give the word and we can handle this."

"That's what I've been saying!"

"Yeh, Boss!"

"It's been long enough already!"

"Over in no time!"

"Let's start with that one you got right there, why don't we…"

But he silenced them all with a slow shake of his head, seeming to have magnified in size.

"No. This one is for the barber."

Their gazes again fell upon me where I was half shielding my face as if to avoid a nightmare. Since I was weakening in the legs like that, Peter Napakakos crouched to my level before he next spoke, resting the turtle on his knee, his voice intimate like it was still just the two of us.

"So as to save you the hand-wringing, we will do it like this, Slide. I will give you a choice. Both options result in your shop making us back our money. The first is that we hand Yat over to you and you take care of it." Hot tears were streaming from the sides of Yat's eyes. His snapped fingers were dangling like a pair of loose flaps and the turtle's mean beak seemed to smile at a job well done. "But I will only tell you the second option if you refuse the first," said Napakakos, "at which point you will have already accepted it. Do you understand what I am saying to you, pal?" He repeated the question instead of letting me blurt something silly, as he'd seen I'd been about to do. "Do you understand?"

I wasn't too proud to admit it: I was in over my head.

"Peter, I'm in over my head here," I said. "It's no choice if I can't hear 'em both, it's a gamble. Oh man, Napakakos, this has gotten seriously out of hand, I really gotta say—"

"Straighten up, Slide." I straightened up. "No more whining from you, alright? Don't let me hear it. Take your pick, it's one or the other. And whatever you choose, make sure to surprise me." He grew earnest. "Please."

Far, far away and deep into the recesses of my mind did I retreat. I felt the entire world shrinking to a moonlit pinpoint within the dark morass of chaos, in danger of exploding into a new cosmos or being snuffed out completely. If there was any place else in Polis that existed in that moment, I could not be convinced of it. There sat Yat, a shattered version of himself, weak like a crab with no shell. I felt the power I had over his fate at that moment and grew scared for myself. *Give him to me?* For me to do what? Oh man, I could think of all kinds of things, none of them good. The onlooking Dread Merchants hovered above their own hostages with a pent-up eagerness, in the depths of that trash yard where no one would hear the screams. Damn, I couldn't believe I'd been so foolish! It wasn't all fun and games, being raised by wolves: they'd expect you to share their diet too. How did I end up here? How were those *damn* cats still strutting idly by like nothing was happening? Meeting Yat's gaze, I tried mustering every inconvenience he'd put me through, but they felt so silly all of a sudden. *You dope!* I wanted to yell. *You should have just left me alone, and then neither of us would* be trapped here in some unwinnable test... What *was* it that Napakakos wanted from me? To *surprise* him? I didn't like this. I didn't like this at all. One thing was for sure: whatever he expected me to do to Yat, I knew I could not do it. I tumbled in the pit of my mind for several eternities before emerging on the other end ravaged by time.

"I can't do it, Napakakos," I said. "It wouldn't be right."

A long pause ensued. I couldn't tell if it was the answer he'd wanted or not, and a new wave of resentment washed over me for worrying about such a thing in the first place. The Dread Merchants gazed upon me with their large faces. I remembered on first meeting how bovine they had seemed, like a wild herd grazing, and now within those deep, cowlike eyes something akin to disappointment was welling up. Without knowing why, I hung my head.

"Say no more," said Peter Napakakos.

Handing the turtle to Cannibal, he rolled up the sleeves of his tracksuit and signaled a few commands. The giants one by one took hold of their hostages and began dragging them deeper into the maze. Those defeated office rats were pleading for all they were worth, *Please!*, *Oh no!*, *I have kids, I have kids...!* Napakakos took out his walkie-talkie in time for an incoming message and, facing me again, spoke with a disinterested remove.

"With what I'm about to tell you, I want you to know that Gallon has checked the numbers and everything works out. The building is insured, so I don't want you whining." He then responded to the walkie-talkie to confirm something.

"What's that you mean, Peter?" I was feeling sick and afraid, already ambushed by hopeless outcomes.

"I am sorry, my friend," said Peter Napakakos, "but even as

we speak it is happening. There's no use resisting." With that he smiled. "We are burning your shop down."

And right as I lunged for him, screaming, two heavy hands thudded onto my shoulders and pinned me to the ground too.

I kicked and screamed and tossed and cursed. I used up every traitorous name I could think of. They lifted me like an angry sack and carried me all the way back through the tangled path, and in a matter of minutes I was dumped outside the chain-link fence onto the hard asphalt where the bikes were parked. Paramount, who'd been the one to carry me, laid a heavy foot on my chest. "Calm down." It was me, him, Siren, Monsoon, about five others, and, all of a sudden, Gallon, who must have been waiting outside. He was leaning on his motorcycle with a sorry look, his glasses frosted over from the wind's chill. Every time I so much as fidgeted, Paramount leaned harder on his boot. How could you! I was yelling to Gallon. I don't believe it! You swine! There's no way.

"I see you've heard. These aren't easy decisions, kid," said Gallon, quite easily. All this time he'd been playing my buddy when really he was a double-crosser biding his time. "Listen, I tried telling you some of this."

Napakakos soon exited through the fence.

"Let him go," he said, causing Paramount to step off me. I stood at once, readying for fisticuffs if need be.

"He hates all of you, you know!" I screamed to the Dread Merchants in a continuation of my spewing. "I just heard the whole thing. You're expendable riffraff! A bunch of nothings!"

I must have been hoping to start a mutiny. Instead, not a single one of them batted an eye, as if they'd known as much already. Napakakos settled me with the same paternal grip he'd used on Yat.

"We like you, Slide. You helped us in a moment of need and as a result we have helped you. These are the dealings of men. You came to us with nothing, on the Mount, and here you are with new clothes, friends, a place of your own, and responsibility. I have even heard there may be a little woman who is interested in you.

"But we are running a business here. You are too behind on your payments to make them up in any reasonable time. The insurance will cover part and you will get back to work eventually, to pay off the rest of your debt. I'm doing this for your own good, you understand? In the meantime, I do not want to hear of you leaving Petit Julienne. How are you feeling?"

I told him to shove off, that I was feeling like shit and he knew it. What was he trying to do here, play with his food? They let me expend the last dregs of my bitterness with a stony silence. That abominable moon was prying everywhere like a no-good gossip.

"I don't believe it, Napakakos," I said. "I think you have to be joking. This is a test to see how I would react. I *definitely* failed it but it's still just a test." My own voice sounded both near and faraway, like a transmission by telephone.

"It's no test." Hearing him confirm as much was the last twist of the dagger in my heart. I was afraid. I'd known it all along, but now I was so afraid I knew nothing else. I was frightened by their enjoyment, and by death's lingering presence on the edge of the night. Most frightening of all was what I noticed in Peter Napakakos's small eyes peeking out from beneath the ridge of his brow. I saw in those eyes that there was no less love nor more hate in them than when first I had met him as a total stranger. And I saw that no amount of time would change such a thing, the distance between him and the world would remain the same, regardless; that he was as likely to offer me a pat on the back on Monday as a stab in the same spot Tuesday. He did all he did without malice or passion, as if a coin were in place of his heart, a danger matched in its terrible detachment only by Polis itself. When next I spoke it was with a whimper:

"I have to see it. This is something I have to see with my own eyes or I really won't believe."

He considered my request with blank reflection, eventually saying, "Whenever you're ready," and indeed headed straight to his own motorcycle and started the engine, the others then doing the same. I moved on rubbery legs to sit on the back of his, and we rode off through the night's alleys in a somber convoy, the harsh wind numbing my face, my chest, my heart. Whether the howls I heard were those of the wind or of the Dread Merchants screaming to the moon, I didn't even know. We rode through the territories back to Little Levant and I saw Debrandt Way's approach by the glowing spot of sky above it. We had to stop some many feet away for the thick crowd that had packed the alley to watch the show. Getting off the motorcycle, I shoved my way through the onlookers as they murmured, *Look look, it's the barber, he must have heard, oh, he's not going to like this...* The closer I got, the hotter the night's heat. Loud pops and crackles peppered the crowd's noise. Then there it was, orange and roaring: the entire building up in flames. It was down almost to its fire-licked bones, exuding a blistering wall of heat that kept everyone a good ways back, except for one. It was the woman who lived upstairs with her flightless parrots. Two of them were with her, covered in soot, but the others were nowhere to be seen and she was wailing, wailing, wailing, gripped by an unholy madness that no one dared approach. Me I thought that was about the right reaction. But I was fixed rigidly in place like a charred corpse myself. It was all gone. I didn't even notice that Napakakos had followed me. And there was Uglygod again, looking mischievous and incredibly cruel, his walkie-talkie in hand. The flickering light danced his tattoos into evil green shapes. Coming close, he exchanged a few whispers with Napakakos, then spoke to me in a heavy tone:

"Tragedy what happened. One of the woman's birds must have knocked over a candle and started the whole thing. We're all deeply sorry. Isn't that right, Barber?"

"That Lady Is Swallowing a Sword"

I fell into a serious slump after that night. Some kind of an ache lodged itself in my chest and couldn't be removed no matter my efforts. I stopped doing laundry and developed a sore throat. My diet, which already hadn't been much to speak of, devolved into fried foods from the deli and artificial juices. If ever I ate a vegetable, it was by accident, or ketchup. Beneath my bed grew a graveyard of styrofoam boxes and my shit turned black in the toilet. My expression met any attempts at a smile with a stubborn resistance. No one would have noticed one anyway beneath the unwieldy beard eroding my face. I had stopped shaving. Without anything to occupy my hours, the prospect of sleep seemed forever at my side, as if to offer me an escape from life. Every morning when I awoke into the thin sliver of bliss in which I didn't yet remember, it seemed like any old day in my own apartment at last, I'd make it as far as putting one foot on the ground before a vision of the fire paralyzed me. From there, it was either a return beneath the covers, or onward into empty hours spent twiddling my thumbs. Dark half circles clung to my eyes like hammocks. I seemed always to be smelling smoke. All who saw me haunting the alleys of Petit Julienne with no regard for territories, like a roughed-up zombie impersonating a man, knew right away to give me a sympathetic berth. *Ah, it's the barber, there he goes again, that accident at the shop must have struck him right in the heart...* I heard the world like that: as warbled echoes traveling an underwater distance. All of its sights passed before my eyes like a reel of leftover footage. I saw the fetid markets crammed with fly-covered meats. I saw the brown-toothed children playing tag in the rubble of abandoned tenements. I saw the amputees kicked out of hospitals, waiting in long lines for some welfare soup. I saw my burned-out barbershop covered in detectives. I saw the Locoperros rob me of my green tracksuit as if I were witnessing a matter that didn't concern me. Three of them caught me on a shivering night, put a cord around my neck, and sliced me on the cheek, too, so I knew it was serious. *Cabrón*, they growled, *you want to die...?* I must have ended up in the wrong area. If I ran into someone I knew, there was no guarantee I could offer them anything more than reflexive babble, as if the drainpipe of my words had been clogged and only the dregs could get through. *Oh, hi, FatBoy, yes, I'm fine, no, nothing for me today, I was only going for a walk, as you can see...*

In the interminable slog that had become my life, I would occasionally bump against the new parameters hemming me in. I was not to leave Petit Julienne. To ensure such a thing, black motorcycles had taken to patrolling my neighborhood, mounted by faceless teens who followed my every move, making surreptitious phone calls to unknown interlocutors as if I were out on parole. Any attempts to contact Uglygod, Siren, Monsoon, and the others were met with voicemails, and as for Peter Napakakos himself, I didn't even try. At Gallon's chicken spot the Dread Merchants watched my onetime approach like I was a pariah trying to come in from the cold, and it was clear even from a distance that no one wanted to associate with so blatant a coward. I turned around. Instead, someone I'd never met called from a blocked number every morning and afternoon to check in on me, or, as he put it in his modulated voice, "To make sure we don't end up with another vendetta situation on our hands. No one needs that, you least of all. Understand me, Barber?" "Who is this? Is this Monsoon? Lantern? You changing your voice with one of those machines! Huh?" I tried asking, but they'd hung up. Whether Yat was limping about free, whether he was still tied up in some godless heap, or whether he had nothing but earthworms for company, I could not know. One thing for sure was that the trash had been cleared up—one day, as if it had been nothing at all, the trucks resumed their routes, though manned now by the Dread Merchants' underlings. That one made me want to cry for every accidental tragedy I'd ever had a hand in! I was living the outcast's life of missed invites and unreturned eye contact. I didn't know if I was still allowed to wear the black tracksuit I had left, so I didn't bother. Not that I thought it would work, but on the occasion when I passed that old third-story gym, I found a beefy new henchman blocking the entrance, telling me it was closed. Fine, I didn't need them. I didn't need anyone. Hope had abandoned the sinking ship of my heart. Rock bottom was above me. My friends, I was running out of effort. Every sour prediction I'd ever heard felt like it was coming true. That is until, on a sorry afternoon like any other, I came home to see a wrapped package waiting right outside my door. I tore away the plastic and opened it. It was a new purple shirt. There was a note attached that I read once inside: *For tonight! It's her favorite color. Have fun, you two! Xo, Mrs. W.* Oh shit! Time had really flown. It was already the day Judith Abernathy and I were supposed to have our date...

It was a horrendous date. Judith Abernathy had heard what happened to my shop and offered that we postpone but I insisted anyway and dragged along my dark mood. I didn't see what difference it would make. We met in the courtyard of her building on Basilica Trace around seven. I was in the purple shirt and black pants, with pointy-toed shoes and a gold belt buckle. With great effort had I managed to splash some water on my face and go over my features in the mirror, as if readying to impersonate myself. Alright then, Slide, it's all straightforward, keep it together a few hours and it should be okay. But that had taken so long I hadn't had time to trim my beard. When Judith Abernathy came down the stairs, she wore cream pants, short-heeled suede shoes, a purple halter top beneath a black cardigan. Long pins held up her hair, emphasizing the arch of her neck, as well as her constant expression of someone overcome by the sight of a beautiful painting. She looked nice. "Hello, Slide," she said, pecking me on the cheek such that I could smell her bergamot perfume. "We're matching." It was one of those warm winter days that seem misplaced. We began walking toward Avenue VIII so we could get a taxi to the part of Petit Julienne bordering Downtown and still suited for tourists—I'd asked the voice on the phone earlier if it was okay for me to go and he'd said fine as long as I was back before the sun rose. Judith and I talked about this and that, nothing at all, silly things not worth mentioning. "Any news on the shop?" she soon asked. I told her Not Really. "Perhaps you can all start rebuilding soon, no? I heard the insurance paid out," she said. Again I said Not *Really*, kicking a paper cup someone had littered on the ground. "I don't want to talk about it is the thing," I said. She agreed with me. She was always agreeing with me. Wrapping it up, she said, "Such a tragedy. We should just be glad everyone's alright," as she raised her arm to hail a taxi.

We went first to an introductory salsa class in a converted warehouse on Ezekiah Lane in the Merchant District, where at the door she presented the guy with two coupons and we took a set of spiral stairs to the music. The space was a chilly gymnasium. In the center, a large square had been cordoned off by trellises covered in fake vines and multicolored lights. There was a three-man band of bongos, trumpet, and guitar playing according to the needs of the class. The teacher was a Spanish-looking guy, I didn't know from where, and he had his shirt unbuttoned down to his navel plus sequins on his tight pants. The way the class worked, he stood at the front talking through a wireless headset and everyone was following the step-by-step lead of him and his partner, a brown woman with dimples and loose hips. Judith Abernathy and I weren't doing too well. I kept missing the turns, she kept making up for it by saying, Don't worry, it's fine. She leaned in: "He's my least favorite instructor anyway, he changes the routine too often." Oh no! She'd done this before. She was one of those people who picked up dancing when they got older, the introduction was only for me. Well, I was *just* about getting the hang of it by the end of the hour, when the class ended and the doors opened for regular dancing. Just like that, all these well-dressed Spanish guys—I didn't know from *where*—were filling up the room and whispering in women's ears to ask them to dance. It was like an ambush. The whole thing was a ploy where the instructor offered free classes for couples then invited his friends to come steal the girls, suddenly it was plain to see. Me and the rest of the introductory guys we didn't stand a chance. There I was with Judith, trying to match the trumpet and bongos and stepping on her toes, when one of them invited her to dance. "Would you mind, Slide?" she asked. He was a suave ladykiller with a regal nose and a hand on her back. That one made me shuffle to the edge of the room while the bongos started back up and a cloud of glitter erupted from the ceiling for no damn reason. I mean, it was glitter in my hair, on my clothes, down my pants. What a drag, stuff like that, it doesn't get out just by doing your laundry. I tried having a conversation with one of the other wall-clingers between swigs from his flask but neither of us was in the mood. I caught glimpses of the ladykiller leading Judith through a series of whirls and twirls, one-two steps where they turned back-to-back and floated around. They danced two songs, she danced one more with a taller fellow who asked after, then broke off. By then I'd started pretending I had something to do on my phone. I could see her looking for me but I didn't wave. Soon she spotted me and came over. Her skin looked flushed and alive, her hair tangled like from a good romp in the sheets. "This is boring," she said. "Let's leave."

She had planned that next we'd go to Duke's Plaza, where there'd be street performers and street foods. It would be a walk only down to Forsyth Street, still in Petit Julienne, though far enough south that parts of the area resembled Downtown.

We returned to the pulse of nighttime life, every breath of the cool air fresh, crisp. After so long in Petit Julienne's cramped confines, I was having a hard time adjusting to all that open space, feeling a little like exposed prey along those tree-lined boulevards. I couldn't shake the suspicion that we were being tailed by just about every black-coated teenager I saw supposedly checking their phone. Judith was telling me about her life: she had grown up in a stable family, her mother had made soaps, when she was nine she and her father had... her voice trailed off. "I'm sorry, I must be boring you," she said. I told her, No, no, it's okay, all this is great. Duke's Plaza was a cobblestoned oval bordered by small cafés, with two fountains in the middle around which all kinds of street performances were in full swing. A man rode a unicycle on a tightrope between two lampposts, short acrobats stood on each other's shoulders, matching children made a pack of sweater-wearing dogs do tricks. People had come out as families or on dates and were laughing and applauding amongst the soft glow from the lampposts. At one of the food carts Judith ordered two sticks of grilled marshmallows sprinkled with nutmeg and at another two cups of hot cider. I paid for them all. To get home she would probably want another taxi too. We sat on the rim of one of the fountains where a cherub stood on one toe, the water turned off for the season. In front of us, one of the largest audiences was gathered around a man balancing a chair on his forehead and cracking jokes. I couldn't see much of him past all the butts in the way, but the jokes were loud enough, all romantic puns. Things like "Why so gloomy? Let's go on a date and I'll chair you up!" or, to a giggling, blushing woman: "Well, don't you look lovely tonight, my seat-heart." Geez, he was a real riot. I didn't even know how he'd gotten such a crowd. Everyone was laughing with him, even Judith Abernathy right next to me, who was chuckling as she held her stick of marshmallows on either end with dainty fingers. She took tiny nibbles with her small, delicate teeth like those of a baby that had never fallen out. Over her shoulder, near another side of the fountain, was an ethnic woman swallowing swords. I mean she had a full-on *sword* she was dangling above her mouth and slowly sliding in. Only when I saw it did I realize I'd never seen that before in real life, only on TV or the internet. I could hardly believe it. But the thing was, she didn't have a crowd around her at all. *Maybe* there were a few people glancing as they walked by, but mostly they were focused on something else, like the guy making jokes with the chair. Judith was saying something again but I interrupted her: "That lady is swallowing a sword…"

It wasn't totally clear what I was talking about so I pointed with my marshmallow stick.

"The woman over there behind you is swallowing a sword. Look, right there, it's not a figure of speech."

Judith turned to see.

"Oh." The woman was guiding a saber down her throat, selected from the many kinds of swords laid out on a cloth before her. "She's quite talented."

"I mean *geez*," I said. "Someone's right there taking swords down her throat and people aren't even paying attention." I shook my head at everyone's backs. "What are they even paying attention to? Some guy with a chair?"

"He's one of the regulars around here, Slide. He's been doing it for years," said Judith. By her tone I could tell she wanted me to quiet down.

I stood up.

"What's he even *doing*, though?" I said. "He's just making jokes and balancing a chair. Those don't even have anything to *do* with each other. It's not like he's juggling, which'd make it harder. He could make jokes *then* balance the chair and there'd be no real change in difficulty."

The three men directly in front of me glanced back like I was a freak on the subway. In the clearing ahead the man was strutting with his hands on his hips and going on about his ex-wife, really corny. "She really didn't chair-ish me!" I looked to the woman again. All that was left of the saber was its hilt resting upon her lips. This was ridiculous. This was ridiculous and no one was doing anything about it.

"You, sir." I tapped one of the guys on the shoulder. "Are you aware that the woman over there is swallowing swords?"

He didn't want to answer me (he stepped away) but his friend did, a bearded dandy with excessive freckles:

"Yes, we noticed her earlier," he said.

"And what did you think?"

"She's alright, I suppose," said the man.

"You *suppose?*" I said. "Is that all we are doing here?"

"Slide, come here." Judith had stood up behind me and was massaging my shoulders, probably to calm me down. I shrugged her fingers off and walked around the audience until I was on the side closest to the sword-swallower. I looked at them but pointed at her with my marshmallow stick.

"There is a sword-swallower *right here* and none of y'all are paying attention." It was loud enough that a few people looked my way, about five. The woman was gently extracting the saber with her eyes to the sky, her delicate gags audible now that I was nearer. "Are you seeing this shit? You could swallow a whole sword and it's not enough for some people."

Some of them laughed, which was annoying because I wasn't being funny. "I'm not being funny," I said. "Do you know how hard this must be?"

Judith had trailed me around the edge of the crowd but now stood a little ways back. A vendor of toys on the other end of the plaza set off a whistling firework into the sky, which everyone turned briefly to watch explode. (I flinched without meaning to. A sound like that in Petit Julienne, it meant something different.)

"Did you feel those sparks? I knew we were having a connection," said the man telling jokes with the chair. Everyone chuckled.

"That one wasn't even about *chairs*," I said. "I mean, he's not even *funny*, this guy."

"Hey, what's your problem, alright? The man's trying to work," said a scowling woman. Her date had turned to glare at me too.

"*Everyone's* trying to work," I said. "This guy's getting all the credit is the only difference." My sword-swallower had moved on to a longer saber for a routine where she first twirled it around her and did quick spins in the air. She was seriously focused. "Look, I'm no comedian. You wouldn't call me an acrobat either. But you give me a couple days and I can come back here with a chair on my head, a couple jokes written down. But this? But *this*…"

"Then why don't you then?" said someone else.

"Are you even *listening*?" I said.

Some of them were starting to grumble as they turned my way.

"No one has to listen to you. You're interrupting the show," said the same someone.

"Where is the *order* in this place?" I moved on by saying. "Everywhere I go I see lines and lines but never any order. It's just a bunch of skipping. Doesn't matter how hard you work at what you got, there's always going to be some asshole with a chair on his head in front of you." More laughs; others shook their heads. Poor Judith. She seemed really far away. "And if it's not that, then it's something else. It's always *something* in this place."

"Hear! Hear!" I didn't know who'd said that. They must have been farther back.

"I'm not trying to make a scene," I said, "this is just the log that broke the camel's back. *Swallowing swords!* It's enough to dis*cour*age you."

"Shut! Up!"

"Hey, let the man talk."

A plastic bottle was thrown my way, but it might have been a coincidence, because of how bad the aim was.

"You *see*?" I said. "It's a risk having an opinion nowadays. It's like a dictatorship, except it's worse because there isn't even a dictator. We're just doing it on our own. What are all of you going to do after this? Go home, I bet. This lady, she probably has to use all sorts of *lozenges* for her throat when she goes home. In order so as she can make it back here to be ignored again tomorrow.

"I'm really sorry, ma'am," I yelled to the sword-swallower, "I'm not trying to make an example out of you or anything."

"Cheese left," someone was saying.

"What?" I said.

"She's *deaf*," they repeated. "Plus she doesn't put on a show."

I looked at the woman again. She was going on with her routine same as ever. There were for sure a whole lot more people paying attention to her than before, but she was so wrapped up in her act she didn't seem aware of it. Oh no. She must really have been deaf.

"This is just the worst," I said, turning my back to her. "Stuff like this will make you cry if you aren't careful. All night she's here swallowing swords for people to ignore her for this other guy, and she doesn't even *know* how shitty the jokes are. That's the way it is out here in Polis—you never know what's biting you on the ass until you try taking a seat."

"Amen, brother!"

"You could be rushing to catch the train but they've all been canceled. You could have ten dollars in the bank but it costs twenty to keep it there. I mean, it happens to *me* too. I've been living this life pay as you go for so long it feels like the ladder I'm climbing is a wheel. Who's progressing here? I don't think anyone's ever progressed here in all their lives. At least not anyone I know. Oh, Rosa! I've seriously failed you. Oh, Calumet, you were right all along. Me I'm supposed to be at my barbershop but they burned the whole thing down. Typical, it's so typical. What if she sneezes, this woman? It's cold out here and that could happen. This is her *life* we're talking about."

I was hardly seeing who was in front of me anymore. I was every type of angry I'd ever been. Sad too. That crowd in Duke's Plaza was looking at me like I could immolate myself and all they would reach out to do was warm their hands. Lordy oh me I must've really been going crazy. I must've sounded like every madman who'd ever wasted my time, except now I knew there was a *reason* they'd gotten that way.

"Sure, okay, I get it, everything happens for a *reason*, of course," I went on, "but what if the reason's bad? You see so many people like this out here, maybe it's no coincidence, maybe it's the way they want it to be. Geeez-uuus, have I seen too many stickup kids. Too many hooligans, vagabonds, rogues, and perverts, too many sad stories asking for change. The worst thing is you get accustomed. Too many widows with old photographs and truants with unlikely alibis. At first it was fun but now I've walked by too many vagabonds on the street corners plotting poor outcomes. I've met too many smart alecks and just as many dunces. As a matter of fact there's hardly a difference. You can't ask a simple question out here and not get five thousand answers, none of them useful. Too many drunkards reeking in the morning and tourists lost at night. Too many bums, too many weirdos, too many pregnant ladies standing on the subway because no one will give them a seat. Sometimes I get indigestion, it stresses me out so bad. Why have signs if they just get covered in graffiti? Why have lights at the crossings if we're going to jaywalk anyway? I've seen too many hit-and-runs where no one's to blame and been in too many traffic jams with no answers at the end. How do you figure *that* one? Oh gosh, I really wish I was kidding. I wish I was kidding even a little bit. Where are people's parents? Where are the politicians? Does anyone have a number? *Geez* do I have a few suggestions. They should have given us warnings before they told us all to come here. Instead it's been a whole lot of mumbo jumbo. It's not supposed to be a *career*, chasing your dreams, it's supposed to be temporary. You're supposed to catch them eventually, aren't you? But oh man, it never happens, not out here. Not for the big things anyway. DREAM WITHIN YOUR BUDGET, that could have been a warning. Or here's another one, REACH FOR THE STARS, BUT STOP WHEN YOUR ARM

HURTS. See? That's thinking realistically. It's some kind of number they've done on us, I tell you. We've been scammed so bad we hate anyone who points it out. That's called pride, and it's no substitute for the rent. We're picking the lint out of our pockets to look for flecks of gold, but they must've fallen through the holes. Ha! As a matter of fact: Ha! Ha! Ha! What to do? What can you even do? I'm not suggesting we burn the whole thing down or anything like that, that's definitely not it. Except what if we did? Ha! Ha! Ha! Who loves a cage just because of how big it is? Fling open the doors! Raise the roof and break the windows! At least someone rattle the bars or something. Stomp on the floors! Pick the locks with the fillings from your teeth! You'll see that the wardens are cowards and won't do anything. What I mean is, there aren't any wardens at all—they've left. They told us to stay put on the way out and that's what we've been doing since, like dummies. Melt the mortar! Dig tunnels! Set off the alarms and make bonfires on the roof! Am I the only one who feels this way?" I was gone and gone and gone. Someone from the crowd yelled, "Whataya want, an end to all your problems?" and I yelled right back, "What? No, don't be ridiculous! I just want some better *problems* is the thing. You see some people out here and they're hogging all the good ones. Meanwhile, what are ours? Ours are that it costs one arm and a leg to go to the hospital and then costs the other two for a plot in the cemetery. Pah! The food causes cavities. The air makes you cough. Everything's on sale which means nothing is—those were the prices all along. I mean, please, someone. I'm a kite with no string here. I'm treading water. I'm jumping up and down. I feel like I'm running out of time but I don't know for what. It's bad..."

*   *   *

I trailed off. It wasn't like I'd had a whole *plan* of where I was going with it or anything, so all of a sudden I found I was trailing off. There was the same ol' crowd. The woman swallowing swords was still going. The guy with the chair must have been done, or else enough people had lost interest for him to have called it quits. In any case, he'd ended the routine and had taken a seat on the chair. With a groan he said, "Wrap it up, buddy," in a whole other voice from his showtime one—more tired, serious. That was all it took: he said, *Wrap it up, buddy*, then one by one people began to dissipate. A few of them clapped. They strolled away to different attractions or the food carts. Judith Abernathy was there by the fountain with a pinched, furious look. I'd made a mistake, oh gosh it was obvious now. A young girl with pigtails came up to me. "I liked what you said." She was digging in her purse to find some change to give me. She must've thought it was just another show.

SOME STRANGE THINGS

My shop was rebuilt, except shittier, without love. The slapdash job took less than a week, by the end of which I was reinstalled behind a stiffer chair, no TV or music, locked glass doors like a rat under observation. Rough adjustments had to be implemented to account for the fire, such as temporary drywall everywhere you looked, slathered with a strong industrial paint that induced slight headaches. Instead of the red couch there was a line of plastic stools with no backs. From the ceiling hung a string of air fresheners to combat the charred smell. I had been excluded from these renovations as I was excluded from everything, summoned only afterward by the voice on the phone that informed me of my new situation, which also included Paramount's daily presence in the shop. "For security, of course. We don't want any other incidents," the voice said by way of explanation. He was less than happy about it himself, Paramount. Morning to evening he sat reading comic books on a tiny stool, like an immovable pillar, eclipsing half the light with his enormous head and oozing a humorless mood. Despite his long mane and the ragged beard clouding most of his face, it was clear to everyone who looked that he was not there to have his hair cut, and the bulk of his presence implied a similar-sized danger against which such bulk must be needed. Which isn't to say there was a whole lot of people for him to frighten anyway: the new, shoddy Cuts Supreme had way fewer customers. Half were the die-hard paranoids who had difficulty trusting another barber with their hair, and the other half were the few neighborhood locals motivated more by pity on seeing me sunk so low. For any of them to get in, they first had to knock and speak through the muffled glass, at which Paramount would then take his sweet time lumbering over with the keys and ask them a bunch of questions. Sometimes if he didn't like them he'd send them away regardless of my input. What's more is that Rufus (he really was a bunch of nerves) said that his sleep had been affected since the fire and he had it on a doctor's good orders to take some downtime. He quit. It looked at first like I was to man a sole chair, until Gallon showed me in the numbers that I had to find a replacement or there'd be no hope of me ever making up the remainder of my debt. It was the first time I'd spoken to any of the higher-ups since the fire, but the whole affair was an officious transaction conducted without so much as a handshake. I tried avoiding it, and really I weighed all kinds of alternatives, but in the end I gave in to Roger J's requests to man the other chair. He had heard of the opening. He set up the next day with a multitude of complicated instruments fresh out the pack and made it right away apparent that he had no idea what he was doing. To cover that up, he spent the whole day pretending to ask my opinion on various haircuts whenever he got stuck, as if to trade notes. It was like having to cut *two* people's hair at once—the one in my chair and the one in his. You should've seen it: he'd make a misplaced swipe at whoever's hair with his clippers, nod solemnly like he'd heard a good argument, then turn to me and start running his mouth. "Just like when we met, right, guy? Back when we used to talk shop, remember? Who thought it would've gotten so literal! Say, you see where this fella's skull back here is getting all bumpy, what setting do you like to use? I have some ideas myself but it's always nice to compare techniques..."

I hated Paramount, who never moved. I hated every haircut that wasn't a bald fade with a line-up around the sides. Hatred was making me see what I had been ignoring: that this wasn't what I wanted—I had been settling. Life had pulled a fast one on me and swapped out my dreams for lesser ones. I couldn't believe I was back here again, bunkered in a shitty apartment and saving up just to be poor. I might as well have stayed with Calumet and Eustace, at least *there* there had been a TV. I hated the snow that made it hard to walk and the wind that made it hard to think. I hated that Peter Napakakos seemed to have washed his hands of me and I was no longer invited to

Council. I hated that Judith Abernathy wouldn't speak to me when I hadn't been that interested in the first place, and even the coughing Mrs. Watts (as if on orders) no longer asked for help with her scratch tickets. She must've seen that my luck had run out. It seemed the rest of my life in Polis would have continued like that—a festival of wallowing, jerking awake at every bump in the night—if not for some truly strange things starting to happen.

The first was a text message in the morning's early hours. I'd been dreaming of piranha-infested waters when the *ping-ping* of my phone roused me. *Wait!* it said. *Is this Slide? Darling how have you been??* My heart skipped two beats seeing the name appear on my screen: it was Monica Iñes. I held the phone an arm's length away, stunned. I messaged her back saying what's up and how had she been. *My dear*, she responded quickly, *it's been so long! I still remember our lovely dinner! Are you still in Middleton? We must hang again soon!* That did the trick: I was smiling like a dope. Monica Iñes! There was a ray of light if ever there was one. We went back and forth over the next half hour—she explained she'd only just transferred her contacts from her old phone was the reason for the delay, life for her was going well, she had so much on her plate at work, anyway what was I up to and were my ears still cute? *We really should get together! I owe you a tour of Point James*, she wrote. Gosh it was a lot to handle. All the thoughts of her I'd extinguished were heating themselves back to life. *Sure*, I wrote. *That sounds good.* I had to play it cool. I couldn't let on that I was pacing my room in excited circles. *Let's do lunch at Café Pampillon!* her next message said. *You must tell me when works for you, soon or it'll never happen...* Oh wow. I practically died. I replied saying

I'd definitely check my schedule, even as beyond my window one of the black motorcycles forever tailing me puttered on by. I would have to figure it out. Well, my friends, I walked to work that day practically whistling, my hands in my pockets and with a jaunty step too!

The following day, I was taking my recycling to the faraway dumpsters near the park, where about four teens on skateboards were making a lot of noise. Soon they were shouting loudly to each other, saying, *No way!*, *I doubt it*, *You think so?* I passed by them after I was done with sorting my recycling and one of them with a nose ring approached me a little smirkingly. "Can we have a picture?" he asked, waving his phone. I was a bit put off but I was in Six Bricks territory and I didn't want any trouble either. I took his phone from his hand and told them to get closer together while I looked at the screen. But that wasn't it. Instead they gathered on my either side and the nose-ringed one turned around his phone to face us. They wanted a picture with *me*. He snapped one, five, eight pictures, each one capturing successive gradations of my annoyance. No doubt I was part of some prank. "Ooh wait wait wait," one of them said, having had an idea. He picked up a tree branch he'd seen on the ground and held it in the air like a scepter. The others thought that was hilarious. That was the last picture: all of them laughing, me in a scowl, and that one guy holding his stick. I went off from them sorry to have taken the time. "You're a legend!" one of them said. Me I didn't even look back.

But it didn't take so much as another day before I was again asked for a picture, at my shop this time, right around dusk when my senses were on high alert. In the intervening hours

Monica Iñes had kept on texting—she was excited for lunch sometime soon, I definitely had to meet so-and-so, this-one-that-one, so much to catch up on, so many things to do. Hopes of seeing her again swelled in my chest. It was another rainy evening of imprisonment with Roger J my cellmate and Paramount the warden. They were on the stools doing nothing. A man and a woman in all denim descended the stairs and were trying to explain themselves through the glass.

"We just want a *picture*," they were saying.

"A what?" asked Paramount, playing oblivious. He'd gone right up next to the glass.

"A picture!" they repeated.

"What you want a picture for?"

They'd had enough of him: instead they were standing on tiptoes and speaking past his shoulder: "Come on, Glitter Guy, it'll be a quick one, tell this man to let us in."

Paramount got upset. He took out his gun and waved it.

"I don't like your look. Beat it." *Geeez-uuus* did they get out of there fast, backing up *whoa-whoa-whoa* and scampering their way up the steps.

"You can't keep *doing* that, Paramount," I said. "It's my clientele we're talking about here." He grunted as he took his seat again. That had me in a funk. I kept on with what I'd been doing, trimming the hair of a shady seller of newspapers who only ever paid in coins.

"You know, guy," said Roger J, "Paramount might have a point there, though. I had to invest in some security myself when I went through my own notoriety. It's more worth it than you think, some of these fans can be nutjobs. Why, I remember, one time I was signing autographs and my hand catches a cramp right as—"

"What are you talking about, Roger J?"

He did his nod. "I'm just saying. You're going to want to be a little more careful now that people are getting to know you. Take it from *me*. This cramp I was telling you about, it comes on right as I'm signing a cast for this brute-looking fellow, no offense, Paramount, and he was ready to—"

But I cut him off again because I still didn't understand. He took out his phone. "You haven't seen this?" he said.

The name of the video was "Must See! Glitter Guy Goes on Legendary Rant" and it had already been viewed four hundred thousand times. In it, I was being filmed from an oblique angle by a steady hand a couple feet to my left. I was wearing the silky purple shirt and holding the marshmallow stick, which I waved about, the sword-swallower lady in the background. And, because of that silly salsa club, I was twinkling almost head-to-toe in glitter. Alternating bits of it caught in the streetlight as I moved about looking as ridiculous as a costumed masquerader.

"What is this, Roger J!" I said, not even hearing myself. That other me was going on and on about sword-swallowers and mocking the guy with the chair on his head, to whom whoever was filming momentarily panned for effect. "... hard you work at what you got, there's always going to be some asshole with a chair on his head in front of you..."

"Who filmed this?" I said again. "Are you joking with me?"

"I thought you knew," said Roger J. "Playing it cool, you know? That's what I like to do."

The man who paid only in coins stood up from my chair. "Oh shit," he said. "That's you?" He squinted at my face and poked his neck out. "You're the Glitter Guy!" he said, throwing his hands to his head. "Yo, I can't believe this shit. It *is* you. I'm gonna need a video, my man." He, too, started reaching for his phone beneath the apron.

Me I was feeling woozy. "Rog, what is going on?" I said, wobbling on my feet.

"It's been everywhere, guy. You're the flavor of the week. Look." He scrolled down the page to show me some comments. One of them said, *Wait... how can I marry this man?*; another said, *Truth to power!!*; and another said, *Lame*. Roger J was scrolling too fast; I took the phone from him to go through them myself: *So glad someone said it!*; *Another unemployed whiner spewing garbage*; *This should be required in schools*; *Why hasn't he finished his marshmallows??*; *O Homem Mais Legendario De Todo Tempo*; *Dude looking like a fairy with all that sparkledust...* Meanwhile the people from earlier had returned to the door, but with three others and greater insistence—Paramount was on his feet fending them off. Meanwhile the man who paid only in coins was pointing his phone at me, making *another* video. "Yo, Glitter Guy, speak to the people, my man!" Meanwhile I sat down on one of the shitty stools and tried to feel my body. Meanwhile Roger J was coaching me on how best to handle the situation. Meanwhile claps of thunder from the night's ridiculous rain sounded off as if in snide applause. Meanwhile my own phone was vibrating with a text from Monica Iñes: *Darling! So excited to get you over here. I've heard of a few parties that we absolutely must attend!*

POINT JAMES &
HAVERFORD

(in which what glitters isn't gold, escapes are orchestrated,
and—on the highest of heights—some final
betrayals are turned in before the deadline)

You think you're doing one thing when really you're doing something else. You think, Today I'll save some change for a show at the cinema, but instead those are the dollars you end up handing over to the bandit in the alley. You think, *Click click click*, these are such good photographs I am taking!, and then two blocks too late you realize the lens cap was on. You go to the beach and the water is bright with sparkling colors, but then when you jump in you realize it's because of jellyfish. And just when you figure you've done the one good deed you *won't* get punished for, the world comes tapping on your shoulder to collect its debt.

GLITTER GUY

Two days later there seemed not to be a place I could go without my video having been there first. I was seriously blowing up. I was getting recognized in the grocery store, the drugstore, the dollar store, along every other stretch of sidewalk while trying to mind my own business. Hour by hour the view count online kept racking up and at each new plateau did there seem another consequence for my life. At five hundred thousand views, sidewalk idlers whispered to each other as I passed, wondering if it was me; and at six hundred thousand they followed along just to be sure. Eight hundred thousand was when even the meekest amongst them took to snapping pictures of my face. Nine hundred thousand was when people I already knew began to regard me with a bit of wonder, as if I had been someone else all along and had only now been revealed. Mrs. Watts, who'd been ignoring my luck, stopped me again for some help on her scratch tickets, and to cough her way through a few adulations. "That was one heck of a speech, Slide. Have you been writing a long time?" Me I scratched away and won her four hundred dollars. But all the while thinking, *Writing?* What on earth was she *talking* about?

Well, *she* at the very least was still using my name. To everyone else I was Glitter Guy—as in: *Glitter Guy, I know how you feel!*, *Glitter Guy, tell us about the warnings again!*, *Glitter Guy, you're a real inspiration, you really moved me, you know...?* I really hated it. In Petit Julienne, which had always been a land of the strictest demarcations, those demarcations seemed to loosen for me, and if it was the case that some rivals on the west side of the street saw me walking along the east, it wouldn't stop them from calling me over for a bit of a word. A half dozen Terror Boys did exactly that while I was on my way to the bodega one day. Their leader, a red-eyed blackman in the midst of a cracking game of dominoes, addressed me: "You the one they're saying was in the video?" I nodded a timid *mhm*. "Thought so. They evicted my granny in the middle of the heat wave. Didn't care that we were a day away from getting the paperwork in order. You think anyone listens to us? It's good what you said. Anyone give you any trouble, you show them this." He handed me something: an evenly balanced switchblade, cool to the touch, with a writhing dragon engraved along its handle. I could only sputter out a few thank-yous as he patted me on the head. "You're alright by us. We like those messages you've been putting up too." And when I asked them what messages they were talking about, they all said *exactly* and flashed me smirking winks like we were in on some secret... That one forced me to keep my eyes open while walking about, and in fact it was true: here-there-and-everywhere had someone been vandalizing surfaces with snippets of my speech! DREAM WITHIN YOUR BUDGET, one such inscription read, scrawled across the glass display of a fur coat emporium on Brandeis Way. TOO MANY HOOLIGANS VAGABONDS ROGUES + PERVERTS, said another, on the wall of one of those municipal buildings responsible for handing out checks every month. I was walking along Dorset Trace when I turned a sudden corner to find a large group gathered beneath the billboard of an unpopular politician. A black bar of paint had been slashed through her eyes and the question WHO'S PROGRESSING HERE? sprayed across her mouth in a hasty hand. Everyone looking up at the billboard was sharing stories of all the times the politician had gone back on promises, or given their babies a cold when she kissed them. Suddenly they saw me. "It's him!" someone said. And: "Glitter Guy, you rascal!" And: "You seriously stuck it to her, she's a real lout, you know!" Oh no! They thought I'd been the one to do it! Listen, I have my faults same as anyone, but smearing public figures definitely isn't one of them. I was trying to explain as much but they were moving in on me with a flurry of hands, patting me on the back before I even had a chance. "She's another criminal, of course, except they get away with it sitting behind a desk!" said a veiny Arab with a tall hat. "You thinking of giving another speech?" asked a trio of big-bosomed women corralling two children apiece. "We have a couple suggestions for what you should tackle next." "Glitter Guy, are you doing anything right now? You must come see the hole she put me to live in, it's just like you described." "Yes!" "That's true for me too!" "We've been on the waiting list five years, seven of us jammed up like rats, every month some new excuse!" "Mine was asbestos!" "Black mold for me!" It went like that: one sad story setting the stage for another. Their irritation built to a furious current until a man sitting on another man's shoulders shouted the politician's home address for everyone to hear. They all picked up the nearest rocks they could find and began marching over that way. Geeez-uuus! It looked like they meant business. I might've been dragged along, too, if I hadn't slipped into an abandoned building during the haze of their stampede, catching my breath with my hands on my knees. Shit, it was getting hard to go anywhere. I might as well have stayed at home.

But it was no better there either! Whether or not because of Mrs. Watts, the rest of my neighbors had taken a sudden interest in me, such that there was hardly a time I couldn't expect another one of them to come introducing themself. A bookish man with thin hair and a wet upper lip, whose off-tune cello you could usually hear groaning at night, gave his name as Professor Koolanis once I opened my door to his shy tapping. He nervously launched into a long, boring lecture on the technical principles of my speech, as originally laid out by the rhetoricians of antiquity, some of whom I might or might not be aware of, but with whom, it was no bother, he was more than happy to foster an acquaintance should I ever be so inclined, seeing as it had, after all, been his good fortune to write a number of seminal texts on the subject in his own youth—a youth, if he dared say so himself, that had been unregrettably spent on society's front lines tackling the important issues of the day, animated as he and his colleagues all were by the zeal of progress, a zeal he'd once feared had

been extinguished but that, he hoped this was not too pre-
sumptuous, he now felt certain had in fact been reborn in none
other than the young man it was currently his pleasure to be
presenting himself to at last. *That* was interrupted only when
a passing Indian woman dropped her laundry basket to squeal
and grab my hands and say she had known there was something about me from the first day I'd moved in. Even though
the only other times she'd spoken to me had been to inform
me that she was taking the parking spot reserved for my unit
since it didn't look like I'd been using it. The nudist with
the pistol collection, the gaunt family of five, the pockmarked
adolescents who I suspected lived without supervision—
now they all wanted private words, or at the very least a pho-
tograph. Sometimes on coming home I'd see a couple of them
from a distance waiting out front of my door, having brought
friends, and I would turn right around to head back whence
I'd come...

I couldn't walk along Circuit Row because the Armenian shop-
keepers played the video on a loop on their TVs for sale; along
Charlotte Street because this one school, Rosebud Elementary,
was full of vile, pebble-throwing children who sang mean
chants. Neither Emissary Lane, where the Trinidadians cranked
up calypsos and made a party wherever I walked; nor Dame's
Circle, where the Senegalese always had a newborn they wanted
me to bless; nor Friedman Street, where the Czechs tried
pouring me full of lager; nor Fynn Road, since the Locoperros
around there could give a damn who I was; nor Baruch Street,
because I'd violated some Hasidic law I didn't even know; nor
Eckleman Way, where the graffiti from my speech was at its
worst. Which was to say nothing of the zones my affiliation

with the Dread Merchants had barred me from all along, or the boundary of Little Levant that Napakakos himself had said I was to go no farther south than. One of the inane detours I was having to take given all these restrictions ended me up along a wintry alley where I was too late in spotting the dozen black-clad figures closing in upon me. With more wonder than shock did I notice their gold piercings and carefully wrapped garb, their rich, oily skin like that of a painting come to life. I recognized them all the way from Calumet's long-ago tale even before they introduced themselves: the Brothers Seven, those enigmatic mystics he'd once considered joining. They had made the pilgrimage from their usual haunt of Avenue VII to come here, their expressions the tentative, relieved sort of those who have been searching a long time and have found what they are looking for.

"Brother," one of them said from the circle they'd formed around me, "we welcome you."

"And we commend your grandiloquence."

"A mighty feat."

"Agreed."

"Indeed."

"A little unfocused, naturally."

"Yes, yes, most unfocused."

"But that will come with practice."

"With which we can help."

"There's much to do."

"Our leader, Brother Maglucius, has requested your presence."

"A great honor, of course."

"Much is brewing Downtown."

"You have heard of the unrest, of course."

"The time is ripe."

"We have been prepared."

"History can be ours if we play today right..."

"Yes."

"Of course."

"Well, alright," I finally interjected, looking for the best gap in the circle to squeeze my way through. "Look, I'm seriously flattered. Thank you, I mean. Is there some sort of website I can look you guys up on after I think about it a little?"

One of them referenced his pocket notebook and gave me the address of their website. He was an elegant Nubian scented in musky aromas.

"Brother!" he held my shoulder and said. "You must join us. Incredible things are happening now that you have spoken..."

On the night the video hit one million views I was awake in bed watching it for the umpteenth time, still incredulous. There was that other me, ranting like a doppelgänger set loose. There was my sword-swallower, probably still unaware to this day. Spinning upward on a ticker beneath it was an ever-increasing view count: 999,478 "... lines and lines but never any order..."; 999,662 "... feels like the ladder I'm climbing is a wheel..."; 999,901 "... hooligans, vagabonds, rogues, and perverts..." Then it happened: the ticker went over: 1,000,002 views. Wow. I sat up. My head felt light. I'd never had a million of anything before. Soon after that was when the first journalist called. Things had been bad enough with my phone number having gotten out and my inbox flooding with a thousand messages a minute. With declarations of love, with penises and breasts, with death threats, with cartoons of myself eating marshmallows from a stick. I mean, I could hardly *find* the ones I wanted to find. Searching for Monica Iñes was like wading through an ocean of spam. *Darling*, she'd last said, *seriously, why won't you respond? We need to pick a date or we'll never see each other. How about Saturday at five, we can do Café Pampillon!* Oh man. I really wanted to confirm, but how to explain that I wasn't allowed to leave? In fact, just that morning Paramount had delivered a spot of ominous news: Uglygod wanted to talk to me. He'd jostled his way through the growing crowd of teenagers gathered outside the barbershop, Paramount had, and closed the door against their pressed-up bodies with enormous effort, clearly itching to draw his gun. It was becoming a serious madhouse around there. Less and less often were people coming for haircuts and more often to see if it was me, knocking on the glass as if having paid for an attraction that had yet to begin. *Glitter Guy, come sign my sneaker, come on, step outside for a little...* Paramount he was as mad as a prodded ox. "Ug says he needs to talk to you," he said through clenched teeth. It didn't look good. I thought of what I'd said in the video about them burning my shop down and feared I might be in trouble. Come to think of it, now would have been a good time for them to shoot me in the head and throw my body amongst the fish. I was starting to get paranoid. I told Paramount okay, but that night instead of going home I went and booked a stay in a wharf-side motel for a while and didn't return to my shop the next day. It was getting impossible to get work done in there anyway.

So that's where I was when the journalist called. I heard my phone buzzing from the dingy carpet and picked it up. "Hello?" "Yes, is this the Glitter Guy?" I told her maybe. She said she was calling from the *Looker* and did I mind if we spoke On the Record?, then launched into her questions before I could ask her what that meant. What was my name? Where was I from? Could I tell her a little about the inspiration behind the speech? Had I studied politics at any reputable institutions or was I self-taught? Geez was I stumbling over my words until, suddenly, *click*, she hung up, and two-three days later an article appeared in the weekend edition. WHO IS THE GLITTER GUY? read its headline, right there on page 14. I'd picked up a copy from the fresh stack the motel manager kept next to a bowl of expired candies on the front desk. "It was a warm March night and there he stood, fully rehearsed, ready to make his mark on the world," the article began, which was about all I needed to read of such balderdash. I wouldn't recommend you find a copy, it's a bunch of lies. Nonetheless, people ran with it. Its various misquotations further fueled my depiction as an intrepid crusader railing against injustice, and from north to south that image of me brandishing a marshmallow scepter propagated more and more. Suddenly I was inspiring others to take bold action, to renege on their shitty leases, to reenact my rant on their office floor as a means of quitting their jobs. From Lower Middleton there came a video of an irate fry cook at a Tasty Burger branch nailing the whole thing word for word, then dumping a fresh batch of fries onto the counter. Downtown in the Financial Plaza, some bigwig at a bank must not have been treating his underlings too right, for a coalition of them banded together and chained themselves to the bank's doors in protest, all wearing purple shirts. That one ended in a hail of billy clubs and nine-ten arrests. Three million views and half the students at the Hochoy-Shucster Institute of Law marched out en masse to camp in the Financial Plaza and bang plastic buckets. *Ten* million and the other half joined the next day. Things were starting to get exponential. It seemed no sooner had the views doubled in the morning than they had quintupled by the afternoon. Marches and sit-ins. Strikes for no reason. Sales of purple shirts reportedly going through the roof. Overnight, murals of my face were appearing on the sides of fancy residential buildings, while an outpouring of self-recorded testimonials—from evicted tenants, from homeless wards, from the most hopeless of house hunters whose pain, they said, matched my own—kept sprouting online. "I thought I was the only one," so many of them said. At any given moment, I was being called a savant, a fraud, a man touched-by-fire, a fad, an avatar of lost hopes, a joke, a huckster, an anointed one, a sad excuse for culture, a solution, a whiner, a wide-eyed puppy in need of a bowl of milk... Well, it was all fun and games until the bomb went off.

They had waited until the courthouse closed, so as to avoid any casualties, then detonated the charges they had hidden there earlier that day—shadowy figures, with no faces to speak of, and lists of grandiose demands they delivered to lawmakers the next morning. The blast shattered every window of that elaborate edifice's northern wing with an ear-piercing *boom*, crumbling the gilded dome and igniting a trail of gasoline on the front lawn that spelled out the words WHAT IF WE DID? in flaming letters. "It is our stance," read the demands, "that that which has been can no longer be, and that which is to be must be by the many and not by the few. In our insistences we stand with the Speaker, who is dubbed the Glitter Guy, offering the promise of the blast until such day as we are met with the promise of the pen." And so on. As a matter of fact, Jim, Jean, I seem to remember you two covering that one as well...

*   *   *

These happenings and more I watched on the fuzzy TV in that musty motel room with its stain-soaked bed. I was scared to leave. Scared even to return to my apartment and pick up the rest of my stuff. Now it was clear the Dread Merchants were looking for me, given all the missed calls and furious texts from Uglygod: *better call me back barber*; *u hidin frm us bytch??*; *if this is what I think it is ur going 2 b sorry!...* It was only a matter of time until they found out where I was. The weekend had come-and-gone and I hadn't made any plans with Monica Iñes. I'd worn the same clothes for four days and eventually stopped smelling myself. My latest habit was peeking out the blinds to see if any black motorcycles were patrolling, no matter how unlikely—the surrounding area was one of those rare zones so destitute that no crew had laid claim to it, a sorry mess of boarded-up ratholes filled with sand blown in from the beach. That there was a motel here at all felt more to do with the fur-clad women forever smoking suggestive cigarettes in the lobby than with anyone truly needing somewhere to sleep. Well, I was standing there anyway, looking out the blinds one Thursday evening, when yet another ring sounded from my phone. I was ready to hit IGNORE on instinct except this time it was Monica Iñes.

"Darling! It's like I can't hear from you! Are you getting my messages? Hello?"

"Monica," I said, touching my chest.

Her voice slipped down my ear like a hot unguent, quickening my blood into feverish action. It was really her.

Wherever she was it sounded busy.

"There you are! Slide! It's been a while, hasn't it? Darling, what happened to last weekend?"

"Hmm?"

"Saturday! We could've gone to that novelist's launch if you'd gotten back to me in time. Oh, it was a fabulous reading, Slide, tears all over the place, I bought an extra copy that I can give you, you know?"

"Right. I'm really sorry about that."

"It's in the past now. So listen, I figured I had to call or we'd never see each other. It shouldn't be this hard to set something up, my dear, if I have to confess, I think you're being a little lazy about it. These things aren't one-way streets, right? That's me, Theo, put it right there, if you don't mind. Fine, no no, the agave's fine. Slide? Okay, let's do Saturday, that's in two days. It's at the point where I really must insist, dear. Are you into polo? My friend Portia invites me to matches, though I think it a bore, and she herself only goes because of a referee she in*sists* is a dead ringer for a lumber magnate she still hasn't gotten over. I don't see it, the bone structure's different, but there'll be good drinks at least. We can meet at my office and grab lunch first. Sushi? I miss you, silly. How are you, by the way?"

"Monica, I..." By now I'd run a washcloth under some cold water in the bathroom to wipe across my face, plus I was kicking a path through the room's trash as if preparing for a guest. Heaven and a *half* was I in one hell of a fluster. I was on the verge of unraveling all my heart's contents, a knotted-up yarn of venom, pity, fear, longing and loneliness, frustration, the worst kind of confusion, despair, shock, awe, and anxious excitement at hearing her voice again. Instead I said, "I got held up."

"Oh, Slide..."

We went on for five-six minutes. She rattled off some more fun options for me to consider before choosing the ones she liked best. She had me Hold On for about thirty seconds to quickly complain to someone about a rickety table leg then picked right back up explaining what stop on the subway I'd need to get off at. I was moving here-there-everywhere around the room like an agitated fly, first to the bed, next to the ironing board, and finally back to look through those blinds, where through the gaps between the dead buildings lining the road I was convinced I could make out the shape of a motorcycle anyway.

That one made me blurt out with a choked-up dread: "Monica Iñes! Oh, it's all horrible! You have to understand, I have a whole lot going on. Ah shit, it would take me so long to explain and no one has the time. I don't think I'm going to make it there this weekend, I'm sorry, and I really did want to see you too." It was seriously getting me worked up, the thought of not seeing her after all. "I apologize, okay? I'm in a boatload of dangers is the thing and it's not fair of me to share them with anyone who didn't ask."

"Shhh, shhh, shhh!" She'd been trying to calm me down since I started. "Hush, Slide. You're talking nonsense, of *course* we're seeing each other."

"Oh, Monica, I really wish I could make you understand."

"There'll be plenty of time for that. The subway, Slide, I was saying, what stop's nearest to where you are now? I'll walk you through it."

"There aren't any stops near here."

"Come again?"

"No subways! Or at least I wouldn't be able to make it to one without something happening to me."

"Who ever heard of that? Where are you these days, then?"

I told her where I was.

"You're *where?* Oh dear. How'd you end up all the way there, darling?"

"Monica Iñes, it's such a—"

"Long story, yes, yes, I'm sure."

A sharper, less leisurely note had entered her voice, of either impatience or concern. She'd gone somewhere different as well, a little quieter.

"Here's what we'll do, Slide. I'll send over a car. We get them at work all the time. I'll have one pick you up in the morning and bring you out here. Jacob. Jacob! I'm booking a car for Saturday morning, it's to pick someone up. See, Slide? You won't have to do anything, you know?"

Closing the blinds, I moved over to the bed in four quick steps. I sat down. I got up. Suddenly I thought of Calumet. I can't say why for sure, but I did. Then I had a plan.

"Tinted windows," I said into the phone.

Monica Iñes said, "What?"

"The car has to have tinted windows, Monica Iñes, that's the only way." I was picking up the leftover bags from my takeout orders and gathering them into the trash. On the phone, Monica Iñes was relaying my request to the same someone in the background. Me I was sweating harder, flustered as if already pursued. Her voice came back on.

"Darling, that works. Send me your address so we can confirm."

FLIGHT FROM THE SLEEPLESS PATROL

My friends, to escape Petit Julienne was no easy feat. The next day I called Roger J to give him the location of the hidden

key to my apartment, so he could go inside and pack my suitcase with the things I cared for most. These he was to ferry
to Judith Abernathy's place at night. Such precautions avoid-
ed many problems. Hers was the address I'd given to Monica Iñes, since I obviously couldn't go back to that apartment
myself, and having Roger J come all the way out to the motel
with my stuff would certainly arouse suspicion. But more important was how useful Roger J would be in covering my tracks
later on—I didn't expect Napakakos and them to be too happy
when they discovered I'd gone. Already could I imagine them
turning over every stray stone they came across to track me
down. Having Roger J as one of the few people with a clue, it
was about as close to disappearing as could be managed. Liars
like him, the one thing you can be sure of is that they make
horrible witnesses. They wouldn't believe a *word* he said, even
if it was the truth.

The car was scheduled to come at dawn, so I made the furtive
walk to Judith Abernathy's a little before that. She and Roger J
were in the living room of her tiny, neat apartment going over
photo albums of her as a girl. It was the first time I'd seen her
since our date, not counting the video in which she appeared as a
meek background figure during quick pans of the camera. It's no
use lying about it: things were a little awkward, seeing her again.
When she met me at the door we both almost flinched, and I was
slow in taking off the sunglasses and hat I'd worn on the way over
to keep from being recognized. Still, she let me inside without
complaint, offering me the plate of sliced cheese on the table.

"Okay, Rog," I said, once I'd checked to see that my suitcase
was alright, "remember what we said. If anyone asks, I mean."

He looked up from the album and gave a solemn nod, glad to be of use.

"You're visiting someone in the hospital."

"Correct. I have a sick relative and it couldn't wait."

"That's right. Cancer of the esophagus."

"No, Rog. I didn't say that part. Don't add that in."

Geez, you really had to keep an eye on him or he'd lie about what color the sky was, which, at that moment, was the steely blue of an approaching sun. I checked my phone. As usual I had a million messages from unknown sources. There were some missed calls, too, but I couldn't be sure which one was the driver I was expecting.

"Judith, can you do me a favor? Keep an eye out the other window in case the driver gets it wrong and comes from that side."

I was busy staring out my own window but heard her getting up to go over there.

"Would you like anything else, Slide?" Judith Abernathy asked.

"I'm fine, thanks," I said. "It should be a black car."

"Are you *sure* you do not want anything else, Slide?"

Something about the way she said it the second time made me turn to look at her. There she was by the other window looking small again, her features tightening. Five kinds of fury seemed to be vying for a turn in her eyes.

"Judith...," I began.

"You know, come to think about it," said Roger J, oblivious, turning to another page of the photo album, "I do have a camera I've been meaning to brush off."

Then the driver came. It was a sturdy black car, moving in the creeping, unsure way of someone who's a bit lost, and its windows had a deep, deep tint just like I'd asked for. The car pulled up in front of the building and turned on the hazard lights. A call came in that I didn't even bother to answer. I put my shades back on, grabbed my suitcase, and headed down-stairs as fast as I could. Roger J was right behind me and Ju-dith Abernathy was farther back, as if undecided. Me I was al-ready outside a couple steps ahead, opening the car's back door.

"Prism Media?" I asked. Monica Iñes had given me the name of the PR firm where she worked.

The driver turned around to confirm yes. He was an upright senior citizen with two hands on the wheel. A crimson livery hat allowed for only glimpses of his silver hair, in neat contrast to the trimmed black mustache clinging to his upper lip.

"Pop the trunk, please," I said.

I threw my suitcase in there then got into the back seat, rolling the window down for some final farewells.

"Okay, Roger J. Okay, Judith Abernathy. I'm usually better at goodbyes, but this will have to do. It's best you don't know where I'm going for real, so you won't be compromised. You're welcome to anything left in my apartment too."

From the curb Roger J reached in to shake my hand.

"Alright then, guy. If ever you're back on this end be sure to hit me up."

"That won't be happening but I appreciate the offer."

He did his nod again. Man-oh-*man* was I tired of seeing him do that nod. When he stepped back, the fingers of his retracted hand fell by his side and lightly grazed those of Ju-dith Abernathy, who didn't come over to tell me anything. At the last second I saw it: the two of them were falling in love and waiting for me to go. The sudden sense of it hit me like a lightning bolt. I almost wanted to get back out the car.

The chambers of my heart were beating in competing directions—toward my impending escape, and back to the missed opportunities of an alternate past. I didn't even know why. But time had run out on me and the driver was already tapping the touch screen in the central panel. It was quite the fancy car. He asked if I was ready, I told him yes and rolled up the window as we got going, looking backward as Judith and Roger J got smaller and smaller before ultimately disappearing when we turned our first corner.

The driver had a route already planned, but on checking it over I saw it was a bad idea—it was shorter, yes, but would take us through all *kinds* of territory. Leaning toward the touch screen I asked if he didn't mind, then pointed out here, here, and here, where he should go instead.

"That's quite the long way, sir," he replied.

"Trust me, it's for the best," I said.

In the back of the car I settled down on the floor and started adjusting my coat so it covered my curled-up body. The windows could be tinted all they wanted, I wasn't going to trust them to keep me one hundred percent hidden. Bunkered like that, I got to talking to the driver—things like How's it going?, Where was he from?, This is some weather we're having, don't you think? Stuff to keep him calm. He was chatting along well enough, though I could tell he was still nervous.

"You nervous?" I asked.

"You hear things about the area is all, sir." He had a direct way of speaking that didn't mince words.

"I'd be lying if I said some of it wasn't true. We'll be alright."

"Is there a reason you're down there, sir?"

"I didn't get a lot of sleep last night."

"Alright."

We made stop-start progress through the alleys. Of course I couldn't tell exactly where we were at a given moment, but I knew he was a professional and would stick to my directions. Beneath my coat I was going mad with excitement. I was really pulling it off! Soon I would be out of Petit Julienne and never look back. Every bump on the road from my prone position was the turbulence of a rocket ship escaping the orbit of a doomed planet. At last! At last! Well, we were going along fine like that when I heard him shifting gears and felt the car reversing.

"What's that?" I asked.

"A wrong turn, sir."

He backed up, made the proper turn, and kept on going. Six minutes later he was reversing once more.

"Again?" I said.

"A minor confusion. There were stalls in the way."

That time we made it a bit farther before he stopped yet again.

Me I was practically snapping: "What's the holdup?"

"I'm being told to pull over, sir."

Shit. He'd gotten lost somehow. We were in Locoperros territory, I was almost sure of it.

"What do you see around you?" I said from where I was.

"Only some signs, sir."

"What *kind* of signs?" I had to emphasize. He really wasn't doing too well. Someone knocked on his window and I could hear his heart stop.

"What should I do here, sir?"

"Who's it knocking?"

"The gentleman has a lot of tattoos."

Oh shit! Oh no! If there was worse luck to be had, I couldn't think what it was.

"Is he big?" I asked, though I already knew the answer.

"Yes, sir."

"Listen, open it a crack and talk to him. Don't let anyone know I'm here! You have to be calm, you understand? Being calm is extremely important."

"Sir, if I may only ask—" but there was another, angrier knock and he couldn't get to what it was.

I heard him roll the window down a bit.

"Good morning," the driver said.

"How you doing, pal?"

It was Uglygod, of course. I was petrified.

"I am well, thank you."

"That's swell. Let me ask you something, pal, you know where you are?"

The driver must've first looked at his touch screen with the directions.

"I believe this is Freeman's Trace, sir."

"That's cute. I believe you're in the wrong place, is where you are. Roll your window down some more."

He hesitated. The poor guy, he had no idea.

"Now," said Uglygod.

The window went down more, cool morning air pouring into the car. Around the sides were the taps and murmurs of the others I knew were also surrounding us.

"So what brings you to our neighborhood, my friend?" Uglygod asked.

"I made a wrong turn, sir."

"A wrong turn to where?"

"Excuse me, sir?"

"Where were you trying to go that you made a wrong turn to!"

"For a pickup, sir."

"I'm not seeing anyone back there."

"I haven't picked them up yet, sir." That was good. He was a quick thinker, this guy.

"Oh, I see."

I felt the car sink beneath the weight of someone climbing onto it or taking a seat on the hood, as I'd seen happen before.

"Well, we would hate for you to be lost," said Uglygod. "Why don't you tell us where you're looking for and one of us will show you the way."

"I'm afraid that's confidential, sir."

"Come again?"

"Company policy, sir. The pickup is a private client."

"That's not fair, is it? You trying to be rude now? Imagine if I came to where you lived and told you it was confidential why I was there."

"I have told you why I am here, sir. It is only the matter of whom that—"

"Don't correct me."

That shut him up.

An eternity passed. Uglygod had either stepped away for a moment or else simply turned his head, for now his voice was speaking to the others in the coded terms I had come to know. They were planning to rob the driver of everything except his socks and sell the car engine for scraps. Their only holdup was in debating whether or not to make him take them to where he was going so they could see if there was someone worth robbing too. This was bad. This was about as bad as it could possibly be.

Me my heart was going *doom doom doom* beneath the coat and time had slowed to the detailed pace of final moments.

Soon his voice returned. "Turn the engine off, pal."

Tense, shuddering breaths. The driver didn't say anything and the engine was still on.

"Let me ask you something: You have trouble hearing?" Uglygod said, followed by a sound I knew all too well by then: of a gun's chamber going *click-click*.

I leaped up from beneath my cover and shouted "Drive!" into the driver's ear even as he was already mashing his foot down onto the accelerator. He didn't need me to tell him. We lurched into sudden motion, the world disintegrating into a blur, and a loud *pa-pow* that must have ruptured our eardrums rang out as the window to my side shattered into pieces. The car's motion had knocked the arm Uglygod had been pointing inside with his gun, squeezing out a bullet. It was Uglygod, Reverse, Two Piece, Kid Vicious who'd all been flanking the car on their motorcycles. Still clinging to the hood was Monsoon. The driver hit the brakes once, from the shock of that shot, or to shake Monsoon off, which happened with a wild cry from Monsoon as he clattered into a row of cloth-sellers. We were on Freeman's Trace, the edge of Little Levant that bordered Windbreaker turf. The day was just getting started and there weren't yet many people along those colorful stalls where embroidered tapestries were sold for bargains. The driver took off again, swerving to avoid Monsoon's legs and clenching the wheel with two hands while he dipped down the first turn he saw. "Fasten your seat belt, sir!" he shouted. Me I thought that was ridiculous. Suddenly the noise of dual engines caught up to us and Two Piece and Kid Vicious appeared on either side riding motorcycles. Peering through the fractured hole where once my window had been, Kid Vicious nearly gasped upon seeing me. "Ug, it's the barber! He's in the back seat!" he yelled. Uglygod was farther behind but was gaining on us too. Kid Vicious was trying to reach for his gun but kept having to navigate the quick turns on which the driver was leading them. *Geeez-uuus* could he drive! He had the alert pose of a diving hawk and was honking the horn every two seconds to let people know to get the hell out the way. We were passing beggars, deliverymen, gaggles of aunties on their way to church. With a hand brake maneuver he swerved the car's tail end and knocked Kid Vicious off his bike, then dove down a sharp-turn alley for which he would normally have had to slow down. *Pow pow pow*—Two Piece was still there shooting inconsequential bullets that hit nothing. Uglygod caught up and was right next to me. "Where do you think you're going, Barber!" The fierce collage of his tattoos took on a monstrous aura. He didn't have his gun anymore so was trying to reach inside again and get at my throat. "Pull this shit over now or there's an unhappy ending ahead!" I scuttled back to the far side where he couldn't get me, shards of the shattered glass piercing my palms. "Hold on, sir," said the driver. We hit a stretch of terrible potholes that made the car's trunk pop open and my teeth chatter. Uglygod, his hand still reaching inside, rode them all out with no loss in speed. Suddenly he grasped the door handle and pulled it open. Oh *no*! I don't know how but he was managing to ride his motorcycle at the same time as he held the door open, glancing back and forth between the two as if preparing to jump. Then: he jumped. For all his weight, it was a swift, catlike move in which one moment he was on the bike and the next he'd abandoned it to tumble away, one foot inside the car, the other dangling, and his hand gripping the rim of the window where the teeth of glass were biting his palm. "Driver!" I screamed. "Help! Do something!" He flashed a quick glance behind and almost screamed himself. Uglygod was righting his footing against the wild momentum of the car. Now he had both feet inside and was crawling toward me, reaching for my ankle, looking horrendous, the points of his filed teeth gleaming like the mouth of a shark. "We should have left you on the mountain," he growled. The driver was focused on the road and couldn't help. Soon we'd both be strangled and that would be the end of everything. Who would have thought it would be like this? Right at the edge as I was about to cross over. Now Uglygod was pulling me toward him and the lethargy of death was numbing my mind. How easy it would be to let him bite me on the neck and drain me of all this troublesome life at last… But my hand alone had other ideas, for suddenly I had gathered a handful of glass shards from the broken window. I waited right until Uglygod was close enough and threw them into his face. He shrieked, and in clutching at his eyes, freed my leg. "You son of a bitch! You rotten cunt! I'm going to rip your balls off! I'll stab you in the neck with your own bones!" So he was saying, but he couldn't quite track where I was now that his eyes were closed, fumbling about to grab me. "Brakes!" I yelled to the driver. He mashed them with a loud *scccrrrrcccch* that slammed Uglygod and me both into the backs of the front seats. But it was I who recovered quicker. With both legs did I load up a mighty kick and shove Uglygod out the still-open door, and bruised and blinded he tumbled out onto the dirty sidewalk of Gortat Street, knocking into a mailbox and swearing like a sailor's uncle, venomous to the very core. I shouted to the driver Go Go Go and he was off again, leaving Uglygod behind in a spate of dust and gravel. The others, who'd just caught up to find Uglygod on the ground, stopped to help him, firing some last-resort bullets our way for good measure. Those missed too. The morning was entirely electric with our manic breath, the bright, ignorant sun, the clattering sounds of the shot-up car. Holy shit. Soon our breathing settled. At the first possible safe stop (a gas station miles and miles away), the driver got out to have a brief panic attack, then called his wife. He devoured a bottle of water, snapped the trunk shut, and sat on the curb with his head in his hands for several minutes. Once he'd composed himself, he got back in. "We should be there in forty minutes, sir." And other than that, it was a pretty regular drive.

BEYOND THE ARCH

My friends, is there anything quite like entering Point James for the first time? No, I'm afraid there isn't. The only reason I pity those already from there is that they never get the chance to arrive. For those of us who are not—who must instead approach by cutting west across Downtown until the sea comes into view, then wade our way north along Avenue XIX through the last remnants of pedestrian life—we know something has changed when passing beneath the Septennial Arch. It is an impossible structure of elegant, translucent glass, straddling the road from end to end and dancing with refracted light. It looks like an overgrown gem, glimmering with such radiance that I spotted it from several blocks away and kept my mouth open the whole time. Oh my, I said to the driver. Even close up, something about it seemed less built than discovered, like a futuristic ruin from a civilization that had yet to come.

One passes beneath this arch as if through a portal between realms, and finds on the other side a Polis separate from the rest of Polis, where the light shines brighter, where the smiles are easier, where if it wasn't necessarily the case that the grass is greener, it is only because nowhere else has any grass to *begin* with. "What's the forecast supposed to be today?" I asked the driver while slipping off my down jacket—for here in Point James the weather was already balmy, and the breeze coming in through the broken window was of the warm, uplifting variety that inspires those to jog who have never jogged before. "It's spring, sir," he said, keeping his eyes on the road ahead. We were traversing a grove of dainty gardens dotted with blue ponds to which the ducks were returning from their long absence. Those soon gave way to a stretch of museums with imperious pillars, competing exhibits of great deceased artists, and one of which had a bridal party along its steps waiting to catch a bouquet. We navigated a corridor of stone towers connected one to the other by overhead walkways that I gazed up at through the car's sunroof as if into the underworking of an intricate clock—that's how I proceeded, dazed as a time-traveler, ogling each new sight with disbelief. A plaza of nude statues covered in doves. Two suited men riding a tandem bicycle. Long, elegant dogs with luxurious coats, cantering like horses. A lawn of laughing women playing croquet. Town houses, towers with recessed courtyards, walkway after walkway where liveried doormen on soft carpets tipped their hats just for you looking at them. Now a stretch of residences, now a bit of commerce featuring shops of stunning variety—for antiques, for marble countertops, for cheeses, mushrooms, foreign herbs and rare books, for well-designed furniture already arranged as if in a living room. Coffee sellers with sixty-eight kinds of beans sorted into wooden bins. There were people and people everywhere but never any *traffic*. Instead it seemed a giant choreography where no sooner did one light turn red than two others turned green, and for every vehicle that slid into rotation around the botanical roundabout, another had just left, such that there was never a pause in the whirlpool of their gleaming bodies. I'm not even kidding. But was Point James old or was it new? My friends, looking out the car, I couldn't quite tell. For at one moment was I noticing the black horses lugging ornate carriages, the handmade streets of misshapen stone, the lichen-dyed alcoves, the rusted suit of armor sitting on a bench, the weather-stained edifices overrun with gargoyles, or the tailor in his window working with needle and thread; and at another all I saw were cars sliding by with sleek, silent engines, public touch screens offering information, automatic doors that opened at the slightest irritation (leading into buildings of such experimental design I could not tell what they were *for*), tiny robots delivering packages through the air, kids on motorized skateboards typing on their phones. At the bus stops there were *timers* saying when the next bus would arrive. Even from afar I could tell everyone's clothes were of a higher thread count, their chatter devoid of violent concerns. I would have pressed my face against the window if there had still been one left. Us, in that busted-up car, we stuck out like a bruised toe on a pedicured foot.

We drove to the peninsula's western edge, along the water where the radiance of its blue spilled over into the rest of the world. I shouldn't have been surprised, but of course every strip of beach had pearly white sand and golden dogs chasing after frisbees. We went by the marinas where the anchored boats bobbed playfully in the sun. Now everyone I saw wore breezy pastels and flip-flops, and was gladly waiting in line at the seaside ice cream parlors atop which giant pelicans were perched, pruning themselves. It seemed that with every passing minute the memory of winter's cold days became more laughable, dubious, a kind of fanciful nightmare only those of us from elsewhere had ever endured. We eventually slowed at a dual row of hedges lining a sandy walkway, and the driver called someone and told them we'd arrived. A rustic sign reading FINNS BAY MEADOWS hung from a wooden post. But to my horror I spotted something else too: a gaggle of photographers crowding the path, their preening lenses already focused with anticipation as the car slid to a stop. There must have been *twenty* of them, split half-half on the entrance's either side, straining to see who was in the car. *Let me get an angle there*, *Anyone with a clear line?*, *Move over just a little, please*—that's what I heard them telling each other as I kept my head tucked down beneath my cap. The driver got out and fetched my suitcase from the trunk (somehow it hadn't fallen out during all the commotion), then opened the windowless door for me to exit. I counted to three and stepped out onto the sidewalk, taking my suitcase from the driver and gripping it for dear life despite the pain in my cut-up palms. The photographers leaned in. One serious ponytailed woman in particular, with a furrowed brow and glasses, was deciphering my face. She was the first to raise her camera to her eyes and press the shutter.

"It's him."

That first click set off a wave of others like a cascade of dominoes.

"It's the Glitter Guy!"

"Hey!"

"Turn this way!"

"Smile!"

Cameras were going *snap snap snap* all over the place, their flashes stunning me like so many zaps to the brain. It was nearly the height of morning but they *still* had the flashes on. If I'd thought the driver was going to be of any more help, I was sadly mistaken, for he'd walked back around after handing me my suitcase and gotten into the driver's seat before taking off. I never saw him again. I swear, my whole life in Polis has been me never seeing people again.

"Let's have a better angle now!"

"Glitter Guy, any comments on the councilman's comments?"

"Who are you wearing today?"

"Glitter Guy, were you in an altercation?"

Their calls for attention had me looking first one way then the other, sputtering silly nonsense for answers—What? Me? No, it's not anything special that I have on; Everyone calm down, it's a long story; Ouch!; You're giving me a headache... I couldn't make out but one of their faces in the induced haze of the flashes. Gone already was my sense of orientation; I put my hand up to my eyes and tried making my way forward by feel. But that only had the effect of driving them into a fit of desperation. To get angles on my shielded face they got shovier still, and a pink-haired punk who must have been seriously nuts blocked my way to snap a photo himself. Others did the same. Soon I was getting swarmed, barred from the way forward.

"Glitter Guy, where'd you just come from?"

"Any plans for a second speech?"

"What are your concerns about the lawsuit against you?"

I might have dawdled there forever, trying in vain to answer their useless questions, if not for a voice cutting through that cacophony.

"Slide! Dear! This way, quick!"

Yes! Yes, oh yes! I shoved my way through the throng until she came into sight. She was standing beside a maître d's podium, beckoning for me to hurry. "Come! Let's get you inside! Don't just stand there!"

I pushed my way along the sandy path, stronger now with something to push *for*. They stayed on me hot, the photographers, getting their last shots in, all the way to the maître d's podium, where they desisted as if encountering a force field, and where, on the other side, at long last, life had returned me to Monica Iñes.

"Geeez-uuus, Monica Iñes," I was already saying, "holy shit! Did you see all that? That's about the worst it's ever been."

"Slide! Language!" she said, ferrying me past the hedges so I'd be out of sight. We made it to a wider expanse, a few guests waiting to be seated in one of the open-air pavilions decked out with chatting brunchers. Except what I'd taken to be just a restaurant was really one of many stands surrounding a green field, where a half dozen horses were topped by riders swinging mallets. Wow, she hadn't been kidding: there really was a polo match after all. The commotion of my arrival had turned a few people's heads our way, but they soon returned to the slim binoculars with which they were watching the action on the field. "Yes, it's very unusual, someone must have tipped them off. Oh, Slide, I really wish you'd called me earlier, you know?"

"Monica. Geez do I have to talk to you about stuff."

"I'm sure! So do I, it's been one hell of a morning, let me just say. Oh, I've been up since forever, dear, some problem with my alarm and..."

She had on a chic oversize navy jacket, a button-up white top tucked into flowy silk pants, thin plimsolls, and a wide hat. Her nails, lacquered with French tips, were already going *clack-clack* on the screen of her phone as she kept on with her recap of the morning. My oh my, I was really here again! There were her red lips; there was her tongue moving delicately across her teeth like a balanced acrobat. She was just as I'd remembered her but different too. Her painted face was as smooth as ever and the long braid of her hair had so lengthened that its ends now sat comfortably upon her buttocks. She looked sexy.

And yet the easy air with which she had waltzed into my life that first Sunday many lifetimes ago seemed gone, replaced by a displeased fidgeting as she looked me over—my roughed-up shirt and bruised palms, the nicks and scrapes from pieces of glass. Come to think of it, I hadn't looked too good the *last* time I'd seen her either, she must've thought I was like this all the time.

"Monica, something's happened," I finally said. "I've been in this video, you see. It's everywhere now and I can't do anyth—"

"Yes, Slide. Don't be silly, of course I know all that. And I read that horrid article too. Oh, Slide, I really wish you'd responded earlier. You can't go trusting everyone who puts a microphone in your face. We're old friends. I have your best

interests at heart, you know?" she said, taking my free hand
into both of hers. Her perfume was an intricate, woody fra-
grance with undertones of crushed berries.

"I'm sorry, Monica," I said, sighing. "There's more to it
than that, though. Look, I'll tell you the whole thing over
brunch like we said. Sushi, right? And what are the rules for
this game? I've never had the chance to learn, although I've
been meaning to."

One of the riders had pulled a slick maneuver where he
juggled the ball a few times on his mallet before whacking it
downfield, to the light applause of the crowd. I was making
my way to the pavilion when she tightened her hold on my
hand.

"You know what, Slide?" She looked me over again. "I just
remembered, I do have a few quick errands to run. And the
match is quite stale, these Andalusian teams are practically
professional so it can get rather one-sided, you know? Let's hit
the road. You'll meet everyone later on. Come on, I'm parked
out back so we can avoid those fiends."

She pulled me with her, almost a tug, along the backside
of the pavilion without ever setting foot inside. She made a
quick call telling whoever it was to meet us so we could get
going. A slope of manicured vegetation led away from the
stands and toward the parking lot, where we waited a few
minutes for the car. I thought I heard someone behind us call
her name, but it must have been for someone else, because she
didn't turn around. Soon the car came, a burgundy convertible with cream leather seats. It was fancy and everything,
but the real shock was the driver behind the wheel: another
Monica Iñes. Gripping with proper two-handed positioning
was what seemed to be an entire *replica*. Her smooth features

were the same, her sandy complexion no different, though her outfit of plain jeans and sweater was about as unfashionable as could be.

"Slide, you remember I have a sister, of course," Monica Iñes mentioned as she took my suitcase from me and threw it into the back seat.

"Of course," I managed.

"Marissa is trying out as my assistant for the time being, while between jobs." On the other side she opened the front door for Marissa to hop out, then settled behind the wheel herself. "There's nothing like family, you know?"

The other Iñes made her way over to me in soundless steps, shaking my hand with averted eyes, bloody though my palm was. "It's very nice to meet you." She was thinner than Monica, her hair in a pixie cut barely covering her ears. Looking back and forth between the two of them, it was as if I were witnessing a single life split into opposing fates. From the slight bobbing of her mouth, like that of a fish, it seemed Marissa was about to say something more. But she thought twice of it, and opened the front passenger door for me.

"Quickly, dear. We really should get going," said Monica Iñes.

I did like she said and hopped in, Marissa settling into the back. Monica Iñes cut a winding way out the parking lot and onto a road along the lot's side, such that some of the photographers who were still there spotted us anyway. However many there'd been when I'd arrived, they'd *multiplied* in the minutes since. *Glitter Guy, look over here, you bastard!*, *Give us a shot, we have bills to pay, don't you know!* I buckled my seat belt, pretending I didn't notice them, as Monica Iñes peeled off toward Avenue XIX heading north.

Monica on the Move

She drove with the pedal almost to the floor. The radio was playing a song she liked, a wireless headpiece stuck in her ear. She was saying to Marissa, Call this one, Call that one, Cancel that thing at five o'clock but schedule that other one for six, to which Marissa would frantically nod and hit buttons on her own phone. The sun was warmer still and the wind was whipping Monica Iñes's braid into an auburn contrail. The only thing faster than her weaving from lane to lane was her chatter through her phone, on which she was placing one call after another with hardly a pause in between. "Yes, I'm on my way." "Don't worry, he's expecting me." "I'll be there later, so stop asking, please." I couldn't imagine the people on the other end were getting much of a word in. If ever more than a few seconds extended between one call and the next and I thought I might ask her a few things, she'd preemptively squeeze my knee and say, "Slide, it's been so long. You look well. I've missed you, you know?," which just about melted away anything I'd been thinking. Oh, Monica, I wanted to say, what a long circle it has been, how endless the months. Can you even imagine what these miles have done... *Ring ring, ring ring*: she'd be on to the next call.

We jetted straight to a place she liked to get some quick things to eat, the Cranston Liverwurst on Coolander & XVIII. For me she ordered the foie gras burger and raspberry seltzer, and for her and Marissa Iñes a pair of complicated salads. We could eat in the car as long as we used paper towels to cover our laps. We made our way to a fantastic plaza of clothing boutiques, each with identical white interiors and hanging black signs. She told the person on the phone One Sec and, turning to me, asked, "What are your sizes, Slide?," and when I wasn't quite sure she measured me with her eyes then stepped into a store called Two Snails, leaving the engine running. In six minutes she was back with a salmon-colored shopping bag that she handed to Marissa before hitting the pedal again. We stopped by a perfumery, where she got me a mature cologne. We stopped by a jeweler and picked me up a simple watch with a brown leather band. Oh wow, Monica, I kept on saying. You really don't have to. Along the way I was getting recognized all over the place, on sidewalks and street corners, by passengers in parallel cars during stops at red lights. In one of them two loud Asian men and a stylish blackwoman yelled as if frightened and nearly veered into our lane trying to ask me questions. They started playing the song, the electronic remix of my speech that had grown popular. "Glitter Guy, is it you for real? My brother loves you! Wait, please, don't go, say the part about the jaywalking…" That one caused Monica Iñes to fold the roof up and close the windows. It wasn't that we were being followed, but we weren't *not* being followed either—the ending of one such scene often caused another to begin in a transfer of commotion, as if we were hopping our way through Point James along sinking lily pads. It was a real roving circus, I'm not kidding. As if to take my mind off things, Monica Iñes took a break from her phone and said:

"So how have you been, Slide? We have such catching up to do. What's the latest?"

I breathed a sigh of relief. *Gosh* did I have a lot to talk to her about.

"Well, Monica Iñes, you really wouldn't believe it," I began. I got going, but it was all out of order: I told her of the camp on Millennium Mount and then of Osman the Throned,

I mentioned something about the juices I'd poured down Rosa de Sanville's throat and followed that up by saying I'd become an entrepreneur and opened my own barbershop. I swear, it was a real mess, my thoughts shook about as if from the torque of the car's turns.

"Mhm, mhm," Monica Iñes kept saying, her eyes on the road. "That's so interesting. And how are the boys doing? Eustace and that other one? I have to say, Slide, it was very rude the way things ended last time. The poor dears." I opened my mouth with five things to say all at the same time. But glancing over my shoulder I saw that Marissa had been eavesdropping and I didn't really know her like that.

"Everyone's fine," I said. Monica nodded.

"That's good. Honestly, though. So rude. That tall one especially. What was his name again?"

When we pulled up to a varnished wooden gate, flanked by tremendous stone birds, along a tree-covered street named Dorsicund Trace, even the security guard at the booth slipped out of his stoic demeanor to ogle me before letting us through. The gravel drive beyond the gates led to a tucked-away spa spread out amongst seven Japanese bungalows. We parked in front of the main one and all got out, following Monica Iñes into a cool lobby, where she checked in. "Iñes. One guest. We're in a slight hurry. He'll have a charcoal rinse and a trim, if Naseema is in." A voluptuous woman with soft, milky skin manned the desk. She responded Right This Way in a soothing voice and handed me a towel and a pair of cloth slippers. I followed her outside and slightly uphill, past the bonsai groves and trickling fountains and guests in white robes being led by attendants of their own, Monica Iñes phone-chatting by

my side while Marissa waited in the lobby as instructed. One of
the bungalows had a steamy interior, wood paneling, and hot,
shallow pools. The attendant handed me off to a short woman
in a kimono, who told me to disrobe and get into the water.
I hesitated: Monica Iñes was right there. Placing her hand over
the phone speaker, she said, "Slide, we don't have a lot of time."

I was like a shy mule being led to a pond: "Is there a changing room or something?"

"It's all the way at the other end. We'd have to get you a
robe too. Come on, we're in a hurry."

Oh gosh. What now? There was no way out. I took off my
clothes and got in, naked, covering up with my hands, winc-
ing at the water's scalding touch on every one of my wounds.
Fine pebbles covered the base of the pool. The attendant used
a wooden scoop to douse me all over, then took handfuls of
pebbles and scrubbed me from head to toe. *Geeez-uuus*, it hurt
so good. She scrubbed away the thin crust of blood, the residue
of my panicked sweat. I heard myself groaning in embarrassed
delight. By the time it was done and the attendant was drying
me off, Marissa Iñes had brought up the shopping bag of my
new clothes. These I changed into right there: a pair of skinny
black pants, a black shirt, a black cardigan, a black belt, and
a pair of black shoes too. I put on the watch. Looking me over
afterward, Monica Iñes settled at last into a soft repose, as if
she'd satisfied an itch.

"You look nice, Slide."

She applied sprays of cologne behind my ears and along my
neck. And before it was all done, we made a final stop at one
more bungalow: a hair salon of the utmost pristine beauty.

That part was like it wasn't even happening to me. All of
a sudden I was being reclined in a soft chair, my hair getting

washed by the massaging fingers of the stylist Naseema. She was a stalwart Iranian with no smiles and few words. "Turn" was mostly what she said, when need be. Aware of our short time, she made quick work of the wash and got me into her chair, setting into my frazzled mess with scissors so sharp you could hear them slice the air. She took some off here, some off there, moving around me with the swift motions of a dancer who's given up her dreams. Try as I might to see what was happening in the mirror (I thought I might give her some feedback as one professional to another), she always managed to position herself in the way. I didn't see the results until she was done. Oo-la-la. I had a low, neat afro perfectly tapered at the sides and a sharp line done as if with a precision machine. My beard had been groomed to elegant proportions and the surrounding skin brought back to life with a mild astringent. My eyebrows were trimmed, my protruding nose hairs cut away. I looked good. Contemplating myself, I knew what was true right then and has remained true to this very day on which I speak to you—it was the best haircut I'd ever had.

It was just around midday and I'd been in Point James for four hours. I had new clothes, a new look, a growing attachment to wearing my shades since they kept me from being recognized. I felt discombobulated and spun about, ricocheted by the madcap tour Monica Iñes was taking me on with hardly a pause for reflection. I wanted to know: What's happening? Who keeps calling? When's it going to be just me and you like you said? Wowed as I was to discover each new luxury around the corner, I was equally aware of a growing irritation at so late a discovery, as if my life in Polis so far had been but a mocking prelude. Point James seemed separated from the rest of everything not by that spectacular arch, but by an invisible

moat of eighty crocodiles, or unwritten agreements. It hadn't
occurred to me as an *option* to come here. Not really, I mean.
Calumet had mentioned a few things, sure, but he hadn't mentioned enough. Before getting back on her phone, Monica Iñes
rattled off a schedule of events for the rest of the day, a dinner
at this place, cocktails at that one, so on and etcetera. It was as
if now that I was cleaned up, she could speak to me freely. On
our way out of the spa, the security guard from earlier came
up to my window and leaned in, while Monica Iñes revved
the engine and waited for an opening in the passing cars. He
was a weary blackman with coarse stubble and a vein down
his forehead, his skin darker still for the tint of my shades.
He seemed shy. "I was—" he began to mumble, "I was very
moved by what you said. For people like us..." He ran out of
words. His hand was there on the windowsill, and for a moment, I thought I would pat it with my own, if only to have
done something. Monica Iñes saw her opening and took off
into the street with a whiplash turn, the car belting down the
road like a horse on fire.

We then returned to the marinas. The polo match was all done
but there was still time to catch Xander Durant, a colleague of
hers whom I absolutely had to meet.

"He's the one we would have gotten lunch with last weekend, too, Slide. Oh, I really wish you'd called me. You should
have called me, but it's okay. You're here now."

Ordinarily he worked at Neptune Studios, in the La Fontana
District, along the eastern bay, though, today being Saturday,
he was working away from the office. Her wireless headpiece
ran out of charge and she had to connect her phone to the car's
speakers, right as the water's shimmering edge came into sight

again. She called one number and no one picked up. She called another that rang twice before a woman's voice answered hello with a lot of commotion behind her. She and Monica Iñes had a loud, halting conversation, interrupted often by the woman squealing at whatever was happening around her.

"Monica, love... where'd you go... next thing I knew... eek!"

"Never mind that. Where's everyone now? Hurry, please."

"Listen... over to Pier Nineteen... send Dicky for you... simpler that way."

"Oh, alright, I suppose, but it really wouldn't have killed you to wait, you know?" The woman laughed at a joke in the background and Monica hung up.

This time we parked along the street and walked all the way to the end of a wooden dock slick with moss. Five people were on the deck of a nearby boat watching a car race on TV. Three little kids ran around us playing a game, their mother right behind holding ice cream cones. I was about to ask what we were here for when the sound of an approaching motor cut across the water, a yellow dinghy bouncing toward us over the waves. Operating the engine was a deeply tanned man with blond dreadlocks, who soon docked the boat perfectly before us.

"Iñes, Iñes, Iñes," he said, extending a hand to help her onboard. "Never on time."

"Save it, Dicky," she said.

We followed her onto the boat, Marissa Iñes, then me, and Dicky pointed out handles along the railing for us to hold on to and set off. He wore a blue sailing outfit and a dopey grin, bobbing his head to some song no one else could hear. Once we had cleared the docks and were in the open water, I saw he was ruddering us toward a long, spectacular yacht, gleaming white on the horizon. "Well, we're just getting started, fortunately," said Dicky.

Along the way Monica Iñes redid her look. She shed her hat and jacket and took her top off to reveal a cream swimsuit she'd been wearing all along. Taking an elastic out of her purse, she tied her hair up into a coiled bun. From a small white tube she applied dabs of sunscreen first to her fingertips and then to her face and arms, and swapped her lightly tinted sunglasses for a heavily mirrored pair. Dicky cut the engine for us to drift the remainder of the way to the larger boat, and we passed four-five beautiful people swimming in the clear water. "Would you look at that, it's Monica," one of them said. "We were just asking for you, we missed you at the rest of the match!" A rope ladder extended off the yacht's side, which we one by one ascended. The yacht had a hard, varnished deck of reddish wood. Many people were milling about and drinking from flutes of champagne, pop music playing from somewhere. Without exception were they tall and good-looking, imbued with an aggressive health that began at their teeth. One was a slim-waisted blackwoman shaped like a dream, another a mixed-blood fox with lips like inviting pillows. A chiseled adonis, a debonair gent. *Geeez-uuus*, I'd never seen so many tall, healthy-looking people all in the same place before, usually they're more spread out. Some of the women in bikini bottoms alone had breasts that shone like pinpoints of light. I had to keep my eyes up. Monica Iñes instructed Marissa to go occupy herself elsewhere while leading me through the revelers.

"Where are we going, Monica?" I said, for the umpteenth time that day.

"Xander's over there," she said, pointing ahead.

"The front?" I said. "I'll meet you there. Let me catch my breath a second." I was feeling flustered and anxious. A little bit ugly, too, since we're already on the subject.

"The bow, Slide. It's called the bow."

She charged me through the women clinking drinks and the men in animated chatter, saying hi to some she knew, until finally at the yacht's edge we climbed over a low railing beyond which three people were spending their time on the prow. Two of them were women halfway asleep on long towels, their backs exposed to the sun, an ice bucket of champagne sweating between them. But the other, as if to survey the world, stood right at the tip with his hands on his hips—a languid man with a mane of wild black curls, in a pair of skimpy orange swim shorts over which his stomach hung. Without a shirt covering him up it was easy to see the extent of his tan and the traces of flab beginning to congeal upon his athlete's body in decline. He had a sharp ridge of a nose, razor bumps under his chin, a thin crease for lips. His eyes left the water and turned toward us, full of the uncontained energy of a child at recess. It was Xander Durant. At his feet sat a gray poodle.

"Iñes! You've returned. Tell me something, what's it take to get a man like Hector on the phone." He indicated a wireless headpiece fitted into his ear.

"Hector's leg's broken," said Monica Iñes.

"Broken? I heard it was a sprain."

"Broken."

She'd taken up the bottle of champagne from between the sunbathing women and was pouring herself a glass. Xander Durant shook his head.

"What's that mean for the Centennial then?"

"I'm hearing they may go with Clementine's team, but you know how she can be. Is there another glass for my friend?"

"Broken leg doesn't mean he can't get on the phone."

"Xander! I mean, he's probably on all kinds of *medications*, you know? He must be really woozy, understand?"

He looked unsatisfied. "Broken leg doesn't mean he can't have someone answer his phone."

"A glass for my friend, Xander?"

He retrieved a glass from where it had been nestled in the crook of one of the sunbathing women's necks and tossed it to me underhand. Shit! I juggled it around and nearly fumbled the catch. A group of four leaned over the railing behind us and asked Xander Durant if he wanted to try the cake, to which he said no and they ran off giggling. It was a loud day with all that music, the babble of fun, the hum of other boats buzzing by.

"So what then? We're supposed to sit here waiting while the bone sets? While Clementine's team is *allegedly* running the show?"

"I can have someone get on it as well, there are things in place. Oh, Xander. You really are so rude. Hasn't it occurred to you to introduce yourself to my friend?"

"Your friend's on my boat."

"Oh, Xander. Too rude. Come here, Slide."

She introduced us. When shaking hands, his remained limp, like a gift offered, leaving me to do the work of moving it up and down. Pleased to meet, I said. Charmed, I'm sure, he said.

"Slide and I are just catching up today. We're old friends and it's been some time."

"Mhm," said Xander Durant, pulling away.

A pair of bubbling streams broke the water's surface a couple feet out. Suddenly there rose two scuba divers in wetsuits, paddling their way to the yacht while dragging a nylon net between them. They hooked the net's corners to a pulley contraption that Xander Durant then pushed a button to raise. In the net were countless black oysters.

"Which are these?" he stood near the edge and asked. One of the divers took off his headgear to respond, a long-faced man with a hard jaw and dark dots for eyes.

"We got thorny and European flats in there. Good spread couple fathoms down."

From the pocket of his small swim shorts Xander Durant took out a shucking knife, grabbed an oyster from the net, and shucked it open. After slurping down its insides he tossed the shell back into the water.

"Okay, these are fine. See if you run into any goldclasps like last time."

The divers both nodded. The one who'd spoken refitted his headgear and they disappeared beneath the water.

"You all want oysters?" he said to us. Monica Iñes said no even as I was nodding yes. He woke up the sunbathing women to ask if they wanted oysters and started rapidly shucking one after the other. The poodle at his feet yawned.

"Slide, don't you think you should take off those sunglasses. It's a little rude in company," said Monica Iñes. I would really rather have not.

"I'd really rather not," I said.

"Alright then, Iñes," said Xander Durant. "I'm getting Clementine on the line and we're going to get to the bottom of this. I already told the Arctics they'd be performing at the Centennial and no one's going to call me a liar if I can help it."

He pushed a button on the earpiece and instructed it to call Clementine.

"That sounds good. Slide." Her focus returned to me. "Those sunglasses *are* a bit rude." She was getting insistent, antsy again like when we'd met this morning.

I looked around. People everywhere were wearing sunglasses.

Xander Durant said, "Let the man keep his sunglasses on if he feels like it. What are you, his mother? Yes, hello? Clementine? Listen, it's Xander, your people are really fucking us over with the Centennial, I thought we'd talked about this?"

She marched up to me and took off my sunglasses, folding them into her purse. "Not everything needs to be a whole issue, Slide." That one stunned me twice: once at the audacity, and once again at the flood of sun-bright colors. I hadn't realized how *blue* things were. The ocean sparkled like a field of watery diamonds and in the sky above were the fluffiest of clouds wafting on by. We were a couple leagues out from Point James, its skyline a brilliant assembly of spires.

I didn't know what to do with the hand not holding the champagne glass. I put it first into my pocket, but then took it out to let it hang all nonchalantly at my side. The women, who were slurping oysters, were both very pretty, lounging about like rare cats. I was doing my very best not to look at their breasts—at least with the shades on no one would have noticed. Gosh was I feeling ugly, roughed up like a piece of coal. From the party going on behind us came a lot of laughs and commotion as a new song started. Xander Durant was ranting to someone on the phone and shucking oyster after oyster, going, "Well, how'd he even break it?" or "For the umpteenth time, no!" or "Are there no more surgeons in the world..." Such yelling was causing him to pace. And only because of that did he once come my way, in the midst of his circular march, his eyes passing over my exposed face for a split moment. He moved on. He did a double take. A look of consternation occupied him.

"Do I know you?" he asked me.

Oh Lord. I could see where this was going.

"I doubt it," I said, angling so as to face the water.

"I told you already, it's Slide," said Monica Iñes. "We're old friends. The last time I saw him we had the most lovely dinner together, didn't we, Slide?"

"Yes, it was splendid!" I said. I wasn't sure why but my voice was a little higher, and I'd said "splendid" without meaning to.

"I can swear you look familiar," said Xander Durant.

"Oh, Xander, you are always harassing the people I bring around. Never giving them a chance to breathe, you know? Ignore him, Slide," said Monica Iñes.

But I couldn't ignore him. There out of the corner of my eye did I see him scrutinizing my features, except for a sudden break to snap at someone on the phone and tell them to hold on.

"Wait." He took off the earpiece. "You're the guy from the video, aren't you?"

"Xander! Really! Do you *have* to be so embarrassing?"

"What video?" I whimpered.

"Holy shit, it *is* you!" he said. "You're a goddamn unicorn, you know that? This is a unicorn sighting!" He opened his mouth. He was really getting amazed.

"Xander, don't be so crass! Really, you would bring that up as the first thing? You're such a crass, Xander, it's hard to introduce you to friends. Everyone I introduce you to it gets harder and harder," said Monica Iñes. And yet her movements had loosened up at last and her arms were going through the exaggerated pantomimes of weariness, such as pressing her champagne glass against her forehead as if to fend off a swoon. One of the sunbathing women was taking a closer look at me for the first time, too, her mouth slowly opening into an astonished O.

"You're the Glitter Guy!" exclaimed Xander Durant. "Monica, you old devil, you naughty bitch, you brought me the Glitter Guy, didn't you! Ooh, this is just like you, isn't it!" His face was growing animated with delight as if he were unwrapping a gift. All of a sudden he was wiping his palms so he could shake my hand again, properly this time. "I can't believe it's you! I have all kinds of questions for you," he pulled me in to say. "The things you were saying, they're exactly right. *Exactly* right. Someone had to say it so here you are. It's wrong the way things work in this place." He swept his hand across Polis. "They're calling you the voice of a people, you know that?"

"No, I wasn't aware," I said.

He nodded yes, yes. "What's that line you had? 'One hundred in the bank but it costs two to keep it there'? See? I know the best parts by heart. Say it for me, won't you?"

"I don't remember it all," I said. Geez was I feeling uncomfortable. Now the other woman was looking at me too.

"That's what I thought," Xander Durant said understandingly. "Impromptu, wasn't it? You were touched by the muse, weren't you? I recognized it in your eyes, you have the same eyes as in the video." Such was his excitement that the poodle had picked up on it and was bounding around us in hind-leg jumps. His earpiece rang in his hand and he tossed it aside. "I'm a poet myself, I know how these things are. Monica! You are such a devil! Why didn't you tell me you knew the Glitter Guy?"

"Oh that?" Monica Iñes was back on her phone. "Well, I was hardly thinking about *that*, you know? Slide and I go way back, before any of the video nonsense."

He hadn't heard her. He'd gotten the bottle of champagne and was pouring me the last drops. "Oh, this changes everything. Everything! My friend, my friend, my friend—welcome to my boat."

Xander Durant Offers Representation

Opening a hatch in the prow that led belowdecks, Xander Durant ushered us down a set of narrow steps and into a small office, clearing a bunch of papers from the desk as he settled behind its five computer screens. The room was an elegant mess of hardwood paneling and soft-cushioned seats. The music upstairs grew warbled and distant. But his chatter hadn't slowed one bit. He was having *this* idea, *that* idea, so many things that could be done but we had to act immediately. Can he sing, Monica? Can he dance? How does he do onstage? Then he froze, too excited—almost nervous, even.

"Iñes, do you know what this means?" He drummed his fingers frantically. "We can carry him to—" but she was already nodding her head six times: "I know."

"Oh, you naughty bitch. You naughty, naughty bitch."

From somewhere on the ground he'd found himself a dress shirt and an unlikely pair of glasses, though the orange trunks were still all he wore by way of pants. His typing on the keyboard was constant, his attention flitting from one screen to the next like a hummingbird between flowers. And Monica Iñes, she was growing just as lively, saying, No singing, no dancing, he's a friend, not some puppet.

"Xander, I was thinking this as well, but you need to tell me your opinion. I was thinking we could start him at Berni—"

"Bernicio!" They finished the name at the same time, trembling in anticipation of whatever that meant. Xander Durant nodded *of course* and sent off a quick email. But one minute later he had an issue: What had happened to my beard?

"The beard had to be trimmed," she said. "He looks better this way."

He threw his hands to the ceiling as if to a jury of angels. "We need the beard from in the *video*, Iñes. You can't just go changing it. Not everything's a fashion show."

"Well, nothing to be done about it now."

"No worries," he said, "he'll have to grow it back is all..." and let his words trail as he resumed typing.

The clacking of his keys, their ping-ponging of ideas, their jargon-filled chatter of which I was simultaneously at the center yet somehow entirely excluded from, as if I were overhearing arrangements for my own funeral. We can do so much, Xander Durant kept on saying. There's no limit to how much we can do.

"Ah, before I forget," he said. Opening a drawer by his side, he took out a stack of papers and slid them over my way. "It's your standard agreement but you can skim it over if you would like." That's the one that stunned me. I looked at the top page, the heading of which announced a contract between management and client. Flipping through didn't make a difference: I couldn't understand anything. For the first time that day I felt a familiar rage returning, my time in Petit Julienne not even a single day gone.

"What is this?" I cut in. "What is any of this?" I'd said it slightly louder than I'd wanted to. Xander Durant stopped typing, more than a little excited. You could tell he was thinking I might go on another rant. Damn, that about nixed that option.

"I haven't been given a single explanation of anything since I *got* here," I continued, trying to regulate my voice. "Who is this man, Monica Iñes? Why're we on this boat? And that party going on upstairs, I mean, everyone has their *breasts* out for crying out loud! What's a guy suppose to do? Shit, oh shit, I really need a seat." I sat down with my head between my hands. My mind was hours behind in processing the day's events—part of me was still in that final tussle, with Uglygod's large fingers around my ankle. Oh man, I was feeling a little nauseous: the boat must have been rocking or something. "Is this boat rocking or something? Monica Iñes, all I'm asking for is a little time with you. Aren't we supposed to be catching up? How come that hasn't happened yet..."

"Iñes. You want me to handle this? I can—"

But she was already on the chair next to me, pulling in close. Monica Iñes put her hand on my back.

"Oh, I'm sorry, Slide. Come here. Let's talk. You're absolutely right," she softly said. "I should have explained more. I'm sorry." She rubbed my back. "I'm sorry."

A couple sighs eased out my chest without me meaning them to.

"It's like everything's gone all crazy for me all of a sudden." I steadied my shaking hands. "I'm hardly getting the chance to *speak* anymore."

"Poor thing! Oh, my dear. It's okay, Slide, I know how it must be. You're going through the stages."

"The stages?" I looked into her eyes.

She nodded. "It happens a lot to people in your situation. Xander and I, it's what we help our clients deal with every day, Slide." From where he was behind the desk, Xander Durant straightened the angle of his glasses and nodded. "Let me ask you something, dear, has your phone number gotten out?"

"Oh wow, Monica Iñes! How'd you even know? I've had about nineteen calls since I've been on this *boat*, even."

"That usually happens first. All sorts of nasty messages, I bet. And you've been hearing from the lawyers too?"

"Yes, Monica."

"Full of hollow threats and empty promises. You have to understand, Slide, people are going to try to take advantage of you now. It's different for you. Poor dear, I can only imagine." A wave of cheers sounded from the deck above. "These things don't come with a rule book, I'm afraid. There's no rule book, only a few people you can trust and a lot that you can't."

She removed the contract still on my lap to a coffee table on the side. Noticing a spot of fluff upon the collar of my new shirt, she pinched and flicked it away, and, her hand already there, stroked me once on the cheek, her fingers softly bristling through the strands of my beard.

"Remember when we met in Middleton, Slide? We talked about the apartment you were going to have. You spoke so wonderfully that night. I was so moved. Well, Slide, you're luckier than most. You finally have a chance to make it happen. It's a nasty business, the one we're in, but if you know how to work it, things can turn out alright. That's all we're trying to do here. Aren't we friends, Slide? Yes? Well, Xander's my friend and that makes him yours too. We're experts, you know? We've seen how these things can go and we know how to avoid the sad stories."

Here I was again, staring into the depths of her eyes, really just the two of us.

"You can't imagine how long it's been, Monica Iñes. Longer than the days in between."

"I know, Slide. It's alright now, though. Now we're here." She returned the contract to my lap. "We're here, and you have to trust me, you have to trust Xander. You have to sign first, Slide. I really did miss you, you know…"

It was still a clean, bright day, with that eerie warmth the sun seemed to have saved for Point James alone. A view through a porthole showed the endless waves of the dappled sea. I rubbed my temples and looked back at the papers. "What does it say, Monica Iñes?" I mumbled.

"It says we're the ones helping you." She squeezed my leg. "I'm going to get you a pen." She got me a pen from the desk. "Here, Slide. On these pages. Here, here, here, and here. You sign and we can begin."

The pen had a dense heft and a fountain nib. Engraved on its side was Xander Durant's name. "Monica, are you sure?" She said she was sure. I watched my arm move toward the dotted lines, Monica Iñes turning each of the pages. I signed, signed, signed, and signed.

The day regained its absurd pace. Clapping three times in glee, Xander Durant took away the contract to fax it to someone, then locked it in a drawer. Next he summoned Dicky from where he'd been enjoying a slice of cake upstairs and told him to make a couple loops before returning to land.

"Lotsa good people here on this boat, Slide," said Xander Durant, leading me with a hand on my back. "This is about the best boat you could've picked to be on, and I've been on plenty."

Monica Iñes (forever one step ahead) was clearing our way on the deck as if I were a dignitary coming through, her short, bustling figure in danger of losing itself amongst the sea of statuesque bodies. We maneuvered our way in and out of the dancing revelers glistening in the sun. Upon reaching the uppermost level overlooking the rest of the party, Xander Durant cut the music and with an arm around my shoulders announced, "We have a special guest with us today I'd like everyone to meet…," only for people in the crowd to start shrieking *Glitter Guy!* before he was even done. And, my friends, what a sea of waiting faces it was…

I was surrounded on all sides, shaking hand after hand. "Holy heavens!" "Pleased to meet!" "Is it really him?" "Move, let me get a look." "This tops the time we had the chanteuse for sure…!" A princely rogue, Julius Woodswam; Portia Avery-Kim, an Asian beauty; Victoria Pernét; Salman Goldnickel; Renata Montelier; a dark-skinned belle, Dyan Mishka; Frederick Chatterwine; Amaka Coppermill; Raphael Filipi; Fernando di Bravi, the exiled heir; Konstantinos Hatzis, of Hatzis Brewery fame; Avery von Pompernol; Cristina Oliver; Majla Radiç; Yørrick Sprasberg; Lucia Mynofsky—they all had names like that. They worked in PR and in media solutions, as ad execs, as brand ambassadors, or as VPs of communications, information offered up immediately upon touching palms. Which is to say, they were all a bunch of *professionals*.

"Simply stunning work," said a blond amazon, slipping me her card. "We should get together and go over your options. I'm a huge fan." Only for Xander Durant to snatch it right away and tear it to bits.

"Hands off, Maria. Besides, you still owe me for the parade incident, let's not forget…"

They wanted to know *this* thing about me, plus *that* thing as well. How are you liking Point James? Is it really your first time? I would have told them myself that it was pretty alright so far except that Monica Iñes cut right in: "Oh, Slide is practically a regular by now. He's very adaptable, isn't that so? You should have seen him today, posing for pictures!" She threw her head back to laugh and everyone followed suit. From there she insisted on staying right at my elbow no matter which way I turned, so as to better intercept any questions coming my way: Where was I from? Slide's been all over the place, he's a natural roamer, you know? What did I do? What *doesn't* he do, he has so many talents, this one… In the moments I did speak, everything I said was funny—I'd never made so many people laugh before in all my life. A grinning ginger named Henry Talsbury asked if the video had been staged and I was almost taken aback.

"*Staged?*" I said before Monica Iñes could get going. I shook my head at him. "Why not have *everything* be staged then?"

They thought that was hilarious. Everything I did they thought was hilarious. Champagne bottles kept opening and before I knew it I'd had five glasses. The boat was piercing the waters like an ornate fin. Trios of experts were bouncing around ideas of what they thought my best media options were. Soon my opinion was needed over by the hot tub, where an animated discussion about the state of affairs in the other boroughs was being spearheaded by a broad-chested gentleman with a bored, nasally voice.

"You hear some of these stories coming out of Middleton and it's perfectly criminal. Criminal! Wouldn't you say, Glitter Guy?"

They turned in unison to regard me like I was an authority. I told them, Yes, it's pretty crazy out there for sure, to which they murmured in agreement.

"It's the policies," offered a smoking woman, elaborating no further. Meanwhile Xander Durant was loudly explaining the meaning of my speech to anyone who would listen, the poodle crooked under his arm and Marissa Iñes (whose existence I'd nearly forgotten all over again) at his side, nodding along. The hours rolled by in a wave of tiring delights. Evening came and I'd had to pose for a thousand pictures. Yet another bottle was opened and someone held up his glass. "A toast! To spring! To too many smart alecks and just as many dunces! To the Glitter Guy!" Everyone laughed, then raising their own glasses said: "To the Glitter Guy!" Oh *Lord* was I a little embarrassed. It's the last thing you really want, a couple dozen people applauding you when you haven't done anything. And there was Xander Durant, back to yelling into his earpiece and flashing me a thumbs-up. And there was Monica Iñes, returned to my life after so long. She was off to my side (still near enough to reach me if need be), chatting up a storm with a pair of hazel-eyed beauties who worked in marketing:

"...was quite natural to see the first time I met him, of course. We had a lovely dinner, just me and him. And his eyes! You know, such passion, it's hard to come by nowadays, right..."

Back at the piers the group disembarked in a drunken herd and dispersed into sleek sports cars, taking off with waving promises to get lunch sometime. The four of us loaded into Monica Iñes's convertible (after I'd checked the trunk to make sure my suitcase was still there), me and Marissa in the back so that the two up front could go over the day's events like tactical agents debriefing post-mission. Whom had I met, who'd said what or expressed notable interest—tidbits of which they were having Marissa Iñes write down. *Zip, zoom, zip*—if Monica Iñes had been driving fast earlier, it was nothing compared to now with the roads clear. Point James's evening lights were the brightest of any kind I'd seen in all of Polis. "Slide, dear," she found my eyes through the rearview mirror and said, "did you intend to go back to Petit Julienne today or would a longer stay be alright?" Even so casual a mention flooded my mind with images of the Dread Merchants lying in wait to dish out a vicious retribution. "A longer stay sounds fine," I said. She said, "Lovely."

We drove to Ampara Street between XVII and XVIII, into the half-crescent driveway of a glass tower where a valet took the keys. "I have a couple free nights here I've been meaning to use. It ought to hold you over for a while," said Xander Durant, leading us inside to check in. Hotel Satilon—a sleek cornucopia of modern amenities. My room, on the twentieth floor, had chic gray-and-white decor, floating tables and angular chairs, contemporary art pieces of balancing stones, plus a computerized voice that asked me upon entering what temperature I'd like the bedroom set to. I told her it was fine the way it was. Monica Iñes had Marissa lay my suitcase at the base of the bed and availed herself of one of the mini-fridge's sparkling waters. "Alright. Let's everyone get some rest then. Slide, darling, we'll see you soon, okay? Lots of exciting things to come. Expect a call from us." She swooped in to kiss-kiss me on the cheeks, then Xander Durant vigorously shook my hand. Marissa Iñes, following a soft prod from Monica, came forward last to say, "I look forward to working with you," focusing on my nose. While they were receding down the hallway, I could hear Monica scolding her.

Then there was no one. I changed into one of the scented bathrobes I found in the closet and walked about touching things. The metallic lamp. The wall-embedded TV. There was a pair of complimentary bedroom slippers I slipped on and did a little dance in. It was all so nice. I wasn't sure why, but something about being there, on my own again, felt no different from if I had been back in that vile motel. Falling backward onto the bed, I stared blankly at the ceiling.

"Would you like me to adjust the bed?"

"No, Computer, that's fine."

A minute passed.

"Actually, Computer, make it a little softer, why don't you."

"Okay. I'll make it softer."

Some whirs and clicks; the bed softened to perfection. My mind was going fast and loopy in the moments before sleep, blending the day's happenings into a nightmarish hodgepodge. The flash of cameras. The car's broken window. The scuba divers surfacing. I checked the video again and it was up to thirty-eight million views.

"Computer, do you ever want to cry sometimes?"

"I'm sorry. I don't know what you mean by 'Do you ever stop to fly from time.' Would you like me to do a search?"

STAGES

That contract marked the final blast of my life in Polis, setting off a dizzying string of happenings from which I never recovered.

"What you have managed," Xander Durant was saying, "is right up there with your meteorites, your black swans, your blood moons, northern lights. Eclipses, even."

It was two days later and we were on our way somewhere else, in Xander Durant's ride this time, a custom-fitted black truck with a leather interior. I'd spent the intervening Sunday

watching bad movies and asking the computerized voice difficult math problems. If there was an item from the hotel's room
service I hadn't ordered, it must have been in the fine print.
When Monica Iñes had come to rouse me that morning with
yet another change of clothes, it was with more than a little
relief that I escaped my putzing about.

"Rare phe*nom*ena is what we're talking about," Xander continued. "You've struck a *nerve*, Slide, and it's not to be wasted.
We have to move fast! We have to move now! We have to
break some things along the way but it'll be alright."

I nodded along to show him I got what he meant. "Like
thunder in a bottle," I said.

He cast Monica Iñes a slow look. "Right," he said, returning
to the road. "That's exactly it."

I was in the back seat next to Marissa Iñes, a closed book in
her lap, her attention forever flitting to whoever was speaking
next. Occasionally she would have that look of being on the
verge of saying something herself, only for the moment to pass
as quick as the blur of traffic. Pedestrians at a crosswalk caused
Xander Durant to mash the brakes and blast the horn at them,
three ballerinas running in a hurry.

Monica Iñes took the moment to turn and face me, resting
a hand on my knee. "It's a lie what people say, Slide. Not all
exposure is good exposure. That's been your problem but it's
what we'll fix first, dear. Slide, you still trust me, of course?"
She squeezed.

"Of course, Monica Iñes."

"Alright. Well, I think you're going to like what we have
planned."

*   *   *

What they had planned was a steady diet of meetings aimed at exploring my career options at this juncture. Meetings with the advertising agency New Horizon Solutions; with Club Jack Aesthetics, which did work in the digital space; with Aura Scope, and so on. To these we would arrive late, always without apologies, wearing sunglasses indoors while teams of hasty execs in striped shirts went through their pitches slide by slide. I had the impression they'd been up all night preparing, eager to pull it off if for no other reason than to return to their beds. Geez, what a big fuss! And the craziest thing was that each pitch, without fail—it truly was crazy if you think about it, my friends—had to do with me being some sort of rabble-rouser...

"... hope you don't mind, but we've taken the liberty of putting together a few mock-ups!" the first of such execs was saying, Bertham Bellamy of New Horizon Solutions. We were on the fifteenth floor of their Courtsford Street branch, at the head of a long table lined with nodding associates. The office was an air-conditioned glass cube in the middle of an open space of mobile desks where hip young people sipped beer while they worked. "Joshua, show them the mock-up!" said Bertham. He was an excitable yuppie with pudgy hips and muttonchops, forever snapping at a hapless intern for not changing the slides on time.

The mock-ups flashed on-screen—in one, a digitized version of myself wore jeans and a stylishly ripped jacket with nothing underneath, in seeming ignorance of the thin-limbed models stroking my bare chest. AMBROSIA FRAGRANCES, read a logo at the bottom, LET YOUR SCENT DO THE TALKING. In another I was on a hill overlooking a landscape of burning towers with my hands on my hips, so as to best reveal the glimmering watch pictured in sharp relief. AVERY. THE TIME IS NOW, read that one.

"And you've run this by Erondu and them?" Xander Durant asked in a bored tone.

Bertham broke his neck nodding. "Oh, they're onboard. Very onboard! Everyone wants a piece of the action."

"These do seem a tad on-the-nose, no?" said Monica Iñes, equally unimpressed. Me I was saying nothing, as had been the plan.

Bertham shook his head. "Oh no no no." He snapped at the intern to go through more mock-ups, but they whizzed by so fast nothing registered besides the continual renditions of anarchic scenes. "It's sexy business right now," Bertham was urging with a jitter in his voice. "Revolution is very in…"

44 Promotions was on Dauphine between XVI and XVII, another airy, open-plan space, this one in the heart of the Arts District. There we met for lunch with their Aesthetic Development Team, headed by Claudia St. Ames. *They* were the ones to offer me my first commercial—in it, I'd be back at the site of my rant, Duke's Plaza, reenacting it all, except this time at the end I'd take a bite from the stick of marshmallows. It was a commercial for marshmallows.

"It's all natural ingredients, of course, and one quarter of the proceeds will go to an urban community outreach program of your choice. Concept's been testing well with the twenty-to-mid-thirties and Van Nummond's signed on as well, says he can shoot as soon as next week," Claudia St. Ames was saying. She was a twinkle-eyed bohemian with silver hair and necklaces all over the place. They'd even brought along a pack of the marshmallows for me to try, which I was currently munching on since I was still hungry after the light sandwiches they'd served us with cups of seltzer water. The marshmallows were strawberry-flavored and delicious.

"It's certainly something to think about," said Monica Iñes, moving the bag out of my reach. "Although with all the new research on sweets... We're not sure if our client's values align on this one, you know?"

Knock Socks was a trending clothing brand specializing in comfortable home-wear and they wanted me on as one of their models for their summer line; I'd wear their hoodies and comfy socks in various relaxed poses throughout the home that it was implied I had found at last. At Phoenix Athletics they had a similar idea, except for them it was sneakers—an*other* mock-up, of me leading the charge of a torch-bearing crowd while wearing their latest pair. By the end of the week there were other things too. We visited the campaign headquarters of an up-and-coming statesman who'd wanted to meet me real bad, a plainly handsome smooth-talker with a hard, square chin, who had no sooner thumped me on the back than was launching into his spiel for me to endorse him. "When I heard what you said, why, I could have written it myself. Powerful. That's the only word for it. *Powerful.*" He went into detail about the type of speech he'd want me to give at his rallies while his staff photographers snapped pictures of us shaking hands. We met with Richard Bolt, attorney at law, a gruff boor of a man with a loosely done tie, who didn't have a lot of time to spare but handed over the paperwork he'd filed against the various entities that were using my image without permission. We were bustling to keep up with him along the bends and turns of the courthouse halls, where he was due in a trial any moment now.

"None of these will pay out, but it sets the tone. Oh, another thing, couple criminal suits coming your way as well, though that's easy enough to nip in the bud. Turns out you can't go around inciting unrest then frolic off wherever you want. I'd advise you to get security, Glitter Man, or you could be a martyr. Durant, what time are we teeing off Sunday?"

"Nine."

"Can't do nine. Ten."

"What you got at nine?"

"I'll see you at ten."

Bolt slapped him playfully on the cheek, then flung open the oaken doors to a packed courtroom and disappeared inside.

"Want to know what he has at nine?" Xander asked Monica in a salacious whisper.

"Those were only rumors, weren't they?"

"Ernie Horsham ran into them going at it like rabbits. If you consider that a rumor, then sure."

"Xander! So crass..."

We met with Vibrant Designs, who pitched us an audiobook. With Platinum Solutions, who could arrange a clothing line of purple shirts. With 4th Planet. Open Plane. Alahora. AVM, LMM, QZ8. Werbermeir Inc. Bedford & Buford. Second Phoenix, whose film and TV branch had put together a couple cameos in the latest movies. Some of the meetings felt as if they were held for no other purpose than to say there'd been one. Everyone would nod, reclined in ergonomic chairs around glossy tables, speaking of things like *impact* until quite satisfied.

"We're lining them up here, my friend," Xander Durant said once, after we'd stormed out of yet another office without so much as a handshake. "These suckers are all the same. They hear one of them got a sit-down and they want one too. There's blood in the water, Slide, and we're waiting for the feeding frenzy. We line 'em up, we strike 'em down. Capeesh?"

"Capeesh."

We opened the four doors to his truck.

"But, Xander?"

"Mhm?"

"Whose *blood* is this we're talking about, though?"

"Oy vey! Iñes, this one's for you."

That occupied the weekdays. On the weekends I had a rotation of social appearances aimed at raising my profile. I was to be seen at the right places doing the right things, holding my hand up to avoid photographs, though making sure I was still in them. These weren't exactly *meetings* per se, but they weren't *not* meetings either. Xander Durant would know of a philanthropist's fundraiser, a nonprofit's gala, or Monica Iñes had exclusive tickets to the soft opening of the avant-garde artist's new show. We would go to dinner. We would go to two dinners. We'd have four dinners booked but time enough only to pop into three, slowed as we were by the four-man security detail they'd gotten for me after all. Dressed in another new outfit of which the price was a mystery, my beard enriched by luxurious oils, I would peruse those bustling scenes like the visiting king of a tribal nation, laughing up a storm if that's what everyone was doing, unless otherwise knitting my brow before responding to some societal question it seemed I was now in a position to answer. Zola Birchwood Amos the patroness, a known eccentric, once quieted an entire banquet table to ask me if it was indeed true, Glitter Guy, that in Middleton, where I was said to have lived, there were orphans roaming in hordes, abandoned to the streets with no one to care for them should they have so much as a bruise on the knee...? Wow. It was the first time I'd thought of Soup-Eye in about one million years. I felt my brow knitting without meaning to, answering yes, even though, but, well, what she had to understand, though, a lot of them are good *kids* is the thing. At the Archwood Museum's Garden Gala, where I received a standing ovation just for showing up, I was proclaimed the guest of honor and thrust onstage to deliver opening remarks for their exhibition *Dissent through the Ages*. At the Xenmeir Jewelry Walk, where elegant old women donned the most exotic pieces from their collections and cooled themselves with paper fans, I was summoned by a domineering group of six, later described to me as the Kingmakers, and was viciously prevailed upon to choose sides in various political disputes. I rubbed shoulders with the exiled princes, the bored billionaires looking for causes, with the playboy Mustafa Elmahdi around his table in the back room of Club Malacon, where everyone seemed an assemblage of toned limbs, and where no sooner did you tip your glass to finish the drink in your right hand than another one was being poured in your left. The luscious hair, the laughter like bells, the conversations as easy as stones skimming a surface—every next event seemed a continuation of the party on Xander Durant's boat.

In fact, one time it was just that: we rode the yacht out to Haverford where a friend of his was having a garden party at his country home on the rim of a secluded lagoon along the western shore. That one rocked me out of my senses all over again. It was a sprawling estate of landscaped acres, oaky trees surrounding a manor of thirty-two rooms. Servants in white uniforms met the boat at the dock, where a gangplank was set up for us to disembark—we had ridden over with Raphael di Bravi, Amaka Coppermill, and the captain Dicky. We merged with the rest of everyone amongst the rows of tables with soft white cloths, the garrulous chatter, the freshening up of drinks at an outdoor bar manned by a mustachioed cocktailier in coattails. Gregory Holnut, the rubber heir, whose property it was, invited me for a long-spanning tour of the estate. He showed me the adorned foyers, the painted frescoes, the hall of portraits of his noble Scottish ancestry on one side and the Ethiopian gentry on the other, the aviary of rare birds, the Great Danes, the stables in the distance, the twelve bedrooms and ten bathrooms, the library, the upper-floor observatory with a gilded telescope pointed toward his favorite constellations. It didn't even feel like we were in *Polis* anymore. Back in the garden, at the center of yet another circle of curious eyes, I felt myself swelling full with their adoration, overwhelmed by the pretty angles of their faces in the growing dusk in which the fireflies were awakening from winter's long sleep. Drowsy as in a dream with no exits.

I stayed in a rotation of hotels for which Xander Durant and Monica Iñes footed the bills and told me not to worry. They alternated from the starkly modern to the gilded and elaborate, each more splendid than the last. The one constant from room to room was the appearance of my leather suitcase at the foot of the bed, which it was always Marissa Iñes's duty to see to. For the most part she continued to appear in momentary glimpses throughout the day's hectic whirl, always with some next thing to do from amongst the onslaught of her sister's instructions. Again and again her acute tilting of the chin, her slight opening of the mouth, would lend her the anxious impression of a child about to share the first opinion of their life, only for such suspense to culminate in a mere "I hope you settle in well," before she left me to it. Lying on those feathery duvets, perusing the minibar in nothing but a laundered robe, calling room service for a shrimp cocktail just because—it felt truly ridiculous how nice things had become. Geeez-uuus, what an embarrassment. Though these were but mere intermissions, followed always by Xander and Monica *knock knock knock*ing at the door, telling me to Hurry up, Put clothes on, We have a meeting with this agency, a party in that restaurant with so-and-so, head of studio. The valets would have one of their cars ready-to-go downstairs, unless the night had called for a limousine to accommodate a larger party. *That* one would be a riot of champagne all over the place while they blasted fun music and Xander Durant read aloud from the various tabloids where my ongoing exploits through Point James were being chronicled. Well, it was on one such Sunday night, on our way back to the limousine after the premier of a play, that some of the Purple Shirts first tried to save me...

We were leaving the theater along a carpet of flashing cameras when they burst into hysterics from the depths of the throng: seven men and women in purple shirts. "Free the Glitter Guy!" "Hurry, come with us!" "Viva!" They'd dispersed themselves within the crowd as if for camouflage but were now shoving their way through the photographers toward the barriers along the carpet. A dreadlocked ruffian, a tattooed vandal, two shaved-headed women wielding cans of pepper spray—you could tell they weren't from Point James by the rough cut of their clothes and the wide berth those to their sides were giving them. "Glitter Guy, it's going to be okay!" "We can take you to the extraction point, now's the chance, you must flee!" One of them had succeeded in vaulting his way over the railing, an agile no-gooder now barging through the other attendees as the photographers went wild. "Out of my way, fiends! Glitter Guy, we don't have much time, come with us and you can—"

As for what it was I might've been able to do, I never found out, for the security detail had formed a rough phalanx around me and pushed me into the safety of the limousine, which got going in a hurry.

"Wait! Holy shit! What was that!" I was bewildered, looking out the back window to where they were now being tackled to the ground. Soon they were swallowed out of sight by the hordes of picture-takers. "It sounded like they needed my help."

"Oh, Slide, it's just some silly ideas people have gotten into their heads about you," said Monica Iñes, sighing and straightening out the ruffles in her outfit from the hasty escape. She handed Marissa a bottle of wine to uncork. "They're a little unwell, you know, people like that."

The others in the limousine nodded along, Xander Durant, Lucia Mynofsky, Portia Avery-Kim, two others I didn't know.

"Some of them are dangerous, too, is the thing," said Lucia.

"Yeh!"

"Mhm."

"That's right."

"Remember what happened to the guitarist?" said one of the others.

Their faces saddened.

"Those were good days, when he was around."

*   *   *

Reminders of the ruptures elsewhere in Polis came mostly through the glimpses of TV that I managed to steal back in my room. Geez-us. Flipping through those channels, you got to seeing how things had really gone from bad to horrible. Except it hardly had to *do* with me anymore. From Middleton's tip to its end were there now all sorts of riots clogging up the streets, in a culmination of the hot agitation I'd witnessed while living there. Tenants suffering in the bonds of unreasonable leases were dangling out of windowsills, threatening goodbyes to life unless their landlords agreed to more reasonable terms. More and more Downtown students, up to their necks in debt, were storming out of classes en masse to clog the Financial Plaza and harass bank executives on their way to the office. In one such broadcast I even thought I saw that redhead that I'd replaced at the de Sanville town house, amongst the ragtag groups drumming plastic buckets in protest. For these and all other calamities did the detonators of that bomb take claim, having by then emerged from their furtive beginnings into a guerrilla band known as the Purple Shirts. They were a bombastic organization of inestimable size (either many or a few) for which the price of membership was merely the donning of their eponymous uniform. After each anarchic act, they released a statement reaffirming their support of the one known as the Glitter Guy, despite his current status as an abducted hostage of the nefarious forces of greed that it was their solemn duty to topple. Oh yes, my friends: now that word of my hobnobbing in Point James had spread, there were more than a few opinions on the matter. Some, who saw in my tabloid photographs not some hapless victim but a traitor to the cause, the worst kind of sellout, had splintered into disillusioned bands, beholden only to havoc. Their latest tactic was to block important roads for hours at a time with heaps of flaming trash while terrorizing onlookers, to which they afterward ascribed no deeper message than a couple good laughs. One such incident ended in a night of fisticuffs between rival factions that overloaded the hospitals for days, plus the top-to-bottom looting of the Greentower Mall, which had only just reopened after damage from the flood. Ai-yai-*yai*! I was getting a little depressed, to tell you the truth. Every next bottle-smashed face seemed scarred as if by my own hand; there wasn't a single panicked granny I could think of without some shame. From east to west my words were still being sprayed everywhere. It was a turbulent jubilee, a festival of chaos, true pandemonium, yet all it would take was the remote's OFF button for it to feel like it wasn't happening anywhere at all...

As for the real estate agents, they came practically begging us. Every last one of them wanted to be the one to have found the Glitter Guy an apartment. Monica Iñes had replaced my overloaded phone with a new one that she also hung on to, such that anyone trying to reach me had to first go through her. At any given moment I might overhear her making plans for us to stop by an open house.

"Now, we must be careful, dear," she warned me on our way to the very first. "Some of them will try to take advantage, Slide."

"Advantage?" I said, in the front seat for once, since Xander Durant was busy. "What do you mean 'advantage'?" I was excited in spite of myself. We were in a neighborhood of stately trees and peculiar bakeries, the atmosphere quiet and serene for the first time in weeks.

She nodded *mhm* as she made a left turn down a sun-dappled drive. "With people like this, it's all about them, of course. Everyone's trying to make a reputation."

Those agents of Point James were of a different breed. On none of Polis's other figures were the strands of their hair as fastidiously in place, the level lines of their teeth so like those of a diagram. Where Osman the Throned had been a ruffle of untucked shirts, they were nothing but neat lines and creases; where he had been unshaved, they were smooth. Whatever eagerness their constant calling might have betrayed, it was masked in person by the unbothered air of leisurely tycoons, as if they were giving me a tour of their own homes. Such was the case with Laurie Adlemore, a long-retired pageant queen with the leftover habits of a life spent being admired. She had shining dark skin as taut as a plum's, and was the one to show us the brownstone at 609 Fulsom between Avenues XIX and XX.

"It's a pleasure to meet you. I'm from Middleton myself, and I agree it's a shame what's become of it," she said when she met us out front. "In these matters, a victory for one of us is a victory for all. Shall we, Slide?"

I followed her through that unlocked door and into a world of elegant atriums, a back garden visible through the glass, where the bees were flitting amongst exaggerated flowers. I couldn't believe I was in one of these impossible homes where the only traces of dust were those left to float about in beams of sunlight, for effect. Her company had staged the space with graceful furniture, such that, walking around, I couldn't help imagining spending a lazy afternoon lounging on the plush couch, getting up only to enjoy a quick meal with friends at the mahogany table with gold lace placemats. I was going gooey in the legs just being there.

"Starts at twelve and a half, not including fees," said Laurie Adlemore, with another gracious sweep of her hand, once we'd concluded our tour. "That's a markdown from one-fifty annual, since the first two months are free. We'd like to get it off our hands."

"Wait," interrupted Monica Iñes. "Isn't this the same building where that thing happened to the children?" She opened a kitchen cabinet as if to check. "Oh, Laurie, you should've told me as much earlier, don't you think..."

Another, Seamus Lowe, a coiffed Scotsman preserved by gels, showed us the twenty-sixth-floor condo in the Petunia District, with room enough for nine cartwheels, a view of the parks, and a pitted salon with a clap-on fireplace.

Except, queried Monica Iñes, were there not a lot of musicians living in this building? "Slide, imagine the noise, it simply won't do..."

Tiffany Zupot walked us through a lavish two-bedroom, but Monica Iñes said I'd be needing three if I was planning to entertain.

Or Monica Iñes would say: "Those aren't hypoallergenic, are they?" Or: "And you said that *doesn't* include the landscaping fees?" Or: "Xander, explain to Slide what *bespoke* means."

And so on. She seemed never to have met an apartment in which there was not something wanting, and for all the fanfare of these recurring viewings, they all ended with the same drive back to my hotel.

"You must be patient on this one, darling. I know it's your dream, but it's not everywhere that can become a home, you know?"

I was in the back seat next to Marissa Iñes, since Xander Durant's poodle was riding shotgun on its way to the dog salon. She was reading one of her books, Marissa Iñes.

Suddenly I tried it: "What about where you live, Monica Iñes?"

"Hmm?"

"Where do you live?" I repeated. I even leaned forward. "I'd like to see it, if that's alright. Like you've been saying. It might be instructive, after all."

"Well, of course, silly! I *must* have you over. I ordered a new painting for the space, so as soon as it arrives we'll have a lovely brunch."

"But, Monica—"

"Marissa! Close your mouth! Slide's too kind to say it himself, but it makes people uncomfortable. You know, I always tell you, some of these manners you overlook are really quite essential."

It was a little strange, actually. She mentioned the names of many friends, yet those that I met seemed to be Xander's first and hers second. She dressed as immaculately as anyone around but spent the evenings making unsatisfied adjustments. Though she was forever at the heart of some chatty, laughing crowd, in the moments I spied her on her own (as was once the case in Haverford when she didn't know I, *too*, was outside catching some garden air after the heat of the ballroom's activity), her face loosened into a secret pondering that narrowed her eyes and pulled heavily at her cheeks. With her sister, her usual bossiness took on the harsher, more bitter tone of a public shaming, as if in her she saw the image of a life she had vowed to avoid. For her part, Marissa Iñes endured these lashings without complaint, responding only with a nod, or occasionally by throwing me that meek look, opening her silent mouth. Although what she had to say was anyone's guess, I thought at the time.

As it would turn out, Monica Iñes and Xander Durant eventually agreed to just about everything we'd been pitched. I did the photo shoots. I did the guest lectures. I did that marshmallow commercial, not in Duke's Plaza itself (to which I swore I'd never return), but in a true-to-life replica out in Haverford. They even had a lady to play the sword-swallower, although she wasn't deaf, plus she required makeup to make her look ethnic. That was a whole day of shooting, a young, irate director with a cascade of a dirty hair yelling at me to do the speech right, with better energy, more force. The thing is, I could hardly *remember* the way I'd done it the first time. I was having difficulty feeling as angry as I'd been. Half my mind was already on to the next obligation. I did the speaking engagements in which eager-eyed attendees listened to me go over my travails in Polis and clapped at the worst moments, when my life had been at its most shit. I did the radio call-ins at five in the morning for commuters on their way to work and recorded jingles for later use. Forty-six million, sixty-eight million, eighty million—if the video's views showed any signs of slowing down, I must not have known what they were. March became April and I was already more fatigued than from nine lifetimes' worth of notoriety, dragged along as always to a gala, an opening. Sometimes from within the senseless whirl of that pretty morass I would say to Xander Durant, Xander, I don't get it, I can't remember why I'm *here* anymore, what's it that I did?, and Xander Durant would say back, Don't be foolish, my friend, it's never about what you did. I would say to

Monica Iñes, Monica, what about those people, the riots, we can't just be here doing nothing, can we?, and Monica Iñes would say back, You *are* doing something, darling, this is the best way you can help. And once, on the brink of one of my increasingly rare moments of bravery, I exclaimed to them both:

"Do I have to *do* this?"

We were in an elevator heading to a function at the ambassador's residence and I was struggling to tie my bow tie.

Xander Durant shook his head and grabbed the tie's ends. "It's simple once you get it down. The trick is in keeping one end longer than the other."

"No," I said. "I mean any of this? Not just the tie. The function. Tonight. Tomorrow. All these *engagements*. Do I have to do this? I'd like a vacation, or something like that."

They flashed each other looks. Whatever the silent transaction, Monica was the one to answer.

"Of course, dear. I couldn't agree more. A vacation in a couple weeks sounds lovely. We're all booked up until then, I'm afraid, and you're not quite allowed to cancel on a whim, Slide. It's all in your contract, if you would give it a look..."

At least I was earning a pretty penny. The baseline fees charged for my various appearances were stipulated in strict terms on page 19 of that same contract, still a hefty enough sum after deductions for taxes owed, and the thirteen percent cuts for Xander Durant and Monica Iñes (each), for me to have more leftover than I knew what to do with. What I mean is—I was becoming a little rich. In my bank account for the first time the balance was undergoing a steady surge and one of my newest habits was to stop by the nearest ATM just to pull it up on the screen and stare. I couldn't believe I could take it all out if I wanted to and run away with my arms full like a bandit at the end of the world. In two-twos I paid off every debt I'd ever had and sent a check to Peter Napakakos for an amount way more than what I thought I owed him, just to be safe. That made me want to cry. To have struggled for so long, to have endured so many nights of greasy food, to have suffered the itch of falling-out hair that is the worst of debt's symptoms, only to have it all evaporate… More and more were those agents leading me through tours of glorious apartments like choreographed dances and me I watched the whole thing as if from afar. There it all was, like I'd imagined from the magazines—the in-vogue duplexes with Scandinavian furniture, the big-windowed high-rises with members-only gyms, elevators that opened directly onto your apartment and nowhere else, all of them available for lease if only we could talk business—except it was *still* like in the magazines, unreal. There was no *nothing* to any of them. I would walk through the freshly painted chambers knocking on each of the walls, not to test their quality, but to see if they would fall over. For the first time I understood Napakakos's fear of the world's hollowness, of there being beneath Polis's mask not some hidden face, but nothing. "What are we thinking?" whatever current agent might be saying. "Going rate is ten thousand a month, but I can finagle a ten percent knockdown if we can guarantee the first three months paid up front…" Oh gosh. The world had become my oyster but I'd lost my appetite. Now that's sad.

The Last Viewing

I was becoming lost in there. I was spending my waking moments caught in that opulent labyrinth and my sleeping ones

in dreams just as confused. You see, you two, you have to understand: Point James was disconnecting me in a terrible way. My
life before living there had begun to feel distant and unlikely,
an imagining. Sometimes, when hastily moving my things
from one hotel to another, I would encounter the paraphernalia
of those other lives—my black tracksuit, the book of haircuts,
Calumet's map—and the shock of seeing them again was of a
dull, unconcerned sort, as if I were encountering a limb I'd lost
long ago. I had so much footage being taken of me that I was
starting to walk around life in the third person. There Glitter
Guy goes, getting into another limousine; there's Glitter Guy,
reciting that same old speech again; oh, look, that's him on
the front of a T-shirt; there he is up until the ungodly hours in
some backroom club surrounded by sycophants. I had to talk
and talk and talk. I was not to shave my beard, because it had
been that way in the video. It was a fate more preposterous
than even the most stone-faced of impostors can bear: I was
impersonating my own self.

One day the video hit 100 million views and I hardly cared
anymore. One day we met with a team of security professionals because the threats on my life were becoming really
quite serious. And one day, and this day was a Monday, I was
pulled from the morass by Marissa Iñes saying something
after all.

I'd answered the *tap-tapp*ing on my hotel room door to find her
standing there in the hall. I spent a stunned moment waiting
for her sister to appear at her side—it couldn't have been more
than six minutes since they'd dropped me off at the lobby
downstairs. Marissa must have circled back on her own.

"You going to sleep?" She spoke in the kind of loud whisper everyone can hear anyway, her eyes lit with an energetic zeal I'd thought them incapable of. She wore a raggedy sweatshirt and jeans.

"Not necessarily," I said. "Is this about the Hansworth opening? Okay, listen, tell Monica I don't need to practice, alright? I remember what she said about cutting the ribbon."

"It's not about that." She held my arm. "I want you to come with me."

Uh-oh. What was this about? Some kind of hanky-panky?

"Uh, listen. I should let you know, I think you're a great girl and everything, Marissa Iñes, it still doesn't mean that—"

"Whatever you're going to say, don't. I need your help. Come with me, it shouldn't take long." She tugged me in the direction of the elevator. "Slide. Please."

We drove in a strange silence, north along Avenue XV in the plain sedan she had parked in a shadowed corner of a lot. Her position at the wheel was a low, two-handed hunch, as if she had only recently learned, and she would speed in bursts before reminding herself to slow again. The night's late hour had reduced the world to its most forlorn sights—clubgoers waiting in line, a shop's last employee sweeping the floors. My toes were clammy in the hotel slippers I'd managed to put on. The air was warm. A dusting of stars lingered overhead. The radio didn't work and we didn't have anything to talk about. I mean, I *tried* and everything, mostly small talk since she wouldn't say where we were headed, but the distraction would cause her grip on the wheel to tighten, and the car to swerve ever-so-slightly, so I dropped it. That's how we rode, as if in separate vehicles overlaid by an accident of time. Still, if ever I glanced her way, I could see Marissa Iñes's lips moving in the slight motions of a silent monologue.

Soon we arrived at yet another of Point James's pretty neighborhoods, one more tree-lined street in an elegant hive of fashionable towers and tasteful shops. Approaching one such building from the back, she retrieved a clicker from the glove compartment and opened the mechanical door to the garage. Down below, she drifted by one spot after the next until parking in A18, then got out. "Come." I got out, too, and walked after her, passing rows of expensive cars like metallic beasts at rest. A red metal door led to a miniature lobby of three elevators, of which she took the third and beeped a key card from her pocket to get us going. When the elevator opened again it was onto a landing of two doors. Using a key, she opened the one on the right.

It was bare in there. A stark, unadorned hallway, without so much as a welcome mat to rub our feet on, led to a dark space filled by the echoes of our shuffling. The lights did not work, leaving a dim gloom so eerily gray that my hand before my eyes seemed as if formed from smoke. Fumbling about, Marissa Iñes first found one candle on the mantelpiece, and, after lighting it with a match, shared its flame with the others dotted throughout the space. Soon we stood in a glowing pocket of light. I looked around. I saw the high ceilings in need of replastering, the hairline fissures along the wall like the cracks in an eggshell. Moving about in a detective's hunch, I studied the grooves in the hardwood and pieced together where the furniture had once stood. Here must have been the sofa. Beside it, a loveseat, or chaise longue. A bookshelf. Two small stands. And there, in the space on the floor next to the ragged curtain covering the bay window, were the four grooves where for so long a desk must have stood so as to have a view of the skyline, provided you leaned forward. If it wasn't my heart making all that mad noise, then it must have been a subterranean knocking from the floorboards. My mind was reeling in visions, haunted by foreign memories. When I looked up at Marissa Iñes, the light had deepened the contours of her face. Long legs of wax were running down her candle and dripping onto the space between her feet...

"Our father died without grace," she began. "Mad at the world. Cursing. Whatever disease had come for our mother had come for him, too, and he squandered the last of his fortune fighting a useless war against it. Which of those misfortunes pained him more is hard to say. His wealth was its own sickness long before. In some sense he was only swapping one for another.

"There are those you meet whose entire lives can feel like little more than a prelude to their dying. It sounds bad, but what I mean is they have a knack for it. It is like a great potential visible within them all along, and the longer they live, the more anxious those around them grow to see it fulfilled. I know I was. He'd conjure up long lists of injuries that had befallen him, from childhood till yesterday, and rattle them off whether he was with an audience or not. He moaned through nights of fitful sleep, if he wasn't gnashing his teeth. Boils sprang up everywhere, drying into patchy scabs once popped, and the scent of the salve used to disinfect them made him vomit a sticky mucus he'd let dribble down his chest. His hair didn't have to fall out as quickly as it did, but he took to tearing it out in clumps once he noticed. Trying to help him walk anywhere was an exercise in futility, for he'd refuse angrily, and one day while getting up from the toilet he fell and broke his ankle. With the cane he then required, he'd hit visitors on the knees in response to perceived slights, until weakness robbed him of that ability too. Ghosts came to visit him. He'd point to the blank air where they stood and recited their evil accounts of the room in hell being prepared for his arrival. In his efforts to escape it, he became a Catholic, then a Buddhist, then a pagan mystic. He'd go blind for days only to regain his sight amongst terrible migraines and his bones poked through the skin even as his belly bloated from trapped gasses. He forgave no one, and took back every nice thing he'd ever said about the world. His last correspondences were a series of commands for his attorneys to sue the doctors who had not cured him, but he burned up their refusals along with the albums of family photographs we hadn't managed to hide from him in time. He made a great drama of dying, it is true, yet it was a drama of fulfillment in a way. I had never seen an unhappiness so total. Doing so, you realized that the capacities of the spirit are far greater than you had imagined, as happens when witnessing a master at his craft. It was his best performance in a lifetime of them. I'm certain his last regret was in not getting to do it again."

Her slow sauntering through the room had brought her to a doorway, and with the candle still in hand, she beckoned me to follow down that lonely hall. Me I walked after her like a zombie.

"H-h-he... he *died?*" was all I managed to say.

"Yes," she said, her hand trailing along the chipped wainscoting.

It was an even larger apartment than I had imagined, unless it was the absence of all things that lent it the ghostly proportions of a catacomb. In what might once have been a bedroom, she gave the candle a slow wave through the air, causing our shadows to lean and sway as if moved by winds.

"This building then," I went on, "this is the Rudolph?"

"No. Not anymore. But yes."

She let her eyes fall to a point nearer the walls, as if there still stood a wide bed, a gaunt, angry figure tangled in its ragged sheets.

"At the end, though, he began to forget," she continued. "That is what did it for my sister. You can forgive the dying almost anything. What they suffer, after all, they suffer alone, those by their side only caught momentarily in the whirlpool of their sinking. But who can stand by and watch entire portions of our lives be thrown away as if they were nothing more than clipped nails—those portions it is our loved ones' job to keep safe?

"First he confused the two of us, that much is to be expected. Next we were meeting him all over again in a calamity of tears and reuniting hugs. We did not grow up with him, Slide, I don't know if I said. After that we became our mother, and thereby the targets of those long-ago abuses that must have led her to flee him in the first place. Finally, we were strangers. We would approach his bed to adjust the pillows when he'd seize up, seeing his ghosts, then yell out names of past lovers to come save him from our clutches. Their names he remembered quite well."

On and on we went in that strangest of viewings, through the lonesome chambers, the rusted bathrooms, that forlorn kitchen where they'd heated up meals in the breaks between typing. Like a cat in darkness did Marissa Iñes move about, the candle in her hand going out for minutes at a time before she could locate another of the matchbooks lying everywhere.

In the kitchen she opened the sputtering tap for some water to wipe her face of the night's heat. A hard, bitter tone sharpened the edges of her voice as she clutched the sink's either side.

"My sister, Slide, she does not forgive. I lost something, too, when that man erased half the life I'd ever known, and revealed in its place only a putrid core. But you must forgive. After all, I would say to her, what difference would it have made if he'd died outright? Where would the memories have been then? What vengeance can you take on the dead? She did not think as much. To her, his forgetting was an act of aggression, and my sister only knows how to respond in kind.

"Once he passed she took to ridding the world of every last vestige of him. He'd been in the morgue less than a day when she was already discarding his old jackets and scarves, tearing up his archives in the study before the scholars could come inquiring. She paid a couple quack cousins to light special incense meant to erase the auras of past inhabitants and left it burning for days. Well-wishers trying to give their condolences were met with a shield of smiles they could not get around. At the funeral she stood near the back in order to better step outside and make calls for work. She had him cremated, against his wishes, saying that the demands of a demented man were worse than noise, and as for what has been done with the remains, I cannot say. They wanted to have a memorial for his works at the Howitz but she pulled her strings and had it forever postponed. She held flash sales for any know-nothing collector to come waltzing through here and snatch whatever they could. Anything left unsold she gave away to the staff. That was fair enough, but when I proposed that the walls where the artworks had hung be repainted, or the floors buffed of their nicks and scrapes, she insisted that they be left the way they were. Her only point was destruction. Over that year I watched as she made this home into a nothing of a place. A corpse for buzzards. A graveyard without flowers."

Her jaw hardened into a knot, bulging through her cheek. Ducking out of sight, she rummaged in the cupboard beneath the sink for a few moments. When she stood she had a paint can in her hand that she placed on the counter, its loud clang like the clash of cymbals in an empty hall. She'd gotten out two brushes too.

"Well. I've been painting anyway," said Marissa Iñes. "Come, Slide."

In the farthest room, newspapers were spread on the floor and sections of the walls' trim covered in blue tape. After lighting more candles, she took a stepladder from where it'd been leaning in a corner and unfolded it. She rested the paint can on its miniature platform and opened the lid, the paint inside a smooth ivory tone, almost cream. More than half that wall had been done already. She positioned the ladder, then climbed up to dip her brush into the paint. The other brush she gave to me and showed me a corner to her right where I could begin as well.

We worked side by side, separated by the ladder's reach, in the careful quiet of that unanimous night. The only sounds were the scratching of the brushes along the wall, the distant din of Polis wafting up to us at such a height. Me I'm not really your best painter, but I was figuring it out alright. All you had to do was go up-down-across, over and over, in a couple coats. It was soothing. When I looked over at Marissa Iñes, she was deep in the peaceful concentration of a private ceremony, as if in prayer.

"And you have been happy in Point James, Slide? These past weeks?"

I thought about it. "No."

"You miss the other places?"

"*Miss* them? They weren't any better themselves. In fact they were worse."

"Perhaps you will leave Polis then?"

That one made me pause. An invisible door had opened in the room, letting in cold drafts from unknown climes.

"I don't see where else I would go."

"I see."

We kept painting. At one point she swapped brushes, explaining that mine was better suited for getting the edges. Another half hour's worth of silence went by before she made her way down from the ladder.

"It is my sister's final wish that this place be gone from her life," said Marissa Iñes. "She is already in talks about liquidating her share of the asset. Half of it is mine, but without the means of securing that other half, I will be forced to do the same and see it go up for sale. It will be on the market in two weeks. I don't know how I was so careless in letting her gain such a stronghold on the affairs. In these things, she knows more than me."

She retreated from the wall with her hands at her sides, I thought, at first, to review her handiwork, but when I turned toward her I found her gaze fixed upon me with the same intensity with which she had earlier remembered that phantom bed. A shiver was coursing through her body, causing her brush to splatter paint, and the dance of shadows on her face to vibrate in an anxious tremor.

*   *   *

"We could live here, you and I," Marissa Iñes said to me on that stalled night on the eighteenth floor. "This could be the answer. I know you have been looking for some time, and that the looking has not gone well. Silly boy, when will you stop running in circles like a hen with no head? Yes, I can see you are surprised, but is it really so impossible? There's laundry in the unit to use at your convenience and we'll have room enough to stay out of each other's way. It is a quiet neighborhood where people protect each other. No one here will care that you are some sort of circus show, or try to take your picture when you are not looking. The staff here is lovely and know to keep secrets. They can safeguard against those vampires. And, Slide, it will be somewhere to own. Isn't that a difference?"

She turned both her palms upward and spread her arms. She stood like that, an avatar offering a tiny, tiny world. I had not moved from where I still knelt with the brush in my hand—she'd done well enough to note my shock, which had sent hot rushes of blood to my face. I thought I heard the clack of typewriter keys sounding from down the hall, or saw Calumet's curled-over shadow flickering in the corner of my eye. What sort of a lunatic hope was this! What a treacherous dream! Just in considering it did I feel myself a sort of usurper stepping on fate's toes. What confused luck. How two-sided a destiny. Time had spun its strange tricks and shown me a future overlaid by ghosts.

I opened my mouth in an attempt to say this and more, but all I came up with was "But your father—"

"That?" she cut in. "Ha! Ha! Ha! Ha! Ha! What house is there in Polis in which some bitter sack hasn't died in the worst of agony? Huh? Did you think this was the only one?" She had another good laugh, clutching at her sides and bending over in wheezy cackles. *Man*, all this time I'd been thinking she was regular when really she was a madwoman. While she was busy at it, I finally stood, returning the paintbrush to the can with a slow, sinking *plop*.

"What about the *fees*, though!" I interrupted. "Or, like, the lawyers or whatever. Are we going to have to deal with those? And, I mean, for starters, where would I even *sleep* is the thing? There'd be all sorts of *furniture* I'd have to buy. Also don't buildings like these have co-op boards and stuff? Plus your sister is for sure going to be angry. Oh geez, Marissa Iñes, this *definitely* isn't what I thought we were coming here for."

I was starting to freak out. Half my mind was already decorating every way I looked while the other half was conjuring those other two holding hands and finishing jigsaw puzzles together. Every last candle seemed to burn with a mad light too bright to face directly.

"Slide. Who cares. Those are problems, yes. But there's no time for wringing your hands. If this place gets to market neither of us could ever afford anything like it again, even if we lived ten times. I need you, Slide. And you—don't be too brave to say it—don't you need me? We can be happy here. We'll paint the walls and put new panes in the windows. We'll be roommates. You can do whatever you like. It'll be even is what I'm saying. No one can take it from you."

Not for the first time did I have the sensation that in seeing her I was seeing an inverted life—candid where the other was sly, bare where the other was armored. As if sensing all this, she said next:

"My sister, Slide, she takes. If you let her she'll shrink your world until there's no room to stretch your arms, as she has long done to me. Here we are, trapped together. We can get out, though."

I picked up a candle of my own and looked at her head-on.
"How much do we need?"

She told me the amount.

"I'm short of that," I said. "And how much time?'

"Two weeks."

"Hmm. Alright, Marissa Iñes. I have an idea. But it's something you're going to have to help me with too."

THIEVES IN THE DAY

My schedule over the next four days was the most packed yet. Tuesday alone featured a breakfast meeting at Northridge Publishers to discuss the viability of my memoirs, a panel at the Manthusen Center as part of their ongoing series on civic engagement, followed by a recording session with the Arctics for the opening of their new album. *Zip, zoom, zop*—we were flying through them all at breakneck speed.

"Fernando is absolutely the best, dear, a true savant, which I don't say lightly. Oh, you should have seen what he did for Valatori's spring campaign last year. Completely brilliant! Isn't that right, Xander?"

"For sure. Bit of a prick, though."

"Xander!"

It was another of the endless rides in Xander Durant's truck, the four of us on our way to a hasty photo shoot, since a notable stylist had called with a sudden opening in his schedule. In anticipation of summer, the sky had scrubbed itself of clouds and hung a hot sun high in the east. Me I was running on four hours of sleep, if we're rounding up, though somehow wider awake than ever.

"He's the one that did the visuals for the West Bothridge flower show, right? Fernando, that is?" I leaned forward to ask Monica Iñes.

"Oh no no no, you're thinking of Fernando *Ballati*, this is Fernando Untlever we're talking about. Best not to confuse them, dear, they haven't been on good terms since that business with the adoption."

"My bad, Monica Iñes."

"An easy mistake. But, Slide! You're really picking up on the details, aren't you?"

"What can I say? Some things I can take to like a dog in water."

"That's the spirit!"

"Now, Slide," said Xander Durant, making a turn, "a couple pointers I'd like to go over with you before we get in there with the band this afternoon..."

In the daylight there was nearly the sense of last night having been a game, something silly to forget about. Looking over to where she sat huddled with her nose in a book, you'd never have thought Marissa Iñes some kind of mastermind plotting a silent revenge, which, I guess if you think about it, is the best way for a mastermind to look. We hardly glanced at each other throughout the day. Not that it was that *difficult* or anything: before last night, I don't think we'd exchanged more than six sentences. Now without the candles around to lend her a beatific glow she'd regained the shy impression of a mouse trying not to intrude. Geez: it really is all about circumstances, what makes you notice people... But, lest I should think it all a dream, the moment we found ourselves with a second alone—Monica Iñes and Xander Durant having left us in the reception area while they had a word with some executive, or

Marissa Iñes ferrying all the free goods I'd been given at the day's events up to my hotel room—we would launch at once into a rapid-fire dialogue:

"Have you gotten hold of them yet?"

"No, still trying."

"Marissa Iñes!"

"It's not so easy!"

"Just tell them who I am and that should make it easy, right?"

"Yes, but there are all sorts of numbers to call, and I'm never sure who's who."

"Geeez-uuus!"

"And the bank? What about that? Have you arranged it?"

"They said two days."

"Until?"

"Until they can get back to me. Look, I'm having to do this all by email too. Whenever I try to call I get put on hold."

"We need to hurry."

"I know. How's your sister do it so easily?"

"It's her *career*, Slide. I hardly know anything. No one who I call recog—"

"Wait, hold on, shhh, here they come..."

So you see, Jim? Jean? It wasn't some walk in the park, getting here to the two of you. Those next days extended before me in a fretful confusion, time somehow both fast and slow. Given the sway her sister had over my phone, Marissa Iñes and I were limited to such hasty exchanges, unable even to duck away for a walk because of the instantaneous crowds that formed everywhere I went. Glitter Guy! Glitter Guy! We loved you in that commercial...! It went one day. Two days. Three days, then a fourth. On Friday night I had a panic that Xander Durant was onto the rub, for he'd come across the two of us sharing words in a surreptitious corner of a gala instead of schmoozing with the director like I was supposed to be doing. (We were in talks to make a movie about my life.) I'd been proposing my latest idea of tracking down your address, when, by Marissa Iñes's mortified expression, I could tell we'd been spotted. And in fact, yes, out of the corner of my eye I saw Xander Durant some mere feet away from us and closing in, heretofore cam-ouflaged by the sea of identical tuxedos filling the hall. I had to think quick: foisting my empty glass on her, I finished up an order: "That's right, a neat martini, and I like mine dry. Chop-chop now, Marissa, I don't have all day..." Her mouth opened-then-closed, right in time for Xander Durant's arm to slip its way around my shoulders. "One of those sounds good for me, too, Mini-Iñes"—his name for her—"we'll be by the ice sculpture. My friend, you're being asked for, we might have found an actor to play that roommate you mentioned, I remember you said he was a bit pasty, correct? There's good word he might have been on one of those makeover shows as well...," said Xander Durant, without a tinge of suspicion. He was a bit sloshed himself, luckily.

After that we stuck to phone calls, me using the one in my hotel room, which she would call from home. It was on these phone calls late at night, once we were done with logistics, that I learned of the inner workings of that other Iñes—her fondness for marzipan, which she hid packets of in her purse; her dream of translating old, forgotten books; the things her father said that had hurt, but the ones that were good too. "He was a complicated man," she often said in summation.

"Trust me, Marissa Iñes, I know all about those..."

When we were alone, her voice would again take on the boldness I'd witnessed at the Rudolph, expanding into a mellifluous timbre that recounted life's troubles without flinching. She had been telling me a tale of how Monica Iñes had once fended off a schoolyard bully by gluing the girl's hair to her chair when I piped up: "Geez, Marissa Iñes, so she's always been ruthless, huh? It's a wonder you haven't tried saving yourself sooner, to tell you the truth!" I was ironing my purple shirt for the fundraiser tomorrow where I was due to perform. A long pause extended from her end. I said Hello? into the receiver, thinking we'd been disconnected. "Monica and I love each other, Slide," she finally said. "We're orphans." "Marissa, I didn't mean it like that..." We talked for a few more minutes, but it was clear she was no longer in the mood. She said she'd received word from her bank that my funds were en route, then hung up to get ready for bed.

For all my constant exposure, interviews had seemed like the one thing Monica and Xander hoped to have me avoid. They spoke often of the importance of mystique, and cited other celebrities who'd built entire *careers* on having said no more than one hundred words altogether. In reality, I knew they thought my talking for myself would mess it all up. That was why I looked forward to the fruition of our plan with the restrained mania of a convict digging the last inches of his tunnel. Although it wouldn't have sufficed to simply escape. I needed exoneration too. We worked in stealth to put the pieces in place, me maintaining a happy front throughout the day, Marissa Iñes using every last trick she'd picked up from months spent with Monica. The two weeks she had mentioned at the

Rudolph were down to two days when at last she delivered the news we had been waiting for. We were stepping into my latest hotel room, Xander and Monica farther down the hall laughing about something.

"Slide. It will be tomorrow," she whispered as she placed my bags down.

"What?" I said. "Already?"

She nodded yes. "They moved quickly once I actually got to them."

The room was nice: a plush king-size bed, an aquarium of orange fish, complimentary seltzer. She took out some papers folded many times over and handed them to me with a nervous flourish. Opening them, I looked over the jargon-filled lines that months of signing contracts had made me adept at deciphering, and where in no uncertain terms Acorn Studios claimed the rights to an exclusive sit-down interview. Geez-us: she had really pulled it off.

"Is the amount okay?" asked Marissa Iñes.

I turned to the last page and nodded. With the pen I now kept in my pocket, I signed where I had to.

"The transfer will go through tonight," she said after I'd returned the forms. She looked a little nervous herself as she headed for the door. "Send it to me after. And in the morning we will have to move early. I'll be here at six."

The Tallest Tower

But she came at six thirty! I'd been up, dressed, and worrying myself silly already when her panicked voice came through the other end of the phone.

"We need to go right now!" she yelled.

"Marissa, I know!"

Outside, I was pacing back-and-forth along the curb until she pulled up, opening the passenger door from the inside, the car still rolling forward even as she called for me to Hurry and Get In.

"Slide, I think my sister may know" was the first thing she said once I got in.

"What!" I said.

She picked up a worried speed.

"I'm sorry, Slide. There was a phone call, they were calling to confirm. She was so confused. Oh, it's a whole long thing but we'll be alright. Buckle up. Are you ready?"

I braced myself against one of her breakneck turns. Damn: she had something in common with Monica Iñes after all.

"I'm ready," I said.

"Alright," she said, and kept us heading north until there was no more north left.

So we drove to the Epsilon Building, the tallest tower, where on the very top floor I was due on-air in something like thirty-five minutes. That harsh monstrosity loomed like a slash through the horizon. I can't say how *you* two feel about it, coming to work here every day and all, but me I'm almost *glad* it's so out of the way, at the very tip of Point James, where you don't have to feel its heavy presence like an overlord shadowing the land. If you could count what Marissa Iñes did as parking, then fine, it was more an abandoning of the car halfway between two spots, the windows still down as she pocketed the keys and flung open the door. I scurried after her, past the giant sign with ACORN STUDIOS embossed in silver, to the double doors that slid open from a few feet away. We entered a high atrium with the banners of various TV shows hanging from the ceiling. At the security desk Marissa Iñes gave her name and said we had an eight o'clock. The time was seven twenty-three. But the guard was already waving us through with an air of boredom.

"Yes, yes. Glitter Guy, correct? He's expecting you upstairs. Cutting it close, aren't you?"

That one made us dash for the elevator like it was the last of the lifeboats. She waited until we were hurtling upward to voice what was no less terrifying for its being obvious:

"Slide. There's a chance that she's on her way."

The numbers for the floors ticked off: twenty-four, forty-two, fifty-six, as, in a series of painful pops, my ears adjusted to the altitude, and the next thing I knew the doors were opening onto one hell of a fracas on the sixty-fifth floor. Hordes of people were walking one way along the hall and about as many were walking the other. They had clipboards, flannel shirts, mobile headsets into which they were yammering. A redheaded woman was tearing up pieces of paper and yelling into an underling's face. A stream of beefy men was rolling large cameras to somewhere they were needed, while behind them a teenage assistant pushed along a cart of snacks. "Light check!" "Mics up on P-thirty-two!" "Hey, coming through!" One such PA with a particularly frazzled look had been waiting for us.

"There you are!" she uttered in relief. She was a curly-haired brunette, dressed in plaid, a bit googly-eyed from the thickness of her glasses. "You trying to kill me? Come on!" Geez: it was about the most no-nonsense introduction I'd ever had.

Waving away any obstacles with her clipboard, she cut a path through the melee. We went this way and that along the poster-lined halls, passing more PAs, all-purpose hands, sound engineers, and audience coordinators as they darted through doors below glaring signs indicating FILMING IN PROGRESS. Beside these doors were large screens showing the happenings inside, such that walking through the hall was like peering into an array of dimensions: a high school drama set in a classroom, trivia game shows pitting color-coordinated families against each other, a dance extravaganza with an audience giveaway, a cooking segment where the blond host had organized the ingredients into neat bowls to make cooking look easy. I hadn't realized everything was filmed so *early* in the day. We detoured through one of them, the PA down to her last resorts to get us to where we were going on time. Tugging the door open with a brusque "Let's go!," she ushered us into a darkened studio with the set of a homely living room illuminated in the center. Onstage, a trio of actors was going through a scene before a laughing audience. We were at the top of the stands, cutting toward an exit at the opposite end. You didn't have to be an expert to tell the show was one of those shitty ones that wouldn't be on TV for long: a situational comedy. "Honey," the mother was saying to the daughter while the father sat behind his newspaper, "do you even know how to *spell* Africa?" The audience laughed. We got to the other side and exited back into the bustle. Whether the PA was yelling into her earpiece or at us, it was hard to tell. "Around the corner! We're right around!" she was saying, until we indeed made a hard right and she roughed open another door into a control room like a pilot's cockpit, with lit-up screens, knobs and buttons, and a glass pane looking out onto an adjoining set. In the room were two men. The first was any old someone, an engineer, probably, fiddling with dials beneath the gaze of the other, who held his hands behind his back as he slowly turned around. Wow: sometimes even knowing what's coming doesn't make it any less crazy. There was his silver hair, his harsh features like those of a joyless eagle. Still with his hands behind him, he fixed us with the same steely look I'd last seen a lifetime ago, from a distance of several yards. We'd made it to him at last. It was the news producer from Millennium Mount.

"You're late," he said.

Marissa Iñes was apologizing as the PA was absolving herself of blame, throwing her hands up in defense.

"Yes, we're super sorry about that," I chimed in myself, extending my hand for a shake, then lowering it once he didn't do the same. "Although you're a pretty hard guy to find, if we want to be honest about the whole thing."

The producer raised an eyebrow. "Is that so." We must've been some spectacle, arriving like that, but he just stood there, as if watching a segment unfold. "Well, as you can see, we've been setting up for you," he eventually said.

I looked through the pane into the adjoining room. I don't need to tell the two of *you*, obviously: it was your news studio. Geez, that's some sort of trip, seeing it in real life. I hadn't expected it'd be so small, or that the news desk and the weather room and the sports table were just different facets of one interconnected setup, like the chambers of honeycomb. A variety of technicians were adjusting lighting panels and running long multicolored wires all over the place.

"Well, are they here? I'd like to give them a sense of what I'd like to talk about before we get going," I said.

The producer shook his head. "No pre-meetings. You'll see them when we're on air."

"What?" I said. "What do you mean? That's *nuts*! You can't have me going in there all blind, man, what if I *embarrass* myself?"

"Blind's good. We want the reactions." The engineer had moved a dial in a way the producer didn't like, so he moved it back to its original position. "Or have you become a broadcast expert since you were on the Mount?"

That one snatched the words right out my mouth.

"You're here, at least. Sign these." He picked up a stack of papers and handed them to me with a pen, then was already opening a door to the adjoining set.

I signed the release. Some moments in life you can't hem and haw about. When I handed it back to him there in the doorway, he held my gaze for a long moment. "I hope you know this is an unusual arrangement." I told him I did.

Cutting through the set we stepped over a tangle of cords, ducked beneath the swinging arm of a camera. Marissa Iñes was hurrying along a couple paces behind. "We'll need to get you to makeup then," the producer was saying. "Barbara, see to it."

The frazzled PA directed me toward another slim corridor, back in the direction we'd come.

"Marissa—" I began.

"It'll be okay, Slide. Go with her."

She led me down the hall to a glaringly bright room where six-seven other people sat before a row of vanity mirrors getting their powder applied. I was handed off to a clear-skinned specialist who settled me into a seat and tucked paper towels into the collar of my shirt.

"He's on in twenty-five," Barbara the PA explained to her. The specialist nodded and got to work, dabbing cotton balls with a pink solution and rubbing down my face. "This is an astringent. Hold still, please." To my left was a little girl with pigtails singing scales, a woman in sunglasses standing behind her, and to my right was a man with wrinkles, crying.

"Mother, no, absolutely not!" the little girl interrupted her singing to say. "That should absolutely be B-flat. You've always had the worst ear, Mother. Excuse me, sir," she then said through our reflections. "What note does this sound like to you?" She sang the note again.

"What?" I said, tugging at my collar from the heat of the lights. "Listen, I don't really know much about this stuff, alright?"

She rolled her eyes at me. The old man who was crying stopped so abruptly I realized he'd been practicing, too, then was off on a phone call about some sort of callback he was expecting. The specialist palmed my head like a ball to keep me from fidgeting.

"We need to do something about this hair," she said.

Then I was ferried backstage, stumbling, in the charge of another PA no older than yesterday, a sickly smelling spray puffing up my afro. I was made to stand within a blue square taped to the floor, next to a table of pastries and orange juice. Scaffolds of lighting fixtures extended overhead; peppy teenagers were pushing more cameras on wheels. *Positions! Positions!* people were saying. A timer with red digits counted down from sixteen minutes. Almost by accident did Marissa Iñes return to my side, looking a bit lost. "Marissa Iñes!" I yelled. "Geez, I didn't think I'd be nervous, but I'm kind of nervous." She could only nod in response. Her face was a little green. The producer appeared: "The hell's he doing *here?* Someone get this man on set!" *Thirteen minutes.* Another gum-chewing PA pushed me by my lower back toward the set, Marissa Iñes drifting along. There was the oak table, the stately chairs, the wall of black curtains providing a smooth, formless background. Off to my left was a glare unlike any other. They were so bright, the lights, they made everything else dark, such as the cameras pointing our way, and the murmuring crew behind them. The PA led me to my seat, an armchair facing two empty ones. "We need him mic'd up," he yelled. A sound guy smelling of tobacco came and held my chin up, then fitted me with a pin-on microphone, slipping the wire down my shirt into a radio transmitter he attached to my belt. *Eleven minutes.* The seat had a thin cushion through which I could feel the hard wood on my ass bones. The producer was off to the side overseeing everything like a conductor. Marissa Iñes had gotten lost again somewhere in the jumble and me my pulse was through the roof. The room was a scramble of ants, a cacophony of people yelling *Positions!, Sound check, Ready up....!* And that was when I saw her.

She emerged from the darkness with such poise it seemed a part of the choreography. The ease of her gait, like a steady ship amongst turbulent waves, caused the crew members to let her through without question. She wore heels and a simple white dress that clung just-so. A French braid had tightened her hair into a neat cascade that exposed her elegant neck. Tucked beneath her arm was a scarlet clutch she hadn't bothered to set down, as if this were a mere pit stop amongst the day's other obligations. Her steely eyes were so singularly upon me I thought her an apparition myself, summoned up from the most inconvenient of dreams. Just like that, Monica Iñes was stepping onto the set.

"Slide, honey. I've been looking for you." She closed the last few feet between us and rested a hand on my shoulder. "We're late for the match, you know?" We were supposed to have gone to a fencing contest between two European prodigies that morning, out in Haverford.

"Oh, hi, Monica," I managed to mumble. "I don't think I'm going is the thing..." My heart was thrashing, and when I looked left-and-right for Marissa Iñes, she was nowhere to be found. From the darkness I heard the gruff shoving of Xander Durant.

"Take me to him!" he was saying to whomever. "This is some kind of outrage!"

"Mhm," said Monica Iñes. "Well, that we can discuss, I don't mind if we skip the one. Come on, dear, let's get up."

Her talk comprised the same sweet words as always, but you could hear the fuse of her voice burning low. She was hovering over my chair and casting a long shadow upon me.

"Monica, I don't think I'm going to—" I tried again.

"Slide—"

"Wait! Who is this?"

The crew was only just figuring out they had an intruder on their hands.

"We'll only be a minute," she spun around and said. She returned to me. "Slide. I'm going to need you to get out of that chair and I'm going to need you to come with me."

"Monica Iñes, this really isn't the best time. It's a whole thing that's about to go on."

"I know you've been convinced of some silly things, darling, and that it all sounds very nice. You mustn't be fooled." Here she rubbed her hand along my spine as if to hastily tune an instrument. "Slide. Get off the chair, Slide."

Off to the side Xander Durant was now saying, "That's our client you've got over there! What kind of shenanigans are afoot in this operation!" He'd found the producer and was facing off with a waving of arms and close pointing of fingers. The producer stared back unblinkingly. More of the set hands were now saying things like *We got a bogey on the set!* or *Hey, let's get security in here!*

"People are going to try to trick you, Slide, it's exactly like I warned you," said Monica Iñes.

I leaned back against the chair so her hand couldn't stroke me anymore.

"Monica. I'm really not coming."

"Get off the damn chair, you silly boy."

Just then she looked up over my shoulder and froze. I turned to see Marissa Iñes walking onto the set.

"You," Monica Iñes softly said. "You're some ingrate, you know that, Marissa?"

"Don't talk to her that way," I tried.

"Hush, Slide!"

But it was Marissa Iñes who said that last part. Now that her fear had come true, she seemed freed from worry. The color had returned to her face; her voice was back to its rich timbre.

"Monica, we're going to do this interview."

"Mhm," said Monica Iñes, her hands on her hips like she was listening to a child lie. "I suppose you're very proud of this. And your little stunt with the apartment too. Cross-constituent deeds? Anonymous accounts? Oh, Marissa, it's really sloppy work, I could tell it was you all along."

Doubt briefly shaded Marissa Iñes's features. She let her bottom lip curl beneath the top one before righting it back into a defiant line.

"The trans-referral checks out and it's valid under the Inheritance Statute, Co–Next of Kin."

"Is that so?" Monica Iñes arched an eyebrow.

She countered with a legal term of her own, only to be met by another from Marissa Iñes. This went on a little while. I couldn't quite follow, but it was clear Marissa Iñes had done her homework.

"You must think you're so clever," Monica Iñes finally relented. Her icy composure was melting under the radiant force of her anger.

For his part, Xander Durant seemed to not be doing too hot either, looking on with a furrowed brow at a piece of paper the producer held between them. Plus the security guards had arrived at last—five of them in navy uniforms branching off, three toward Xander Durant, two to the set. As for the rest of the crew, well, just about everyone had stopped what they were doing to watch the spectacle. "Ma'am," said the pair of guards nearing us. "Come this way, please."

Monica Iñes grabbed me—a sharp row of nails into the forearm.

"Slide! Get out of this chair at once!"

"Ouch!"

"Ma'am! We're going to have to ask you to let go!"

"Get off! Slide, we're going right now. Up. Up!"

"Geez, seriously, I think you're cutting my skin."

The guards were approaching with the wide-open stances used for cornering skittish animals.

"Don't you dare!" Monica Iñes was saying, even as Xander

Durant had already been wrangled, his hands behind his back. "You lay a hand on me and there's going to be hell to pay!" she added.

They laid hands on her. A pair of firm clenches on the shoulders, gripping all the more tightly for her resultant struggling. Now she was seriously digging into my arm.

"Marissa, what do you think this is? Come over here! Tell them to call this off, Marissa! Don't make me say it again. Come here! And after all I've done. All I've done for the *both* of you!" With an expert squeeze of her wrist, the guards managed to loosen her grip on me. It didn't stop her from resisting their every tug. "Slide, honey, you're the more reasonable one. It's not too late to undo all this. Call the bank. Get off the chair. *Talk* to her, won't you? Talk to her, dammit! Let me go! Let me go this instant...!"

They were managing to move her away. Soon they'd neared the perimeter of the darkened wings and the exit sign. Xander Durant was already being taken off with a muffling hand over his mouth.

But as for Monica Iñes, they had underestimated a last burst of strength, for she pitched forward once again and was straining her every neck muscle to lean as much our way as was possible.

"He left us!" she shrieked. "That's all anyone ever does, Marissa, they leave. And if you don't leave them first then you *get* left and that's how it works." They dragged her farther off. "What do you think will happen now? You think you'll redecorate and it'll be fine? That's really pathetic, you know. It's sad. It's still the same place he'd lock us out of whenever a new *friend* was staying over, you remember that? We'd have to pretend he was away for work so someone from school would let us stay in their guest room. Who took care of you then, Marissa? Huh? Who handled the shame? It's good what happened to him! Let me go! Let me *go*! It's not going to work, you know? He's just like anyone else, that boy—a disappointment in waiting. He's the rudest one there is. You dummy, *I'm* what you have! I'm the one who'll never leave. Oh, and Marissa? You're fired. You're so, so fired...! Marissa, please, it's me, it can be better. Don't do it like this, sister, we're all we have, you know? Come on! Come on, you ungrateful little..."

They dragged her off. The producer's natural appetite for scandal had let it go on, but once he tired, he lowered the halting hand he'd been holding aloft and had them escort her away. I hadn't noticed it before, but the cameras were recording the whole thing, of course. She thrashed a last few kicks, claws, threats, and screams, was hurled through the exit in a torrent of cries, and that was about the last of that for Monica Iñes.

PRIME

"Five minutes!" yelled one of the hands. The commotion resumed. The red digits were ticking along, the producer continuing to orchestrate with flicks of his hand.

"Marissa," I was trying to say through it all, "that stuff she was saying..."

"It's alright, Slide." She wiped her face before looking at me. "In fact it's a bit of a relief." With a squeeze on the shoulder, she told me, "Good luck, okay?," then stepped off the set.

Three minutes. All at once the red lights of the cameras blinked on. *Quiet on set!* someone yelled. Everyone hushed. It was suddenly so still. I could feel my face trying to sweat but the makeup soaked it up. Someone from the dark-and-lights yelled for me not to look into the camera. And, from the wings backstage, the two of you showed up.

Wherever you'd been, it had left you cool and calm, unless that's the way you always are, of course. It's one thing seeing you on Mr. Borsnitch's shitty TV and another altogether witnessing you gliding toward me as if on private currents. When you sat down it was all I could do to grip the chair's arms in dizziness. It felt strange and unimportant, surreal, yet all too obvious.

"Hi, I'm Jim," you said, Jim.

"And I'm Jean," *you* said, Jean.

"We've heard so much and we're excited to talk."

"We're fans ourselves."

"That was surely some business just now."

"If you don't mind, we'd like to ask you about it once we're on air."

"Everyone's run you through the prep?"

"Always remember, we're here to facilitate."

"If we cut you off, it's only for time."

Wow. You two must get this every day, but you're really good-looking people. It's a little awkward saying it to your face *now*, but it's what I've been thinking half the time sitting here. *Sixty seconds.* The producer came to share a whispered word with you and the weight of everything started hitting me. I had to pee. It was the worst timing in the world but right about then I seriously had to pee.

I hissed it through my teeth: "I have to pee."

The producer, without turning, hissed back on his way to the control room: "Well, Slide, you are going to have to hold it."

The PA yelled, "And we're live in five, four, three, two…"

Well, that about brings us up to now. Geeez-uuus do I need to stretch. Also, I don't know if you can get burned from being beneath stage lights for too long but I'm definitely a contender. Jim? Jean? I have to say, it's been about the most I've ever spoken about myself, sitting down for this interview. The most I've ever spoken about *anything*, if we're really being honest. You're probably going to have to cut this up into a bunch of segments, I bet. Don't leave out any of the important bits if that's what you do, okay? You see some of these segments sometimes and it's *obvious* how many of the important bits they left out, it hardly makes *sense* in some of the worst cases. Things like that should be illegal. Whatever. I shouldn't worry. You guys are professionals.

Gosh, what time is it? I should be getting home. I forgot to mention we've started furnishing the place already. It's nothing too fancy: I got one of those mattresses they say are good for your spine and a vintage trunk to put some of my things in until the bureaus arrive. That suitcase is pretty much falling apart. I'm not sure how many of those clothes I'm going to keep, and we agreed I'd get one of the medium-sized rooms. It's the one with the best view, though. In my opinion. The big one we're saving for Calumet. I know, I know, it's a little crazy. It'll probably feel like one hell of a *circle* to him, going back there. But I think it will be good. It's no use, running from demons your whole life. They don't get *tired* is the thing, whereas you definitely will. Your best bet is to go find them where they live and fling open the windows so they fizzle away in the sun, like dew, or certain kinds of odors. You have to be *willing*—that one you can take from me. Plus it's like I always said: Calumet, he really needs to get out more. I've checked with the building supers and they said bringing the cat is fine, and I don't have any allergies so it can run about wherever. The two of them can *stretch* for once. It's a whole different staff working there as well: I asked around and no one even remembers any of those old people. That's a fresh start. It'll be a little hard, but he can step back into life now, one foot at a time. Anyway. I'm going to have to ask him first.

Me I'm still no expert but I've picked up on a few things at least. I've seen the hustlers and the prowlers and the ones from nine to five. The schoolgirls growing too fast as well as the schoolboys trying to catch up. I've fallen in with some bad types and fallen out with them too. *Neither* of those would I much recommend by the way. I've chased so many horizons around this place you'd've thought I knew how to get to the other side. But no dice. That's Polis for you—an island of life's hostages. Of too many arrivals with nowhere to depart. Of violence as a first resort and fire as a last, of billboards with better options. Tiny tragedies, mute joys, and lonely women seen on the other end of packed subway cars. Of wanting. Of babies born crying who never learn to stop, of cures sold to you first then the illnesses second. Of loose leopards in dark trees, suspicious giants, snipers on their last stand, truants in the back alleyways no map can find, ignoring the bell. Of if it not being the one thing then it certainly being something else. It's no use trying to burn this place down, I was wrong about that. We would just build another. That kind of stuff will make you cry if you're not careful, this stubborn dream we keep agreeing to. Whose only promise has ever been some weary terrain where the city we are looking for may one day be found.

ACKNOWLEDGMENTS

A first and foremost thank-you to my editor, Claire Boyle. Her tireless eye saw this novel through every round of revision and last-minute email. This book and its author could not have been more fortunate in finding such a champion.

To my agents, Andrea Somberg, Sebastian Godwin, and David Godwin, who picked me from the slush. To Caitlin Van Dusen and her eagle vision. To the writing teachers of my life: Ms. Mignon Walters, Aunty Carol, Mrs. Rhona Bisram, Mr. James Connolly, Bret Johnston, Amy Hempel, and Leland de la Durantaye.

My years at Iowa were invaluable in granting me the time to make horrendous writing mistakes without consequence. To that end I would like to express my gratitude to my professors Nimo Johnson, Paul Harding, Margot Livesey, Ayana Mathis, and of course Sam Chang, without whom so many of us would still be lost. For providing feedback on an earlier draft I owe tremendous thanks to my classmates Dini Parayitam, Emma Wood, Nyuol Tong, and Kris Bartkus, whose evisceration of what I thought was a final version made all the difference. To Derek Nnuro, who shared every workshop with me. To Lindsay Stern, who read first. To Mgbechi Erondu, Anca Ro, Christina Cooke, Will Shih, De'Shawn Winslow, Regina Porter, Delaney Nolan, Kevin Smith, Joe Cassara, Jen Adrian, and Stephen Markley. Thank you!

Thank you to Emeka Kanu, Eric Taylor, Matthew Trammell, David Lee, Tomas Unger, Rhoden Monrose, Bradley Booker, Gabriel Fotsing, Hanna Heck, Lauren Pistoia, Alene Rhea, Rashaud Senior, Spencer Hardwick, Justin Dews, Luke Murphy-Baran, Patrick Gordon, Samra Girma, Amber James, Emilia Rinaldini, Dougan Khim, and Sarah Diamond. To Justin Blugh, Omari Bekoe, Kareem Ditzen, Gerard Murrell, Dale Chesney, Quartus Johnson, Alex Joseph, Kienan Faria, Robert DeGannes, Tristan Young, Lawrence McNeill, Aidan Chin-Aleong, and Dominique McClashie. Because of you, I can never complain about friends who did not believe. Thank you to Bryony Cole. Thank you to Kimberlee Chang. Kristina Oliver, I do not know how I would have survived without your open door. To HTK and the Inglorious Basterds and the whole of QRC. Big up! Growing up in Trinidad, we quickly learn to not waste an audience's time when telling a story. Thank you for that fundamental lesson.

A special thanks to Bespoke Education for providing me the means to both write and live in New York City.

This book owes a spiritual debt to the works of Patrick Chamoiseau, J. D. Salinger, Álvaro Mutis, Renata Adler, Jorge Luis Borges, Italo Calvino, Salman Rushdie, Ralph Ellison, and most importantly Gabriel García Márquez, who opened my eyes.

And to my family. My heart is too full to tell you how I feel. My cousin Rene, for whom no dream is too large. My sister, Micere, the wisest reader I know. My mother, Dawn, who holds everything together. And my father, David. He was the one to read us the stories that revealed the world, and that first caused me to ask, What is that, and how do you do it?

Eskor David Johnson is a writer from Trinidad and Tobago.
He currently lives in New York City.